The PUCK decoy

A FAIRFIELD U NOVEL

G.N. WRIGHT

THE PUCK DECOY

A FAIRFIELD U NOVEL

G.N. WRIGHT

Copyright © 2024 by G.N. Wright

All rights reserved.

No part of this publication may be reproduced in any form or by any electronic or mechanical means, including information storage and retrieval systems, without written permission from the author, except for the use of brief quotations in a book review.

This is a work of fiction. Names, characters, places, businesses, companies, organizations, locales, events and incidents are either a figment of the authors imagination or used fictitiously. Any resembles to any person, living or dead, is unintentional.

The author acknowledges trademark status and trademark owners of various products referred to in this work of fiction.

This author does not have any control over and does not assume any responsibility for author or third party websites or their content.

Cover Design - Haya In Design

FOR ANYONE WHO EVER HAD A CRUSH ON THEIR BEST FRIEND'S BROTHER

A LITTLE NOTE FROM ME TO YOU

Welcome to the world of G.N. Wright!

If you are new to me then thank you so much for taking a chance on one of my books. I hope you enjoy & stay awhile!

If you are already a reader of mine then thank you so much for coming back.

The Puck Decoy is the second book in the Fairfield U Series.

It is a standalone and can be read and enjoyed alone but I would highly recommend reading The Puck Secret first as there is an overlapping storyline to enjoy.

Before diving into this book please note that the FMC has Autism Spectrum Disorder and I would like to gently remind everyone that the word spectrum is in there for a reason.

No two people on the spectrum are the same, we are all different in our own way and those differences don't diminish our place on the spectrum in any way.

This character is based on my own lived in experiences through myself and my daughter, and while they might differ from your own, or someone you know, it doesn't make them any less real.

Hallie was written in mind to shine a light on Autism and in particular girls with Autism and I want that to be something we can celebrate together without making the whole story about it, because it doesn't completely define who we are.

Please note this book also contains explicit sexual scenes, alcohol and drug use, forced marriage, discussion of marriage deals for children when they come of age, and political crimes. Please proceed with caution.

Oh and don't miss out of the little bonus scene at the end to get a preview of what is coming next in this world!

PLAYLIST

miss Americana & the heartbreak prince - Taylor swift
peter pan - Kelsey ballerini
complicated - Olivia O'Brien
falling - harry styles
i wanna be yours - artic monkeys
friends don't - maddie & tae
18 - one direction
two pieces - demi Lovato
back to you - selena gomez
eyes don't lie - kingfisher
say don't go - taylor swift
i'll be damned - gavn!
wild love - james bay
your heart or mine - jon pardi
in case you didn't know - brett young
right here - chase atlantic
let me love you - Arianna grande, lil wayne
us - james bay
a drop in the ocean - ron pope
skin and bones - David kushner
call it what you want - taylor swift
so high school - taylor swift
blossom - dermot kennedy
deep end - x ambassadors
no love for a sinner - shay Zamora
love u like that - lauv
my boy only breaks his favorite toys - taylor swift
perfect - marianas trench

CONTENTS

Prologue	1
1. Josh	5
2. Hallie	13
3. Josh	27
4. Hallie	39
5. Josh	50
6. Hallie	58
7. Hallie	70
8. Josh	80
9. Hallie	90
10. Josh	101
11. Hallie	111
12. Josh	120
13. Hallie	130
14. Josh	142
15. Hallie	151
16. Josh	165
17. Hallie	180
18. Josh	192
19. Hallie	202
20. Josh	211
21. Hallie	216
22. Josh	230
23. Josh	239
24. Hallie	247
25. Josh	254
26. Hallie	266
27. Josh	277
28. Josh	292
29. Hallie	303
30. Hallie	317
31. Josh	331

32. Hallie	343
33. Hallie	353
34. Josh	358
35. Hallie	367
36. Epilogue	376
37. Bonus Scene	381
Afterword	387
Acknowledgments	389
Also by G.N. Wright	391
About the Author	393

PROLOGUE
JOSH
DADDY DEALS

I hate my father's office. It's cold and miserable, just like him. What's worse is, he knows I hate it, and it's why every time we have something to discuss, he always makes me meet him here. It's a power move, one that allows him to think he is in control, but the truth is, his games don't matter to me. They never did. I let him rule with his iron fist, and went along with whatever bullshit he demanded, because I knew I would soon be free. I was happy to keep doing that, but then he involved my sister.

There was no way on this earth I was going to stand by and allow him to force her into marrying some piece of shit just because he was friends with his father. Thankfully, it was easier to dig up some dirt on her intended and flush his reputation down the toilet, but I knew it wouldn't be enough. It's the only reason I am here, because I know what I have to do next.

It's another twenty-minutes before he finally deigns to show up, citing overrun meetings as his excuse. Yet I don't miss the lipstick on his collar, rolling my eyes at his sloppiness. I honestly don't know how he ever got elected as Mayor. As he rounds his desk, he loosens his already astray tie, and searches through some papers on his desk until he finds what he is looking for.

"You cost me a lot of money by ruining the Thorne deal," he snaps, leaning over and placing a stack of sheets in front of me. I don't even let my eyes drop, keeping my focus on him as I wait for him to continue. He doesn't have concrete proof that it was me who foiled his plans, but he knows I did it, and it's that knowledge that has me smirking. "Not that it matters now, I know you'll do your duty." He leans over again and taps on the list in front of me. I still don't look at it.

"I will do what's required," I start, measuring my words slowly. "But you will keep up your end of the deal and leave Madeline alone. You won't insert yourself in her relationship, you won't mess with her tuition or place at FU, and you won't disrupt her life in any way. Do you understand?" I hold his stare, not letting the smile that crosses his mouth affect me. I'm not the little boy he used to be able to scare away with just the boom of his voice. I'm a man now, and I will do what I need to in order to protect my sister.

"You should consider following my footsteps into politics, son, you'd make quite the show." I don't take his false praise for anything other than what it is, and his smile drops when he realizes his words no longer have an effect on me. "You have my word that I will not interfere with your sister's life in any way. The Darkmore boy is an acceptable enough choice given his trajectory. As long as you do your duty, I will stay away from them."

I am already on my feet and grabbing the list from his desk before he has even uttered his last word. "Consider it done."

Now I really do try and make it outside before I let my eyes drop to the list, I do, but I've never been good at delayed gratification, and with my future at stake, my restraint breaks. I'm not surprised to find the usual hoard of socialites, and businessmen's daughters, but as my eyes scan to the bottom of the page, I almost stumble at the last name on there, coming to a complete stop.

No, that can't be right, it must be a typo, a misprint, but as I read her name once, twice, three times, I have to force myself to face my father again.

"Hallie's name is on here?" My words come out as more of a question than I'd like, and my father lifts his eyes from his computer to me, but he remains silent waiting for more. "Hallie Rose Sanders, as in Maddie's best friend."

My father shrugs. "Yes, and? She comes from a good, wealthy family, her father runs a respectful, successful business, and Hallie is a nice, good girl." He returns his focus back to his screen as he adds in a mumble, "Lord knows you've done worse."

I know his words are dismissing me, and too shocked to say anything else, I turn on my heel and storm my way out of there, not stopping until I am behind the wheel of my car. Only then do I let my eyes drop to the list again, ignoring every other name on there and dropping back down to *hers*.

Hallie Rose Sanders, my sister's best friend, and the girl who has gotten under my skin since she was nine and I was eleven. I wonder what she would make of her name being on such a list? The thought is laughable. She would be the worst choice I could ever make. But then again, what if she wasn't?

No, wait, this is perfect. Hallie knows all about what was going on with Maddie being forced into an engagement, and she knows I'm the one who ultimately saved her. If I just explained the situation, then surely she would agree to helping me out just long enough to see Maddie and I graduate and get out from under our father's thumb.

Yes, this is perfect. Why tie myself to a real wife when I can tie myself to a fake one?

It's time to ask my sister's best friend for a favor.

#1
JOSH
DEVIL DANCES

I sold my soul to the devil the day I was born, I just didn't realize it at the time, but now he wants to collect with my signature on the dotted line. It doesn't matter that the devil in question just so happens to be my father, or that the deal was made to protect my sister. No, the only thing that matters now is that I have no other option than to marry someone that my father approves of. My father, Hugo Peters, esteemed Mayor of the town of Fairfield, and a complete joke of a family man. I hate him, and I know hate is a strong word, but if I could come up with one solitary word for how I feel about the man who raised me, that's what it would be. *Hate.*

My childhood was basically a silent war that I was ill-equipped to fight at the time, and worse, I wasn't the only person I had to protect from the battle. My little sister Madeline is the only one in this world that I truly love, and I would do anything for her. Which doesn't sound like the burden that it is, but unfortunately, just as I know that fact, my father does too, and he wields it against me often.

The only escape I ever had from him was hockey. From the moment I picked up my first stick and whacked it against my first puck, everything changed. It was my cold solace that eased the burn of the hell I was growing up in. It used to be the one thing I could count on, the one thing that could keep me grounded no matter what was happening, but I haven't felt at home on the ice in a long time. There was once a time where the game felt fun and easy, where scoring a goal and winning a match meant everything to me, but as of right now, I can't quite remember when I lost that.

I guess it started when my father realized I didn't want to follow him into a career in politics. It was a speech I'd heard a thousand times about how his father was in politics, how his grandfather was in politics, and that it was just what Peters' men were meant for. He doesn't care about my love for the game, or my aspirations to be in the NHL. No, the only thing he cares about is the fact that I am a disappointment to the family, something he has made more than clear in private, but that doesn't stop him from singing my false praises in public any chance he gets.

We have never seen eye to eye, not since I was old enough to understand the type of man he truly is, and all I have done since is try and shield my sister from him. A matter that he recently pushed the boundaries of like never before, when he tried to blackmail her into marrying his business associate's son, Bradley Thorne. Something I quickly rectified as soon as I was aware of it of course. It only took a little digging and some phone calls to expose his cheating on his college football team, and he quickly became unsuitable. Unfortunately though, that wasn't quite the end of it all.

I knew my father wouldn't stop. The only time he ever cares about Maddie or me is for reasons that aim to make him look better, and even getting Bradley Thorne out of the picture wouldn't have been enough to stop him. If I didn't step in, he would have just put the next suitor in line on the block and pushed my sister towards him. Maddie isn't like me, she is kind, warm, and innocent. She would never survive the burden of a loveless marriage. So I gave my father an ultimatum, I told him to leave Maddie alone and I would take her place. Of course the bastard made me wait for his answer, no doubt trying to find someone else to take Thorne's place, but then along came Nova Darkmore.

Captain of my hockey team and overall a giant man-whoring prick, yet somehow to my surprise he managed to fall for my little sister. A fact I am still having trouble trying to swallow, but the even bigger surprise is that despite the history of my father fucking his mother Diana, and basically ruining her life, he actually approves of Nova as a match for Maddie. Apparently being the star of the hockey team is good enough to make him a suitor for her, but not good enough for his only son. So I guess in the end she has won, but I will still pay the price to protect her.

The list of names of suitable future wives he gave me has been burning a hole in my desk for days now, and not just the list and the requirements that come with it, but the name that sits on the very last line of that list.

Hallie Rose Sanders.

My sister's best friend, a constant in my life since I was eleven years old, and a fiery tinkerbell-sized rocket who pushes me at every turn. I'm not sure what the hell my father was thinking putting her name on there, but now that it is, it's like I can't see any other. Hallie and I have a complicated relationship, but it wasn't always like that. In fact, I used to consider her one of my only friends, I guess in a way I still do, even if I'm not one of hers, but I had no choice but to push her away. I was already stuck in hell, I wasn't going to drag her down with me. Yet now it might be the only way for me to survive, for me to beat my father at his own games once and for all.

Today is Thanksgiving, and instead of arriving early at my parents' yearly gala, like I know they expect me to, I am pacing my room staring at the list of names in my hand. Fuck my father, fuck him for being who he is and forcing my hand in this way. He knows how much I love Maddie, how I would do anything for her, and now I've got to make a decision that will impact my life forever. And not just mine, someone else's too.

Feeling both stressed and frustrated I storm from my room, move down the hallway, and barge inside my roommate's door to get his take on things. Daemon Forbes plays on the hockey team with me and became a close friend from the moment we both started at FU. He has his own shitty background to deal with, and though I don't know all the details, I know he has it far worse than I do. Something I remind myself of as I find him sitting alone on his bed on a day that should be spent with family.

"Oh, please, do come on in," Daemon drawls, not even looking up from the sketchpad in his hand, as his pencil moves furiously across the page.

I pretty much always find him like this, tucked away and isolated in the solace that is his room, scrawling pictures he never lets anyone see, and avoiding interaction as much as humanly possible. The layout of his room is a mirror image of my own, except Daemon's walls are lined with overflowing tall, black shelves filled with books and sketch pads. We have both been tainted by the sins of our fathers, but where I let my grief spur me into action, Daemon lets his consume him. It pours out of him in waves, and for the last three years I have been doing everything I can to not let him drown.

Daemon isn't the type of person that lets people in, but after three years playing on the same hockey team, and living in the same house, he didn't really have a choice when it came to me. It's why I'm here now, pacing the one bit of clear space at the foot of his bed as I try to gather my thoughts.

"Fucking archaic bullshit that's what it is," I spit, not gaining any more of his attention than I already have. Not that it matters, he has been witness to this particular rant more than once over the last month. "I'm twenty-one, who fucking gets married at twenty-one?"

"You apparently," Daemon grumbles, eyes laser-focused on whatever is on the page in front of him, his pencil still moving.

I ignore him as I continue. "And Christ, the names on this damn list, so many fucking names," I hiss, smacking the list in my hand with the other. "Serena Lock, Callie White, Jessica Farmhouse, Lana Cockworth, I mean really? Lana fucking Cockworth? Her name backwards spells anal for Christ's sake."

A version of a smile graces Daemon's mouth, as the edge of his lips curl. "I'd definitely lead with that in your proposal," he muses, using his finger to blend in whatever he is doing.

"Brianna is on here Daemon, and her friend Georgia, the one always trying to fuck you at parties," I exclaim, but again his eyes don't move from his art, not that I begrudge him that, I know how much it helps him. Instead I forget the list for a second and focus on my father instead. "Can you believe he expects me to just pick a wife, like it's that simple, like I'm just picking what I want to eat for dinner tonight?" I continue pacing back and forth at the end of his bed, wishing the dark hole he has created here for himself could swallow me whole.

Unfortunately I am not that lucky, and as if he has direct access to my thoughts, my phone starts ringing and I spy my father's name flashing across it. I groan, showing Daemon the screen, who does nothing but frown and sketch even harder, and then I accept the call.

"Father," I say in a clipped tone, seeing no point in exchanging pleasantries when I am already late.

"Have you picked someone yet?" he asks, no doubt sitting in his office with an after dinner whiskey and making his party guests wait for his big entrance. He doesn't have to elaborate, he knows I know what he means, he's probably been rejoicing at the fact he now has control over me after losing it for so many years.

"Yes," I lie, hoping he doesn't detect the dishonesty in my words, as my eyes flick back to the list in my hands. "Just narrowing down a few final details," I add, not bothering to elaborate like I know he wishes I would.

"Well don't take too long," he snaps, that temper of his, one of the main things I inherited from him, teetering on the edge of release. "Our position in this society is more fragile than you think, just look at what happened with the Mayor of Black Hallows."

I frown at the mention of Carter Fitzgerald, the infamous ex Mayor of the town just over from us. "Dad, that Mayor was a psychotic serial killer, I don't think this is the same kind of thing."

My father scoffs, "Yes, well, we all have our secrets, Joshua."

When I flick my gaze to Daemon now he is watching me carefully, no doubt hearing every one of my father's words in the otherwise silent room. Secrets, that's what it always boils down to, doesn't it? Secrets are what keep Daemon in this dark spiral, secrets are what got my father into office, secrets are what ruined my relationship with him, and secrets are how he almost stole my sister's future from her.

"Just stop wasting my time and pick a suitable wife or I will do it for you," he adds, interrupting my thoughts, and I don't respond, turning his words over and over in my head.

It doesn't matter what I do, those words still bring me to only one solution. My eyes flick down to the list yet again, and just like they have since the moment my father gave it to me, they stop on the name on the very last line. Despite everything, Hallie is the only reasonable choice he put on that list. She is the only one on there who truly sees me, knows me, knows my family, knows what I am up against here, and will hopefully be willing to help me end all of this.

"I understand," I finally reply in a clipped tone, this time not waiting for a response as I end the call and stare at the name of my future wife.

"It has to be Hallie," I all but whisper, earning another grunt from Daemon. "I just have to convince her, which should be easy enough, right? We're friends." Daemon laughs this time. It's subtle, but it's definitely a laugh, and I stare him down. "What? You think she won't agree?"

Daemon shrugs noncommittally, his pencil paused as he sighs, "She seems nice enough." That's it, four words, more than most people would get, yet they make me smile.

"You're right," I tell him, folding the list in half and shoving it into my pocket. "The choice is simple, she *is* the only choice." None of the other women on this list could ever compare to her, they don't share the same history as we do, regardless of how many of them I have already fucked, her excluded of course. "Thanks, Forbes, you always know just what to say." I don't wait for his response, leaving his room as quickly as I came with only one destination in mind.

Hallie and I might not be close anymore, but I know like me, she would do anything for Maddie. She cares about my sister just as much as I do, and I'm almost certain she isn't seeing anyone right now because I haven't seen any guys around her. Not that she ever really has guys around, except for that one prick from high school who used to brag about taking her cherry until I broke his arm in two places and he finally disappeared.

Regardless, Hallie is better than any other wannabe trophy wife looking for their step up the societal ladder. She is the right choice, the sensible choice, the only choice.

I just have to get her to agree first.

#2

HALLIE

INDICENT PROPOSALS

The clock on my nightstand reads 7:01 pm which means I am officially late. I hate being late, it's something I have never been good at, but after letting my parents collar me into that extra game of Pictionary, I knew it would be inevitable. If it wasn't for me already having plans with them I probably would have lay paralyzed until it was time for the party.

It's Thanksgiving, and as always I enjoyed a lovely home-cooked meal prepared by my father, which my mother meticulously supervised until he eventually threw her out of the kitchen. That was swiftly followed by a game of Charades, with more questionable results, and then finally, Pictionary. It's tradition. One that was cut short this year as I needed to rush back home to get ready for the annual Peters' Family Charity Gala. Mayor Peters throws it every year, encouraging people to open their checkbooks for the needy, when in reality all he is trying to do is make himself look good, and as usual, I am already running late.

It was made worse when I got caught in traffic on the way home, another pet peeve of mine, but I thought I would still be able to make some of the time up if I just stuck to my usual routine of getting ready. Shower, shave, hair wash, dry hair, do makeup, finish hair, and then finally get dressed, it's the same order I always do it in, and it helps me remain calm, even if I am running behind. Now I have my makeup done, and my hair half out of its rollers, as I step into my dress and realize it's going to be a struggle to zip it alone.

Damn it, where is my best friend when I need her?

The only reason I attend these damn parties is for her, and she can't even be here to help her best friend out in a dress crisis. I thought for sure she would be home by now, even though I know she is spending the holiday at the hospital with her boyfriend Nova. They are visiting his mom during her cancer treatments, but visiting hours will have come and gone by now, so I can only presume that he persuaded her into some alone time before she has to leave him. Maddie is being forced to attend her dad's party too of course, although her father conveniently forgot to invite her new boyfriend. I scoff at the thought, imagining several ways I could make him suffer for everything he has put her through, none of them entirely legal, yet still it brings a smile to my face.

Scanning my room for my shoes, and trying and failing to fasten up my dress, and getting annoyed at how the fabric feels, I hear the doorbell ringing downstairs and curse. Who the hell could that be? Sighing, I stalk from my room, pulling out the last of my rollers as I go, and clutching my dress to keep it upright. When I am almost at the door, the person on the other side rings again, and I am ready to rip them a new one with the mood I am currently in, but when I swing it open I find the last person I expected to see, well not until the party at least.

Josh Peters.

The Puck Decoy

I have known Josh since I was nine years old, but in recent years I have for some reason, become the absolute bane of his existence. We used to be best friends, inseparable really, and I'm not sure when that changed, I just know it did. Josh was eleven when I moved in next door to him, and I can still remember the very first time I saw him. My mom and dad were shouting orders to the movers and trying to contain the chaos, as all our earthly possessions were transferred from truck to house, and that meant I was left unsupervised to explore the grounds. It was December, yet still it was unusually cold, but when I came across the boy in the snow with a stick and a puck, the freezing air suddenly melted away.

He was a force on the ice even then, and all I could do was stand and stare in complete and utter fascination, as he flew around the makeshift rink he'd crafted out of rocks. I'd never had a crush before, but I was pretty certain that from the moment I laid eyes on him I was changed forever. That something in me was irrevocably altered, and as if moved by magic, I started walking towards him until I was standing in the middle of the fake rink and completely in his way. I expected him to yell, or at least tell me to shove off, but he just stared at me in wonder and confusion until he finally said, "Well, do you want to play or not?"

That was the first time he ever spoke to me, and the first of many games of hockey we played together, and to this day they are still some of my favorite memories from my childhood. It wasn't long after that, that I was introduced to the rest of his family and met my best friend Madeline. Maddie and I bonded quickly over our shared love for Taylor Swift and our aversion to pickles. I mean, what else do you need at nine years old? Then we quickly became inseparable, sitting together in every class, and spending almost every evening in our rooms gossiping about anything and everything, yet not once did I ever speak of the butterflies in my stomach that occurred anytime I looked at her older brother.

My eyes unwillingly scan him from head to toe as I take in his strong muscular form, completely irresistible in his black tuxedo. His blond hair is tousled perfectly, just like always, and those blue eyes like steel are sharp, focused, and completely annoyed, just as they usually are when looking in my direction. He looks angry, which again is the norm lately, but there is a simmering tension burning beneath the surface, almost as if he is nervous or something, which isn't like him at all.

I clutch my dress even tighter and take a deep breath to prepare for the battle with him. "To what do I owe this displeasure, Joshua," I drawl, forcing my eyes to his, and praying he doesn't notice the blush now burning up my neck. I've become an expert at hiding my feelings for him over the years.

Which is a stupid notion because of course he doesn't notice, he never does. I've been in love with my best friend's brother for almost a decade now and he still looks at me in the same way he did the day that I stepped in the middle of his rink. Yet tonight I can't help but notice there is something different about him and his stare.

"Can I come in?" he asks, those ocean eyes sparkling with an intensity I have never seen before, and it makes it hard to breathe.

"Maddie isn't here," I force out, trying to subtly inhale another deep breath to calm my now racing heart. The only time he looks better than he does right now is when he is burning up a sweat in his hockey uniform, yet still his entire presence is distracting.

He offers me a grim smile. "I know," he starts, clearing his throat. "I, er, I came to talk to you." I was right, he does look nervous, which like I said, is a first for him. I haven't seen him look this unsure since before he learned how to ignore the taunts his father would fire his way when we were young.

Too surprised to say anything, I step aside and let him pass as I try and recall the last time he ever came to me directly for anything. Of course, there is never a time we don't talk. I see him every couple of days since he checks on Maddie often, and I've done my own checking on him in recent weeks given the tension between him and her new boyfriend and everything that happened, but this seems different.

I give him my back, closing the door behind us, and then take a final deep breath before moving towards the stairs. "Can we talk in my room, I am already running late," I say pointlessly, considering him being here makes him just as late as I am.

Josh follows me without a word, slipping into the uncomfortable silence that has become our norm in recent years. Gone are the shared jokes, and teasing taunts, and left in its wake is a stalemate of twisted barbs I can't recover from. I don't think he means for it to be this way, but once he went to college he put this distance between us and now everything from before is lost in the void that is now our common ground.

I move straight to the chair at my dresser and sit down to slip on my heels, clutching the bodice of my dress to my chest to keep it in place as I slip the straps around my ankles. "So what can I do for you on this fine evening, Joshua?" I ask in an attempt to hide my nerves, standing in my heels and checking them out in the mirror while running my fingers through my hair in an attempt to make it look effortlessly styled.

I can feel Josh's stare on me and it makes me nervous, just like it always has. I know it's cliche, falling for your best friend's brother, one who has no interest in me, but when he looks at me, it's like everyone else in the world ceases to exist. If only it were the same for him.

"Okay, well," he starts, trailing off, once again looking intense as our eyes collide in the mirror. He takes a step towards me when his stare drops down my back, no doubt taking in my unzipped dress, and without thinking his hands automatically dance up my spine to fasten me up. I'm sure he doesn't notice the goosebumps his touch leaves behind, and I practically leap away from him as his fingers skirt against my skin, causing him to rapidly retreat his hands. "Sorry, I forgot," he mumbles, moving back to my doorway, and before I can ask what he means, he adds, "Hallie, I need you to marry me."

I freeze, momentarily caught in a time where the boy I've loved since I was nine has just asked me to marry him. No, that's stupid, of course that's not what he said, I'm just letting the fantasies I make up in my head before bed run away with me.

"Sorry what?" I ask with a laugh, knowing I misheard him somehow.

"I need you to marry me," he repeats, more certainty in his voice this time, and somehow I definitely heard him right, though it doesn't make me believe him any more.

We stare at one another without a word, just like we did that day on the ice, only this time he doesn't break the silence. He's looking at me expectantly, patiently even, waiting for a response to his question, but all I can do is stare back blankly, as I try to work out what this interaction could possibly mean. Maybe it's some sort of new humor I am not picking on. I am known to be bad at that kind of thing, jokes don't always land with me, but it's been a long time since we shared any kind of joke with one another.

"Is this some sort of prank I don't understand?" I ask nervously, hating the confusion that stains my tone. "Like when I was twelve and you went to kiss me but then you fell off that rock?" I quickly add, before the nerves building up inside of me explode and render me silent.

Josh smirks now, some of his usual bravado returning as he

leans his huge body against the frame of my door. "First of all, I wasn't trying to kiss you, you had something on your face," he lies boldly, and now I have to smirk at him for still holding onto his version of events for so long. He's such a big fat liar. "Second of all, you pushed me off that rock," he recalls, pointing his finger at me in accusation.

"Eh, potato, potato," I say with a shrug, knowing full well the panic and nerves that burned through me when he tried to kiss me that day. Yeah I pushed him, hard and fast, but I'm never gonna admit that to him. The same way he will never admit to me that he actually *was* trying to kiss me.

"Hallie," Josh sighs, his exasperation returning, and this tone is one I am definitely more familiar with in recent times.

"Joshua," I toss back sarcastically, and his face turns solemn.

"Hals, this isn't a prank," he confirms, leaving his spot by the door and closing the distance between us. "I really need you to marry me." Seven words I have imagined in an entirely different context, yet somehow this one is a lot weirder than my smutty dreams.

"I don't understand," I admit in a whisper, knowing that out of everyone, Josh is the last person who would judge me. He knows me better than almost anyone.

I have always known I was different. It was never something that was shied away from in my household growing up, and when I was diagnosed with Autism Spectrum Disorder at seven years old, it was something we celebrated. There was finally a reason I was different, a reason certain things were so hard for me, and a reason I looked at the world in a way others didn't. It's why I don't feel scared to ask for more context with him, because he understands my need for it, and doesn't hesitate to grant it.

"Do you think my father just accepted that Brad was out of the picture, and let Maddie be with Nova without consequence?" he starts, fury lacing every word as he steps away from me and takes a seat on the end of my bed. "You know him, you know his aspirations, if it wasn't Bradley Thorne then it was just going to be someone else, maybe even someone worse. I couldn't have that, so I stepped in."

I let his words wash over me, nodding at each and every one of them until I focus on the last three. "You stepped in?" I repeat slowly, trying to make sense of exactly what he is saying. "What does that mean? What did you do?"

Panic sets in because I already know the answers to the questions I just asked. I know Hugo Peters far better than I wish I did, and I know about the marriage deal he tried to blackmail his daughter into these past few months. Which means I also know that it was foiled somehow, and what Josh means when he says he stepped in, but for some reason I need to hear him say it.

"I took Maddie's place," he confirms, my worst fear springing to life, and I swear his words feel like little shards plunging into my heart. "My father will leave Maddie alone as long as I marry someone of his choosing."

Oh my god, this can't be happening. Josh has to get married. Josh. *My Josh*. Married. The words tumble through my mind over and over again, clashing together like titans until I can barely focus on anything else. What kind of fucked up bullshit is this? I'm no stranger to coming from a prominent family, but my parents would never do something like this to me, no matter what they could gain in return. And what is the Mayor even gaining? What does he get out of using his children like they are pawns in his games?

It's only then that another thought enters my mind. Josh just proposed. He stepped in and took Maddie's place, his father is forcing him to take on the business marriage, and now he's here proposing to me.

"And he chose me?" I say, completely bewildered, I didn't even think his father liked me, outside of the fact that my last name is Sanders. I've always felt like he thought I was weird and insufferable. Josh opens his mouth to say something, but then quickly snaps it shut and just nods. "Oh god you're serious aren't you? You really need me to marry you."

His face is solemn, nothing like the face I expected from the man proposing marriage to me as he sadly replies, "I wouldn't joke, not about something like this, or literally anything else for that matter." He's right of course, like I said, gone is the boy who participated in something as simple as jokes, and left behind is the man his father molded in his neglect.

I can see his despair as clear as day, something I probably wouldn't pick up on if he were someone else, and I know he doesn't want this. Josh has never even had a girlfriend, not one he has made known anyway. Sure, he fucks around a lot, I've heard the rumors, but I have never once seen him so much as kiss a girl in front of me, let alone anything more. Now here he is, sitting in my room and proposing marriage, to *me* of all people.

Fate has a sick and twisted sense of humor doesn't she, because how many times have I wished for something to happen between us? How many times have I fallen asleep making up scenarios in my head where we end up in bed together? How many times have I wished that my best friend's brother looked at me the same way I look at him? There have been too many to ever possibly count. Yet now here he is, offering me what sounds like the world, only it's completely the opposite. This isn't love, it isn't even commitment, it's a doomed deal made to protect the only person he *is* capable of loving.

As if reading my mind, Josh stands and closes the distance between us, yet he doesn't touch me this time. "Look, Hals, I know I am asking a lot, especially from you, but this is Maddie we are talking about. If I don't do this then my father is going to punish her for it, and I don't know any other way to save her, not yet at least. Please, just help me do this, help me save her," he pleads, and just for a second, he's back to being the lonely boy on the ice again, asking me if I'm playing, and just like that very first day, I can't say no to him. Not to the little boy back then who became my first crush, and not to the grown man now who became my first love... and I guess, my first husband.

"We're going to need some ground rules," I start, knowing that if I am agreeing to this then I need to protect myself. "If we do this then we need to have a solid agreement in place." I push away all the emotions fighting against one another inside of me and focus my mind on logic and reasoning. He needs my help, and I am going to help him, it's as simple as that.

I move to my bedside table and pull out the green notepad and sparkly pen I keep in there. Of course they are both untouched, I hoard both items for their beauty only, but right now I have nothing else on hand, and this doesn't feel like a scrap paper or phone notes kind of deal.

"You're serious?" Josh asks, his eyes fixed on the things in my hands as I move back towards him.

"I am always serious about making lists, Joshua." I don't know why I need to remind him of that fact, he knows me well enough by now, he has been witness to plenty of my lists over the years, and the subject of many more, not that he has seen those ones.

I doubt he'd appreciate all the pros and cons lists about him that I have hidden in my phone notes.

I quickly start jotting on the top of the pad and when I move my hand, Josh snorts. "The never forever rules, really, Tink?" The old nickname rolls off his tongue so easily that I have to fight to keep the smile off my face. He really has no idea of the effect he has on me.

"Number one," I say out loud, ignoring him completely. "No kissing." My hand shakes as I write and I hope he doesn't notice,

I hope he thinks this rule is because it suits us both. I'm sure he has kissed hundreds of girls, and is as skillful at that as he is on the ice, but there is no universe where I could kiss Josh Peters and then walk away with my heart intact.

"Number two, no lying to one another." I am gripping the pen so tightly now that my fingers are turning white. I also feel like a total hypocrite right now considering all I do is lie to him about my feelings towards him, but it's okay because I'm pretty sure I lie to myself a lot more.

"And number three, absolutely no falling love." I finish that last one with multiple exclamation marks and Josh flashes me with that rare smirk of his that has those butterflies roaring to life inside of me.

"Just had to add the exclamation marks to be sure I understood that one, huh?" he asks, cocking his brow at me and I shrug. "Don't worry, Hals, you already know I'm not wired to find and appreciate something as simple as love," he adds with a smile, not realizing his words have just shattered the heart that beats for him.

I'm not stupid, I was present for most of his childhood, for his father's affairs and shortcomings. The only love he ever experienced was the love he has for his sister, and the love he got from his sister, so of course he doesn't believe he is capable or even worthy of feeling the joy that love can bring. The pain in my heart intensifies as I think about the love my parents showered me in, so much so that it was both glorious and suffocating, and I can't help but wonder how Josh would have turned out if he had been offered the same. Would he be different if he had bloomed in the sun instead of wilting in the shade?

"Okay now what?" he interrupts my thoughts, and I have to take a deep breath to keep my emotions in check before I answer.

"Sign here." I shove the pad towards him, and he holds my

stare for a couple of seconds before rolling his eyes and taking the pen from my hand with another side grin.

He signs his name in a neat little scrawl and then hands it back for me to do the same. Then silently I return the pen and pad back to my top drawer for safekeeping, and then steal my spine as I return to him.

"Okay, now ask me to marry you," I demand, and he blinks back in confusion with a dash of exasperation, and it reminds me so much of the boy who used to be my best friend. The same boy who I forced to propose to me with a ring pop on vacation when I was eleven. That was the first time I agreed to marry him, and he promised he would one day swap the ring for a real one, until I ate it, that is.

"I just did ask you to marry me like three times," he states with a frown and I have to smirk. This boy. So strong-willed and defiant, yet I still know every access point to get under his skin and annoy him.

"No, you need to ask me properly," I state, repeating the same line I did when I was eleven, once again straightening my shoulders in preparation for the big question.

"Hallie, will you marry me?" he asks with an air of annoyance, and I roll my eyes, letting my shoulders drop.

"No," I reply.

"No?" he repeats in question.

"Yes, no, that's not how you ask properly," I tell him, and he tips his head back and looks up at the ceiling, no doubt recalling how serious I am when it comes to my hand in marriage.

"I really forgot how annoying you are," he grumbles, and I try to ignore the veins that spill down his neck into the collar of his shirt. Why does he have to be so hot?

It's with that in mind that the next command slips right off my tongue without pause. "On your knees, twenty-two," I say, and his head snaps back down towards me.

"What?" he asks, stumbling over the word and looking at me like I have grown an extra head.

"You heard me, Joshua. You want to marry me then get on your knees and ask me properly." This might not be real, in fact it's as far from true love as I could possibly get, but hell if I am not getting a proper proposal, even if it's a fake one. I wanted it when I was eleven and I still want it now.

"Really?" he asks, looking at me like I have gone crazy. "You're insane, you know that right?" I want to tell him he is the one who makes me insane, that I have been crazy since the second I stormed into the middle of his own personal self-made hockey game, but as always the words die in the pit between us.

"Yeah, I know I'm crazy," I admit freely, not adding that I am crazy in love. "I also know I'd get on my knees if you asked me."

"What?" he asks again, in shock this time, and it's only then I replay the words I just said back in my head, and my confidence stumbles as his shock turns to a smirk. "So all I have to do is ask, huh?" he says, and the bastard knows exactly how to make me squirm.

"No, wait I mean, that came out wrong," I trip over the words as I rush to get them out, but thankfully Josh sighs as he takes pity on me.

Then he drops to one knee in front of me, and every single one of my fantasies blur together at once. Josh Peters was a beautiful boy that grew up to be a breathtaking man, but right now, on his knee before me in his perfectly pressed tuxedo, he looks like a god sent to ruin me.

"Hallie Rose *Tinkerbell* Sanders," he starts, and my breath catches in my throat as he smirks at his own joke. "I don't have a ring pop on hand, but will you please do me the honor of becoming my fake wife so I can save my sister and your best friend from a terrible and lonely future?" he asks, and when I raise an amused brow, he finally adds, "Will you marry me, Hallie Bear?"

The words hang in the air between us, just like they did when we were kids, except now there is no childhood innocence lingering there. Something shifts at his words, and I want to make a joke, to refuse him, to tell him I can't marry him. To keep us in the black and white we have grown comfortable in and not push us back into those shades of gray that I could never understand, but I can't, because it's him. The boy I fell in love with when I was a child, now a man I would do anything for, especially when it comes at the price of helping the one person we both love most in the world.

It might hurt me, change me, break me irrevocably, but if there's one thing I could never do, it's say no to Josh Peters.

"Yes," I say, barely above a whisper, as I force back the tears threatening to break free at what I am about to do. "Yes, Joshua, I will marry you."

And just like that I am once again free falling into his abyss.

> # #3
> # JOSH
> ## GAME PLANS

The drive over to my parents' house is unusually silent given who my passenger is. I've spent years being on the receiving end of many heated debates, and thought out monologues regarding things that interest Hallie, but right now she remains tight-lipped by my side the entire time. In fact, she has barely said two words since she agreed to marry me, something I still can't quite believe she agreed to, and then we were somehow walking out of her house to come here. I'm not sure if her new found silence is a good thing or a bad thing, especially not when her usual M.O. is to talk endlessly until she drives me completely crazy. That Hallie I can deal with, but this one? I'm not so sure.

Her eyes are fixed out the window, her stare blank and uninterested, as if she would rather be anywhere else but here. Her hands are fidgeting in her lap, a nervous tell of hers, and her leg is bouncing up and down rapidly as we pull through the community iron gates that lead to my childhood home. She has been here at least a thousand times, and now I can't help but wonder what she sees when she looks at it. It looks nothing like how her parents' home used to be, even though they resided on this very same estate before they moved. No, her house was warm, inviting, and filled with love. Nothing like the one we are both about to enter.

I'm not surprised when we pull up that the whole place is covered in fall decorations, which will no doubt make all the partygoers swoon, but all I see is the stark truth: that my father cares more about his image than he does anything else.

When we reach the usual valet they hire, I greet him by name as I pass him my keys, knowing he will take it to my usual spot, before moving around the car and opening the door for Hallie. She looks at the house with the same disdain that I am sure is clear on my own face, and it only makes me smile. If anyone hates my father the way Maddie and I do, it's her. I just hope she can hold her own against him because upgrading herself from my sister's best friend to my future wife is only going to put her under more fire. She knows I will protect her, at least I hope she does, but I need her more than she realizes, especially if I am going to beat my father at his own game.

We move towards the front door but I halt, feeling that same dread that drowns me every time I come here starting to consume me. In truth this place hasn't felt like home for me in a very long time, and it feels even less like it now that I no longer live here, but for once I'm not alone. Hallie steps up beside me and loops her arm through mine as if it's the most natural thing in the world for us. She stares up to where my mother and father stand in the doorway, greeting guests as if they are a perfectly happy couple.

"You're not bailing on me already are you, Joshua, because I have to say, that's very bad husbandly form," she jokes with a smile, flicking her gaze to me, and when our stares lock, my heart stops thundering in my chest. That calming effect she always seems to have on me, soothing me from the inside out.

Her green eyes are shining bright as usual, with a hint of mischief just like always, and I can't help but be captivated by her. She will make the perfect wife. She's stunning of course, her beauty only exaggerated tonight by the gold dress that clings to her every curve, but it's more than that. She's smart, funny, kind, passionate, and I know no matter what she will always be there for me. One day she will make the perfect real wife, but for now, we have to fake it until we make it.

It's why I entwine our arms even closer, rolling my neck, and straightening my shoulders at the same time in preparation for the night ahead. "I wouldn't dream of it, Hals, I'll always have your back," I tell her, and I mean it. This thing between us might be fake, but our friendship is real, and I care about her more than she knows.

Saving Maddie is the most important thing to me, but having someone to help me do it is just an added bonus, especially with that someone being Hallie. At least tonight, and for the foreseeable future I guess, I'll have her by my side for support. Which is a strangely comforting feeling I haven't felt– or should I say, let myself feel–since I was a child..

"And I'll always have yours," she replies softly, and before I can thank her, she adds, "But only if we survive our first night as a fake engaged couple."

Those last words are meant just for me as she starts leading us up the stairs towards where my parents wait. My mother is still fawning over guests coming through the door, but my father's gaze is already laser focused on the two of us. His eyes take in our linked arms and pressed shoulders, and a winning smirk tugs at the corner of his mouth. He thinks he's finally got me exactly where he wants me, just like I need him to. This is the start of the game, the one he has been winning for far too long, but tonight, I take back some of that power and push back in the only way I know how.

When we reach the top of the stairs, the guests talking with my mother finally move aside and she spots us too. "Oh, Josh darling, look at you, so handsome in your tux," she coos, stepping forward, and I pull my linked arm from Hallie's to embrace her in greeting.

"Good evening, Mother, you look beautiful," I respond blandly, my ingrained manners coming out in full force, before I step back and nod my head at the man by her side. "Father," I add dryly, and his smirk is still filled with knowing pride that most might mistake for affection towards me, but unfortunately I know better.

Silence stretches between us, and my mother does what she does best, and quickly jumps back in with a smile that doesn't quite reach her eyes. "And, Hallie dear, look at you, just as beautiful as always," she preens, offering her a hug.

"Thank you, Mrs. Peters, I was just about to say the same to you," Hallie replies, perfectly polite as always, before pulling away from my mom. As if on instinct, I put my arm around her shoulders and pull her back into me, causing my mother to flick her gaze between the two of us.

I see wonder there now, and just as I am sure that my father is buzzing inside right now, I am also sure that my mother isn't privy to the deal that forced my current hand. Of course she ignores the obvious, just like always, and decides to change the subject instead. "And just where is your sister, I thought she was coming with you?" she asks, forcing an air of annoyance in her tone, when deep down I bet she wishes Maddie wouldn't come at all.

My eyes stay locked with my father's as I respond to her. "Maddie is still with Nova and his mother, they all spent Thanksgiving together as you know, but she will be here soon."

If I wasn't watching him closely I would have missed the slight tightening of his jaw at that news before he hides it. "Madeline is still coming alone, yes?" he asks, and I have to smirk. I might hate Nova Darkmore, but seeing the effect he has on my father is very satisfying for me.

"Yes, because god forbid she brings another hockey player to your fancy party, huh?" I ask with a scoffed laugh, and finally my father frowns.

He opens his mouth to say something, but Hallie beats him to it. "The place looks great, Mayor Peters, Mads is going to love all the decorations. We won't keep you, looks like you've got more guests coming." She nods her head behind us to where more people are about to ascend the steps, and before my mother and father can say anything else, she is dragging me away.

We brush past my parents, but before I can make it another step, my father grabs my arm and leans into my ear and whispers, "Pretty, polite, and politically respectful. Looks like the apple doesn't fall too far from the tree now does it? Great choice, son."

I rip my arm away from him, but just as I am about to tell him I will never be anything like him, Hallie grips my hand and the words die on my tongue.

"Come on, twenty-two, I need a drink," she softly pleads, and I turn to find her green eyes shining bright once more, and that's all it takes. I don't linger, I don't turn around to dignify my father with a retort, I just squeeze her hand softly, and pull her back into my side as we make our way fully into the party.

The whole place is swarming with overdressed people that blend perfectly into the extravagant decor. All of them have fake smiles painted on their faces as they complement one another, all while ignoring the staff moving around with trays filled with champagne and canapes. I nod at a waiter as he passes, and he stops to offer us both a glass as I give thanks and Hallie watches the room by my side.

"So what's the game plan?" she asks, surveying over everyone with a smile I know to be fake, her mask for the people now perfectly in place.

Hallie hates parties like these, yet has never missed a single one, usually staying by Maddie's side for comfort, and I mildly wonder why she always insists on coming. I mean, yes, she grew up in this world just like I did, but her parents are a far cry from mine. They have never forced her hand in anything, from school to her personal life, she has always been free to make her own choices. I mean, hell, they don't even attend these things anymore, yet Hallie RSVPs yes to every single one. Something I think I have taken for granted in the past, but right now with her here, I feel a little contentment, especially with Maddie running late.

"What do you mean, what's the game plan?" I ask, watching her as she watches everyone else, which is why I catch her signature eye roll that I am always on the receiving end of.

"Holy hell, Joshua," she curses, making me smile, before she looks at me head on and adds, "You've played hockey since you could practically walk, how are you still this dense?"

I almost choke on my champagne at her insult. "I thought making you my fiancé might make you be a little bit nicer to me," I reply, clearing my throat, and she rolls her eyes at me again.

"Well, you thought wrong," she snaps, closing the small amount of distance between us as she lowers her voice to ensure she isn't heard. "Your father is forcing your hand and now in turn mine, and you're telling me you don't have a game plan? I mean, look around, Josh, half of this party is already staring at us in wonder."

I do as she says, flicking my gaze casually towards the

people in our vicinity, and she's right, they *are* looking at us. They are pretending they aren't of course, but every second or so, someone's eyes meet mine and then shift to Hallie with wonder. People are used to seeing us together at things like this, but we usually appear as a trio, with Madeline as a buffer in between us. We are never alone together, not anymore, not since I pushed her away, now here we are completely under scrutiny.

I mean, it's not surprising, I never ever bring a date to my parent's parties, not just because I don't want to bring anyone here beneath my father's watchful stare, but just because I don't date, period. I have enough pressure to deal with without adding a girlfriend to that mix, which I know is ironic considering now here I am with my future wife, but that's a means to an end. Hallie will help me with this and then we will just go back to normal as friends.

I turn my stare back to her and she smirks, shaking her head slightly before she leans in even closer, bringing her mouth to my ear. "If you want people to believe we are engaged, you might want to start pretending a little better and looking at me like you actually enjoy my company," she laughs in a whisper, her floral scent lingering even when she pulls away, and I stare at her dumbfounded.

"But I do enjoy your company, Hals, I don't have to pretend," I respond without thought, and as our eyes lock her smile softens, but just as she opens her mouth to say something, I see a couple approaching us in my peripheral vision. "Incoming," I whisper, before turning to them with a smile. "Mr Sharman, good to see you," I say, as I shake his hand firmly.

Mark Sharman is an associate of my father's, they work in office together, and once upon a time he went against my dad to run for Mayor and failed, and some would say he never quite got over it. He's not a vindictive man by any means, but he is one always looking for a leg up the ladder, which is why he accosts me at every event we attend together.

"Josh, you're about as good a liar as your father," he smiles, shaking my hand right back.

"Oh, I doubt that," I laugh, turning to his wife. "Mrs Sharman, looking lovely as always." She blushes, confirming the rumors that her preference for younger men isn't false, which is why I gratefully pull Hallie into my side. "May I introduce my fiancée, Hallie Rose Sanders."

Mrs Sharman loses her smile, but Mark seems to find the news nothing but interesting, as he purrs. "I didn't know you were engaged, Josh, I bet your father is proud." He winks, as he sticks his hand out to shake Hallie's. "Lovely to meet you, Miss Sanders, any relation to Jeremy Sanders Finance?" he questions, naming Hallie's father's business with ease, which isn't a surprise, they do run in the same social circles after all.

"Yes, Jeremy is my father," Hallie confirms with a polite smile, releasing his hand and curling hers back around my arm. "And our engagement is new, the announcement will be running this week," she lies with ease, and it just cements my mind even further that she was easily the only choice I could have made.

"Well, let us be the first to say congratulations," Mark hums, raising his glass of champagne to us before taking a sip. I almost thank him, but then he adds, "Does this mean you are finally going to follow your old man into politics and hang up that hockey stick of yours?"

It's the same tireless question I always get at events like these, and I wouldn't put it past my father to lean on his friends to ask me stuff like this constantly. It's a well known fact that Peters men are political men, apparently having a passion outside of that is unheard of, especially to my father. Maybe he thinks if enough pressure is applied that I'll bend to his will, but it hasn't happened yet.

Hallie's hand tightens on my arm and before I can come up with the politically correct response that Mark is no doubt searching for, Hallie steps in. "Josh is actually on track to play for the NHL, so you'll see him on your TV screens long before you find him in the Mayor's office," she gleams, looking ever the proud future wife I need her to be, as she smiles up at me. "Maybe you should take a day off from politics and catch a Flyers game sometime soon and you might find yourself inspired," she adds, turning back towards Mark and fitting him with a kind glare.

Yep, definitely the perfect choice for my wife.

"Oh I have no doubt I'd find just as much politics on the rink as I do in my office, my dear," Mark gleams, watching the two of us even closer than before with a look I definitely don't like.

The string quartet in the corner starts playing a fresh song, and I take the opportunity to escape his assessing glare. "If you'll excuse us, it's time I take my new fiancée for a spin around the floor." I grab Hallie's champagne glass and discard it along with my own, and nod the two of them goodbye as I lead her out onto the dance floor.

"You hate dancing," Hallie murmurs with a knowing smile, as she brings her hand up to meet mine, and I place my other at the small of her back.

"Yeah, well, I hate my father's co-workers even more, I guess," I answer her truthfully, and she laughs, as we fall seamlessly into a dance we have done a least a hundred times before.

A comforting silence stretches between us, one that can only be bound by years of friendship, as we sway with one another and block out the outside world. I didn't always hate dancing. In fact, I remember a time when we did this almost daily one summer. It was right before my dad's affair with Diana Darkmore came out, and I didn't have a care in the world. I thought my parents were the picture of happiness, I actually aspired to be like them one day, and Hallie and I would watch their wedding video on repeat and dance like it was our wedding day. I thought I would grow up and be just as happy, just as in love, but I was nothing but a foolish child. The only wedding I will ever have is the one to Hallie in the name of taking my father down, and I'll still be happier than he ever was.

We slowly rock back and forth, and I realize this is the first time we have danced together since that summer, and it now feels a lot more intimate than it did back then. "You know you're nothing like him," Hallie utters against my chest, her head tucked comfortably under my chin thanks to our height difference, and I wish her words didn't affect me. She knows better than most what it does to me to be in his shadow. "Like, you know you're amazing, right?"

I ignore the sentiments of what she is trying to get at and choose humor as my deflection instead. "I mean, I haven't had any complaints, amazing does seem to be the general consensus," I grin, and I practically feel her eye roll.

"I meant at hockey, you prick," she curses, and I chuckle. This I can do with her, our banter, it's simple, easy, and comfortable. I am forever fascinated by how easily I can push her buttons.

I might have spent the last few years keeping her at arms length and not allowing myself to be open and fun with her like this, but those old habits don't just disappear. The same foundation we built as kids is still there, it's just buried beneath all my issues.

"That's not a very nice way to speak to your future husband, Hallie Bear," I tease, and I feel her hand tighten around my shoulder as she digs her nails into me in response.

"My future husband is about to get a dick punch in front of all of his father's friends if he isn't careful," she claps back in her usual, taunting manner, and I smother my laugh in her hair. It smells like cotton candy, and I can't stop myself from inhaling softly.

"Now now, stop flirting with me, Tink, or I'll have to start breaking those pesky rules you wrote so carefully on that pretty pad." My tone is joking, but my words have her pulling back and snapping her stare to meet mine, almost as if they have her intrigued. "What? Don't tell me, little old Hallie Bear enjoys breaking the rules," I tease, watching her closely and she huffs.

"Can we get divorced yet?" she snaps before adding, "I really do hate you."

"No you don't," I declare, but before she can say anything back, another voice interrupts us.

"Damn, Hals, you got him on the dance floor, it's a Thanksgiving miracle." Hallie and I pull apart and find my sister watching us both with a smile. "You both look amazing, have you been here long?" she adds, flicking her stare around the crowd with complete uninterest.

"You're late," I tell her. "Dad was pissed."

Her smile doesn't even falter as she responds, "Yeah, well, dad is always pissed." Usually hearing something like that would have her concerned, but it seems Nova has had a positive effect on her, even in such a short space of time.

"That's true," I agree with her, locking eyes with Hallie and silently conversing that we need to tell Maddie about our arrangement, before I look back to my sister and add, "We need to talk to you about something."

"Ladies and gentleman," my father's voice booms across the room, cutting our conversation off before it even started, as the lights around us lower and a spotlight pins him center stage. "You could be anywhere in the world tonight but you chose to be here with us, and for that we are eternally thankful." The three of us share a look of contempt as we all turn our focus to where he is standing with my mother by his side. "I am always thankful for everything I am blessed to have, but nothing more so than my wonderful children." He raises his glass towards us and a few guests look our way and smile as we all pretend he is the perfect father they make him out to be. "But this year I have even more to be thankful for."

Panic starts to curl in the pit of my stomach at his choice of words. No, surely this can't be going where I think this is going. He wouldn't do that, not here, not in front of everyone with no time or planning. As if her thoughts mirror my own, Hallie slips her hand into mine and squeezes tightly, and when our eyes collide, hers shift nervously towards Maddie.

"Maddie," I grit through my teeth in a whisper. "I really really need to tell you something," I plead, and of course she gives me her full attention, but just like always, my father wins.

"My son is getting married," he booms, and silence echoes around him as the smile on his face widens. "He proposed to his childhood sweetheart earlier this evening and she said yes, so please, raise your glasses to the future Mr. and Mrs. Josh Peters."

Fuck.

#4
HALLIE
AWKWARD ANNOUNCEMENTS

Applause explodes around us as all eyes turn our way, but my only focus is on the way my best friend's face drops in confusion. Maddie looks between the two of us like she is missing something, and before I can make it make sense for her, my stare flicks back towards her father. Mayor Peters is watching us closely, just like every other person in the room, and his face doesn't look as happy as it should be. This is all a game to him, he enjoys the control, and I know how happy he must feel to be forcing his son's hand to get what he wants, and this right here is the proof.

Clearly this is a test, and from the tension I can feel rolling off of Josh, he knows it too. This isn't good, I need to do something, and the first thing I have to do is damage control. The look on Maddie's face right now doesn't scream 'I am happy my best friend just got engaged to my brother', and that's a problem, especially if we expect people to buy our story. So without thinking of anything else, I throw my arms around her neck and pull her into an embrace.

If my actions of affection aren't enough for her to realize we are in an emergency, I hope my next statement is. "We can explain everything I promise, but for right now we really need you to go with this, your dad is watching," I rush my words out in a whisper against her ear, praying she understands the meaning of them, before pulling back and painting a happy smile across my face.

There is a fake smile across her own mouth now too, one I have seen at every single event like this that we have attended together, and I know I've got her. "I'm so happy for you two," she preens, tossing her blond hair over her shoulder and no doubt enthralling all of the guests around us with her beauty. "My big brother finally popped the question," she adds, smirking at Josh, who still looks more than mildly irritated.

"We knew you'd be so happy," I reply, louder than necessary, as I move into his side and place my hand on the center of his chest, which seems to jolt him from his thoughts.

"Couldn't have planned it without you, sis," he responds coolly, pulling her into us for a hug of his own before he adds much lower, "Sorry, Mads, we will explain everything after all of this."

When we pull apart there is no time for any more hushed words between us, because we are immediately accosted by other party goers. Plenty we know, and others we don't, all offering their congratulations in an effort to suck up to their Mayor. We then get asked every question you would imagine for a newly engaged couple to be asked, until I can barely think straight. I'm not very good at communicating clearly all the time, especially to people I don't know, so Madeline does her best to interrupt when she can, answering questions with ease. It reminds me that she has basically trained her whole life for this kind of thing, and all it does is reinforce to me why I am doing this.

Of course the number one question is people wondering where the ring is, which we manage to ignore or move past with ease the first couple of times we are asked, but when a third person asks, Josh jumps in and saves us. "It's being resized, we need to get it done before we get pictures for the announcements to go out." An answer which is met with understanding, because of course what's a high society wedding without an announcement.

There are mentions of engagement parties, bridal showers, and huge event spaces where we could hold the wedding, all of which overwhelm me, but my forced smile of a mask remains in place. Josh is a rock by my side, holding me against him, and any other time I might enjoy his firm body being pressed against me, but right now I just feel like I could collapse into bed and rot.

After twenty-minutes of hell, I manage to slip off and grab myself another glass of champagne, surprised to see that Josh leaves behind Maddie and follows after me. My best friend is still doing damage control after her father's bomb dropped, as her brother accosts me by the drinks table and curses.

"Can you fucking believe he did that?" he seethes, grabbing himself a glass and draining it completely. I shouldn't be surprised at his anger, I know better than most people what his true feelings towards his father are.

I flick my eyes across the room and find the man in question still watching us, which is why I casually brush my hand on his shoulder in what to outsiders would be mistaken as intimacy. "He's still watching us," I reply quietly, bringing my body next to his once more and desperately trying to ignore his alluring scent, as I pretend this whole thing doesn't affect me.

Engaged.

I am engaged. Something I have honestly wondered if I would ever be, yet now here I am, engaged, to Josh of all people.

One of the first people to ever truly get me, to become my friend, and now my fiancé.

How the hell am I going to survive this with my heart still intact?

At that thought I almost tell him I've changed my mind, that I can't do this without ever giving him a reason why, but then he looks at me. He looks at me and the ground beneath me shifts, because right now he isn't looking at me like I am his friend, he is looking at me like I am his savior, as he scoffs at what I said.

"Of course he is, if he had his way he'd have us exchange our vows right here and consummate the marriage in front of him and all his pathetic guests," Josh spits, turning towards me and pulling my body into his with little to no effort. I swallow my gasp as he presses up against me, and silently pray he doesn't see the blush no doubt staining my cheeks. "This has to work, Hallie, I cannot let him win again, we have to make him believe this is real."

His words and his body rob me of any response, because for just a second he isn't the harsh and brutal Josh I have come to know. No, instead I see a flash of the boy I fell in love with, the soft and gentle boy who became my best friend when I was nine years old. When I don't say anything, he jolts back a little, breaking his intensity as if now realizing our close position. He moves to separate us, but knowing his father's gaze still preys upon us, I grip the lapel of his jacket and hold him in place. Then I use my other hand to turn his cheek away from his father and other prying eyes, making the moment look more intimate than it is.

"It will work, Josh, I can make them believe it's real," I all but promise him, not adding out loud how easy it will be for me to do that.

A real marriage requires trust, lust, and love, and unfortunately I just so happen to have all three for my fake fiancé.

Something he thankfully doesn't notice as he sighs and nods at me, pulling our bodies apart, but looping our arms together, turning us back towards the rest of the room. Most people's eyes are still on us, and I try not to shudder under the countless female stares looking at me with distaste.

"Let's just make it through the next couple of hours, which should be easy considering we have the wrath of Maddie waiting for us," he muses, our eyes flicking over to her, and though her smile is still in place, I can still see some betrayal in her eyes as she looks at us.

"I will handle Mads, don't worry," I tell him, knowing that whenever the two of them argue, though it's rare, it always gets heated. "Let's just get tonight over with, and I'm sure everything else will be fine."

Everything but my heart that is.

We spend the next two hours blurring the lines between the stories of our friendship, and creating the fake relationship we now have, until people are making comments like 'they always knew we'd get married'. By the time we leave, I feel the mask that I have kept perfectly in place all night slipping. I'm not stupid, I know how these parties work, I have been attending ones like them for as long as I can remember, but I have never let myself be the center of attention at any of them. If anything, I go out of my way to be invisible, always staying on the outskirts, only speaking to the few people I like, Maddie and Josh included on that very short list, and then leaving without incident, and honestly I expected tonight to be the same.

Of course as usual I underestimated Mayor Peters, and it seems I am not the only one struggling with tonight's events and revelations, because when we leave the party and climb into the car, Maddie slides into the back seat silently. Which leaves me to take the front seat with her brother once more, as we endure the world's most silent and awkward car ride. Not one to ever feel comfortable in the spotlight, I don't bother breaking the tension, and by the time Josh pulls up at our house, I have practically picked all of the skin off my thumb in my anxious state.

Maddie slides out of the car first, moving right up the steps of the house, not even greeting her bodyguard Hector on her way, as she unlocks the door and stomps inside. Josh and I sigh in unison, as we both unbuckle our seatbelts and head inside to face the music.

When we reach the living room, Maddie is standing in the center and all she does is grit out one word, "Explain."

I move to take a step forward, but Josh puts out his arm and blocks my way, taking the steps necessary to put himself in the center between me and Mads. I guess he knows how to handle this situation more than I do, so I let him take the lead, it's their father's demands after all. What I don't expect is for him to totally ream her out.

"You knew this was going to happen, Maddie, what else did you expect?" His tone is harsher than I anticipated towards her, and she opens her mouth to respond but he cuts her off. "You chose Nova, remember? And I chose to step in and take your place so you could have him, so what else is there to explain?"

Of course growing up with him I am more than used to the anger that clings to him right now, but so is his sister. Maddie stalks towards him with nothing but contempt in her eyes for her brother right now, and I know this isn't going to be easy.

"What else is there to explain?" she repeats with disbelief, a humorless air about her tone. "I don't know, how about how my best friend became involved, how about why you didn't tell me this was happening, how about why you didn't pick literally anyone else in the world, huh? Why don't you explain that?" Her tone is just as harsh as her brother's, and I doubt telling her that her father picked me would make her any less angry right now. I know stepping between them will do nobody any good, so I remain quiet.

"Father made his demands and I met them," Josh replies flatly, and I wish his words didn't sting me the way they do, despite knowing how fake this all is. "Demands that were given so you could live your own life however you want, remember?"

I'm not stupid, I knew all about the deal that my best friend's father was trying to force on her. He threatened her tuition at Fairfield U if she didn't marry the guy he picked out, but when everything happened with Nova, I just assumed it was all off the table. They might not see eye to eye, but Josh has always been his golden boy. Smart and athletic, and someone he could brag about to his fellow political sycophants. I never expected him to make a new deal with his son, and even more so, I never expected Josh would ever actually accept such a thing. Yet the Mayor knew the one weakness that would get him.

"I didn't want this, and I'm not accepting it, pick someone else," Maddie urges, and panic flows through my entire body at the thought of Josh playing happily ever after with someone else, even if it is pretend.

"The deal is already done, Madeline, it was you or me, you or her," he states simply, moving to stand beside me. "And we both chose you."

Maddie looks between us, shaking her head in refusal, but when her brother doesn't budge, she turns her attention to me. "I won't let you do this, Hallie, not for me." Tears gather in her eyes now, and I push away from Josh, and pull her hands into mine.

"Maddie, you're my best friend and I love you, but you can't stop me from saving you, not when I've seen how happy you've been lately." And she has been so happy, Nova has changed her completely, it's why I didn't hesitate in saying yes, not just for

Josh, but for her too. "You can't ask me to take that away from you," I tell her with a smile.

"And I can't ask you to throw away your life to marry Josh," she cries, and I almost laugh. Laugh at the thought of anyone thinking they were throwing their life away getting to marry someone as kind-hearted as Josh Peters, but instead I just try and reassure her.

"It will be okay, we have a plan," I start but Josh cuts me off.

"Our marriage isn't really any of your business, Maddie. I asked Hallie to be my wife and she said yes, end of discussion." His words are said with such finality that I flinch, but of course his sister doesn't back down.

"No, not end of discussion," she yells back just as there is a knock at the door, and neither of them even look in its direction as they stare each other down.

I roll my eyes at their melodramatics and move to answer it, not surprised in the slightest at who waits on the other side. Nova Darkmore greets me with a smile that I'm sure would make most women's knees go weak, including my best friend's, but apparently my affliction to blond haired assholes, who are now technically my fiancé, makes me immune.

"Hals," he greets me warmly, not showing any disappointment at me being the one to answer. "How was the party?"

I step aside to let him in, given he finds his way here most nights and I am more than used to him frequenting our house now, as I grunt back, "It was... eventful." Only then does he hear the shouting coming from the living room and his smile drops as he looks at me in concern. "Like I said, eventful," I add with a sigh, leading him towards the living room.

"Did you honestly think you could just choose your boyfriend and skip off into the fucking sunset?" Josh scoffs. "Wake up, Maddie, dad wanted a deal and he got one, and it no longer concerns you." I approach the two of them with Nova by my side, and only then does Josh notice his arrival. "Why don't you enjoy the aftermath of my decisions and stay out of my business," he sneers, gesturing towards the captain of his hockey team.

"Everything okay here?" Nova asks, his question tinted with a dark edge, as he moves himself in between Maddie and her brother.

Josh's stare only hardens as it flicks between them. "Everything is fine, Darkmore," he spits, silently staring down at his sister, and ignoring Nova's presence completely.

Maddie stares right back, but I see the moment she knows her brother isn't going to back down, and her fight dissipates. She sighs heavily, looking at both of us with regret, before she turns her attention to Nova and pleads, "Just get me out of here, Charmer."

Nova looks between the three of us confused before he nods slightly, pulling his girlfriend from the fray of tension circling around us, and we both watch in silence as they leave. That silence lingers a few seconds after the door is slammed behind them, before Josh curses.

"Fuck," he yells, reaching up to loosen his tie, and cracking his neck at the same time.

"She'll come around," I tell him with more hope than I have, and he almost gruffs a laugh.

"Why are you always so optimistic that everything will just work out?" he snaps, and I can practically feel his shields going back up around him. Shields I have been trying to penetrate ever since he found out what kind of man his father truly is, and failing every time.

"I guess I just see things black and white. She is your sister and she loves you, she will get over this fight and you guys will go back to normal," I shrug, not really knowing how to answer him in any other way.

I have barely even finished my sentence when he interrupts me again. "None of this is fucking normal, Hallie." His anger flows off him in waves, and all I want to do is reach into them and pull him out. "Normal would be a father who doesn't force his children into ridiculous archaic notions just to satisfy his own needs to stay on top." He turns away from me, placing his fists on the back of the sofa and dropping his head down towards the floor, inhaling deeply as if trying to catch his breath.

Moving towards him, I place my hand on his shoulder, something I have done multiple times tonight, only this time he flinches completely. His head shoots up, and he pushes away from me like my touch is poison, and looking back at me is someone I both recognize and hate. It isn't the little boy who gave me a ring pop when we were kids, it isn't even the man who asked me to marry him just a few hours ago. No, the only person who stands before me now is his father's son.

"You did good tonight," he tells me flatly, like I'm nothing but a damn show pony, and I steel my spine against his whip of words. "We can work out whatever other issues if and when they arise, but for now we should be good." Then without waiting for me to respond, he turns on his heels and heads towards the front door. I don't bother following him, I know when it comes to Josh Peters that I have to pick my battles, and right now this isn't a war I want to wage with him.

So I let him leave, and just like always he takes half of my heart with him, and when I finally hear the slam of the door, I let my first tear fall. I don't know why I cry, but I do. I let the emotions of this entire night rush to the surface. All of the people, the music, the foods, the smells, the faking it, all of it consumes me until I barely even make it up the stairs, and I don't bother taking off my dress before I crawl into bed.

I pull Percy the Penguin, a soft toy my husband-to-be won for me when I was a kid, towards me and cuddle him tight, knowing that just like every night I wish there was someone to hold me while I cry. I also know that Josh might make my heart hurt now, but it will be nothing compared to how it will feel when this is all over. I don't care how temporary this thing between us is, I know I will barely make it out alive. Love really is the worst disease, isn't it?

#5
JOSH
CLASS CLAIMED

The announcement ran in the newspaper the Monday following our engagement, not that I was surprised. My father was efficient enough to have an affair while still running this town, so of course he was efficient enough to get the engagement in the paper less than 72 hours after it was announced. He is the mayor after all. A mayor that people bend over backwards to accommodate, hence why my phone has not stopped ringing for the last four days with the wedding planner on the other end of it. I only answered the first call, and only because I didn't know who the number belonged to. Then I stayed long enough to discover the wedding plans that were already made for my sister's forced wedding in the spring–that I botched–were now going ahead as my own. *How delightful.*

I haven't spoken to Hallie or my sister since the night of the engagement, though I'm sure they both saw the announcement. I imagine my father sent them a copy as he did me, but the only thing on my mind has been taking him down. After asking a few trusted friends, I was given the name of someone who might be able to help me. Someone I plan on paying a visit to this week, but first I have to find my fiancée and make her aware of the dinner my parents have invited us to. One to celebrate our engagement with just the family, which I know is just a ploy for my father to keep a close eye on us, but if he wants a show, I will give him one.

It's Wednesday now, and thanks to a girl in the main office, for whom I promised an introduction to my teammate Levi, I now have access to Hallie's class timetable. Hence why I am waiting outside the building that houses Hallie's last class of the day. It's late in the afternoon, but there are still a few people milling around, some of which pass and nod in greeting to me, but mostly I am left alone to wait.

After twenty-minutes or so the quiet building before me finally comes to life as people start filing out of it, and my eyes scan the crowd looking for her. Knowing Hallie she will probably be the last one out, waiting for everyone else to leave so she isn't jostled and pushed as she makes her exit, especially given her aversion to most people's touch. Unfortunately for me I am only half right.

I spy her at the back of the crowd like I thought, her brown head of curls piled in a bun on top of her head, with a few pieces at the front left down to frame her face. She is wearing leggings, tucked into a pair of black boots, matched with an oversized FU sweater and a bag slung over her shoulder. Except that isn't the only thing over her shoulder. A large arm engulfs her tiny frame, and I follow the length of it around her until I find its owner.

Archer Gray.

Archer plays on my hockey team and just so happens to be Nova's best friend. We aren't enemies, but we aren't friends either, just teammates. Kind of in the way that Hallie and I are just teammates in this fake marriage, yet that doesn't stop me from storming towards them in a rage.

Hallie spots me first, her eyes flaring wide in surprise, as I interrupt whatever Archer is telling her. "I suggest you get your hands off my fiancée, Gray, or playing pro hockey will be a distant dream," I seethe, holding him down with my stare as he takes in my arrival.

"Your fiancée?" Archer laughs, looking between me and Hallie as if this is just one big joke, but when neither of us join him in his humor, he goes from amused to confused.

"Yes, my fiancée, one who doesn't like to be touched, so I'll tell you one more time, get your fucking hands off her."

Hallie still looks surprised at the turn of events, but at my second warning, she goes from shock to anger. "Don't threaten him, you big egomaniac, he wasn't even doing anything," she argues, stepping out of his hold on her and moving towards me.

"He was touching you," is all I respond, and she has the audacity to laugh.

"Fucking hell, Joshua, he had his hand across my shoulder, not in my damn pants." Her defense does nothing to deplete my anger, especially with the people still milling around us and listening to our every word.

I close the gap between us and lower my voice to only be heard by her. "Yes and think about how this looks," I tell her. Does she not realize what being fake engaged to be married entails?

"It looks like my financé is a raging psychopath," she spits at me, that fiery temper that only I ever seem to bring out of her finally making an appearance, which brings the attention of our current problem even closer.

Archer steps into her side once more looking concerned. "Hals, what the hell is going on?" he asks her, and the nickname breeds more familiarity between them than I thought.

I stand back and assess the two of them again. She doesn't look uncomfortable in his presence, there is no fake mask on her face, and she lets him touch her. "Is there something going on between the two of you that I should know about?" I demand, and while Archer now looks amused by the direction of my thoughts, Hallie just looks exasperated.

"Of course there is nothing going on between us, Archer is my friend." Her tone sounds sincere, and I soften slightly, knowing she isn't one to lie, but then Archer cuts in before I can answer.

He slings his arm around her shoulder again, only this time his focus is on me as he gleams, "Well, that's not technically true, Sanders, what about our night on Halloween?" He wiggles his eyebrows suggestively, and I watch a blush spread up Hallie's neck.

"What the fuck happened on Halloween?"

"Nothing, it was nothing, just a stupid kiss in a game," she rushes out the words in desperation, none of them making me feel better, and all the while Archer just smiles in a way that reminds me why his best friend is Nova Darkmore.

"Oh I wouldn't call it nothing, Hals, I still think about it when I'm all alone in my room at night," Archer muses, moving towards her and making kissing noises.

"Archer, I swear to god," I start, taking a step towards him, but Hallie is quick to step in between us, pressing her hands into my chest and pushing me backwards.

"Think how it looks," she repeats my words back to me, and I lift my gaze to the people still surrounding us and waiting for more of a show.

I huff, but let her body restrain me as she turns towards my teammate. "Archer, just go, I'll call you later, okay?"

"No, she won't," I mutter at her back, and she cuts me with a scathing look as Archer laughs.

"Whatever you say, Sanders," he shrugs, looking between the

two of us one last time before he saunters off in the direction of the gym.

We both watch him leave, a few other people joining him in their retreat until we are mostly alone, which is when she turns on me. "What the hell was that?" she snaps, pushing me in the chest, and I stumble back in surprise at her outburst. "You can't just ignore me for days and then show up at my classes and accost me, Joshua, I'm not your fucking pet."

Her anger shocks me, and the only thing I can do in defense is go on the offense. "No but you are my fiancée, and people need to believe that, so the only hockey player who should be hanging off your damn neck is me." I know my argument is ridiculous, but for this plan to work, everyone needs to believe that our engagement is real.

She rolls her eyes. "Oh, please, he was not hanging off my neck, Archer is just like that, he is touchy feely with everyone." She shrugs, standing her ground completely, and all it does is infuriate me even more.

"Well he can be that way with everyone except the person who is going to be my wife," I tell her, not backing down from our heated discussion.

"Do you see a ring," she claps back, holding up her empty finger. "I'm not your wife yet, Joshua." She drags my name out like it offends her, and I have to crack my neck to stop myself from losing my temper any further.

"No, but you will be, come Spring," I tell her in contempt, shoving my phone at her, allowing her to read the countless emails that discuss the venue, the flowers, the food, and more.

I watch as her eyes scan across my phone reading message after message until she finally sighs in defeat, "Well, shit." Shit indeed. I see her shoulders tense as she takes in the amount of information about a wedding neither of us wants until she shakes her head and shoves my phone back at me. "None of this is ideal, but it's not an excuse for you to be rude to me, or my friends," she scolds, her mask of indifference now perfectly back in place.

"Archer Gray is not your friend, he's the campus whore," I snap in anger, and I see the corner of her mouth tug up into a slight smirk, yet still she holds her ground as she stares at me. "Fine, I'm sorry," I add, not even sounding convincing to my own ears and still she just glares. "Hals, come on," I plead in a softer tone. "I'm sorry, okay, it's just everything is stressing me out, my father has invited us to dinner which will no doubt be another test," I snarl as my phone starts ringing in my hand, and I spy the number that won't leave me alone. "And this damn fucking wedding planner won't stop calling me and I just feel like everything is out of my control."

The words tumble out of me and I see Hallie's demeanor finally soften as she sighs, stepping towards me, plucking my phone from my hand and rejecting the call. "So take back the control," she tells me simply, her thick lashes fluttering as she looks up at me.

"This wedding *was* me taking back control, but apparently I can't even get that right." I don't mean to sound so self-deprecating, but when you spend your entire life being told you are good for nothing in private, and god's gift in public, it's bound to give you a complex.

Ignoring my outburst, Hallie looks at me the same way she always does, without pity, without shame, without reason, and for a second I get lost in her stare. Just like always it calms me, but then she opens her mouth. "Let's get married," she states simply, so simply that I can't help but laugh at how infuriated she makes me.

"Hallie, we are getting married, I asked you like four times, remember? You made me get on my knees," I recall for her, and that almost smirk turns into a full on knowing smile.

"Oh trust me, Joshua, I remember you on your knees for me vividly," she purrs, in what sounds a lot like flirting, that it almost throws me off, before she adds, "I meant now, let's get married now, this week, our way, take back the control."

I mull over her words in my mind, thinking she is crazy at first, but then I realize her idea is perfect. My father wants control over every little detail so he can boast about it to all of his friends, well not this time. This time I am going to beat him, and Hallie is going to help me.

"My father wants us over for dinner on Sunday afternoon," I tell her, and all she does is shrug.

"So let's get married on Saturday," she replies simply. So simple and matter of fact that I can't even respond, I just stare at her. There is no one around us anymore yet still she closes the space separating us and places her hands against my rapidly beating heart. "Josh, the only upper hand your father has is holding the wedding over your head, so take it from him, then take him down."

Her floral scent surrounds us, as I clear my throat and respond, "I have a lead on that too." The name and email address given to me is tucked away in my pocket for when I can give it my full attention later, and Hallie just smiles.

"Good," she nods, stepping away from me, but then looping her arm through mine. "You can tell me all about it later, after we plan our shotgun wedding." She begins leading us away from the building that her class was in, but not in the direction of her house.

"Where are we going?" I ask, completely confused by her total agreement in this, but not missing that eye roll of hers.

"To your house," she states matter of factly, like I'm nothing but a dumb jock.

"And why are we going to my house?" I ask, and she shakes her head with a laugh.

"I see Peter Pan still hasn't grown into his adult brain," she muses with a smile, waving hello to a friend across the quad before lowering her voice. "Because people need to see us together, Joshua. You want to marry me, then you walk with me, those are the rules."

It's at this very moment that I know my father will always regret putting her name on the list, because he only thought of her as who she is to him, a powerful man's daughter, an asset, a business deal. Yet he didn't factor in who she is to me, a friend, a confidant, a person I can trust. All of which will lead to his demise, which only makes me smile as I focus back on my future wife.

"Rules, huh? Do we need to get that pesky little list out again?" I ask, letting her lead me home, and she digs her nails into my arm until I yelp.

"Don't make fun of your future wife, Joshua, or you will be on your knees again, only this time you'll be begging for forgiveness," she tells me with a smug smile.

"I told you, Tink, you want me on my knees again, all you have to do is ask," I tell her with a wink, and her answering blush makes me laugh out loud.

There has always been this tension between us, this friendly banter that I always like to test the boundaries of, and she has never been one to shy away from it. In fact she pushes every single button I have and somehow still finds more. So maybe being married won't be so bad afterall, especially to someone who used to be your best friend.

#6
HALLIE
RING POPS

The walk back to Josh's house is nice. We talk back and forth about nothing really, both of us avoiding the predicament we have forced ourselves into, and it almost feels like old times. Like the old Hallie and Josh who would spend hours together, with and without Maddie, and never got bored or tired of one another. I can still feel the anger and stress radiating off of him, but I can also feel his playfulness that always used to appear between us. He teases me, makes fun of me, but then asks about my classes, and what I've been reading lately, and I can almost forget that he's about to become my fake husband.

That is until we reach the path that leads up to his house, and he pauses, pulling his arm from mine and looking at me solemnly. "You should know that Daemon knows about us," he starts, and when I look at him in confusion he adds, "About our arrangement I mean, that this thing between us is fake."

I blow out a slow breath, wondering why out of all the people he would have told him, but all I can say is, "Okay." The word fake makes tears burn at the back of my eyes, but like I've practiced a million times I force them away.

"Levi probably also suspects something is up considering he was privy to information when I dealt with Thorne, but I haven't told him anything, and I know he probably won't care enough to ask. Landon is my friend and teammate, but I am keeping him in the dark along with everyone else," he tells me, and I nod along knowing he's right, but hating the reminder anyway. "So the only people that know the truth are me, you, Maddie, and Daemon, and possibly Levi" he tells me firmly.

"And Nova," I add mindlessly, and he pauses whatever else he was going to say and looks at me with a frown. A frown that makes me roll my eyes, because it seems even the fact that his own sister is now dating him has not made him like the captain of his hockey team even a fraction more. "Look, I know you hate him, and I also know that deep down you know hating him for something both your parents did is ridiculous, but Nova and Maddie are together now, and you have to accept that."

He scoffs at my reply. "In what way am I not accepting it? I'm only marrying you so she can be with him," he snaps, and his words are like a slap in the face.

I try not to let it knock my ego too much given his stress about everything, but still I can't help but snark, "And what a prize that is for me."

His face softens in regret as he rushes to say, "Hals, I'm sorry, you know I didn't mean it like that, it's just the guy's a douche. I don't know what she sees in him." I don't bother listing the many assets that not just Maddie, but half the female population here at FU see in Nova Darkmore, and instead just laugh.

"And I'm sure there are some people who are going to wonder what I see in my lovely future husband," I muse in response, and he smiles, shaking his head.

"Look, all I'm saying is this has to look like it's real," he pleads, reaching out and pulling my hand into his, and I try my best to hide the effect he has on me as I smile and nod.

"So let's go and put on a show." I hold out my hand to indicate for him to lead the way, and he only pauses for a couple of seconds before he nods, and turns and leads us up the path towards his house.

When we enter I brace myself for the smell of sweaty jocks, but am pleasantly surprised to find it smells fresh and almost like oranges. This isn't my first time here, but with the exception of a couple of parties, Josh made it perfectly clear to Mads and I when we started at FU that this was his space, which we both respected. Unlike on the nights of parties, the house now is clean and organized. Sure there are some shoes tossed by the door, a couple of discarded hockey bags, but everything else is mostly tidy.

We find his three housemates all home and occupied, until we walk in that is. Two of them are sitting on the sofa playing video games, and the third is in the kitchen alone, headphones on, and humming quietly to himself as he cooks, but it's clear they all note his arrival.

"Peters, finally man, come and help me kick Cooper's ass, he's..." The guy I know to be one of Josh's friends, Levi Jones, trails off when he realizes that Josh hasn't come home alone.

Levi moved to Fairfield when Josh was a freshman in high school and with their shared love of hockey they struck up an easy friendship. Most people mistake them for being best friends, and they are really close, but I know Josh well enough to know that he still keeps him at arm's length for most things. Being close to Josh myself means I knew him pretty well before we went to FU together and right now I'm not sure if that's a good thing or a bad thing.

"Hallie, hey, didn't expect to see you here," Levi adds, looking between us in confusion, which only intensifies when his gaze drops down and he notices our interlocked hands.

Levi doesn't get a chance to add anything else because his words have now brought the attention of his buddy beside him. "Oh my god, Josh brought home a girl, Christmas miracles must be coming early this year," Landon Cooper booms, pausing the game and tossing his controller on the table in front of him as he makes no secret of checking me out.

"Alright you pair of neanderthals, no need to be dramatic," Josh starts, his words casual, but I don't miss the not so casual step he takes towards them, while tucking me half behind him. "You'll be seeing a lot more of her, so get used to it," he tells them, and despite now being half-hidden, I still see both their eyes widen.

"Damn, Peters, I know you had a no touching rule for her, but I didn't think it was because you were banging her yourself, you dog," Landon drawls, diving off the sofa and holding his hand up for a high five.

"Watch your fucking mouth, Cooper, or I'll watch it for you," Josh snaps, making both his housemates look at him in surprise, and I notice we now have the attention of Daemon Forbes from the kitchen, but all I can focus on is what Landon just said.

I know you had a no touching rule for her

What the hell does that mean?

Landon holds his hands up in defense as Levi comes to join him at his side. "Sorry man, we just didn't realize you had a girl," Landon says carefully, noting the protective stance Josh has in front of me, and I can't help but feel bad for him.

"She's my fiancée and you and everyone else in this house will treat her with respect," Josh grits, not backing down from his anger, and Levi's eyes flare wide.

"Fiancée?" he splutters, clearly taken aback by this whole

situation, and I can feel this thing falling apart before it's even begun, which is why I know I need to take a stand.

I step out from behind Josh, squaring my shoulders and standing firm at his side. "You can't honestly be this surprised, Levi, I mean how long have we known each other? You must have known how I truly felt about him," I tell him with as much conviction as I can muster, which isn't hard considering everything I just said is true. Then I lean into Josh and add, "I just had to wait for this dumbass to realize how amazing I am." I mix it with my signature eye roll for effect, and Josh scoffs a laugh, placing his arm around my waist.

"Oh yeah, with every barb from your lips I just fell head over heels," he drawls sarcastically, selling the lie even more.

"Don't think I won't dick punch you in front of your friends," I tell him, and both Levi and Landon laugh.

"I guess I've been a dumbass too," Levi admits, appraising us again, and it's an effort not to squirm under his stare, but thankfully his friend lightens the mood.

"I knew you were a kinky fucker, Peters, but dick punching, really?" Landon laughs, shaking his head, but I feel Josh tense around me at his words, as if Landon just uncovered a secret, yet still I smile.

"Careful now, the dick punching is widely available," I warn him, coming to Josh's defense, and Landon narrows his eyes at me, but I don't back down.

Josh takes one warning step forward, ready to intervene, that tension back in his hold on me, but Landon rolls his eyes. "Whatever," he snarls, stomping back to the sofa and picking up his controller to continue his game.

"Alright, Tink, let's go," Josh tells me, pulling me away from the living room, towards the kitchen.

When I turn I find that Daemon is still watching us, the knife in his hand paused as he takes in the situation before him. He is still wearing his headphones, but there is no longer any humming. In fact, it seems the only thing he is listening to now is our conversation. There is a look in his eye that I can't seem to decipher, a look so intense it makes me shiver in Josh's hold as he moves us towards him.

"What's on the menu?" Josh asks, slipping away from where I stand to check out the ingredients on the island. "Oh chicken piccata, nice," he adds, answering his own question, as if he expected that Daemon wouldn't, especially given that the man in question is still watching me silently. "Can't wait, it smells delicious," Josh continues on, not seeming to care that his friend isn't responding.

No, Daemon Forbes continues to stare at me, as if his eyes can dissect every secret I have ever had, and it unnerves me completely. We aren't exactly familiar with one another, and I find myself thinking back to the game of truth or dare we played a few weeks ago with some of his other teammates. Alexander Reign dared me to kiss Archer, something that was only slightly awkward given I know Archer pretty well thanks to the economics class we share. Yet it isn't the kiss that sticks in my mind, but Daemon's reaction to it. He didn't say anything, just like now, but he watched it like he both enjoyed it and hated it at the same time. Yet I could still feel Daemon's stare, except he wasn't looking at me, he was looking at Archer, and I can't help but wonder if he has some secrets of his own to divulge.

"Well we've got some wedding planning to do," Josh interrupts my thoughts, and I watch as Daemon finally turns his way, sharing a knowing look with him and Josh nods.

Then he leads me away from the kitchen and up the stairs, and I feel Daemon's stare on us every step of the way.

When I decided earlier that we needed to come here, I don't

think I thought it out fully, because as we reach Josh's room, and he pushes open the door, I find that I brace myself slightly. It's been a long time since I have been in his bedroom, and despite the fact I agreed to marry him, this feels really strange. Of course I am used to him in my space. He is over at the house all the time, and has found himself in my room on numerous occasions, but since his dad's affair he has always kept his own space private. I feel like I am entering Narnia or something as we walk inside, and I can't help my eyes from flying everywhere.

His room is just as clean and tidy as it always was when we were kids, confirming he is still a total neat freak, and I can't help but smile. His bed is made, curtains drawn open, desk tidy, no clothes on the floor, and I roll my eyes when I see he still keeps a checklist on his notice board, yet he makes fun of my lists any chance he gets. I walk around the whole room, inspecting everything my eyes land on, and even smiling at the shelf with photo frames on it. Something personal in this cold and tidy world of his.

In the first frame there is a picture of him and Maddie from when they were kids, but it's the other picture that grabs my attention. Not just because I am in it, but because I have seen it before. I used to sleep with it under my pillow when my crush for him was really bad, but I didn't know he had a copy. This picture was taken on my prom night. Maddie and I were all dressed up, and she forced Josh to take a picture with us. He stands tall and broad in between the two of us and I can remember the feeling of his arm against my bare skin like it was yesterday. When I got my copy I folded my best friend out of it until there was only me and Josh, and the fantasies I created in my head of that night are still used in my nightly rotation to fall asleep now. Of course I had to tuck the picture deep into a box when I moved in with Maddie, but seeing it now, here, makes me smile.

By the time I turn back to Josh, I realize I must have been looking at his room a lot longer than I realized, because he is standing in the corner, watching me carefully, as if waiting for me to make a comment about his room. Feeling both exposed and nervous, I don't comment on his room, and instead go with, "So what's the deal with Daemon?"

My question throws him completely and his frown is instant. "What do you mean, what's the deal with him?" He throws back, not seeming to know what I'm referring to in the slightest.

"I mean, you know, he seems really intense, scary even," I shrug, knowing I'm not really explaining what I mean how I want to, but Josh is already shaking his head.

"He isn't scary, he's particular, misunderstood," Josh states coldly, moving towards me, and letting his stare flick to the picture of us over my shoulder, before coming back to me. "Daemon Forbes is one of the best people I have ever met, you just need to get to know him."

I nod, knowing that if Josh is vouching for him, then I can believe it, and because his closeness to me is intoxicating, I push away from the shelves and move to take a seat on the end of his bed. "So, wedding plans?" I say, clearing my throat and pretending all of this is completely normal, and he turns to me with a look of surprise.

"Hallie, you are doing me this huge favor, one I will never be able to fully repay, so please don't worry about a thing. I will sort everything, the minister, the location, the rings, just leave it to me," he tells me, moving across his room towards his desk. "And speaking of rings," he adds, opening the top drawer and pulling out a back velvet box. He moves back towards me, his height towering over me as he reaches where I sit on the end of his bed and holds out the box towards me. "This is for you."

I know what's inside the box, I'd have to be stupid to not know what a little black velvet box houses, even if we weren't already fake engaged. Yet I can't make my hand reach out and take it. Not when it's currently shaking so hard that all I would do is drop the thing. Again, I'm not stupid. I knew there would be a ring, but I guess I didn't truly think about this moment, and what it would mean to walk around with his fake claim to me on my finger.

I flick my stare up to Josh and find him watching me closely with an amused grin as he purrs, "Do I have to get on my knees again for you to take it? I know how much you'd enjoy that."

I scoff at him, yet still it takes everything I have to keep my hand steady as I slowly reach out and take the box from his hand. He doesn't move away like I expect him to, even when I take it. Instead he keeps his eyes on mine as I slowly open the box and reveal the most beautiful piece of jewelry I have ever seen in my entire life.

I'm not sure what I ever expected in an engagement ring, but it's as if he climbed inside my brain and curated the most perfect design for me from the very essence of my desires. There is a large oval diamond sitting in the center, with green sapphire petals perched on either side of it, all set on a shiny platinum band. It's simple and elegant, and takes my breath away completely.

"I don't know what to say," I tell him truthfully, not trusting myself to not get emotional. "It's so beautiful it almost looks real," I add in a whisper, still just staring at it, and to my surprise he drops to his knees before me.

"Don't insult me, Hallie, of course it's real," he snaps, rolling his eyes as if the idea of having a fake ring for a fake marriage is totally ridiculous, yet still I say nothing. "I know it's no ring pop, but as soon as I saw it, I thought of you," he tells me innocently, not realizing he is making the heart that beats for him and only him, soar even higher. "Like *Tinkerbell* in a ring," he laughs, taking the box back from my hand and plucking the ring from it.

The very real ring with three very real, very huge, gemstones.

Then he reaches out and takes my left hand, slowly pushing the ring into place for where it will remain for who knows how long. It's as if that thought resonates with both of us, because as soon as it's on my finger we both just pause and stare at it for a few seconds, and then when our gazes collide it's like something shifts between us. Like this ring, and this lie, will change everything. I see something in his eyes similar to the day on the rock when he tried to kiss me, and just like that day I panic and shoot to my feet.

"Okay, so if you're sorting the wedding stuff out, then talk to me about your dad," I blurt, forcing myself to breathe deeply as I pretend to casually move around his room.

I ignore his sigh, and don't watch him get back to his feet, and before he even speaks I can feel the coldness seeping back in. "I can handle my father, leave it to me." Words I have heard a hundred times before, and they sound less believable every time.

"No," I tell him flatly, and when I turn back towards him I find him watching me as if he misheard me. "That's right, I said no. Someone dares to have the audacity to say no to the golden boy." I throw his family nickname out and feel a little regret when I see him flinch, but I push on. "I'm in this now, Joshua, whether you like it or not you brought me in, so let me in, let me help," I plead, moving towards him and pretending I don't feel the weight of his ring on my finger. "Not just as your almost wife, but as your best friend," I add, using a title I haven't dared to use in years.

Josh stares at me, absorbing every one of my words until he sighs, "You're a pain in my ass, you know that right?"

"And yet you want to marry me, so it sounds like you're the problem to me," I fire back, and he laughs, shaking his head, sitting on the bed and gesturing for me to take a seat on the chair by his desk.

"So I think we can both agree my dad is an asshole," he starts, and I don't bother voicing my agreement, Josh knows how I feel about Hugo Peters, and it isn't pretty. "Well I've been watching him for years, waiting for him to trip up, just so I could have something, anything on him, and I think I finally found it."

My interest is fully piqued, because if anyone needs knocking down a peg or two, it's the Mayor. "What did you find?"

"I'm not sure exactly. I heard him talking in his office a few weeks back, before I offered myself up to him, about making new deals even if he has to wait for a return on his investment. It was then I saw some papers on his desk that looked like they were from an offshore account, but before I could get a good look he came back. Then I knew I needed help, so I asked around, disguised my interest for what I needed until I was given a name." He leans back and reaches into his pocket, pulling out a piece of paper and handing it to me.

"Lincoln Blackwell?" I read out loud, the name not sounding familiar at all. "Who is he?" I ask, returning my stare to Josh, and he shrugs.

"Apparently he is the go-to guy for finding shit out and getting shit done. He works over in Black Hallows, and only takes meetings in person if he deems you worthy." I'd say Josh almost sounds impressed by him and his reputation, and I wonder if he is jealous about the fact.

"And are you worthy?" I ask, not joking, but he smiles anyway, standing and walking over to where I sit at his desk, spinning my chair, and leaning down beside me to open his laptop.

"Let's find out." I ignore his scent as it surrounds me, the heat of his arm as it presses against my own, and watch as he opens up a new email thread, writes a quick summary about needing his services, and then uses the information on the piece of paper to send it away.

"Now what?" I ask, and I feel his answering shrug against me.

"Now, we wait."

#7
HALLIE
DICK PUNCHES

We spend the next few hours making a variety of plans. Plans to be seen together more, plans on how to handle his father over the next few weeks given we are about to botch the very plans he's made himself, and even having a silent and almost completely awkward dinner with Daemon. Josh fills the silence with chatter about their upcoming hockey game of course, something I have presumed he must do often for his teammate, and then Josh offers to drive me home. We bumped into Landon on our way out, who seemed to be confused as to why I wasn't staying over given the bomb we dropped on him earlier in the night, and I quickly lied about an early workout class. Something which Josh almost cackled at, given I haven't worked out a day in my life aside from the hockey games I have played with him. Then we were on our way across campus.

The drive is silent yet comfortable, and as always Josh takes the scenic route around the lake that runs by my house, while I try not to think about the weight of what I am actually doing by marrying him. When we pull up in the driveway we both spy Hector's car by the sidewalk, and the lights on in the house, meaning Maddie is clearly inside.

"Do you want me to come in?" Josh asks, staring at the house, and I'm almost certain he and Maddie haven't spoken since their argument on Saturday night, which is probably the longest they have ever gone without speaking.

"What, so I can try and play referee again? No thank you," I tell him, no stranger to their feuds over the years given my close proximity to both of them. I reach down and grab my bag as I add, "So I will see you on..." I let the sentence trail off, thinking he will adhere to our arrangement of being seen together, given the plans we made.

"Saturday," he confirms quickly, still half-distracted by the house, yet still I almost laugh. Of course, a few hours together isn't going to change his personality of being a complete asshole the majority of the time, so I'm not sure why I thought becoming his fiancée might make him any different.

"Right, yeah, of course, Saturday." I roll my eyes with a fake smile as I fling open his car door and climb out, before leaning down and adding, "I'll be the one in the wedding dress, just text me the details I guess." Then before he can say anything in defense, I slam the door and move to leave.

"Hals," he shouts, opening his door, and I can hear his footsteps behind me. "Hallie, wait please."

I pause, turning on the spot to look at him and he almost slams right into me as I snap in frustration, "What, Joshua?"

He opens his mouth but nothing comes out at first, as if he had no idea what he was going to say to me, but he came after me anyway, and then he sighs. "I'm sorry, okay? I'm not used to having to lean on someone else and it's going to take some getting used to."

It's more of an apology than anyone else would ever get, but

I'm not letting him off that easily. "Josh, we've been friends for over a decade, that excuse isn't going to fly with me, not as your best friend, and certainly not as your fiancée," I tell him, putting my hands on my hips and standing my ground, because this isn't how our marriage is going to be, fake or not.

His stare trails over me from head to toe, so slowly that I feel my knees wanting to buckle beneath his glare, as he starts to smirk. "Come on, Tink, we both know you can't stay mad at me, you're not capable." He's right, because of course he is, but that doesn't mean I have to like it, which is why I smile right back at him as sweetly as I can manage as an idea comes to mind.

"You're right, Joshua, I really can't," I purr, reaching up so I can bring my mouth closer to his ear. "I like to get my aggression out and then move forward," I whisper, before bringing down my fist and slamming it into his groin, relishing in the deep groan he lets out as it's *his* knees that buckle.

"Fuck," he yells out, dropping down and bringing his hands to his no doubt now aching balls. "Hallie, what the hell?"

I bend down beside him, and shove his shoulder to push him onto his back so he is looking at me as I say, "I warned you I'd hit you in the dick, so you only have yourself to blame. Now remember that I'm doing you this huge favor and that you need to start being nice to me, okay?"

He throws his head back into the grass and closes his eyes with a long groan, a groan that has me thinking of the other ways I could make him make that noise, yet still I stay silent. "I forgot how fucking crazy you are," he gasps through his teeth at me, bringing his eyes back to mine. "Fucking hell, Tink, I'll make sure you're the happiest wife in the history of the world to make sure you don't do that to me again."

I nod with a smile, satisfied with his answer before standing to my full height and saying, "Now, be a good boy and go home and plan our wedding." I once again don't wait for his response, turning to leave and heading up towards the house.

When I enter I hear music coming from the living room, and find Maddie sitting on the sofa by the window with a glass of wine. She doesn't look up at me from the magazine in her hand, but she does ask, "Is there a reason my brother is out there on the grass writhing in pain?"

Dropping my bag by the other sofa, I sit down facing her and shrug. "He was being rude to me," I tell her simply, and her eyes flick up to mine in question, but I don't elaborate.

Maddie just laughs, shutting her magazine, and reaches out to pour herself more wine. "And to think I've been worrying about you, when I should have been worrying about him." She watches me carefully, closely, as if she is trying to see something before she asks, "You're home late, have you been with Josh this whole time?"

I know she means since class ended, considering Wednesday is usually the day we both get home early, and I nod. "Josh and I had to sort some stuff out," is all I respond, not really having the energy to get into it right now, but of course my best friend doesn't relent.

"Hallie, are you really doing this?" she asks, discarding the magazine by tossing it on the table so she can sit forward on the sofa to look at me. We haven't talked much in the last week, we've not been alone much, so I guess now is finally time for our one on one interrogation.

"Yes, Maddie, I am really doing this," I grit back, getting tired of being pushed on this. It's my life, my decision, a decision made between me and Josh, and I am already sick of people questioning it.

"But why?" Her question throws me, not because she is asking it, but because of how she is asking it, like she knows the answer, the real answer. The one where I am secretly in love with her brother and would do anything for him including becoming his fake wife.

I could tell her the truth, I should tell her the truth, but that honesty would ruin everything, so instead I give her something else. "You're my best friend, Madeline, you have been by my side since I was nine years old, but there is no you without him. He's my best friend too." I see the disbelief in her eyes at my words, and I understand it. Josh and I haven't exactly been making friendship bracelets for one another these last few years, but that doesn't mean I don't still consider him my best friend.

"You guys fight all the time," she says in defense, as if that argument alone is reason enough not to do this, and I almost laugh.

"So? Four months ago you and Nova absolutely despised each other, but look at you now." It's a low blow, we both know it, but surely she has to understand where I am coming from.

"But what Nova and I have is real." I can hear the conviction in her words, see the sparkle in her eye at just thinking of her boyfriend and how they came to be, but still she has to understand.

"And you're basing the decision to be with him on the last couple of months. You trust in it, which you should, I have never seen you happier, but I'm basing my decision on the last ten years. Our marriage might be fake, but our friendship isn't, and that's what I'm putting my trust in. That, and him."

I see the moment she realizes that I won't back down on this, not even for her, and I watch as she takes a deep slug of her wine before she stands and moves to sit next to me. "I guess I just don't understand how you can do this," she tells me honestly, and I get her concern, I really do, but it won't stop me.

"You don't have to understand, but as my friend you do have to support it." I ensure my voice remains strong and clear, despite how I feel inside, and I see her entire body deflate.

"Hals, you're my best friend, I'll support you through anything, you know that." Words I've heard a million times, yet I really needed to hear them again now, and I smile a little as I reach out and pull her hand into mine.

"Then you know why I have to do this," I tell her, squeezing her hand gently.

We stare at one another for a few seconds before she sighs in defeat. "Then I guess you're not just my best friend anymore, but my sister-in-law too." Tears gather in her eyes, and I feel my own burn with emotion as I laugh.

"Well that's what they tell me these things mean," I say, holding up my other hand to showcase my newest accessory, and her jaw drops.

"Oh my god, he got you a ring?" she squeals, snatching my hand up in hers, and studying it closely. "Hallie, this is real, like real," she gushes, and I have to laugh considering her reaction is similar to what mine was.

"Yeah I know, Josh said it's like Tinkerbell in a ring," I repeat his words, and her eyes snap to mine, a curiosity in them that wasn't there before, but she hides it with a smile.

"Well, it's beautiful, really, and it suits you." Her words have me examining the ring myself, still so foreign feeling on my hand given I never usually wear any kind of jewelry, and it's definitely going to take some getting used to. "So let me guess, you guys are having a spring wedding?" She stands, rolling her eyes, clearly knowing her father better than he would like, and it reminds me so much of her brother. They are so alike.

I follow her into the kitchen, cringing a little as I say, "Actually we are getting married on Saturday."

Maddie stops abruptly and I almost slam right into her, like Josh just did to me, and when she turns around, her mouth is open. "On Saturday? As in Saturday, meaning like, the day three days from this one?" She rambles, and I nod slowly, before quickly explaining that she was right. Her dad did try to force the spring wedding on us, but we are taking back the power and doing it our own way. She looks at me in disbelief before she laughs. "Of course he did, god he's such a fucking asshole, no wonder Josh gave himself over to him. He's always been smarter than I am, smarter than *him*, if anyone can ruin him it's his own son molded in his shadow."

Her words have me pausing because she's right, Josh has a heart of gold that was turned to stone when he grew up and realized the type of man that was raising him. And instead of following in his footsteps, taking the easy route and privilege available to him, he's done the opposite. He's stepped up, stepped in, and done whatever he can do to protect his sister from their father and his cruelty, and now he's willing to risk it all to show everyone just what kind of man their Mayor is.

Most men would be proud to have a son like him, one with a solid moral compass and compassion, but not Hugo Peters. No, he will see this as a betrayal, as an attack against him, and he won't let the fact that Josh is his son deter him from retaliating. Which means we have to make this work, we have to make everyone believe in us, and then dig up what we can on the Mayor so we can take him down before he ruins us all.

Maddie and I catch up over ice cream, shit talking both her father and brother, until I know she has our backs in this completely. Then I head upstairs to wash off the day. I shower and change into something comfortable to sleep in, climb into bed with Percy Penguin, and then load up an episode of Criminal Minds so I can get my nightly Dr. Spencer Reid fix. What's a better fantasy to fall asleep to?

That's when my phone lights up with one new text message.

Peter Pan : Wedding sorted. 5pm Saturday.

That's it, four words that entail an invite to my own wedding, and all I can do is laugh, because I know Josh will have seen this message as completely fine and informative. Which is why I don't even bother calling him out on the impersonality of it as I type out my response.

> Hallie : It's not even been two hours since I dick punched you, how the hell did you sort it out so fast?

I watch as he begins typing instantly.

> Peter Pan : You forget you can get people to do anything for the right price

I roll my eyes at his response because of course I know that. You can't grow up in our world and not know that, but it doesn't make it any less weird. Before I can respond my phone lights up again.

> Peter Pan : Oh and my dick is fine by the way

His message is innocent, too innocent for the thoughts it immediately provokes in my mind that I have to block out instantly.

> Hallie : I also forget what an asshole you are, hence why I'm marrying you

> Hallie : And I have no concern for you or your dick

Lie. A big, bold-faced lie, but what's one more in a sea of thousands when it comes to him.

> Peter Pan : That's the first time a girl has ever told me that

> Hallie : What a shame that girl just so happens to be your future wife

> Peter Pan : A good wife would kiss it better

I almost drop my phone when I read that last message, my thighs clenching together involuntarily as I imagine doing just that, yet I snap myself out of it. This is Josh, my best friend, who is used to women falling at his feet for his affections, but that won't be me, it can't be, not if I am going to protect myself. I will not flirt with him.

> Hallie : And a bad wife would punch it again

> Hallie : Now stop flirting with me I'm busy

> Peter Pan : Watching Criminal Minds while cuddling Percy is not classed as an actual activity, you know that right?

I look between the Penguin I am cuddling in my lap and the TV screen, and scoff. Silently cursing the stupid prick for knowing me so well.

> Hallie : Neither is punching you in the dick, yet I enjoyed it just as much

> Peter Pan : You better stay away from my dick in future

> Hallie : But I thought a good wife would kiss it better?

> Peter Pan : You're a bad wife

> Hallie : And yet you're stuck with me. This is going to be fun

> Hallie : Sweet dreams Joshua

Peter Pan : See you Saturday Hallie Bear

When I finally fall asleep it's to images of my future husband and his dick.

#8
JOSH

INTERESTING INFORMANTS

It takes two days for me to be deemed worthy enough to be granted a meeting with the elusive Mr. Lincoln Blackwell. A man known for his reputation more than anything else, which is how I find myself skipping my classes on Friday afternoon and heading to Black Hallows to see him. Black Hallows is a wonder of a town. It was built on power and old money, with a clear wealth divide right down the middle that still remains to this day. Considering it resides right next to Fairfield, it's not a place I visit often, especially given my father's disdain for it, but now with the hope of taking him down, I can't seem to get there quick enough.

The office that Mr. Blackwell works for is on the North Side of town, the side that houses the wealthy and elite, and it looks every bit like the uptown security office I imagined it to be. When I asked around for someone who could do some discreet digging, the name of this firm was the top contender, along with the name of Mr. Blackwell himself. He was described as smart, cunning, capable, yet completely ruthless. So imagine my surprise when I am ushered to an office by a secretary, only to be greeted with a face as young as mine.

"Thank you, Eliza," the man, no, the boy before me, says, gesturing to a seat in front of his desk as he adds, "Take a seat Mr. Peters."

I look around confused, as the secretary, Eliza, nods at him with a smile, closing his door and leaving us alone. I look back to him in wonder, before I clear my throat and say, "I'm here for a meeting with Lincoln Blackwell." The guy before me can't be any older than twenty years, and my words cause the corner of his mouth to tip up in what I imagine is his version of a smirk.

"I'm aware of what you are here for, Joshua Peters, first and only son of Hugo and Louise Peters, the former being the well respected Mayor of Fairfield, and I use the word respected ironically," he muses, watching me closely as if his stare alone can seep into my soul. "You attend Fairfield University alongside your younger sister, Madeline. You play for FU's hockey team, and word through the grapevine is that you want to play for the NHL, despite the fact your father wants you to follow his footsteps into politics."

Okay so the guy knows his shit, big fucking deal. I still try not to let the surprise show on my face as I reply blandly, "Is that your way of telling me *you* are Lincoln Blackwell?"

His smirk only grows. "You may call me Lincoln." He opens a drawer in his desk and pulls out a brown file, tossing it on the desk between us. "I took the liberty of digging up some surface level stuff on your father," he shrugs, as I reach out and take the file, flicking through it until my eyes widen at the tidbits of information he has already found. "But it won't be enough to take him down, not with friends in the right places and pockets as deep as his."

All I can do is stare at the information in disbelief as he talks, both impressed at him knowing what I came for, and annoyed that he was able to work it out so easily. There is stuff in here that dates back to before I was even born. Hell, there is a copy of my damn birth certificate, and Maddie's, yet none of it is enough to truly do enough damage. Not the level I require anyway.

I flick my gaze back to him, and he is watching me closely, his face giving away nothing, his eyes telling me I shouldn't question this, yet still I do. "I never said I was here to take down my father," I state matter-of-factly, and he rolls his eyes in a way that reminds me of Hallie.

"Josh, I'm sure you've heard the stories they tell about this town, the nightmares that happened here, and the tales of the Mayor and his friends who used to reign over it." There is no smirk on his face now, in fact I am starting to see why they call him ruthless, he looks nothing like a kid anymore. No, now he looks like a man who has seen far more horrors than I could ever imagine. And he's right of course, I have heard the nightmares of this town, and all about the men who used to run it. The rumors about it are rampant all over the state, yet no one really knows the truth, but looking into the sharp green eyes that currently watch me, I know he does. I know he's seen it all and didn't even blink. "Well they're all gone, and I'm still here. Do you know why that is?"

The question throws me a little, especially considering I am recalling all the news reports about what allegedly happened in this town. So I'm not sure what he's getting at, but given the manner of his office and the place it resides, I don't really think too much when I respond, "Money?"

There goes that eye roll again, as he scoffs, "No, power." He says the word like it's beneath him, like he doesn't really believe in it, or maybe has other meanings for it.

Now it's my turn to roll my eyes. "Same thing," I toss back, knowing that all the privileges I've known in life have come from both money and power.

"No, they're not, and thinking so is a mistake, one you should learn from if you want to take back the power from your father." I blink back as he stands from his desk and moves around it to sit on the edge right in front of me. "I know about the marriage deal you foiled between your sister and Bradley Thorne, and I also know about the one you are about to make yourself, so please let's not waste each other's time."

We stare at one another until I finally relent, thinking about my words carefully before I say them. "If I were here to take down my father, how might I do that?"

His smirk returns, as if he knew exactly what I was going to say and he was the one to get me to say it. I imagine he could get anyone to do anything for him if I'm being honest, and that's only confirmed when he replies, "You'll be busy with your wedding tomorrow, but after that you need to find your father's weakness."

I ignore the fact that he knows I am getting married tomorrow when I have told no one, and focus on what else he said. "My father doesn't have a weakness."

"Everybody has a weakness, Josh, you just need to find it." He rises back to his feet and moves towards a locker in the corner. He puts in a code, and then his fingerprint into a scanner and it pops open, revealing a bunch of tech. Taking out a phone and something smaller, he shuts it again and moves back over to me. "This phone is untraceable, only contact me on this going forward, and this is something to help you find his weakness." Lincoln holds up a small black device that sits neatly between his fingers. "You plug it into his computer."

I take both without question, still confused as to what he does, and what I'm supposed to do now. "Plug it into his computer, and then what?"

"Then I'll do the rest," he holds out his hand towards the door and I stand and walk with him. "But you either need to do it this weekend or wait until after next week as I'll be out of the country."

This weekend? How the hell am I supposed to get this thing into my father's computer this weekend?

I follow him out of his office and back into the main area of the building where the reception desk is, and find the secretary from before talking to another young man, one I recognize instantly and I scoff, coming to a stop and causing Lincoln to look at me.

"You have the audacity to tell me this isn't about money when you have one of the richest men in the country standing right there," I tell him, pointing to the man I know to be Asher Donovan.

Asher is like me in many ways, he went to private school, was raised by wealthy parents, and constantly overshadowed by his father. Fairfield Prep used to play Hallows Prep frequently when we were in high school, and though he wasn't on the team, his name and presence at any game was always something to talk about. His father had more money than god, and from what I hear he also had more sins than the devil. One of the rumors of this town is that Asher killed his father and brother so he could take over the family business, and when his cold, soulless eyes collide with mine, I just might believe it.

"Josh Peters," he nods simply at my presence, recognition clear in his stare as he abandons his conversation with Eliza and moves to stand beside Lincoln who is still watching me closely.

I don't bother responding to him, moving my focus back to Lincoln as I snap, "The world revolves around money, you can get people to do anything for the right price."

Lincoln looks between the two of us, as if seeing our similarities for the first time before he sighs, "And with the right power you can change that world."

This time I look at Asher, look at him and see the changes

that weren't there in high school. There is no grinding of his jaw, no straightening of his shoulders, no dark shadow from his father lingering around him, he looks free. "Are the rumors true?" I ask, knowing he knows what I mean, and his returning smirk is even more sinister than his friends.

"Some of them are true," he muses with a shrug. "And some of them are a lot kinder than the truth." His words make me realize that whatever the sins of his father are, he made him repent, and though my own father's might not be as bad, he too must pay the price.

"I'll get it done this weekend," I say, moving my focus back to Lincoln, and he nods.

"Then I'll speak to you soon," he responds, not waiting for anything else before he turns and heads back to his office.

I watch him go and then flick my eyes back to Asher, to find that he watched him leave too. When he notices that I caught him staring, he turns on his heels and heads in the opposite direction without so much as a goodbye, which shows me he hasn't changed too much in the last few years.

Still reeling from the whole interaction, I head back out to the parking garage, and pull my phone from my pocket to find a text from Hallie. Well, multiple texts actually.

> Tink : Do you know I hate shopping?

> Tink : Like I really fucking hate shopping

> Tink : And do you know what's worse than shopping???

> Tink : Wedding dress shopping!!!

> Tink : Why are there so many?

> Tink : And why are all the fabrics itchy?

> Tink : Do you think this one is okay?

> Tink : *image attached*
>
> Tink : No forget that one it feels weird on my skin
>
> Tink : What about this one?
>
> Tink : *image attached*
>
> Tink : *image attached*
>
> Tink : *image attached*
>
> Tink : *image attached*
>
> Tink : Nevermind I hate them all
>
> Tink : And I hate your father
>
> Tink : And I hate weddings!!!!
>
> Tink : *image attached*
>
> Tink : What about this one?

There is message after message and picture after picture, and it's clear she is in some sort of wedding boutique trying to find a dress. I skim over the messages with a smile and then flick through all the pictures. She looks gorgeous in every dress like she does in everything else, but none of them are really her. Not that I know what any woman wants to wear on their wedding day, especially for a wedding that isn't even real. Yet still I feel kind of bad that she is suffering through this for me.

> Josh : Isn't it bad luck for the groom to see the bride in her dress?
>
> Tink : It's like you think I won't smother you with the fabric of one of these dresses
>
> Josh : Damn! Bridezilla alert

> Tink : Do I need to punch you in the dick again?

> Josh : A smooth stroke would be preferred

> Tink : Remind me of the til death do us part bit of our vows again?

I smile at her response, because despite the threats I am glad she is taking this thing seriously. Especially now that I have a secret weapon in my pocket.

> Josh : You look beautiful in everything you wear
>
> Josh : Just pick the one you will be most comfortable in

Even as I type the words and send them I know they're pointless. None of those dresses are really her and despite this whole thing being fake, her feeling comfortable on our wedding day is important to me. So instead of pulling out of the garage and heading home like I originally planned, I pull up the map on my phone and search until I find what I'm looking for. It seems I need to make a little detour on my way home.

~

IT'S ALMOST nine by the time I make it back, and because it's a Friday night I expect to find my house either empty or in full on party mode. Yet when I make my way inside all I find is Daemon sitting at the island in the kitchen, with half a bottle of whiskey already gone.

"Drowning our sorrows?" I ask, stepping towards him, surprised to find his usually dark and gray stormy eyes looking a little brighter than usual. He's not a big drinker, not after what happened to him, but once in a while he will let go of his trauma and indulge a little. It seems like tonight is one of those times.

"Celebrating actually," he muses, swirling the amber liquid in his glass before taking a slow, savoring sip.

"Well that's a change," I gruff with a smile, as I pour myself my own drink and hold it up to his. "What are we celebrating?"

"You," he confirms, clinking his glass against my own as he gestures to our drinks. "This is your bachelor party."

I can't help but bark a laugh. I told Daemon about Hallie's idea to get married on our own terms and he agreed it was a good plan. I even managed to persuade him to attend as a witness on my behalf, with Maddie of course being Hallie's, despite the fact she is still barely talking to me. Yet not once did I ever imagine he'd actually participate in anything beyond attendance.

"No strippers and just us two present, what kind of bachelor party is this?" I ask with a smile, taking a sip of my own drink.

Daemon rolls his dark eyes, which are for once glossy from the drinking. "Please, you haven't touched any woman in months, and you basically hate the rest of the team."

Okay so he's perceptive even when drinking, I'll give him that, but still I find myself getting defensive.

"I do not hate the rest of the team." Okay, so maybe I do hate Nova and his goofy housemates who think they are all god's gift to women, but the rest of them are okay.

"Fine, then *I* hate the rest of the team," he says with a tipsy smile, clinking his glass against mine, and all I can do is laugh because this is the Daemon I love.

This is the broken boy who became one of my best friends in Freshman Year, the one I bonded with over shitty fathers and obscene demands. The one who has silently been by my side for three years and helped me through everything, whether he realized it or not, and the one who will stand by my side tomorrow when I promise another friend a fake forever.

As if reading my thoughts he nods his head towards the garment bag in my hand. "What's in there?"

I glance down to the bag gripped between my knuckles and sigh, "This is something to try and soften the blow of being married to me."

A silence stretches between us at my response because he knows the burden all too well. I'm sure it's why I never see him trying to force a relationship with anyone, because how can you manage a relationship with a partner, when the one with your own father is a mess? Why invite someone into your issues when you haven't even figured them out yourself?

Tomorrow is my wedding day and I can't even fully comprehend the weight of how it will change things. Not when, in some ways, my father will still have the upper hand and I will no longer be the only one in the firing line. Hallie might be my best friend, or at least she was once, but becoming my wife will be a whole different game, and despite me thinking she is the best player for the job, it's still going to be one hell of a match.

Oh well, for better or for worse I guess.

#9
HALLIE

DRESS DILEMMAS

I'm getting married today, and instead of waking up well-rested after having plenty of beauty sleep for my big fake day, I am sitting in my car wearing my pajamas and freezing my ass off. Why, you might ask? Well because I'm getting married today and I haven't even told my parents yet. My kind and loving, accepting parents who have supported me through everything for my entire life, and me, their only daughter, didn't tell them I was getting married. What kind of terrible person am I?

Everything just happened so fast that I forgot all about them, but last night just as I was drifting off, I realized that as soon as Mayor Peters finds out I tied the knot with his son, and not on his terms, he will do whatever he can to spin it to his advantage. Which will include spreading the news like wildfire. Now it's not like people don't already know that I am engaged to Josh, the Mayor practically told the whole of Fairfield between his party and the announcement in the local paper, but my parents no longer live in Fairfield and they tend to keep to themselves.

So here I am, sitting in the driveway of their house, contemplating between going inside, or turning back and driving off the bridge that leads into their town. Both are just as terrifying to me. The skin around my fingers is almost bleeding because I have picked it that hard, and I couldn't listen to any kind of music on the drive over because I was rehearsing the conversation I am about to have in my head over and over. They're not awake yet, I know because none of the lights are on in the house, which isn't surprising considering it's only 6am, but still I nervously gnaw at my lip as I wait.

I skipped all of my classes yesterday and went full wedding mode. I know Josh said he would sort everything out himself, but as a girl I still felt there was plenty of stuff I needed to do. So I went to the salon and had my hair freshly cut and blown, then I had a manicure and pedicure, before I moved on to being waxed within an inch of my life. It wasn't until I was as slippery as a damn eel that I left and finally went shopping.

I bought makeup, shoes, and accessories, until I finally stumbled into a wedding boutique to look for something to wear. Around thirty dresses later, I finally settled on one I didn't totally hate, which even left me time to run to a jewelry store and pick up a wedding band for Josh. I'm not sure he will even want one, as he didn't mention wearing any kind of ring, but I thought it was best to have one just in case. I still can't quite believe that I am getting married, and not *just* getting married, but to him in particular. Him, Josh, my best friend and the boy I have tried not to be in love with since I was nine, who will now become my husband by the end of the day.

Before that thought can take full flight and force me into panic, a light illuminates my parents' house, and I know my father is now up to make my mom her morning coffee before she does her yoga. Something he has done every single day of their entire marriage, and the kind of thing I'd hoped my own husband would do for me one day, but I guess I'll have to pray for a second marriage for that.

I've always aspired to have a relationship like my parents. They call themselves star-crossed lovers, which is actually total bullshit, but they have been together twenty-five years and still look at each other as if they are the only people on the planet. They have been through everything together, and not once has their love ever waivered. If I were to believe in soulmates, I would believe in them, because Jeremy and Beth Sanders are one for the ages.

It's with their love in mind, and the love they have for me, that I finally find the courage to climb out of the car and trudge up to the front door. I don't bother ringing the bell, using my key to let myself in, and when I round the corner into the kitchen my dad turns and smiles. A smile that turns into surprise when he realizes the sound of my footsteps doesn't belong to my mother.

"Hallie Bear, what are you doing here?" he asks, using the nickname that Josh stole from him when we were still kids, while moving towards me with worry staining his face.

"I really need to talk to you and mom," I say softly, my voice not holding any confidence in what I have to tell them, and it only deepens the frown on his face as he looks over my shoulder.

"Hals?" My mom's voice hits me from behind before my dad can even respond, and I turn to offer her a smile.

"Hey mom," I croak, the nerves frying me from the inside out, and without hesitation she pulls me into an embrace, not lingering for longer than she knows I can stand, before pulling back and tucking an escaped curl behind my ear.

Her stare is unwavering as she studies me closely, before she glances at my father. "Jer, it's a hot chocolate kind of morning," she tells him, giving him the order of my favorite drink they

The Puck Decoy

always used to make whenever I was feeling sad, before she focuses back on me. "Come and sit in the den with me."

I don't bother with a response, not when she tucks her arm into mine and leads me through the kitchen into the room they had converted into a space where they can relax. It's stacked with bookshelves and a big chair where my mom likes to read, and a large oak desk with a computer where my dad likes to work. There is also a corner sofa by the window surrounded by plants where we usually sit and have our game nights. It's probably my favorite room in their house and somehow feels like it's been around forever, despite the fact they have only lived here for a few years.

It isn't long before we are joined by my dad, who comes with a tray of hot chocolates that are overflowing with whipped cream, tiny marshmallows, and chocolate sprinkles. Clearly he thinks this is a major emergency, yet I can't help but smile as he bows while he serves us, before taking a seat beside my mother and focusing entirely on me.

"Did you kill someone?" he asks without pause, totally serious, and I stare at him wordlessly, praying that he's joking, as my mom laughs. "What? You know if she killed someone, I would totally go to jail for her, but I just need to get some things in order first."

Knowing that he is dead serious, I force myself to reply, "No, Dad, I didn't kill anyone."

His relief is clear as his shoulders completely untense. "Oh, great, you had me worried for a second there kid." He takes a deep slug of his hot chocolate, not caring for the cream mustache that it leaves across his lip, as he leans back on the sofa and relaxes.

"But there is something really important I have to tell you, and I'm just going to say it all to get it out there, and you can ask questions at the end, okay?" I flick my stare between the two of them, and my dad looks relaxed now knowing I didn't kill anyone, but my mom still looks a little on edge.

"Okay," they both nod in unison.

"Mayor Peters tried to force a business marriage on Maddie but she fell in love with someone else, so Josh stepped in to take her place under the conditions that he leave her alone. So now Josh has to have an arranged marriage, and I agreed to be his wife so I could help him dig up some dirt on the Mayor and give Josh the upper hand, and we are getting married today." I rush through every word barely stopping for a breath, and then holding it slightly as I wait for their refusals and judgment, but it doesn't come.

In fact, my mother bursts out laughing, and I mean full on tears in her eyes laughing, making my father join her, as I sit there dumbfounded while they both lose their minds.

"Oh, Hallie," she chokes out in between laughs. "I thought it was drugs, or you really did kill someone," she gasps, giggling all over again. She holds her chest as she tries to calm herself down, my dad wiping tears of joy from his eyes, as they both compose themselves.

"But didn't you hear what I said, the part about where I am getting married today?" I repeat, looking between them in total confusion.

My dad laughs again, but my mother looks at me in sympathy as she replies, "We know you're getting married, honey, Josh told us."

My jaw hangs open in shock. "What? What do you mean Josh told you? No. I'm telling you, I'm getting married today."

They both share another look, doing that silent communicating thing they always do whenever they think I am being ridiculous, and it stresses me out. I have to reach for my hot chocolate and take a sip, just to ensure I can actually taste it and that I am really here right now having this conversation.

As always, it's as if my dad can read my mind, and he puts his own drink down and leans forward, gently pulling my hand into his. It's something he would do as a kid when I couldn't stand to be hugged, he would come and sit by my side and hold my hand and tell me about his day. It feels just as comforting now as it did when I was younger, and I can't stop myself from squeezing his fingers.

"Hallie Bear, Josh came to see us the morning after Thanksgiving. He told us everything about what has been going on with Hugo, and apologized for allowing you to be involved in such an elaborate plan." His voice is loud and clear but it's as if I'm not hearing him right, because what? Josh came to see him on Thanksgiving, how the hell is that possible? "The three of us talked everything out, and then he asked for my permission to marry you, and I said yes."

So many words to process but all I do is focus on the last three. "You said yes?" I repeat. "He asked for your permission to marry me, and to be clear you know this is a fake marriage, and you said yes?"

I look between the two of them again, and once again they nod.

"We know you guys have history, and Josh ensured us that he wouldn't let anything or anyone hurt you, and we trust him," my mom finally says, smiling at just the mention of him. She always did have a soft spot for him. Like mother, like daughter, I guess.

Still failing to comprehend this whole situation, and the fact that Josh not only came here and spoke to them, but he told them the truth, and asked for permission to marry me. Even more unbelievable is that they said *yes*.

"So what you're saying is, the existential dread I had all night about this, that caused me to get out of bed at 5am and drive over here, was pointless then?" I say slowly, curling my hands around my hot mug just so I don't pick at them.

"Yeah," my dad nods, as my mom adds, "Pretty much."

Perfect, just perfect. I've been in a manic hellhole all night, and all along they knew everything anyway and were completely fine with it. Why the hell didn't Josh tell me?

We talk some more and they insist I stay for an unofficial wedding breakfast, before politely declining my invite to attend the actual wedding. Apparently watching me fake getting married doesn't count. So with that all squared away, I tell them it's time for me to leave, much to my father's dismay.

"Oh, let her go, Jer, you know she needs to go make herself look good, she's always had a crush on the Peters boy and now is her chance," my mom cuts in with a laugh, as she follows me to the door.

"His name is Josh," I scoff, as if they didn't live next to him for almost a decade and treat him like their own son. "And I do not have a crush on him." I don't add on the fact that 'crush' is now a tame word in comparison to what I feel for him, but hey, everyone lies to their parents right?

Unfortunately for me, growing up in such a loving and accepting household means my parents can see through my bullshit, and are never afraid to call me on it. "Yeah alright," my dad roars with laughter. "You just loved freezing your ass off and letting him beat you at hockey because he's your *friend*." He says the word friend with an exaggerated tone as he rolls his eyes at me. "A friend you've now agreed to marry," he adds with another laugh.

"I hate you both," I grumble, throwing open the door and accepting another hug from my mom. "And I never let him beat me at hockey."

"It's okay, Sweetie, we hate you too, now hurry up and go, so me and your dad can do hot yoga together," she replies with a playful wink, and I groan.

"Gross, now I really do hate you," I say in disgust, darting between them before they start making out like teenagers under the bleachers. "I'll call you tomorrow," I add with a vague wave, as I rush out of the door and head for my car.

"Give Josh our love," my dad calls out after me with a gleeful tone.

"That is if you're not too busy giving him all *your love*," my mom adds, with a giggle that turns into a squeal as my dad pulls her against him.

I give them both the middle finger like the mature adult child of theirs I am, and then dive into my car before I am forced to assault my ears with the sounds of their moans. I already have enough childhood trauma of that, I certainly don't need anymore. Yet still I can't help but smile as I leave their driveway and start on the road back to Fairfield.

What must it be like to be married to the love of your life?

I guess today I will find out, even if he doesn't love me back.

When I get home, I head straight for a shower to freshen up, and then even though the wedding is still hours away, I slowly start to get ready to try and calm my nerves. I do my makeup, tidy up my hair, and then slip on the dress that made the final cut. When I look in the mirror I expect to feel something. That thing that people talk about when they see themselves ready to get married for the first time, but I don't feel anything. All I see is a girl in a pretty dress, wondering if she is about to make the biggest mistake of her life.

Which is how my best friend finds me.

Maddie knocks and then pushes open the door, but then halts on the threshold as she stares at me. "Oh my god, Hallie, you look amazing." She rushes towards me and joins my stare in the mirror as we both take in my reflection. "I mean you look beautiful every single day, but wow, you're an angel."

The dress is simple and elegant, tucking in at the waist and then flowing down to the floor. There is a slight floral detail on the bodice, but it's mostly plain yet compliments my figure well.

"Do you think it's okay?" I ask, knowing it doesn't really matter because one day I will have the perfect dress that does give me the perfect feeling, it just won't be with the perfect guy.

"Are you kidding? I think you look gorgeous, but if you want a second opinion, there is a hockey player at the door asking for you," she states casually, and I almost vomit over the butterflies that flood my stomach.

Josh is here? What the hell is he doing here already?

I don't bother voicing my questions out loud and instead just push past her and head downstairs, not caring if he sees me in the dress. Hell, he saw me in like twenty others in pictures yesterday, and it's not like bad luck can affect a fake wedding right? Yet when I reach the bottom of the stairs I don't find my husband to be like I expect. No, instead I find the last person I ever thought I'd see here.

Daemon Forbes.

He is standing in the open door frame with his eyes on the floor, shifting slowly from side to side, like just being out of his bubble unnerves him. He isn't dressed in his usual attire of a black hoodie and dark jeans, and is instead looking both handsome and smart in a dark colored tux with his usual messy hair slicked back a little. There is a large garment bag in his hands that he holds up straight, and when he hears me approach, he lifts his chin so his stare can meet mine.

Neither of us say anything right away, and I am reminded about the couple of encounters we've had, and the words Josh said about him.

Daemon Forbes is one of the best people I have ever met, you just need to get to know him.

So with that in mind, and knowing that he is close to Josh and knows the truth about today, I step towards him. "Hi

Daemon," I say simply, not really sure what else to say, and a small smile pulls on the corner of his mouth.

"Hi Hallie." His gaze sweeps up and down my entire body with a small frown, before he holds out the bag in his hand. "Josh asked if I could drop this off for you."

I notice he is holding the hook at the top of the bag on one finger, meaning when I grab it from him, our hands don't touch at all. "What is it?"

"Open it and find out." His response isn't meant to be funny, but still a small laugh falls from my lips as I hang the bag on the top of the front door beside us and gently slide down the zip.

When I look inside I gasp at the sparkly green tulle that greets me and before I can even take it all in, Daemon steps a little closer and says, "He wanted today to be perfect for you, and he said that meant having the perfect dress."

At his words I look at him, and I know the moment he sees the unshed tears in my eyes because his own take on a whole new look. Like he's assessing some new information he just discovered, and I can't even find the strength in me to hide it. I let him see it, I let him see the real love I have for his friend. Not the fake kind, or the showy kind, and all I can do is pray that he won't tell him. He steps forward, almost as if he is about to try and comfort me but then stops himself.

"You won't tell him will you?" I ask, the tears no doubt ruining my makeup as I turn back to the dress.

"You don't know me very well, but if there's one thing I'm good at it's keeping secrets, trust me." The tone of his voice has a dark edge to it now, and for some reason I feel he's the one who needs comfort more than I do.

I turn towards him, taking a step to bring us closer together, before I lean up and gently press my lips to his cheek. "Thank you, Daemon."

His entire body freezes when I kiss him, like he's not sure

what to do with that level of affection, and a blush stains his cheeks, but I pretend I don't notice as I move back to unhook the dress from the door.

Daemon clears his throat and nods his head outside, "I'll be waiting for you when you're ready." I must look confused because before I can even question him, he steps aside to reveal a white wedding car idling by the curb, and he pulls the keys from his pocket indicating he is the driver.

Josh really did think of everything, and as my fingers clutch around the bag in my hand that houses what I know will be the most perfect dress, I can't help but feel bittersweet.

I might be marrying someone who doesn't love me back, but I'm also marrying my best friend. A best friend who asks permission for your hand in marriage, and hunts down a dress he thinks will be the one, just to make me feel comfortable, and that's worth more than any other kind of love.

#10
JOSH
UNINVITED GUESTS

A wedding day is something I never thought I would have. Once my dad's affair came out, I always swore I would never get married, and since then I have kept that promise to myself. I have never led girls on, never had a girlfriend, and never let myself get into anything more serious than a few strung together one night stands. After growing up under the guise of my mother and father's bullshit marriage, it's not something I ever coveted for myself, yet here I am, standing before an aisle waiting for my bride to appear.

Planning a small wedding in an even smaller amount of time actually turned out to be easier than I thought, especially with all of the privileges that come with my last name. I blocked the wedding planner's number and spoke to a minister from out of town, paying him extra to keep quiet and get our license sorted in time for today. This meant that the only thing I needed to focus on was getting my mother and father out of their estate, which I enlisted my grandmother's help for. After some gentle name and event dropping, she has taken them out of town to a fundraiser, giving me the whole place to myself.

Knowing Hallie as well as I do, I know she is like me in many ways. She doesn't like a lot of people, or being around huge crowds, and truly despises all of the attention being on her, so I knew a small wedding was the only way to go. With that in mind, and over a decade of friendship behind us, there was only one place I could think of that would be perfect to do this. Now as I stand under the two oak trees that used to form the goal on my makeshift ice rink at my parents' house, I know I chose perfectly.

Long gone are the stones that used to make up our playing area, and in their place is a long black runner lined with white roses, a few petals leading towards me, and large black and white candles in glass cases on either side. Classy, elegant, and beautiful, just like the girl who is about to become my wife. The minister is to my right and a photographer to my left. I mean, what's the point of a fake wedding if there is no one here to document it? So all that's left to do now is wait for her to show up. I sent Daemon with a car to pick her up a while ago with the instruction to get her here for six, just in time for the sun to set, which should be any minute now.

I'm also expecting Maddie, who is clearly running late, but when I hear footsteps on the other side of the outbuilding I know she must be here. So imagine my surprise when instead of my sister, I lock eyes with her boyfriend and the captain of my hockey team.

Nova fucking Darkmore.

"What the hell are you doing here?" I snap before I can help myself, because there is no love lost between either of us, no matter what his relationship to my sister is, but of course all the prick does is smile as he strides towards me in a suit.

"Maddie invited me, I'm her plus one," he shrugs casually,

looking smarter than I have ever seen him, just as more footsteps sound out, only for Archer Gray and Alexander Reign to appear in his shadow, also in suits.

What the fuck?

"I didn't give Maddie a plus one," I grit, watching as my goalie and left wing walk down the aisle behind him. "And what the fuck are they doing here?"

Nova flicks his stare over his shoulder, smiling at his two best friends, before turning back to me. "They asked me what I was all dressed up for and then got sad because they wanted to come. What was I supposed to do, tell them no?" he asks, as he comes to a stop beside me.

"I don't give a fuck what you tell them, but you three pricks are not invited to my goddamn wedding, go home," I demand, as Gray and Reign fall in line beside Nova like some sort of fucked up groomsman party.

"Nova gives Maddie a plus one all the time," Archer gleams with a wink. "It's about time she returned the favor."

"Careful now," Nova warns, at the same time I seethe, "Gray, I swear to fucking god." But of course all the bastard does is laugh.

"Come on, Peters, we can be witnesses for your little shotgun wedding," Reign drawls, exuding the kind of energy only someone with his nepo net worth could. "So how far along is your wife to be anyway?"

I blink back at his casual accusation. "Hallie is not pregnant," I respond with as much finality as I can muster, desperate for this conversation to be over and for them to fuck off.

Alexander wrinkles his nose in disgust. "If you didn't knock her up, what the fuck are you marrying her for?" he asks, completely perplexed.

"Yeah, dude, do you have any idea how much pussy you are going to miss out on now?" Archer chimes in. "I mean, just last night I had this girl's lips wrapped round my cock, her mouth like a damn vacuum, and that was without my wingman here." He nudges Nova with his elbow as he talks animatedly about his sexcapades.

"I am not your wingman," Nova replies, picking something off the sleeve of his suit, before he sighs, "And leave Peters alone, he and Hallie have been secretly in love for years, it's about time they made it official."

My eyes collide with his and I see the truth in them, the truth I know Maddie will have told him, which means right now he just had my back over his friends, and I can't even thank him.

Archer makes a fake gagging sound that brings both our stares back to him. "Fuck, dude, ever since you have been getting regular pussy you have become so fucking whipped."

Nova and I both open our mouths to offer up another warning to him, but before either of us can say anything, my sister finally joins the fray.

"Sorry I'm late," she gasps, trotting round the corner and down the aisle, making all of our heads turn towards her. "I had to make a pit stop on the way," she explains, holding up the one thing I asked her to bring. "I even managed to get a blue one," she laughs, passing it to me just in time for Nova to sweep her into his arms.

"You look absolutely stunning as always, Princess," he drawls, stealing her response with a kiss that has me rolling my eyes as I turn away from them.

"You scrub up quite nicely yourself, Charmer," Maddie gasps when she finally pulls free.

"I can't wait to rip this—" Nova starts, far too loudly for my liking, and I cut him off.

"Nova, I swear to god, if you finish that sentence I am going to kill you and then myself," I promise, as Maddie mutters a quiet apology, and Gray and Reign crack up in a fit of giggles. "If you're all staying then pull it together, Daemon and Hallie will be here any second."

My statement does the trick in shutting up Archer almost instantly. "Daemon is coming?" he asks, and I nod.

"You invited Daemon Forbes but not us?" Alexander cuts in with a pout that I am almost certain he must have practiced in the mirror.

"Yes, because unlike you assholes, Daemon is more than just my teammate, he's my friend." I crack my neck in exasperation at having to deal with them.

"The dude is weird," Reign grunts, and before I can curse him out, Archer beats me to it.

"Don't be a dick, Reign," he warns, and I see both Alexander and Nova's eyes flare in surprise as they look at their friend.

"Yeah, don't be a dick, Reign," a cold dark voice cuts in, and we all turn to find Daemon standing at the end of the aisle with his arm linked with Hallie's, his stare cunning and cold, and locked completely on our goalie.

The tension in the air is thick, but any other words that are spoken are completely lost on me, because once my eyes collide with Hallie's, everyone else just falls away, and the only thing I can focus on is her. She looks perfect, even better than I could have ever imagined, and despite the nerves I can see in her eyes, she still offers me that sunshine smile of hers. Her arm is linked around Daemon's and I can see her fingers digging into his bicep, not that he seems to mind, and when I flick my stare to his in wonder, as he walks her down the aisle towards me, all he does is shrug his free shoulder slightly.

Seems I have a best friend turned best man.

By the time they reach me, the boys are flanked on one side of me, with Maddie moving to the other while still leaving space for Hallie, and when she shares a look with her best friend, I see tears shining in my sister's eyes.

"Joshua," Hallie smiles, by way of greeting. "You don't look completely horrible today," she muses, her eyes dropping down the full length of my body as she slowly takes in my tux-clad form. She has seen me dressed like this at least a hundred times, but from the look in her eyes it's as if it's the first time.

As I return the favor I find myself a little speechless. The dress I picked is perfect, just like I knew it would be, but I guess I never truly imagined what she would look like in it. A traditional white wedding dress wasn't made for the likes of her, no, she deserves something better, something more fitting of her, and when I take her in, I know I made the right choice.

The green bodice fits tightly around her chest, showing a perfect amount of cleavage to still leave something to the imagination, and with it dusted in sparkling jewels, flowers, and butterflies, it looks like something straight out of a fairytale. Two thick straps sit snugly on her shoulders, with the rest of the green tulle and silk fabric fluttering out from her waist all the way down to the floor. She looks like a princess, one far too beautiful for the likes of me, and something like regret pulses deep within my gut as Daemon hands her off to me with a nod.

"Thank you, Daemon," Hallie whispers quietly to my friend, and I swear I see him smile at her, as he moves to take up a spot beside my sister. I make a mental note to ask her later how she roped him into walking her down the aisle, but as she looks up at me, every thought in my mind evaporates.

"You look perfect, Tink," I blurt without thinking, and then curse myself as her eyes widen and a blush stains her cheeks.

"Now now, save the sweet talking for our wedding night," she jokes in response, and I hear the guys cracking up beside me, but right now, in this moment I wish she wasn't joking.

Wait what?
What the fuck is wrong me with?
She's my best friend.

She's doing me a favor.

I can't look at her like that, no matter how perfect she looks right now, and thankfully the minister clears his throat to get started, and I push away the inappropriate thoughts about the girl who is about to become my wife.

My wife.

"Welcome loved ones," the minister starts, looking between the five people standing on either side of Hallie and me as if he were expecting more, and I can't help but smirk because he's lucky he's got this many. "We are gathered here today to join Joshua and Hallie in holy matrimony."

Hallie smiles as she mouths the word "Joshua" to me with a wink, and I can't help but smile back as I shake my head at her.

"Joshua and Hallie, the two of you are the embodiment of young love," the minister continues. "You found friendship and unity in your years of getting to know one another, and now, those gathered here today get to bear witness to what that relationship has become."

His words ring truer than I expect given this whole thing isn't real. We do have friendship and unity, and over a decade of getting to know one another, so even though this is fake, it still very much factors into the reason we are standing here right now.

Hallie is now silent beside me, and I can't help but panic that maybe this whole thing is too much and she is going to change her mind. So I can't stop myself from slipping my hand into hers and squeezing it three times just like when we were kids. *Are you okay?*

Her eyes flick to mine, a look I can't decipher lingering there as she smiles softly and squeezes back three times. *Yes, I'm okay.*

"I understand the two of you have prepared your own vows," the minister interrupts our thoughts, and I see Hallie's eyes widen. "If you could turn to one another and join hands," he instructs, and we join our other hands with one another, which means I feel when Hallie's start shaking in mine.

Before the minister can instruct any further, or push one of us to go first, the words are already falling from my mouth. "Hallie, you're my best friend," I start, surprised by how fast that revelation falls from my lips. I mean, it's true of course, but I'm not sure if she even knows that anymore. "I know I haven't always made that clear between us, but you are, and you have been since the first time I laid eyes on you on this very spot."

I still remember that day like it was yesterday. I was sick of listening to yet another of my parents' fights, and was still too young to know what they were about, I just wanted out of the house. So I headed down here to work out my frustrations with my stick and puck, playing under clouds of gray. I honestly didn't know what to think when the girl with the sunshine smile walked into the middle of my game without saying a word, and for some reason she looked as lost as I felt. Yet from that day forward, she was like a beacon of light I clung onto.

"You didn't care that you were ruining my hockey game, and have pretty much been a pain in my ass ever since, but you're still my best friend in the whole world," I tell her truthfully, because outside of my sister, she is the one other person I truly care about and the only person I could picture myself doing this with. "You've been by my side for ten years, and I can't think of another person I would want to take this journey with." I ensure to choose my words carefully given the extra guests in attendance, but I hope she knows how much I mean them.

"Joshua," she all but whispers, her knuckles white as they fist around mine, but I squeeze them right back, letting her know that no matter what, I will always be there to hold her hand.

"I mean it, Hals, I'll always be your best friend. No matter what."

I hear a sniffle from behind her, and my gaze flicks to my

sister who has tears streaming down her face, and I watch as Daemon silently hands her a tissue. Yet when I hear another sniffle, I look behind me to find Nova handing Reign a tissue too, while Archer grins like an idiot.

When I turn back to Hallie she is watching them with a smile, but when her eyes flick back to mine, I find them glossy with unshed tears of her own. Then she exhales a slow breath as her thumb works back and forth over the top of my hand.

"Josh, you're my best friend too, and it feels special to admit that to you when we are standing somewhere I consider to be our spot," she admits softly, before turning to my sister and adding, "Sorry, Mads, you know I still love you." Everyone laughs and when she turns back to me, her eyes are shining bright. "I still don't know what I was looking for the day I met you. I think I was just anxious about moving to a new town, and wanting somewhere quiet to clear my head. I guess I know you well enough now to realize you were doing the same." Her smile is sad now, as she no doubt thinks of the parents I grew up with and the reason we are truly here. "You've always been a lost boy to me, the Peter to my Tinkerbell, and well, I guess I just want you to know that from the moment I found you I knew that you were special, that you would be important to me, I just never imagined how much, and I'm glad we get to take this journey together too."

A choked sob leaves Reign now, which has Archer cackling even more, much to the minister's dismay, as he huffs at them both before focusing back on us. Yet my eyes remain on Hallie's, on the way she is looking at me, and not just looking, but seeing me, all of me. The good, the bad, the awful, and yet still, deep down I can tell she meant every word she just said, and it should make me feel good inside. I should be thankful to have someone like her beside me, but all it does is remind me of what a dick I've been to her for the last few years.

The Peter to my Tinkerbell.

Stupid, childish nicknames that I used to detest, yet now they remind me that no matter how bad my father and mother might be, I still have a sister who loves me, and a friend–and almost wife–who would do anything for me.

"Now for the exchanging of rings," the minister declares, interrupting my thoughts, and I turn to Daemon who is already holding the ring I got for Hallie between his fingers for me.

I take it from him and focus my attention back on my bride. We let the minster speak and repeat the words after him, me going first and slipping the matching band I got with her engagement ring onto Hallie's finger. Then she goes next, surprising me with a ring of my own which is a simple platinum band with a small emerald strip down the center. It matches hers perfectly, and as rings go, it's one I won't mind wearing everyday. The feel of it is a welcome weight as we hold each other's hands and wait for this whole thing to become official.

"By the power vested in me by the state of New York, I now pronounce you husband and wife. You may kiss the bride."

#11
HALLIE
BROKEN RULES

"You may kiss the bride."

Five words. Five simple words that have my heart thundering in my chest. And not just the words, but everything else too. The groom, this place, the dress. Oh the dress. It's so beyond perfect that I can't even begin to describe it. Then this place, the place where I first saw him, first met him, first heard his name, now scattered with flowers and candles that led me straight to him. *Him.* The boy. The perfect boy with the broken smile, now looking at me like I have just given him everything, and just like the first day I met him, all I can do is smile back.

You may kiss the bride.

Five simple words and the first of our rules goes right out of the window.

Without hesitation, Josh pulls me in until I am flush against him, then reaches up and gently cups the back of my neck, his thumbs tipping my chin back towards his full height, as he whispers with a smile, "It's okay, Tink, we both know you love breaking the rules anyway."

Then before I can even bother denying him, his lips are on mine and every other thought apart from how he tastes evaporates from my mind. The kiss is soft, yet insistent, dominant in a way I have never experienced before, and probably never will again, as Josh ruins me for everyone else, just like he always does. His mouth moves against my own, his tongue gently teasing the seam of my lips, and just as I'm about to open and grant him access, he pulls away, his breathing heavy as he stares at me in wonder. His eyes are glazed and a little unsure as we both ignore the hollers of congratulatory cheers around us.

Josh is looking at me like he has never seen me before, and it unnerves me enough to make a joke. "Well that was about as awful as I imagined." I tell him boldly, lying through my teeth as I try to get my heartbeat to return to a normal pace. One more kiss from him and I might just be ruined forever.

Josh just smirks. "Oh yeah? Imagine me kissing you often, do you?" He is still holding me against him, and with the noise everyone is still making, the only one who can hear him is me.

"You wish. I never think about such things, which is good because I would be greatly disappointed." Another lie considering I can still feel the warmth of his lips against mine, and it's taking every ounce of self control I have to not lean in and kiss him again, just for one more taste.

"You're a terrible liar." *I am.*

"And you're a terrible kisser." *He's not.*

"Well, anytime you want to test that theory, Mrs. Peters, all you have to do is ask." *Mrs. Peters.* Be still my beating heart.

Ignoring his attempts to rile me up, I take a step back from him and square my shoulders as I quietly toss back, "I wouldn't hold your breath, I'd rather choke."

His fingers slip between mine, and we turn towards where

everyone is waiting to congratulate us as he softly adds, "That could also be arranged, there is no rule against that after all."

Heat engulfs me at his words, and I force myself not to react as I look towards my best friend who is smiling wildly at us both.

"You guys, that was so beautiful," Maddie sniffles, wiping another tear from her eyes, and I stare at her confused considering she knows this whole thing is fake and I know she isn't that good of an actress. So why the hell is she crying? "Here, I brought your 'something old'," she adds, pulling a polaroid picture from her purse and handing it to me.

The picture is of me and Josh when we were kids, taken by her in this very spot as we played one of our many hockey games together. "Maddie, I can't believe you still have this, it's perfect." I remember the summer she was obsessed with taking pictures with that camera, no activity of ours was safe from her lens.

Maddie shrugs with a smile. "Maybe I always knew you guys were meant to be," she tells us, as Josh moves to hand me something else.

"This is something new and blue," he winks, handing me a ring pop exactly the same as the ones we used to have as kids, and I can't help but laugh.

"You guys are the best," I tell them, taking the candy from him with a laugh, wondering how lucky I got to snare not one, but two Peters siblings for myself.

"Here I can cover the 'something borrowed'," Archer cuts in, swinging a pink garter belt around his fingers and offering it up to me.

"Hell no," Josh cuts in. "She isn't wearing something you stole from one of your whores."

Archer blinks back in offense, "Hey, don't be rude, this is mine, no girl has ever even seen it, let alone wore it."

We all turn to him in confusion, Damon snorting a humorless laugh in the process and making Archer blush, as Alexander finally clears his throat. "Well, who else needs a cup of tea after that?" he asks, still wiping his tears.

"You guys are the weirdest fuckers I have ever come across," Josh tells them, shaking his head. "But thanks for coming, I guess." And I can't help but smile at his words, ever the political son of the Mayor.

"I'm sure your wife will be saying that to you later," Archer gleams, tossing me a saucy wink, and I tighten Josh's hand in mine before he can even react, holding him at my side.

"Don't be a little bitch, Arch, just because Josh is getting laid tonight and you aren't," I toss back, hoping to keep my new husband's temper in check by fanning the flames of our ruse.

His hand squeezes mine as Daemon laughs again, and I can't help but take pride in seeing him coming out of his shell a little today. Especially after I accosted him into walking me down the aisle.

Archer clutches his chest dramatically. "Damn, Sanders, you wound me, I thought we were friends." I smile at the ridiculousness of him, because for some wild reason he is actually my friend, yet still I stand my ground.

"Actually it's Peters now, and stop trying to piss off my husband or I will dick punch you," I warn him carefully.

"She's not joking, I have it on good authority she will actually dick punch you," Josh cuts in, and I can almost feel his shudder as if he is remembering the pain I inflicted on him the other day.

Before anyone can say anything else, the minister interrupts us to sign our licenses, and then we are pushed towards the photographer to gather up some evidence. Then we spend the next thirty minutes taking as many pictures as possible, in as many configurations as possible, from Josh and I alone, to all of us together, me and Maddie, Maddie and Nova, all the guys together, until Josh finally tells them they have more than enough.

"So, tea?" Alexander suggests again, and for some reason we all say yes.

Which is how we find ourselves back at Josh's house, with Alexander in the kitchen next to Daemon making everyone drinks. Drinks that are definitely not tea. Josh's other housemates aren't home, so we all decide to settle in the living room to enjoy a drink. Nova is sitting in one of the chairs with Maddie perched in his lap, and I am sandwiched between Archer and my new husband on the sofa as we wait for whatever the boys are mixing up in the kitchen.

Josh's carefree attitude from the ceremony has dissipated completely, and now he looks more annoyed than I think I have ever seen, especially when Archer says, "Don't worry, Peters, Cap said we can't stay long since it's your wedding night and all." Archer waggles his brows at him and I swear I hear Josh curse.

"Give it a rest, Arch," Nova scolds his best friend, making his shoulders slump, before leaning in closer to Maddie and whispering something that has her blushing.

"How are those drinks coming?" Josh shouts louder than necessary, and I can only presume by the mixture of Archer Gray, and his sister getting mauled by her boyfriend, that he is close to the edge.

"Alright don't get your knickers in a twist," Alexander tosses back, as he loads up a tray with drinks and heads our way.

He walks around us all, until each of us have one of the drinks, and then takes the free chair beside Nova and Maddie, leaving Daemon to take the final seat on the sofa beside Archer.

Archer of course doesn't hesitate to taste his drink, swallowing it down faster than necessary as Daemon stares at him with a look I can't decipher.

Ignoring them I take a sip of my own, the fruity and tangy mixture of alcohol and juice exploding on my tongue, as I ask, "What is this?"

Alexander smiles at me as he downs his own. "It's my own creation, I call it the Baby Maker," he purrs with a wink, and I almost choke on my second sip, as Josh once again curses beside me.

Which is how the night proceeds for the next two hours. We enjoy the Baby Maker, the Cock Blocker, the Pussy Power, the Wedding Whacker, and the Puck Chaser. All of which are stronger and more ridiculous than the previous contender, until I can feel a warm sensation spreading throughout my entire body.

Tensions between the guys seem low considering that Josh and Daemon aren't really friends with their teammates, but then I have to remind myself of how much time they actually spend together between practice and games. Of course they are used to each other's company, whether they enjoy it or not, and as fake wedding nights go, it isn't half bad.

"Okay next game," Archer slurs, having had double the amount of drinks than all of us. "Truth or dare," he declares with a wink in my direction, and I instantly blush thinking about the last time I played that with the members of this group, my new husband excluded of course.

Yet before I can voice my refusal, Daemon shoots to his feet and leaves the room without a word, as Nova and Alexander both snap, "No," at the same time, making Josh blink around in confusion.

"Why can't we play truth or dare?" he asks, making Maddie choke on her drink, and now it's my turn to look at her in confusion, but her eyes are firmly on the floor.

"Oh I'm glad you asked, Joshy boy, because the last time I played truth or dare I got to kiss your new wife there." He exaggerates his words by pointing at me, as if Josh doesn't know who he is referring to, and as if he hasn't already taunted him with this fact before.

I expect an outburst, knowing Josh, but apparently when drunk he is a little more relaxed. Leaning back on the sofa behind me, his arm resting along my shoulders, all he does is laugh darkly. "And tonight will be the last time you ever speak of it because I will break your jaw if you bring that up again," he warns him, and it sends a thrill up my spine.

Which is ridiculous considering I know he is only protecting me in the same manner he does Maddie, like a sister, not a wife, not a real one anyway, and the thought is sobering. It also has me standing abruptly, causing all of them to flick their eyes my way as I try to clear my thoughts rapidly.

"I need to go," I say without thinking, before quickly adding, "To bed, I need to go to bed." Remembering to keep up appearances of the facade that is my life now. It's our wedding night, I can't exactly go home while everyone else is still here, I will have to wait for them to leave.

Alexander clambers to his feet. "I'll make you another Baby Maker for the road upstairs," he claims, stumbling towards the kitchen.

"We should go too," Maddie cuts in, climbing from Nova's lap, and he follows her instantly, like magnets to one another.

"Oh I am more than ready to go, Princess," he replies, pulling her in by the waist, making Josh groan out loud.

"Yes, please fucking leave before I have to bleach my goddamn eyes," he complains, rising to his feet alongside me, and putting his arm around my waist.

The perfect show.

"No, it's not even ten yet, the party can't be over," Archer drawls from the sofa behind me and Josh looks at me and rolls his eyes.

"See what shit I have to put up with," he whispers, making me laugh, before turning to Archer. "You and Reign can see yourselves out when you're done with the drinks, but we are going to bed."

The words are said with such finality that even I believe them, and when he starts leading us towards the stairs, my stomach floods with anxiety about how this is going to go.

"See you at lunch tomorrow," Maddie calls out to our backs, reminding me of the dinner we have on the schedule with her parents, and not wanting to think about the bomb we are going to drop on them, I let Josh lead me towards the stairs.

"Can't we just stay here?" Alexander calls from the kitchen, and Josh huffs.

"Fine, whatever, but don't make a fucking mess," he snaps, and whatever is said in response is swallowed by Archer's cheer as we leave the rest of the them downstairs and head up to his room.

When we get there Josh doesn't seem to be as phased as I am, because all he does is stroll inside and throw himself down on his bed, whereas I let the door shut behind me before sliding the lock into place.

"Why did you say they could stay, I'll never be able to get out of here now?" I complain, and he flicks his eyes to me, completely confused.

"Aren't you staying here?" he asks, as if we had somehow already discussed our current predicament, and my heart races in my chest.

"You want me to stay here?" I ask, treading very carefully as I move slowly away from the door, but still stick to the perimeter of the room, coming to a stop in front of his closet.

Josh shrugs, sitting up and slowly peeling off his jacket and loosening his tie. "I just presumed you would," he replies casually, as if it's no big deal.

"Isn't it weird?" I question, desperately wanting him to both agree and disagree with me.

"Why would it be weird? It's not like we haven't shared a room before." He stands, moving to his dresser and unclasping his watch, before undoing the buttons on his shirt, and all I can do is stare in awe as he reveals his perfectly chiseled stomach and abs.

"I think it's a bit different now than when you were twelve," I scoff, gesturing towards him, and all he does is smirk.

"Don't tell me, my little Hallie bear, is scared of a hot body?" he asks, peeling the shirt from his skin and tossing it over the back of his chair, and suddenly the temperature in the room skyrockets.

I scoff again. "Please, you are not that hot."

His smirk only widens as he moves towards me. "Once again, you are a terrible liar, Mrs. Peters," he gleams, with a wicked look in his eye as he leans in close to me until I can feel his breath on my neck. "Now step aside so I can get a blanket, I'll sleep on the floor."

I push away from him like my ass is on fire, and ignore his sinful laugh as he reaches into the closet to retrieve some sheets and an extra duvet, before moving to set up a place to sleep at the end of his bed without another word.

Well, I guess I'm spending the night with my husband.

#12
JOSH

BEDTIME BUDDIES

Hallie is being weirder than usual, and I'm pretty drunk, so that's a keen observation on my part, but the girl is acting like she has never been in close quarters with anyone before, let alone me. We practically grew up together, and living next door to one another meant there were plenty of family vacations and camping trips we had to endure. So the fact she is being all skittish just because we have to share a room is very amusing for me. I continue to undress while she acts like every piece of furniture in my room offends her, and then I move to start setting up a bed on the floor for myself.

"I know you are a master of many talents, Tink, but sleeping standing up isn't one of them, just make yourself at home," I try to coax her into relaxing a little, but all she does is scoff.

"*Just make yourself at home,*" she mocks. "Joshua, do you have any idea the level of effort that goes into my sleeping routine every single night?" I roll my eyes at her words, because again we practically grew up with one another, of course I know. "I don't have any pajamas, I don't have Percy, a fan, my sleeping mask, my ear defenders, how the hell am I supposed to just make myself at home?"

Swallowing my laugh, I move to my dresser and pull out one of my spare jerseys and toss it on the bed, before retrieving my phone and pulling up a fan noise that lasts almost ten hours. "Okay, two out of five eliminated, which is the best I can do for you right now, I'll do better next time," I tell her, making a mental note to be more prepared from our impromptu sleepovers in the future.

"Next time," she laughs without humor. "Next time you can come and stay in my room where I have everything I need," she snaps, clearly stressed, and I am already missing her sunshine smile, so I can't help but tease her.

"Inviting me for sleepovers already, wife? My body must be better than I thought."

She drops onto my bed and leans down, pulling up her dress, to reveal a pair of sparkling heels that she begins to unbuckle. "It's like you think I won't dick punch you on our wedding night," she grumbles, totally serious as she struggles with her shoes.

I drop down on one knee before her and unbuckle both shoes with ease, eyeing the length of her smooth calf, as I reply, "I mean, now you mention it, my dick does need some attention."

Her eyes snap to mine and I swear I see a flare of interest there before she masks it with a scowl, "I'm sure the hoards of girls that would give it some are going to be weeping in their beds this week when they find out it's no longer on the market."

Rising back to my full height I flash her a mischievous grin. "Hmm, note to self, my wife is jealous and feisty, I like it." I turn my back and head into the bathroom to give her some privacy, but not before the back of my head is smacked with a pillow.

"Next time it will be a brick, asshole," she curses at my back, and I hide my laugh on the other side of the bathroom door.

Then I take my time brushing my teeth, and changing into some shorts, until I am sure she has had enough time to get out of her dress and ready for bed. Then I give her five more minutes for good measure until I am almost certain she must be done by now. Yet when I venture back into my room she practically dives away from the mirror that hangs on the door to the bathroom, almost giving me a heart attack.

"Everything okay?" I ask, flicking my gaze up and down to see she is very much changed into my jersey, and that the dress I bought her is hanging neatly on my closet door.

"No, Joshua, everything is not okay," she grits out through her teeth, gesturing to her jersey clad form. "Look at me." I already am, so all I do is widen my stare in confusion to try to figure out what the hell is wrong with her. "I'm wearing your jersey," she confirms, and I have to smile.

"Hallie, I know you don't have a very high opinion of me most of the time, but contrary to what you might think I'm actually quite smart. I gave you my jersey to wear, I now see with my eyes that you are wearing it, therefore, confirming you're wearing it seems a little pointless. What is the problem?"

Another pillow is thrown at my head.

"I am wearing your jersey," she snaps again, as I pick up her weapon of choice and toss it back onto the bed.

"So? You wear my jersey all the time," I shrug, not seeing what her point is. "In fact, you have bugged me every single year since I have known you to make sure I always order extra jerseys, just so I can give them to you, so again, what is the problem?"

"I'm wearing your jersey and nothing else," she whispers, looking down at her bare legs as her fingers pull against the hem that reaches her mid thigh. "Yes I wear it all the time, but it's usually with pants," she adds in exasperation.

I open my mouth to respond, but the visual she just painted has me pausing a little. *I'm wearing your jersey and nothing else.* Damn. That's not the first time I've heard something like that, but it's definitely the first time I've cared. I mean I'm not blind, I know she is hot as fuck, I have just never allowed myself to look at her like that. She's my little sister's best friend, she's my friend, but right now as she stands in nothing but my jersey, the thoughts I am having about her are far from fucking friendly.

It takes some effort to force my stare back to hers, and I clear my throat as I say, "Well if you're asking for my opinion, I much prefer this look on you."

She groans at my response, moving toward the mirror to check out where the hem reaches again.

"I was not asking for your opinion, asshole, but maybe some pants?"

This time I can't hold in my laugh. "Hallie, you're like 5ft barely nothing, do you really think I'm gonna have pants that fit you?" I shake my head as I crouch down and ready myself to sleep on the floor. "Just get in bed and stop being ridiculous." I move to turn off the light, leaving the room in just the glow of the lamp on my nightstand, before lying down.

Her stomps back to the bed shake the floor, and I smirk as I sink down into my sheets, knowing she won't let this go. "Easy for you to say, your body is fantastic," she grumbles, throwing herself into my bed with a huff.

"Glad to know my new wife is so attracted to me," I muse, relishing the way she once again curses my name. "And trust me, Hals, if anyone else was lucky enough to see those legs, I'm sure they'd be thinking the same bad thoughts I am."

I swear she doesn't realize how gorgeous she is sometimes. Hence the campus-wide no touching rule that includes her and Madeline. Maddie because she was my sister, and Hallie because she was, well, my Hallie. None of the assholes here are good enough for her, even more so now she's my wife.

"Only if you are thinking that I should wrap them up in some pants." she laughs, and I can hear her getting comfy, so I try to do the same.

"You could definitely wrap them somewhere," I reply without thinking, and the silence that follows is deafening, and I ruffle around in my sheets. "Sorry, that came out by default, I forgot you weren't a random hot girl for a second there."

She scoffs again, "Man whore."

"Brat," I toss back, not bothering to correct her statement considering I haven't slept with anyone since the beginning of the year, and enjoying our back and forth too much to care. It reminds me of when we were kids, before I pushed her away, now here I am pulling her in even tighter than before.

"Asshole." *She won't stop.*

"Drama queen." *I can't stop.*

"Nice abs," she coos sweetly, switching tactics just like she always used to do, trying to catch me off guard, and I laugh.

"Yeah, and nice legs," I reply instantly, shuffling around trying once again to get comfy.

"Oh my god if I have to listen to you move around one more time I am going to scream," she snaps, sitting up to glare at me. "Just get in the bed."

My entire body freezes. "You want me to get in the bed with you?" I confirm, almost sure I misheard her. We've shared a room before, but never a bed.

"Yes, I cannot listen to you fidgeting all night, not when things are already dire for me right now, so just get up here," she demands.

Well, who am I to disobey my wife?

I stretch out my limbs before grabbing my pillows and making my way over to the free side of the bed she has left space on. It's weird to see someone in my bed, even her, mostly because I never have girls in my bed, ever. Once you let them in your bed it's hard for you to get them to leave, so I just don't do it with any girl. But Hallie isn't any girl, not before today, and definitely not now she's mine.

Slowly climbing into bed beside her I am immediately assaulted by her scent, and have to force myself to not make any sort of joke. Especially when I feel her stiffening as I lay down beside her. It has me wondering if she has ever shared a bed with someone before.

Only once I'm settled does she reach out to my nightstand and turn out my light, the soft hum of the fan noise from my phone, the only company surrounding us. Other than that and the sound of our breathing it's silent, and it's in that silence that I think about the magnitude of what we did today. *We got married. I married her. I am someone's husband, she is my wife.*

"Josh," she whispers into the dark. "Can I ask you something?" She's so quiet that once she stops speaking I could almost pretend she isn't here, yet I can feel her everywhere. Which is strange since we aren't even touching.

"You can ask me anything," I tell her the same thing I've told her since she was nine, and prepare for one of her unusual questions or topics.

"Well, it's two things really."

I bite back a smile even though she can't see me as I reply, "I'm sure I can manage both."

"Why didn't you tell me that you went to see my parents?" Her question shouldn't surprise me, but it does. I know she's close to her parents, and I knew at some point she would tell them herself and that it would be the truth. When I don't reply right away she adds, "And why did you go and see them? Why did you ask for my dad's permission?"

"That's three questions," I remark, and three seconds later a pillow is bashed into my stomach. "Okay, okay, relax," I huff, tossing the pillow to the floor and thinking carefully about my answer before I respond. "I guess I had so much on my mind that I forgot to tell you. It didn't feel important to me that you know, but I knew it was important for me to go. You have great parents, Hals, they are smart, kind, supportive, and have always been there for you no matter what. I see what you have with them and I know it's a gold mine, what every child should have, and not enough do. I went to see them because I respect them, and I respect their daughter, and I didn't want them hearing about it from anyone else. And I asked your dad's permission because despite this being fake, my caring for you is very real. You're important to me, you're my family, and I needed him to know that no matter what I have your back, always."

She's quiet for so long that I almost think she has fallen asleep, until she eventually replies, "Do you really have an off limits rule on me around campus?"

Now that's something I am definitely not answering, no good will come of me admitting that, or giving her my reasons why. I like my dick unpunched and still attached to me, thank you very much. "That's too many questions, go to sleep," I snap out into the dark, and I can practically feel her smile.

"Oh my god you do, don't you?" she accuses happily, bashing me with yet another pillow. *Where the fuck does she keep geeting them from?* "Damn, people better be careful around me, apparently my husband is a psycho."

I laugh as I toss the pillow on her head as I reply, "Yeah so you better tell all your boyfriends to back off."

She pulls the pillow into her arms and turns onto her side to stare at me. Even in the dark I can feel her looking at me as she laughs, "All my boyfriends? The only boyfriend I've ever had went running to the hills as soon as we graduated with no reason why, so I think you're safe there."

I'm not sure she means to sound wounded by it, but she does. "Are you talking about Joey?" I ask, remembering that prick's name more than I care to admit.

"Or Jockstrap Jerkoff as he is more affectionately known in my house," she tosses back, and I can just imagine all the other names her and Maddie must have called him over the years.

"Yeah that suits him to a tea," I can't help but snort, thinking about the couple of encounters I had to endure with him.

Hallie is silent for a few seconds before she whispers, "I didn't realize you really knew him."

Fuck. Busted.

I aim my response to be as casual as possible. "We may have spoken once or twice."

Another pillow right in the head.

"What did you do?" she yells, hitting me with the pillow three more times before I grab hold of it to stop her.

"Fucking hell, will you stop with the pillows, and what makes you think I did something?" My voice is that of pure innocence, but she still scoffs a laugh, and I just know she is rolling her eyes.

"Because it's you. You always do something. Remember when your cousin Jason tried to kiss me at that party, and you broke his nose? Or when that guy from your class was taking pictures of Maddie and me in our swimsuits, and you drowned him in the pool? And don't even get me started on that creepy guy who used to work for your dad, he ended up in the hospital, you could have killed him," she rants, listing off only some of my conquests, and I smirk into the dark as I recall them.

"Barely, I only gave him a few crushed up pills in his drink, it's not my fault he shit himself so bad," I toss back, low key wishing I'd have done a lot worse. "That's what he gets for being a fucking pervert, you were fifteen, besides your dad thought it was hilarious."

"What did you do to Joey?" she grits, not sounding as amused by the storytelling as I am.

"Nothing."

"Joshua."

"Nothing, I swear."

"Remember the second rule on our contract?" she fumes, reminding me of the little agreement we signed on her notepad.

"No lying," I huff out, knowing she isn't going to let this go until I tell the truth. "Fine, I broke his arm."

"Josh!"

"What? He fucking deserved it, Tink. You should have heard the fucking shit he was saying about you, about what you guys got up to. I couldn't stand hearing it, so yeah, I broke his arm and told him to stay the hell away from you. You're welcome."

I hear her quick intake of breath and I know I've fucked up somewhere, I just don't know where. "He told people stuff?" she finally mutters into the dark.

My brain instantly goes on the offense and blocks out all the bragging about how tight and untouched she was, as I grit my teeth. "Yeah, of course he did, he was an asshole."

More silence lingers, and I wish I could see her face right now so I could gauge how she is taking all of this. "And you did that for me?" she asks, almost sounding shocked. I don't know why, I've always had her back.

"I'd do anything for you, Hals, you know that," I tell her truthfully.

"Thank you." Her voice cracks a little on her words, and all I want to do is pull her into my arms and make her feel better, but I know how she is about physical touch, and I'm sure just laying in the same bed as me is difficult for her to manage.

"You're welcome, now stop talking about your boyfriends, I thought we already covered that your new *husband* is a psycho," I joke, aiming to lift the mood, and finally she laughs, turning away from me.

"Goodnight, Mr. Peters," she sighs into the dark, as I stare up at the ceiling, still not believing we are here right now.

Yet still I smile as I reply, "Goodnight, Mrs. Peters."

#13
HALLIE
MORNING WOOD

Warmth surrounds my entire body. I feel safe, wanted, needed, cozy even, as my eyes flutter from their deep slumber. My bed is a lot comfier than I recall, and my blanket is more weighted than I remember, but it's so welcome. I feel like I am waking up from the most rested night's sleep I have ever had. It's only when I roll my body to appreciate my comfort that I feel something long and hard against my ass, and my eyes snap open. I'm not at home, I'm at Josh's house, in his room, in his bed, with him, as his wife.

The warmth is him, his entire body is molded against mine, his arm slung loosely over my waist, his nose nestled neatly into my hair. I can feel him everywhere, and I do mean everywhere, every part of him. His breathing is even and flat so I know he is still asleep, which means I know he doesn't mean to be cuddled up to me right now, and I'm sure he definitely doesn't mean the erection he is sporting right now too. Yet that doesn't mean I can't feel it, and it sets every fantasy I have ever had about him on fire in my mind.

I roll my body again, this time pushing my ass out a little just to see what he is working with, and almost moan out loud as his long, thick length presses against me even more. Damn, no wonder the rumor mill is always running rampant about him, if that's what he is toting around inside his pants. I bet he could satisfy every girl on campus with it. Just the thought has me wiggling against it again, teasing no one but myself, but before I can let my mind run too far away from itself I am startled.

"Should I always expect to wake up to my wife rubbing her ass on me, or is this a one-off?" Josh purrs in a sexy, gruff, still half-asleep tone, and I throw myself away from him so fast that I fall off the bed onto the floor.

He doesn't even flinch.

"I was not rubbing my ass on you," I lie boldly, forcing myself to jump to my feet and act casual, while the bastard is still lying in the same position, and all he does is cock one eye open to glare at me in disbelief. "I was trying to escape you, you were the one who was on my side of the bed with your arm wrapped around me," I accuse, flipping the situation back onto him.

This time he rolls his eyes, rolling onto his back, and his side of the bed, as the sheet falls down and reveals his delicious strip of abs. "It's my bed, all the sides are mine," he declares with a yawn, and I want to punch him in his stupid, pretty face.

"I hate you," I tell him, and he smiles.

"No you don't," he gleams, putting both hands behind his head as he watches me squirm, but all I can focus on is the flex of his muscles.

"Then I severely dislike you," I amend, as I stomp towards his bedroom door in desperate need to get away from him.

"Now that's not even slightly true," he muses, sitting up and running his hands through his hair. "And where the hell are you going?" He flips the sheet off his lower half and then stands, stretching upwards, and it takes everything in me not to drool.

"To get coffee, I can't deal with you when I haven't even caffeinated yet, I might murder you." I throw open his bedroom door in the hopes of escaping him, but he is hot on my heels as I head down to the kitchen.

"Death by dick punch seems like a terrible way to go," he jokes, as I come to a halt on the threshold to find the kitchen already occupied. "What the fuck are you guys still doing here?" Josh grumbles, taking in Archer and Alexander sitting at the breakfast bar, and Daemon standing by the fridge silently watching them.

"Ahhh it's the newlyweds," Alexander cheers, holding up his coffee in the air to us like he doesn't have a care in the world.

"We were too hungover to leave before coffee," Archer confirms, flicking his stare over the both of us before he adds, "Nice legs, Mrs. Peters."

Josh pushes past me and smacks him across the back of the head on his way to the coffee machine. "Keep your eyes off my wife, and her legs, you little man whore." And all I can do is pull on the hem of his jersey as I remember I am in fact, sans pants.

I skirt around the edge of the kitchen until my lower half is covered by the island, as Josh serves me a cup of coffee. When my eyes flick down to it, I can't contain my smile when I realize the mug he has served it in is the one I got him last Christmas. When I look back to him, he is busy making his own cup, but of course Daemon is watching me carefully.

"Morning, Daemon," I say brightly, still on a mission to become one of his friends, but all he does is offer me a nod.

Archer watches our interaction closely before focusing back on Josh. "Peters, we are heading to the rink later for a game if you want, nothing major, just us and a few of the guys off the team."

Josh is already shaking his head. "I can't, I've got family

dinner at my parents' house, where I have to tell my father I ignored his wedding plans and went ahead with my own."

"Well that sounds fun," Alexander drawls sarcastically, his half british accent thicker than usual for a change.

"Oh yeah, it will be the perfect family catch up," Josh grumbles, turning around and moving so he is next to me.

"No worries, man," Archer tells him genuinely, as if they have been friends all along, and I watch as Josh studies both him and Alexander climb to their feet and move to leave, in total confusion. "I guess we'll just see you at practice tomorrow, and Hals, I'll see you and your nice legs in class," he adds with another wink, before Alexander pushes him out of the room muttering something about a death wish.

"I'm gonna kill that fucker one of these days, he's a pain in the ass," Josh snaps, and I use the opportunity to slip from his side and climb onto one of the stools at the island, tucking his jersey tightly under my thighs.

I wave my hand in the direction they just left. "Ignore Arch, he's like that with everyone, I swear it's just a defense mechanism. He's not as bright and happy as he seems," I muse out loud, sipping my coffee as I think about the faraway look he gets in his eyes sometimes.

"Then what's he like?" The question comes from Daemon, and it has my new husband's head snapping towards his friend in both surprise and intrigue.

I think about his question, and about what I have observed in the little time I have spent with his teammate, and I answer honestly. "I think he's lonely. I think he just needs someone to want him, to need him, and I mean truly need him so he can live up to his full potential. He has a big heart, I'm just not sure he knows how to use it yet."

Daemon takes in every one of my words, absorbing them

whole, and I swear I can see him turning each of them over in his mind, like a puzzle with a piece he can't quite get to fit. Then when he notices that Josh and I are still staring at him, he dumps his coffee into the sink and stalks from the room without another word.

"Okay was it just me, or was that weird?" Josh asks, turning towards me totally bemused, but my mind is still on his friend, on my friend, on the way they act around each other, and something in my mind clicks.

"Are they always like that around one another?" I ask, wondering if Josh has seen it too.

"Who, Daemon and Archer?" he replies and I nod, sipping some more of my coffee which of course he made exactly how I like. "Yeah pretty much, they have hated each other since first year, but no one knows why."

Oh, I think I know why.

"How interesting," I muse out loud, looking at them in a whole new light now, especially after how Daemon reacted on Halloween during truth or dare, and last night when Archer brought it up again. Yes, very interesting indeed.

"What's interesting?" My new husband questions, and I can't help but smile at how clueless he is. Boys can be so dumb sometimes.

"Oh nothing," I tell him, focusing back on him and my coffee. "Now are you making your wife some breakfast, or do I have to starve and beg first?"

Josh's eyes meet mine instantly, his mouth taking on a wicked smirk as he leans across the island from me and purrs, "I could definitely get down with some begging."

The breath clears from my lungs and it takes every ounce of respect and self control to not react to his flirty remarks, especially when I know he doesn't really mean it. Especially when I also now know what his lips taste like, what his body feels like against mine. It would be so easy to give in, to taunt and tease him in return, and rip up that list of rules and forget all about them. Yet if I let myself do that I won't just fall, I'll break. I'll smash into a million pieces at his feet and he won't have the map to put me together.

So instead I smile and say, "Just because I have your ring on my finger, doesn't mean I wont dick punch you again when you act like a douche."

His smile turns to a laugh, one so carefree and familiar that it almost knocks me off balance. "I forgot how fun you are to hang out with, Tink, I've missed you," he tosses back without a care, as he turns to the fridge and starts rummaging through some ingredients, not realizing the hope his words flutter into my heart.

"Yeah, I've missed you too." *More than you'll ever know.*

The rest of the morning is spent with us having breakfast together, him breaking our wedding news to his very hungover and confused housemates, Levi and Landon, when they walk through the door, and then Josh getting ready for the dinner at his parents, before we drive over to my house so I can do the same.

By the time we arrive at his childhood home with Maddie in tow, all of us are feeling the tension this place represents. So when Josh slips his hand into mine to play our part, I can't help but silently squeeze it three times. *Are you okay?* He only squeezes it back once. *No.*

When we walk through the door I see the same thing as always, an immaculate and beautiful house that somehow still feels cold and uninviting. And when Hugo Peters appears, I remember the reason why. His stare is on us in an instant, taking in our proximity to one another, my hand in his son's, before flicking it over to Maddie and giving her a once over before dismissing her completely. Same as always, except now I am in the lion's den with them, and not just watching from the sides.

"You're late," he drawls, even though we are right on time, before he turns on his heels and we are forced to follow him.

We are led to the dining room like lambs to the slaughter, where we find Josh's mother and grandmother already waiting in their usual designated seats. This isn't the first time I have joined them for a family dinner, having frequented many over the years, but this is the first time I feel nervous to be an unwilling participant.

Of course Hugo takes his usual seat at the head of the table, with his wife on his left, and his mother on his right, gesturing for the rest of us to take our place. Maddie takes the spot next to her mom, and Josh leads me to the other side, where he chooses the space next to his grandmother, and pulls out the chair next to him for me, leaving me the furthest from their father.

"Mom, grandma," Josh greets them politely as always, taking his seat beside me, and then eventually flicking his stare full of contempt to his dad. "Father," he adds, in a less polite tone, and I prepare my shield for an onslaught of battle before the dinner has even started.

The tension is thick in the air as Josh and his father have a silent stare off, neither one of them willing to back down, and when I flick my stare to my best friend, she looks just as nervous as I'm sure I do. The silence continues to loom around us as the servers bring out the first dish, and when I cast my eyes down to the plate placed in front of me, I have to swallow my groan. Years of posh parties and fancy dinners means I am more than equipped to know that the dish in front of me is lobster bisque. *Shellfish*. My worst nightmare.

I have always struggled with food, often sticking to the same comfort meals that I am used to just to get by, but it's hard when you are eating out, or at other people's houses. Of course, given the years of enduring meals just like this, it means I also know not to make a scene, and I remain tight-lipped as everyone else is also served. I don't mind staying quiet, but apparently my new husband didn't get the memo.

"Is this lobster?" he asks, breaking the silence, looking at me with nothing but concern, and I curse inwardly. Both he and Maddie know the issues I have with food, and have never had a problem catering to them, but I don't expect his family to.

"Josh, it's fine," I whisper, praying he just lets this go.

"What's the problem?" his father booms down the table, all ready to tuck into his own appetizer, and I cringe a little at his tone, but Josh doesn't even flinch.

"The problem is Hallie has been coming to dinner here for almost a decade, surely you know she doesn't like lobster, or shellfish of any kind for that matter," he snaps right back, glaring at his father with nothing but hate.

"Oh, Hallie, I'm sorry dear, I didn't realize," his mom jumps in to say, trying to placate the situation, but of course like father like son, neither of them can let it go.

His father's eyes are a mixture of amusement and intrigue as he takes a sip from his drink and smiles, "I'm sure she will survive just this once, son."

Like a moth to a flame I can feel him ready to explode, so I put my hand on his leg and plead, "Josh, seriously it's fine, I'm the fussy one, don't even worry about it."

My actions and words are no use as he turns to me and snaps, "Hallie, you aren't fussy, you have a sensory aversion to certain foods that is fairly easy to manage." My heart soars at not just his attention to detail, but his care too, then he turns back towards his father and with a voice like quiet death he seethes, "So, can you cater to my wife's needs or should we find somewhere else to enjoy our dinner?"

His words hit three targets perfectly, as his father, mother, and grandmother all repeat in unison, "Wife?"

Without pause Josh slips his hand into mine, bringing them up to the table where his wedding band is now clear and visible. "Hallie and I got married yesterday in a small, private ceremony," he confirms, brushing his thumb over my knuckles in comfort. "Mom, grandma, I have photos that I can send you both if you'd like, and father, I will send you the marriage license as I'm sure you'll want to authenticate it."

Sarcasm drops into his tone, as his statement leaves the room so silent you could hear a pin drop, and all I can do is hold onto his hand like my life depends on it, no doubt crushing his knuckles in the process. I wait for the backlash but it doesn't come, it appears his mother and grandmother are speechless, as they both turn to Hugo and wait for his response.

For once he is looking at Josh like a father should a son, with nothing but pride and admiration in his eyes, and it isn't there just to fool any potential voters. It's like he is finally seeing his son and heir become a man and achieve something. It should give me some satisfaction to see it, but I know the real man behind the Mayor, and all it does is leave a sour taste in my mouth.

I reach for my water as Hugo finally breaks the silence. "Ariel," he snaps to one of the servers. "Some champagne for everyone, and please bring my daughter-in-law a salad." I choke on the liquid in my mouth at being called his daughter-in-law, and now the patriarch of the house has spoken, both his wife and mother rush to give us their congratulations.

"Congratulations, sweetheart," Josh's mother coos. "And welcome to the family, Hallie dear," she adds sweetly, yet I can see the hesitation in her eyes as they flick over the two of us.

His grandmother however raises her glass of wine in cheers, nodding in agreement with her daughter-in-law, before she adds, "Yes very nice, just try to keep your dick away from women who aren't your wife, young man, you don't want to turn out like your father."

Now it's Mrs. Peters who chokes on her drink, as Maddie's jaw also drops at her words, but as always his father dismisses his wrongdoings like they are irrelevant, and holds up his glass towards us. "Oh, the apple doesn't fall too far from the tree now does it, son, this is fantastic news."

Josh's hand tightens within mine now and I know he is confused by his father's reaction, which I can't say I blame him, because I definitely expected some backlash about our shotgun wedding. "Fantastic news?" Josh questions, flicking his stare to his sister, who looks equally confused, before focusing back on his father. "You're not mad?"

The server comes back with the champagne, pouring a glass for the Mayor first of course, before coming around to the rest of us. When she reaches me, she lowers her voice and whispers, "Your salad will be out in a moment, Mrs. Peters."

Mrs Peters. Fuck.

I almost inhale my champagne after that, even though I hate the taste, and the fact that the bubbles feel like static on my tongue, as his father finally answers him. "Mad? Why would I be mad? My son has attached himself to the sole heir of Sanders Finance, I couldn't ask for a better match."

Bile churns in my stomach at his view of the world, and even worse, marriage, especially when I have, as he puts it, attached myself to his son. And I don't know why I'm surprised, he did pick me for this arranged marriage, I guess he doesn't really care when or where we did it, just as long as we did.

"I didn't marry her because of who her father is," Josh snaps, pulling our hands into his lap, and I can practically feel the anger vibrating off of him.

"No, but it doesn't hurt to have that kind of backing when

you pursue a career in politics. Good campaigns require deep pockets," his father jokes, offering me a wink. "I'm sure Hallie understands and agrees with that, son. A big spring wedding would have been preferred, but we can still spin this in the right way," he claims, tucking into his lobster. "I can see the headlines now praising, 'Mayor's son claims his bride, next stop: his title'." He smiles as he talks, no doubt imagining that exact scenario where Josh and I skip off into the sunset as he becomes just like his father.

Clearly he doesn't know his son very well.

I'm sure Maddie can see the tension rising in her brother as well as I can, because she quickly tries to change the subject. "Mom, this recipe is great, did you come up with it?" she asks, trying to turn the focus away from Josh, but of course his father doesn't relent.

"Hallie, you'll make a great wife, my son can charm the voters with his words, and you can charm them with your..." he trails off, his eyes gesturing towards my chest, and his son sees red.

"Don't fucking look at her like that," he seethes, pushing his chair back as he shoots to his feet. "And how many fucking times do I have to tell you, I am never going to be a fucking politician," he yells, storming from the table, as I am granted a real look at the true colors of the mayor as he watches him leave.

Hugo stands to follow him, but I jump to my feet and stare him down. "I'll go, you stay and enjoy your lobster," I smile sweetly, as I yell *fuck you* over and over again in my mind, until he relents with a nod.

"That's a good idea, dear, I'm sure you can persuade him to calm down and remember his manners better than I can," he drawls with a wink, and I have to refrain from giving him the finger as I leave. It's that or an axe to the face, I'd enjoyed both.

By the time I catch up with Josh, I find him pacing along the corridor of his father's office, tension and anger pouring out of him in waves. Gone is the Josh who joked and flirted with me over breakfast this morning, and the one left standing in front of me, is the one I hate the most. It's the one who has been torn down and berated by his father time and time again, until he is barely a shadow of himself. I hate it, I always have, but I hate Hugo Peters even more.

#14
JOSH
OFFICE ESCAPADES

This dinner is a fucking shit show, and that's before I've even tasted my damn appetizer. I storm out of the room in a rage because if I don't, then I am going to show my father exactly what I have learnt from hockey over the years, and it isn't how to hit a fucking puck. Anger bubbles to the surface of my skin, and to stop myself from going back in there and letting him win, I smash my fist into the wall beside his office.

"Hey, those hands belong to me now, twenty-two, so you better not be wrecking them," Hallie jokes, walking towards me, looking as sweet and sorry as always. I can't fucking believe I dragged her into this mess.

"Not now, Hals," I snap, ignoring the pain now ricocheting down my arm, as I try and fail to control my temper.

Of course she ignores me, coming to a stop by my side, and pulling my now aching fist up in front of her to inspect. "Peter Pan never stops fighting with Hook, eh?" she murmurs, tenderly brushing her fingers over my knuckles until she is satisfied that they are fine.

"Yeah, well, he's a fucking asshole," I curse back, moving until I can lean on the wall and drop my head back to take a breath.

"Oh, he's a major asshole," she agrees, before adding, "But so is Hook."

My eyes snap down to her and I find her grinning at me wildly, and I can't help but return it. "Brat," I smirk.

"Psycho," she tosses back instantly, and I blow out a breath as I shake my head at her with a laugh. "Now what's wrong? Why are you so on edge? So your dad didn't care about the wedding," she shrugs, searching my stare for answers that I'm not used to having to give, but I can't deny her what she wants, not when she has put so much on the line for me.

So instead of trying and failing to explain how my dad makes me feel, I reach into my pants pocket and pull out the small device that Lincoln Blackwell gave me. The one I need to get into my father's office without being detected so he can search through his files and try and find some useful dirt on him. Flicking my stare up and down the corridor to ensure we are still alone, I lower my head to hers and slip it into her hands so she can see it.

"I need to plug that into my dad's computer without him realizing so Lincoln can hack in and make a copy of all of his files," I say in a low gruff tone, hoping she doesn't question me too much about it, not here, not now.

Yet instead of her saying what I think she is going to say, she simply asks, "Is his office door locked?" She nods slightly to the door just behind me on the left, and I shake my head no. "Then let's do this," she demands, before throwing her arms around my neck.

Panic floods my entire system as the hair on the back on my

neck stands on end. "Hallie, what the hell are you doing?" I whisper, letting my hands fall to her hips to keep her in place, so her body doesn't touch mine too much.

"Acting like I want to fuck you." she tosses back without pause, rolling her eyes at me in the process, and I almost choke on my damn tongue.

"I beg your pardon?" I splutter in response, as her hands come to my cheeks and force my stare to hers, her body pressing fully against mine, and I bite back a grunt. *Fuck.* First there was her wearing my jersey with no pants, then this morning with her rubbing her ass on my morning wood, and now this? A good man only has so much restraint, and I'm not a good man.

Yet she looks at me like I am the crazy one here as she states, "Come on, what else would we sneak into his office for?"

My hands tighten around her waist, willing her to stay still considering how long it's been since I have had a girl pressed against me, as I grit, "And why would us pretending to fuck be the answer?" It takes everything in me to not act on her crazy statement, especially when I can feel the scrape of her rings against my cheek, and all it does is remind me that technically she does belong to me now.

"Well, doesn't he have a camera in there?" she questions, and it's only then that I realize she is right.

"Fuck, yeah he does have a camera in there," I mutter back, feeling this plan falling apart before it's even got off the ground.

"Does it have sound?" She questions me further, but I'm already shaking my head.

"No, all the cameras in the house are video only, god forbid one of his conversations gets picked up by anything" I toss back without thinking, and her smile only widens.

"Perfect," she quips, before shoving me forcefully against my father's door like we are locked in some sort of lover's tryst, while she feels around for the handle. The door gives way before I can even move to help her, and she forces me inside before closing the door behind us, never once letting me go. "Now pretend to kiss my neck and back me up to his desk," she commands quietly, and I can't help but laugh at how crazy she is acting right now, but is it so crazy that it might actually work?

"You're insane, you know that right?" I tell her for the millionth time in our lives, as I spin her around and start leading her back towards his desk.

"So you've been telling me since I was nine," she muses with a smile, before she adds, "Now can my fake husband please fake kiss me?" I let out a deep sigh before leaning my head down and pressing my lips to the side of her neck, making her yelp in surprise. "I said fake kiss, Joshua, do you have any idea how sensitive my neck is?"

Fuck. Does she have any idea how hard she is testing me?

My head drops to her shoulder as I grit my teeth and grip her waist even tighter, as her back bumps against the desk, and I force myself to look back at her. "Okay now what?" I ask, keeping my head low, knowing that the only camera in here is behind us in the left hand corner. From anyone watching it, all they would see is my back and given our position, I know what they would presume we are doing in here.

Hallie huffs in annoyance. "For the love of god," she groans, throwing her head back to look at the ceiling in despair. "Pick me up and put me on the desk dammit. Come on Josh, I know your reputation, stop acting like a little virgin and pretend you're gonna fuck me."

Never did I think I would hear such words come from my little sister's best friend's mouth, and even more so I never thought I'd be intrigued by them. What the hell does she mean she knows my reputation? I don't have a reputation, not one I am aware of anyway, and all I can do is respond how I would any other girl, ignoring the fact this one is actually my wife.

"I mean I could definitely think of a better use for your mouth right now other than your attitude," I snap back, feeling my pants getting tight as I lift with her with ease and place her on the edge of my father's desk.

"Atta boy, that's more like it," she winks, pulling me in between her open thighs and then purposely knocking into my father's computer. "Okay, now guide my hand on where to put it," she demands innocently, but all it does is paint a wicked picture in my mind.

"Please stop saying stuff like that to me," I beg, holding onto my restraint by a thread, as I move to fake kiss her neck this time, and help guide her hand to where the device needs to be. "I'm sorry about this," I add in a whisper.

"About what?" she whispers back, her hand finally feeling around to where she needs to insert the device.

"About touching you," I confirm, ensuring I am putting on a perfect show while not overcrowding her too much. "I know how much you hate it."

Her head flicks back from mine, eyes trailing over my face before she admits, "You're touch doesn't bother me, Joshua."

My hand flexes over hers at her words and at the sound of my name. Hallie has always had an aversion to touch, granted she manages it very well, but her admission still leaves me confused. "Since when?" I demand, more bite in my tone than I intend but it doesn't faze her.

"Since always," she shrugs, like it's nothing, and then I watch as her eyes flick up to the camera in the corner, before she leans in and breathes against my neck. "Okay it's in, but I can't see the screen to see if it's working."

When I told Lincoln I was going to try and do this today, he said the program would only take a few minutes and that I'd know when it's done, so I'm presuming we do in fact need to be able to watch the screen. My mind is still reeling when a plan hits me, and without another thought, I push Hallie back onto her elbows so she can see the full view of the monitor, and then drop to my knees between her legs.

Her eyes widen in a panic, as she gasps, "Joshua, what the hell are you doing?"

There is a wicked grin on my face now, as I lift her skirt, thanking the gods she wore one today, before I place her legs on my shoulders, careful not to touch her too much despite what she just told me. "I'm selling the sex, Hals," I wink, ducking my head under the fabric so to anyone watching it looks like I am eating her out. "Now make sure you scream nice and loud for your husband," I tease, bringing my hand up and tickling the outside of her thigh with my finger until she yelps. "That's it, good girl."

Then I have to grit my teeth to force myself to ignore the alluring scent of her, moving my hands until I can grip the desk beneath her thighs, so I don't touch anywhere else as she gasps, "I hate you."

All I can do is smile as I respond, "No, Hals, you really don't."

"Oh god," she groans, and I crick my neck before I give her something to really moan about. Especially when all I can focus on to help me ignore the black lace panties she is wearing, is the sight of my wedding ring.

She's my wife.

My wife.

And here I am on my knees for her, *again*.

Yet we are just faking it, *again*.

This marriage is only one day old and it's already becoming a real problem.

Ignoring my basic instinct, which is screaming at me right now, I remind myself she is just my friend, and I keep focus on the task at hand as I ask, "Is it working?"

Her body, now covered in goosebumps, moves slightly, and I

can only assume she is nodding, until she finally gasps out, "Erm, yeah, it's working, just give me it a minute."

A minute? A minute with me on my knees and my head up her damn skirt. Does she have any idea the kind of torture this is? Her skin is tanned and smooth, and as always she smells like cotton candy, and right now I really want to fucking indulge. What kind of fucked up plan did we concoct here? I blow out a harsh breath to try and calm my racing heart and her body jolts.

"Joshua." Her tone is laced with warning, but all it does is make my cock jump. "Stop, I'm sensitive," she pleads, and god the images it puts in my head of what I could do to make her truly sensitive.

What the fuck is wrong with me?

She's your best friend you fucking animal, not one of your random hookups.

I inhale a deep breath, ignoring the candy scent I can practically taste on my tongue as I grit, "Tink, not once have I ever been on my knees for a girl and she has asked me to stop, so please refrain from trying to ruin the said reputation you told me about." My words are meant to be a joke to pull us out of this awkward position we have found ourselves in, but her entire body flinches.

"Manwhore," she practically snarls, lifting her foot to dig her heel into my back, and I think about returning the pain.

"Brat," I hiss, using my fingers to pinch her outer thigh and she cries out my name once more.

"Joshua," Her entire body jolts again, taking me with her, and bringing me closer to those lacey panties I am pretending to not imagine her without.

"That's it, call out my name, Tink," I praise. "Let the whole house hear how good a husband I am to you." Again my words are meant as a joke, but all I can do is stare at those damn goosebumps trailing along her inner thigh.

"That's it, forget the dick punches, I'm going to slice the damn thing off," she almost shouts, and I smother my laugh against her skin without thought, making her grasp again.

I'm quick to apologize gruffly before I add, "You know they make plenty of sex toys right? You don't have to chop my dick off and keep it." My focus now solely on those damn panties, an image searing itself into my brain for all eternity.

My wife's pussy is just behind that scrap of fabric.

The thought is maddening.

"Okay, it's almost there," she tells me, and I know if we don't get back to dinner soon, then my father will come looking for us.

I don't care if he finds us here, but I do care if he finds us in this position. I don't want anyone seeing Hallie like this, least of all my father.

"Then I guess it's time for a big finish," I muse before warning her, "I'm going to touch you, Hals." Then before my words can really register or I can second guess myself, I lean in and press a soft kiss to her inner thigh, unable to resist it any longer.

"Oh my god," she squeals, clamping her thighs tightly around my head, giving me a glimpse at heaven, before opening them back up instantly. "Oh my god, sorry, fuck I'm sorry," she pants, as she knocks something on the desk over. "I'm done, I mean, it's done, we can go," she panics, pulling her legs from my shoulders.

I lean back, removing the fabric of her skirt from over my head and placing it neatly back down, and when we lock eyes, her face is stained with a scarlet blush. I can see panic and confusion in her stare, and before it fully takes flight I rise to my feet and lean in, pulling her in for a hug.

"Thank you, Hals, I couldn't have done this without you," I tell her honestly, pushing away all thoughts of me on my knees for her, and remembering who she truly is to me.

She isn't some random hook up, or a fucking bunny desperate to bag a hockey guy. She's Hallie, my best friend, a steady rock in my life since before I can remember. I can't fuck that up just because of a buzz of attraction when her legs were wrapped around me, that's stupid, and unreliable. I don't look at her like that, I see past the gorgeous exterior, and know the true girl behind those sparkling green eyes, and I won't ruin that friendship for anything.

Taking the device from her, I slip it back into my pocket, and help her down from my father's desk, knowing that I will look at it in a whole new light every time I am forced to come in here from now on. With that in mind I look at her and smile as I ask, "Ready to go back to hell with me, Tink?"

Replacing her surprise with a smile, she places her hand in mine and smiles, "I think I'm already there, Peter."

#15
HALLIE

COACH PETERS

Once Josh and I made it back to the table with my dignity barely still intact, the rest of the dinner passed without incident. Sure, his father made a snide comment about us looking refreshed when we returned, but thankfully Josh didn't take the bait. We ate the rest of the food without argument, but not before Hugo delighted in telling us that he has already arranged the annual party they throw for New Year's every year. I have attended many times, always with Maddie, but this year I am attending as Josh's significant other, and his father was nice enough to let us know that it will also serve as a wedding party for us both.

Isn't that just perfect?

It's Monday now, and having spent last night at home alone reeling over the events of the weekend, mostly concerning what happened in the Mayor's home office, and not sleeping a wink, I am dead on my feet by the time I make it to my final class. Which is how Archer finds me with my head slumped on the desk and praying for the next hour to fly by.

"Damn, Sanders, how much newlywed sex did you have?" my friend drawls, throwing himself into his usual spot beside me, and ruffling my hair in a way I have learnt to tolerate from him.

The first time he did it I almost screamed from the shock alone, the second time I barely contained my flinch, yet by the third time I had prepared myself for his friendly onslaught. He didn't notice that I grit my teeth every time he touched me, but I did notice that like me, he is also wearing a mask. His happy-go-lucky fake persona he puts out into the world is just that, fake. Yet I noticed that he seems to settle down quicker after some sort of physical contact with people, like he needs the comfort. It's why I let him do it, it's also why I wasn't bothered by kissing him during truth or dare on Halloween. Archer Gray is a man whore to everyone who meets him, but to me he is just misunderstood, and I see right through his facade.

"Don't mess with me today, Arch, I am in no mood," I warn him, forcing myself to lift my head off the desk to glare at him.

All he does is smirk as he drops a takeout cup of hot chocolate on my desk that has the logo from my favorite campus cafe. "Figured you might be needing this," he grins, taking a sip from his own before holding it up in silent cheers.

"Archer Gray, I knew there was a reason I kept you around, and it isn't just for your bad rep and good looks," I sigh, pulling the cup into my greedy hands and taking a sip, letting it warm me up from the inside out.

"Now, now, don't go flirting with me, Mrs. Peters, what would your husband say?" he teases, clinking his cardboard cup against my own, and before I can even respond, a shrill voice cuts me off.

"What the hell do you mean, Mrs. Peters?" someone snaps, and when my eyes flick upwards I find the angry stare of a girl in our class.

Brianna Michaels. She is gorgeous and smart, but is more well known for hanging around the hockey team and trying to lock down one of the players. I've seen her go after Maddie's boyfriend Nova at least a hundred times, but I'm pretty sure she has been with all the guys at one point or another, or most of them anyway.

I open my mouth to answer her, but Archer beats me to it. "Didn't you hear, Hallie and Josh got married over the weekend," he beams, giving her a wicked look I can't seem to work out, as I force a smile to my face in preparation to accept another congratulations.

Our wedding announcement ran in the morning paper, with a picture I hadn't even seen yet, and I am honestly not sure how the Mayor did it so fast, but I can't be totally surprised. Which is how I found myself accepting well wishes from people all day, some of whom I didn't even know, but I accepted them all with a smile, and this will be no different.

Yet no well wishes come. Instead, Brianna looks at me distastefully before she laughs. "Yeah right, don't be ridiculous, as if Josh would ever marry *her*."

Game, set, match, burn.

I've never been one for confrontation, it's not in my nature, and as her words hit me like a brick wall, I have to force myself not to react.

"Oh yeah?" Archer drawls, taking more delight in the situation than I am. "Then how do you explain this?" He pulls the folded up newspaper featuring the picture of Josh and me from Saturday, and displays it flat on the desk in front of him for her to see. "It was a lovely ceremony, half the team was there," he boasts, and technically he isn't even lying.

Brianna snatches it up and her jaw drops, like actually drops open wide as she stares at the picture of us, her smile long gone. "This is unbelievable," she mutters, before casting her dark stare towards me. "I didn't even know you guys were dating, and no offense but you're not exactly his type."

Another hit right in the fucking gut.

Why is it when people say no offense, they always follow it up with something really offensive? I'm all for being a girl's girl, but seriously, right now, fuck this bitch.

I smile as sweetly as I can manage. "Well I'm a private person, and my husband respects that, and I haven't slept with anyone else on his hockey team, so maybe that holds some appeal to him."

Archer snickers beside me as her jaw drops even wider at the sound of someone dishing her the same disrespect she goes around giving others. "That's funny because out of the *many* girls I know Josh has slept with, he didn't respect any of them, and trust me, there are a lot. You might wanna remember that while you're on your knees for him," she smiles, before adding. "Maybe I'll remind him of all the fun we've had together next time I see him."

Bile rises in my throat and I have no reasonable comeback to her statement, because what can I say? That as his wife, I in fact, don't know anything about what he is like in the bedroom? How stupid would that be?

"Oh fuck off you little viper," Archer snarls, clearly done with her mouth. "Josh hasn't touched you in over a year, and I have to be a bottle deep into anything before even thinking about coming near you, so do us all a favor and disappear."

His words have my eyes bugging out of my head, nevermind hers, and I can't help but feel sorry for her a little. That is, until she flips her hair and replies, "Give my love to Nova, he always had the best dick anyway." Before sauntering away to the other side of the room.

"Well that was fun," I say dryly, trying and failing to shake off the whole interaction, when Archer crowds into my space.

"Fucking ignore that bitch, Hals, Josh has had a no touching rule on you from the moment you arrived, and now we all know why. Unlike her, he actually cares about you, hence that pretty little diamond ring you are now toting around. So some people might be jealous, but fuck them, you're the one who gets to keep him forever."

His words are kind and are obviously meant to make me feel better, but really they hurt me more than everything Brianna just said, because they aren't true. Yes I am wearing his ring, and I am his wife, but that's it, it's just a ring and a piece of paper, nothing more. I will never know him like those girls do, and he will never know how much I wish all of this was real.

"Thanks, Arch," I force out, because short of confessing my love for Josh to him– which he wouldn't understand–I have nothing else to say. I focus back on my drink and drain the rest of my hot chocolate, just in time for our professor to arrive and our class to begin.

I spend the next hour making notes, yet not really taking in a single thing our teacher is saying, and by the time we are done and are ready to pack up, I feel so drained that I could literally pass out. I should go home, I have a ton of homework to catch up on from over the weekend, and I know climbing into bed with Percy would make this day feel a whole lot less horrible, but for some reason I can't make myself do it.

"Are you heading over to practice now?" I ask Archer, as he moves to leave, and he pauses to look at me.

I'm not sure what he sees on my face but it has him holding out his arm for me to hook mine through. "I certainly am, would you like me to escort you to the viewing area so you can perve on your husband, Mrs. Peters?"

I scoff a laugh in the hopes of trying to deny what he just said, but then I remember he believes the lie we have painted, the one that isn't that hard a lie for me as I reply, "Yeah, actually, I think that is exactly what I need."

Which is how I find myself freezing my ass off at the rink as Archer leaves me to rush off and get changed, and I move round the bleachers until I reach my best friend. "Looks like we both had the same idea," I muse, as I find Maddie sitting in one of the lower rows with her phone out.

She has always been a staple here, constantly coming to watch Josh's practice and games to show him some support, and I've joined her many times, but I think her presence has more to do with the team captain than her brother these days.

Her eyes flick to mine in surprise, before she moves her bag to make space for me. "Nova and I are having dinner with his mom after this, so I said I'd meet him here," she smiles wistfully, and it makes me so happy to see her so comfortable and in love.

They are still in the honeymoon phase, so it's basically night after night of listening to her headboard bang against the wall, but hey that's what ear defenders are for, right? I'm so happy for her, hence why it was easy to agree to Josh's insane wedding plan, because it means she gets to have this.

"How is my favorite sister-in-law?" she asks with a smirk, and I roll my eyes as I plonk myself down next to her.

"Tired and cranky," I tell her, as I search my bag for a snack and she laughs. "I didn't sleep last night, and then they were sold out of my usual lunches in the cafeteria which means I haven't eaten since breakfast."

"I mean, you could've just had something else," she starts before she trails off and laughs again. "Sorry, forgot who I was talking to for a second there." Then she takes pity on me and reaches into her own bag, pulling out a chocolate muffin and handing it to me.

"Neeve?" I question, wondering if the muffin is from one of her bodyguards' wives who always sends food and treats for us, and she nods. "God, I love you," I mumble, taking a big bite, before adding, "And I love Neeve." The muffin is delicious and hits just the spot, right in time for the players to start filtering out onto the ice.

I spy the number nineteen first, and his eyes automatically search the stands until they land on Maddie, and then he is skating over towards us without pause.

"You're not wearing my jersey, Princess, I thought I warned you about that," he teases, ignoring his coach as he yells at him to start warming up.

"Nova, I can't wear it everyday and then in bed, it would get too dirty," she complains, but all he does is shake his head.

"Looks like I will have to make something else dirty instead," he drawls with a wink, before turning around and skating away.

Maddie blushes, but my focus is now on the other Peters sibling as he skates onto the ice with a face like thunder. I have always loved to watch him play, ever since that first day, and even now, over a decade later, it still feels just as special. This is his home, his comfort, the only place he doesn't let anyone get to him, and as he whisks around the ice I can't help but feel envious of the rink. He pours his heart and soul into this game, and I know it's the only one true love he will ever have.

He flies around the ice twice before he finally spots me, and when he does, he surprises me by breaking from his warm-up and skating over to me. "I didn't know my wife would be joining me today," he boasts loudly, causing both his coach and some of his teammates to look our way, and I hear Maddie groan beside me.

"Oh I'm not here for you, I'm here supporting my team, go Flyers," I reply in the same tone, and his answering grin has my heart thundering in my chest.

"Then I guess I'll just have to show off for you today huh?" he winks, skating backwards away from me as he rejoins his warm-up. It's only then I hear a few members of his team that weren't in attendance of the wedding asking him about it and he snaps, "Yes, I got married, what the fuck has it go to do with you?"

Maddie stifles a laugh. "And there's the asshole we know and love."

I watch as Daemon skates up next to him and gently guides him away, saying something I'm sure no one else can hear as I smile, "Yeah, there he is."

We spend the next thirty-minutes watching them stretch in every manner possible, and I am practically drooling at the end of it. My eyes stay permanently fixed on the number twenty-two spread across his back, and when they finally start practicing, I swear I can feel the blush everywhere. Maddie and I talk back and forth about class, and the disastrous dinner with her parents yesterday, but mostly our focus remains on the ice, and thankfully because this isn't my first time here, she doesn't question my interest in it too much.

By the time the boys are sweating and skating off the ice to get changed, I am beyond starving, and even Josh in his jersey couldn't make me less cranky. I head outside with Maddie to wait with her even though she isn't coming home with me tonight. Usually I would just head straight home, but just as I am about to do that I remember the role I am playing as his wife and hang back.

Nova, Archer, and Alexander appear first with their other roommate Jake Harper, with Nova moving straight for Maddie and sweeping her into his arms. Jake bids them goodbye then, stating that he is picking his girlfriend up from work, as my best friend turns back to me.

"Hals, do you want us to wait with you?" Maddie asks, smiling inside her boyfriend's arms, and I am already shaking my head.

"No, I'm all good, you guys go, I'm gonna head home with Josh," I nod my head to the rink behind me, as I blow out a breath in the cold air.

"Mads, I know you don't wanna hear this, but your best friend is now permanently banging your brother," Alexander taunts her while eying me with a smile, before Nova knocks him in the back of the head.

"You're right, Reign, she doesn't wanna hear that," Nova snaps, shaking his head at his friend, before moving to leave and dragging the others with him. "Come on and leave the girl alone, see you later, Hals."

I watch them leave, waving goodbye, and then turn back to the doorway of the rink to wait for Josh. A number of players leave before him, including his housemates Landon and Levi who I smile politely at, until finally, Josh appears with Daemon.

"Hals, you're still here," he muses, moving towards me and without pause leaning in to drop a kiss on my head. I force myself not to startle, especially as there are still a few players exiting and lingering around, all with their eyes our way. I guess a quickie marriage while we are still in college can be considered quite the scandal.

Ignoring them all, I focus on Josh only as I reply, "Yeah, I figured we could go grab dinner or something?" I don't know why I feel nervous to ask him to dinner but I do, especially when we have an audience.

Before he can respond, Daemon takes a step past us and moves to leave. "I'll see you at home," he mumbles, but I halt him in his tracks.

"You can join us if you like, Daemon, the more the merrier," I smile, and he looks at me with a truly puzzled look, as if no one has ever extended such an invite before. It makes my heart ache for him, and I ensure to keep my smile in place to let him know I truly mean it.

"No, but thank you," he whispers, before turning away from us and pulling up his hood, scurrying away into the night.

I watch him leave, totally confused, until I turn back to Josh and repeat, "So, dinner?"

Josh looks around at a few of the players still lingering, then gently guides me away from them before he starts. "I actually have somewhere I need to be," he says inconspicuously, and I swear I can feel my heart in my throat as I imagine the worst, reminding myself that our deal isn't real.

"Oh, okay, no worries," I grin, my cheeks now aching from smiling, even though I can feel tears gathering at the back of my eyes for some reason.

"Do you want to come with me? And then we can grab dinner after?" he adds, and I look at him in surprise. Even with his ring on my finger I am not used to him actually wanting to be around me. Not when he has spent the last couple of years pushing me away and avoiding me as much as possible.

"You want me to come with you?" I ask in confusion, and his answering grin is blinding.

"Sure, why not? Come on, my car is right over here," he nods his head towards the direction of his car, and then is moving us towards it before I can even answer.

Tossing his gear bag in the trunk, he rushes to open my door for me, before rounding the other side of the car and climbing in.

I pull on my seatbelt as I question, "Where are we going?"

Josh just looks at me with a smile I've never really seen on him before. "You'll have to wait and see," he quips, starting the engine and I scoff.

"Joshua, you know I hate delayed gratification," I remind him, knowing full well that he knows that I hate to wait for anything. Food, traffic, answers, all of them the bane of my life.

All he does is smirk. "Hmm, give me a couple of hours and I

bet I could change your mind on that," he winks, pulling out of the parking lot and driving in the direction of town.

We are only in the car for about ten minutes, talking about our day and practice, when he pulls into another parking lot, one I recognize instantly. We are at the local ice rink, one I know to be shut on monday evenings, yet still he kills the engine and begins to climb out.

"Well, are you coming or not?" he tosses over his shoulder, before he slams the door and moves to grab his bag from the trunk.

There are other cars in the lot and I note that the lights are on inside the rink, which only adds to my confusion as I climb out the door and walk after him. "Josh, what are we doing here? I thought this place was closed during the week."

"It is," he replies instantly, moving towards the door and opening it for me, and then gesturing for me to step inside.

I walk down the hallway, lowering my voice as I snap, "Then I repeat, what the hell are we doing here?"

Josh doesn't answer, guiding me through the reception area until we reach the rinkside and my eyes widen as I take in the numerous families idling around waiting for something. Before I can ask Josh what it is, my ears are assaulted by the sound of multiple kids screeching his name in greeting.

"Josh!" They scream, abandoning their parents and storming towards him in their little group, as I stand frozen to the spot in shock. Yet my husband seems anything but surprised, the kids collar themselves around his legs and torso, all talking over one another, and all he does is smile.

"Sorry I'm late guys, practice went a little over. Are you ready to get to work?" he asks, and they all scream yes, and he nods his head at their parents in greeting as they all start moving past me to leave.

What the hell is going on?

"Okay then strap up your skates and let's go," he calls out, and they all start rushing towards the ice, as he drops himself onto a bench and pulls out his own skates.

I move to sit next to him, mind still totally reeling, and just stare at him until he finally looks at me and admits, "I teach a class here every week, just basic skating and a little hockey, nothing major."

"Nothing major?" I repeat. "Josh, this is huge, why didn't you tell me sooner?" If I thought he couldn't surprise me after the whole will you marry me thing then I was wrong, because watching the brooding boy with the sad smile tighten his skates so he can go and teach some kids has my heart soaring in my chest.

"I haven't told anyone," he admits with a shrug, focusing back on his skates as he adds quietly, "I do this just for me, and for the kids."

How the fuck did someone as amazing as him grow up in the shadow of Hugo Peters and all of his bullshit?

"You're amazing, Josh Peters, do you know that?" I tell him with a smile, as he finishes with his skates and turns back to me.

"Well if my wife thinks so then it must be true," he jokes, grabbing some gloves from his bag, and then zipping it up.

"Your wife thinks she is lucky to have you," I tell him truthfully, wishing in this moment more than ever before, that all of this was real.

As if hearing the direction of my thoughts he laughs sadly, "It's okay, Hals, you don't have to pretend, no one can hear you."

His words have me assessing him in a whole new light, and before I can open my mouth to respond, the doors burst open and a woman with whoI can presume is her daughter comes rushing inside. The mom is dressed in some sort of diner uniform, with her hair piled on top of her head, and a tiredness clinging to her like I have never seen. Whereas the girl looks immaculate with her matching hat, gloves and scarf set, that go well with the pink skates she is holding in her hand. She reminds me a lot of Maddie with her bright blond hair and blue eyes, and I can't help but smile at her.

"Josh, hey, sorry we're late," the mother rushes out, as the girl silently moves to sit on the bench opposite us, as if she has done it a hundred times before.

"No worries, Callia, I haven't even started yet," Josh greets her with a genuine, knowing smile, before eyeing the little girl. "And how's my favorite student, Pen?" The girl says nothing, and when Josh flicks his stare back to her mom she just shrugs. "Okay, well we'll see you at the diner later?" he adds, and the woman, Callia, nods gratefully, and I am left more confused than ever.

"Thank you so much, Josh, you have no idea how much I appreciate this," she tells him, before taking one last look at her daughter. "I'll see you later, okay Pen?"

The girl says nothing and Josh stands to move towards her mom. "Hey, it's no big deal, don't worry about her, okay, we'll be fine." The woman nods at his words, offering me a smile, before she turns and rushes back out of the doors leaving us alone with a bunch of kids.

I flick my stare to the ice, noting there are around twelve boys ready and waiting for their teacher, yet the little girl still doesn't move. Without pause Josh pulls out his phone, unlocks it, and hands it to the girl, before tossing me another wink and then moving to get onto the ice, leaving me and the girl alone.

"Hi," I say in greeting. "My name is Hallie, yours is Pen?" I ask, wondering if it's short for something, and for the first time, she flicks her stare to me.

"Penelope," she eventually corrects. "But everyone calls me Pen."

"Penelope," I repeat, eyeing her. She can't be more than

seven or eight by my guess, yet her stare gives the impression she is much older. "That's such a pretty name, aren't you going to go skate?" Nodding my head to where Josh now has the boys skating back and forth to warm up. I wonder why she isn't joining in, especially since she has her skates still in her lap.

"Josh teaches me after the boys, he knows I like it better that way," she starts, looking at me in wonder before she adds, "I don't get as much time as them, because he has to get me back to my mom, but he always buys me ice cream after."

Ignoring the multiple questions now floating around in my mind about why Josh does this, or why he looks after her, I instead ask, "Why don't you like learning with the boys?"

Her eyes are somber and her voice soft as she admits, "They get a little too rough, and I don't like that."

I return her smile with one of my own, as I glance over her head and spot the place where they keep all the extra skates. "Want me to fill in for him until he's ready?"

Her eyes widen, sparkling with excitement in the same way as my best friends. "You skate?" she asks, locking Josh's phone and finally giving me her full attention.

"I sure do," I nod, mentally trying to figure out the last time I actually skated, and praying I am not too rusty.

"Are you as good as Josh?" she questions, and it lights a fire beneath me to give her the power to do it for the girls.

"Oh sweetie, I am way better than him," I wink, and she smiles for the first time as I stand and move to fetch myself some skates.

I wait for her to tie on her own before I offer her my hand, and when she takes it, I lead us to the ice with an adrenaline pumping beneath my skin.

Looks like I am back on the ice with Josh Peters once again.

#16
JOSH
WIFE SKATING

I've been teaching at the community center for over a year now, and what started as getting in some extra practice alone, soon turned into one to one sessions, and then a full on group. I'm here every Monday without fail, and being around these kids reminds me why I fell in love with ice hockey in the first place. I'm deep in teacher mode with the boys when the flash of something in the corner of my eye catches my attention. I spin and watch as Hallie steps onto the ice with Penelope tight on her heels, the two of them holding hands, and from my vantage point I can hear Hallie instructing her gently.

Penelope has been coming to the class for almost a year, pretty much since right after I first started it, and word quietly spread. I know her mom, Callia, from one of the diners in town, and she has always gone out of her way to be kind to me. I'm not sure what her back story is, but I know she is a young single mom looking after her daughter alone. So when Pen first started coming to the class, and Callia would run late to pick her up, I started offering to take her to the diner instead of her coming here. It took a few more weeks of lateness before she finally relented, but now we have a nice little agreement going, where I not only get to teach a great kid how to skate, but I also get to help out a struggling parent.

It's been a couple of years since I have seen Hallie skate, and I'm surprised by how easy she still glides around the ice. She is holding both of Penelope's hands now and is skating backwards with ease, pulling her along. The little girl has a huge smile on her face, and Hallie pretty much mirrors it. I'm not sure how long I stare at the two of them before one of the boys interrupts my thoughts.

"Josh, is that your girlfriend?" one of the little boys asks with a laugh, and I respond without thinking.

"No, she's my wife." It falls from my mouth with an ease I didn't think I would ever be able to manage, but this is Hallie we are talking about, she has always been like family, and I guess in a way she now legally is.

"Ew, you got married, why?" Another boy cuts in, making the rest of them laugh, but before I can answer him, another voice beats me to it.

"Because I am awesome," Hallie coos, flying around us in a circle with ease, Penelope still being pulled along with her, as she spins them both. "And we all know Mr. Josh here needed some more awesome so he isn't a cranky pants all the time." The kids laugh, falling for her infectious smile instantly, in the same way I did, as she adds, "Besides, who else is going to show you how to beat him?"

The kids all gasp, until Penelope gushes, "You know how to beat Josh?"

Hallie rolls her eyes, flicking her stare to mine. "I taught him everything he knows," she tells them, and their tiny jaws hang open in shock.

This girl.

"You're going to pay for that, Tink," I warn her, skating over to the sides to grab two hockey sticks. If she wants to play then we can play.

When I turn back to her and hold them up all she does is smile. "Bring it on, lost boy."

Skating back over to them all, I toss her a stick and then turn my focus to the class. "Kids, you wanna learn how to score and block a goal?"

"Yes!" They all scream in unison much to my delight, and I quickly grab my phone and set a timer as I look at my wife in delight.

"Then, game on."

Hallie and I spend the next ten minutes in a battle of wills, flying around the ice with the aim of not letting the other score a goal. The kids are yelling furiously from the sides, in support of my new wife mostly, and every time she manages to slip a goal past me, I see Penelope's smile get brighter and brighter. As the only girl in my class I have found that I have taken her under my wing more than the others, which I probably shouldn't do, but everyone has favorites, right?

The score is two to three, and I am sure I am going to win, but just as the timer is about to go off and the kids start counting down, Hallie manages to skate around me with a trick I taught her in my backyard, sinking a goal and making the score even. Screams tear from the kids' throats as they skate towards us both, but all I can do is stand and stare in awe at her.

"I can't believe you still remember that trick," I say in surprise, closing the distance between us before the kids reach us.

She looks at me with a frown. "Of course I do, why would I forget?"

"Because it was like a million years ago." We haven't played in my backyard since we were both still in high school, but apparently that doesn't matter, because all she does is laugh.

"Josh, trust me, when it comes to you, I never forget anything."

Before I can make sense of her words, we are swarmed by the kids both cheering and teasing us, and begging to be shown the trick Hallie just pulled on me, and of course she obliges instantly, picking Pen to be her assistant. All I can do is watch as she digs herself deeper into the world I tried so hard to push her away from, and it's clear to see that this won't be the last time she comes here. The kids have all fallen in love with her instantly, and I know I won't be able to get away with not bringing her back in future.

The rest of the lesson soon flies by, especially given I am not teaching alone, and it seems like the kids get a lot more work done than usual, and are exhausted by the time their parents pick them up. Hallie and I accept some congratulations from those who have seen our wedding announcement in the paper, and when it's just us and Penelope left, we move to leave.

Hallie and Penelope talk back and forth the entire drive to the diner. I swear it's the most I have ever heard her talk before, and by the time we reach her mom's work, she is walking in with a smile on her face.

"Why don't you grab us a booth and we can get some dinner, while I go talk to Pen's mom," I tell Hals, and she nods, before I walk the little girl over to the counter.

"Josh, hey," Callia sighs, clearing away some cups and wiping down the surface before her daughter sits. "How was it?" she asks, directing her question to me, given that her daughter isn't usually much of a talker, but to our surprise she answers instantly.

"It was so much fun, Mom. You should have seen how Hallie

beat Josh, it was awesome," she gushes, and Callia looks at me in surprise as I shrug.

"My wife tends to have that effect on people." Her eyes widen as she moves to grab her daughter a drink

"I didn't know you were married, I didn't even know you were seeing anyone," she replies in confusion, and I can't say I blame her.

I eat here every week after class, and it's always alone, so I can't lie too much. I therefore stick to the truth as much as possible. "The wedding just happened on Saturday, it was pretty quick, but we've known each other for a long time, our families practically grew up together." It's the last part of my statement that has her smiling softly with a knowing look in her eye. *If only she did know.*

"Well, congratulations, I'm happy for you. Do you want the usual?" She goes to the till to start ringing me up, but I stop her.

"Ah no actually, could I grab a couple of menus?" I know Hallie must be starving after watching me practice and then helping me teach, so I want her to be able to read through some food options.

Callia smiles in response. "Sure thing, I'll bring them over."

"Okay thanks." I nod, turning to leave but not before I ruffle Penelope's hair and bid her goodbye. "See you later Pen."

The kid offers me a wave as I head over to the booth that Hallie has situated herself in, and I slide into the seat opposite her. She studies me closely, not saying a word even though I can see a million questions brewing behind those green eyes of hers. I can't say I blame her, a couple of weeks ago we were barely on talking terms. Sure, I saw her all the time thanks to Maddie, but it had been a long time since we ever properly hung out just the two of us. Now here we are married, and I have seen her more in the last few weeks than I have in the last year. It's weird yet comforting in a way, and it's like I am seeing a whole different side to her than before.

Callia doesn't take too long to deliver the menus, and I talk through some of the options with Hals before we finally settle on an order. Then we enjoy an actual dinner together, unlike the one we attended with my parents yesterday, and for the first time in years we talk about everything. I tell her about the teaching, and the interest I have been getting from scouts, and she tells me about her classes, and how the internship with her dad was in the summer, and now she thinks she wants to work there full time when she graduates. It's nice, and it's the first time in a long time where I have spent any extended amount of time with a female and actually enjoyed myself. And even more so, it's the first time in years where I have opened up to anyone.

We also talk about the wedding and I show her the pictures on my phone, forwarding them to her as we speak. "It was a really beautiful wedding, I don't think I told you that," she whispers, studying a picture of the two of us closely.

"A beautiful wedding to go with a beautiful bride," I muse without thinking, and her eyes flick to mine with a smile.

"You're just being nice to me so I won't punch you in the dick again," she claims, and I can't help but laugh, watching closely as she dips another salty french fry into her strawberry milkshake. She's already blown through two cheeseburgers, and is now on her second portion of fries and milkshake.

I steal one, copying the exact same thing she just did and pretending I like it just as much as I respond, "Hals, there are plenty of things I'd like you to do to my dick, punching it isn't one of them."

Her eyes widen a little as she leans back in the booth and purrs, "Huh, think about me and your dick often do you?"

It's only now I realize what I just admitted to, and I can't exactly back down now, so instead I lean forward and double down. "Guilty as charged, but in my defense, you are my wife."

She swirls another fry in her milkshake before she takes a bite and flirts, "And how terrible of you to have bad thoughts about your wife."

Her words make me groan, not just because of how she said that, but because of the images it paints in my mind too. "Come on, Tink, don't say it like that."

Her smile is innocent, her eyes are anything but, as she asks, "Like what?"

I flick my stare around the diner casually, cracking my neck in the process to prolong my answer before I reply, "Like you're mine for the taking."

Now she just looks amused, "How come? What if I were yours for the taking?" I can see the mischief written all over her pretty face, and I can feel how easy this game would be to play with her, but I have to remember the stakes.

"You don't want me to take you, Hallie," I tell her firmly, reminding myself why I never let myself get attached to women, and the light from her eyes vanishes slightly.

"Why not?" she asks, and I can tell she truly wants the answer.

"Because all I would do is break you Hals, I'd take all those colors that burst out of you every day, and ruin them with my darkness." I am as honest as I can be, and I'm sure she understands given she grew up pretty much right alongside me.

She saw the mess that was my parents' marriage, and she knows the scars I wear that were burned into me from my father's words. I'm fucked up and jaded by his lack of love and affection, so how could I ever expect myself to be normal and have a real relationship.

I'm sure my words will have done the trick, but instead of looking resigned or disappointed, all she does is take a slow sip of her milkshake, my eyes locked on her lips and the straw before she purrs, "Well you know what they say?"

I flick my stare back to her. "What do they say, Tink?"

Her smile is blinding as she tosses back another fry with a wink. "You can't have a rainbow without a little rain."

∽

AFTER THAT NIGHT Hallie and I fall into somewhat of a routine. With the goal of being seen together, we spend our time side by side. We meet each other after class most days, she comes to all of my hockey practices accompanied by Maddie, and she even helps me teach the class at the center. All of that also ends with us having dinner together most nights, either with my housemates, or alone at her house, and we have pretty much seamlessly fallen back into the strong friendship we once had. She even manages to make Sunday dinner at my parents' house bearable, to the point where I almost feel like thanking my father for forcing my hand and bringing her back to my side.

There is just one problem in all of this, and that is the fact I am married to her.

Hallie and I have been in each other's lives a long time, so much so that I can barely remember what life was like before that. I've seen her with braces, watched her cry over boys and movies, and yes I admit there was that one time I tried to kiss her and she pushed me off that rock, but through all of that she has been my friend, my best friend even. Except now, instead of just being my best friend, she is my wife, something that our rings and her proximity remind me of daily.

I have to admit I had gotten used to keeping her at arm's length, and though I missed her, it was definitely easier, because now she is everywhere. She has invaded every part of my life just like she did when we were kids, only this time there is no escape.

She's my wife. *My wife*. And to most people that must sound great, being married to an absolute ten who is also your best friend, it would be great. Except this marriage, our marriage, is completely and totally fake. Something I've been having to remind myself of almost daily.

And what's worse than that is she knows me, like truly knows me, which means she sees through my moods and bullshit and doesn't put up with any of it. Do you have any idea how many dick punch threats you can receive in just two weeks? One hundred and seventeen, that's how many.

"I can't believe Lincoln still hasn't sent me anything," I complain from my spot on the bed, and I swear I can practically hear Hallie rolling her eyes from across the room.

"He hasn't even been home for a week, give the guy a chance to get back into the swing of things," she tosses back, as she meticulously coats her lashes in mascara for the second time.

"Hals, the guy is supposed to be the best, and his services aren't cheap, I expected to have something by now."

Lincoln was away for a close friend's wedding last week, but now he's home and back to work. He was grateful for the files I managed to download from my father's computer that day in his office, and has slowly been digging into all the information I found, but is yet to send me anything useful in return.

Hallie isn't convinced he will find anything at all worth my time, but I told her she doesn't know my father the way she thinks she does. I know him too well, which means I know fucking his secretary behind my mother's back isn't going to even crack the top five of terrible things he has done. Lincoln will find something for me to use, I'm sure of it.

"He's allowed to have a social life, Joshua. Damn, maybe he met the love of his life at the wedding he went to and is too busy fucking to go through your files," she muses, moving onto her lipstick, painting and then rolling her lips against one another, spreading the red stain across them.

I can't help but watch her, mesmerized as she takes far too long to get ready as usual. "The things that come out of your mouth sometimes." I shake my head, but when her eyes meet mine, they calm down the anger simmering beneath my surface. "And no one falls in love at a wedding, Tink, that's just a cliche, and besides, love is for fools."

She tosses her makeup back into the bag and turns dramatically clutching her chest. "Oh my husband says the sweetest things."

I climb from the bed and move towards her. "You're such a drama queen, do you know that?"

All she does is smile. "And you're such an asshole, do you know that?" She pushes past me, sitting down on the edge of my bed to finally put on her shoes.

"Please tell me you are ready now, if you take any longer I won't make it in time for warm up and coach will have my ass if I'm late," I tell her, picking up my bag for the game and moving towards the door.

"Yeah, yeah, I know," she drawls, moving to her own overnight bag in the corner to grab a jersey.

She hasn't spent the night here since the wedding, me usually opting to stay over with her and Maddie instead so I can sleep on the sofa, but tonight there is a big party at my house after the game, so we agreed it would be easy if she just stayed here. You know, to keep up appearances to everyone.

Which is how I've found myself here waiting for her to be ready, so we can leave and head over to the rink together. I told her she didn't need to come with me but she insisted. Now here she is, in tight fitted jeans that are practically molded to her thighs in a way that would have my own pants tightening if I looked too long, and a little tank top that shows off far too much of her flawless skin. Thankfully, she covers it with one of my jerseys for the game before I can become too distracted.

"Okay, I'm ready," she finally beams, flashing me that sunshine smile of hers, as she moves towards me.

"Finally, let's go." I toss my bag onto my shoulder and move to grab the door, but before I can, she slides in front of me and blocks the way.

"Ah, ah, hold on a second," she beams with a smile, one that promises my demise, and feeling that anger coming bubbling back, I can't help but huff.

"Oh my god, what now?"

Hallie straightens her shoulders and looks at me with a teasing glint in her eye. "Tell me I look pretty," she demands, her smile not wavering in the slightest. There is no shame or embarrassment, just this girl that is the bane of my existence, making me speechless once again.

"What?" I ask, totally baffled, but it doesn't seem to faze her at all.

In fact, all it does is spur her on more, as she presses herself against the door so I can't open it at all. "You heard me, Joshua, tell your wife, who just spent an hour getting ready for your game, knowing that she is going to be looked at by everyone, that she looks pretty."

"Hallie," I warn, needing her to not try and push me like this, not when I need to get to the rink and get ready for said game, but of course she stands her ground.

"Joshua," she tosses back in a mocking tone, and I have to inhale a deep breath to calm my now rapidly beating heart.

Her eyes are still firmly on mine, a tempting sparkle in them that tells me she knows as always that she is pushing all of my buttons, so, I decide to push hers right back. I close the distance between us, bringing my body just to the point where it's almost touching hers, but not quite. Then I lean in close and bring my mouth to her ear, not missing the blush now creeping up her neck for a second.

"My wife looks like the most perfect doorstop I have ever seen," I whisper, as my hand curls around the door handle, and I use my other to pull her away from it so I can open the door.

"You really are an asshole," she scoffs with a huff, and I have to smother a laugh as she pushes me out through the doorway, slamming it behind us. "But it's okay, maybe I can find a new friend at the game to tell me I look pretty," she adds with a wink, and that anger comes flooding back.

"Only if you want to spend your evening watching him bleed," I toss back, knocking on Daemon's door as we pass.

Of course he opens it almost instantly, as if he was waiting for us, and he falls in line behind us silently, but that doesn't stop my wife from flashing him her smile. "Hi Daemon."

And unlike with any other person, he actually answers her. "Hi Hallie."

The two of them have formed a friendship based on simple greetings, and honestly it's nice to see him coming out of his shell a little more around her. Landon and Levi are barely here when she is, which is good considering Levi gives her a weird look every time he sees her, but at least Landon isn't bothered either way. In fact, he seems convinced that this thing between Hallie and I has been going on for years. I guess he's dumber than I thought. That, or we just put on a really good show.

With the others already gone, the three of us all decide to walk over to the rink together, while Hallie animatedly chats away about some documentary she watched last night. Daemon is as silent as always, but I can tell he is actively listening to her, and I make a note to thank him later for being so nice and welcoming to her.

By the time we reach the rink, I have about thirty-seconds to get to the changing rooms before coach rips me a new one, and before I can even say anything, Hallie moves to walk in the opposite direction.

"Hope you don't fall, break your leg, and die," she tosses over her shoulder, her hips swaying as she moves to walk in the other direction of the seats, and I am reminded of her demands earlier in my room.

So before she can go, I reach out and grab her by the belt loop on her jeans and pull her back against my chest. "If I do fall, will my wife kiss it better? Because just like every day, she looks so fucking beautiful tonight."

I release her before she can reply, knowing I am playing with fire, because even though she has my ring around her finger, she still isn't mine, nor does she want to be. She's my friend, my best friend, and nothing more.

Leaving her behind I head into the locker room, praying that coach doesn't notice my arrival, but of course he does, the man has a nose like a damn bloodhound. "Peters, you're late," he yells across the changing room, and I know better than to argue with him over the sake of a couple of minutes.

"Sorry coach, I was waiting for my wife to get ready," I reply without thinking, causing some of my teammates to start hollering around me.

"I can just imagine your wife naked," Reign quips instantly, and the glare I give him just makes the bastard laugh.

"Don't forget hot," Gray cuts in. "Naked, hot, and sweating, just dripping everywhere," he drawls, taking a bite of his protein bar and giving me a wink.

I throw my bag to the floor and turn to step towards him, but Daemon is there in an instant blocking my way, and when I flick my stare to him, he shakes his head slightly.

"Last fucking warning, Gray," I tell Archer, pointing my finger, but he doesn't lose his smile, not until his Captain whips him with a towel that is.

"Stop fucking fantasizing about his wife you fucking creep," Nova tells him, coming around the lockers from coach's office already dressed and ready for the game.

Archer steps into his pants, his tattooed chest on complete display as he throws back, "Should I go back to doing it about his sister?"

The look Nova gives him is nothing short of lethal, and before I can even warn him, Nova beats me to it. "Not if you value your life."

All the while Daemon stands between us, hands on me to keep me in place, but eyes on Archer, his stare filled with warning, and something else.

"Alright, don't get your knickers in a twist," Reign jokes, grabbing Archer and physically turning him away from everyone else, before lowering his voice and adding, "You really like to poke the fucking bears, don't you kid?"

Archer only shrugs. "Maybe I have a pain kink."

With fucking teammates like these it's any wonder we manage to play a decent fucking game, and when I move my stare away from them, I find Nova watching me carefully.

"Got a problem, Darkmore?" I ask, because I don't care how much my sister cares about him, I still think he's a giant prick.

"You know, Peters? I haven't had a problem since the moment your sister started sleeping in my bed every night, isn't that funny?" he smiles, and it takes everything in me not to react and cause yet another fight with him.

We have butted heads numerous times over the years, but I promised Maddie I would stop starting shit with him, and right now I am finding it very hard to keep that promise.

"If you want a problem, I can give you one, Captain," I spit in disgust, squaring my shoulders, and flexing my fists in preparation, but just as I step forward we are cursed out.

"Will you bunch of little pricks pack it in and get ready for the fucking game!" Coach Locke yells from his office, storming from around his desk. "I have an eighteen year old daughter who doesn't gossip and whine as much as you little shits, and she's a damn nightmare."

I move my focus back to getting ready, heeding his warning, but I still hear Archer wonder out loud, "Damn, I didn't know Coach had a daughter."

"Me either, I wonder if she's hot?" Reign tosses back, only for Coach to come and smack them both on the back of the head.

"Keep your little pervert minds away from my daughter," Coach spits, and then smacks Archer's head again. "And keep them off Peters' wife and sister too."

After that I can't help but smile as I suit up for the game.

#17
HALLIE
JOCKSTRAP JERKOFF

The last two weeks have been a whirlwind. Josh and I went from barely talking to one another, to being married and seeing each other everyday in an instant. It makes quite a change from putting up with him being a complete and total asshole to me, now he's only a little bit of an asshole, but still an asshole all the same. Yet it's nice to be back on common ground with him, and somehow things feel different to how they were before. His barriers are still there of course, but now they feel more like fences I could climb, rather than walls that would shut me out completely. I see the boy from before his father tainted him, and I know it's not the same, that he has been tainted, but it doesn't change how much I enjoy being around him. And I'm not stupid, I know it doesn't mean anything to him, not in the way it does to me, but spending so much time together is not great for the slight crush I have on him.

Okay, so I love him more now than I ever have, but that's not my fault.

First of all, he's hot. Second of all, he's an asshole, and third of all, he's a shameless flirt. How the hell am I supposed to resist that? *I'm just a girl.*

The feelings I've had for him, the ones that I have spent years mashing down, are now alive and burning hotter than ever. Feelings that are never more tangible than when I am watching him spin around the rink like a flash, letting nothing and no one get in his way.

I've never really been into sports, not in the way most people are. My dad was always more concerned with business and spending time with my mom and me to ever take notice of anything else, so I always thought I would be the same. Then I met Josh. From the very first moment I stepped through the trees that separated our houses, and saw him flying around with a stick and a puck, I was hooked. Not just on him, but the game too.

Yet not once during the many times I wrote our names in a heart in the back of my notepads, did I ever think I would grow up to marry him and be rinkside at his games. Sure, I've had the fantasy plenty of times, where he finishes his game all hot and sweaty and then takes me right there on the ice, but that's all it ever was, a silly yet ridiculously hot fantasy.

Now here I am, sitting front row with his jersey name and number across my back, only now it's not just his name, it's my name too.

Both teams are on the ice making porn, and by that I mean, stretching for the upcoming game, and my eyes are focused solely on the number twenty-two. Other members of the team are laughing and joking with one another, but my husband and his housemate are both silent and solemn as they get themselves warmed up. I watch as he stretches himself into every position imaginable, and the fantasy about him taking me on the ice is the only thing I can think about.

"Careful or you might get drool on your jersey," Maddie teases, jolting me from my thoughts as my gaze snaps to hers.

"What? No, I wasn't looking at him," I say far too quickly, before adding, "I mean, I'm not drooling."

My best friend laughs. "You're a terrible liar, you know that right?" she replies, mirroring what her brother has said to me countless times.

"I may have heard that a time or too." I casually flick my gaze around the arena, forcing myself not to look at him, as my best friend eyes me. "But I wasn't looking at anything."

Maddie shakes her head, her eyes moving back to her boyfriend as she smiles. "You know if you bang my brother that's like breaking girl code, right?"

"What? How is that breaking girl code?" I question instantly before cringing and switching up. "I mean, I don't even want to bang him so why would I care about girl code?" I shrug, as if she isn't digging her claws into my biggest secret and spilling it all over the ice without a care in the world.

"I don't know who the bigger idiot is, you or my brother," she replies, shaking her head, as she waves to Nova, and I can't help but feel envious of her and what they have.

The last month they have surprised us all and become stronger than ever. Nova hasn't even looked at another girl, his sole focus remaining on the girl beside me, worshiping the ground she walks on, and from the noises I hear coming from her bedroom at night, rocking her world too. And Maddie is like a different person, her confidence shining brighter than ever, and the barbs from her father that used to make her a nervous wreck barely even matter to her anymore.

They are perfect for one another, and all it does is twist me up inside, because that's what we all want, isn't it? We want to find a best friend, a lover, a confidant, someone who sees all of you, your highs, your lows, and everything in between, and falls for you anyway. It's what they have, it's what my parents have, and it's what I am desperate for.

"I resent that statement," I tell her, but all she does is offer me some nachos with a smile.

"Just go back to staring, you little hoe bag," she tosses back, bumping my shoulder with hers.

And well, who am I to deny my best friend?

By the time the game starts, the amount of fantasies in my head has trebled, each one more filthy than the last. Those thoughts are only intensified when Josh scores a goal and the crowd goes wild. I'm on my feet screaming his name at the top of my lungs and riding the high with him, but it doesn't last long.

A player from the opposing team crashes into him, slamming him into the ice and my heart catches in my throat. The guy manages a few hits before Daemon rips him away, helping Josh to his feet, but even from across the ice I can see the switch in him has flipped. Josh doesn't stop, he doesn't walk away, he is on the guy in an instant, smashing him to the floor and returning every hit he received tenfold until we can see the blood on the ice.

By the time they are pulled apart, Josh is bleeding from his lip, but the other guy is bleeding from his whole face, barely able to stand as his teammates help him to his feet. Proving my theory that he is totally psychotic, and one hundred percent completely hot.

The other guy is escorted from the ice to see a medic and Josh is sent off for five minutes in the sin bin. I watch as he skates across the ice towards where we are sitting, the entire time my eyes not leaving the blood that drips from his mouth, wanting nothing more than to wipe it away. Now it's not like I have never seen him fight before, if I am honest it happens more than I care to admit, he's always been a hot head, especially where Maddie was concerned, but I can't help but wonder what made him snap this time.

When he reaches the sin bin his eyes instantly find mine and I can't help but shake my head in mock disappointment, ignoring the thrill his bloody smile and wink brings me. Yet that feeling soon turns sour when I overhear some girls gossiping behind me.

"Oh my god, Josh Peters is so hot," one girl gushes, and jealousy burns at the back of my throat instantly.

"I know, it should be illegal to look that good on the ice," her friend agrees, and I feel Maddie stiffen beside me, having obviously overheard them too, and I feel her worried gaze hit the side of my face.

I keep my eyes on the game and pray that's the end of it, but then I hear the first girl's voice again, only louder this time. "Hey Peters!" she yells, causing Josh to turn his head toward us. "If you want to score again my goal is wide open."

Anger burns up inside of me so fast that I want to scream, and I can hear my heartbeat as it pumps rapidly inside my chest. I will myself to be the type of person to turn around and tell them he belongs to me, but it's just not me. And that would be a lie, wouldn't it? Yes I'm wearing his ring, but outside of that we know none of this is real.

Josh stands and turns with a smile and a feeling of dread like I have never known curls in the pit of my stomach. Yet instead of replying, all he does is rip off his left glove, bring the hand up to his mouth and bite down on something white around his finger until it pulls away. Only then does he hold up his hand and showcase his fourth finger. His very occupied fourth finger.

Oh my god he's wearing his wedding ring.

My heart starts to slam against my rib cage and I almost think I won't be able to hear anything other than my heartbeat when he opens his mouth, but then his words cut right through the white noise.

"I've already scored the only goal I'll ever need." His words aren't casual, and as soon as they are out he brings his gaze back to mine and winks again. "You look good with my last name on your back, Mrs. Peters."

I hear the girls gasp as we gather more notice from the people around us, now all looking at me in a new light, and I pray my voice doesn't shake as I force myself to reply loudly, "It's my last name now too, maybe I'm wearing it for me?"

A couple of people laugh, Maddie included, but as the clock on his time in the sin bin runs out, he stands and backs out with a wink. "Oh trust me, it's most definitely for me."

Then he's gone, taking my heart with him as my best friend muses out loud, "You're in trouble, Tink."

I'm in so much of a daze from her brother's words that I can't help but reply, "Since the day I met you, Wendy."

The rest of the game passes without incident, and by the time the final buzzer sounds out, I am more than ready for a drink.

Maddie excuses herself to go to the bathroom before we meet up with the boys, so I hang back alone, letting the crowd filter out a little before I start making my way down towards the changing rooms where I know Josh will be coming out.

It's there that my past catches up with me.

"Hallie?" Someone calls in question, and when I turn I find myself face to face with the first boy I ever gave myself to.

"Joey," I say by way of greeting, locking eyes with my first boyfriend, who is already dropping his gaze down the length of my body in the same way he used to when we were in high school.

I remember that look and how it used to make me feel, only now I cringe a little as our time together comes rushing back to me in waves, and I realize how shitty he was to me. Hindsight is a funny thing isn't it?

My stare shifts to the two friends beside him, both of which I recognize from high school, and from the smirks on their faces I'm sure they remember a lot more about me than I do about them. It's only then that Josh's words from a couple of weeks ago come back to me.

You should of heard the fucking shit he was saying about you, about what you guys got up to.

A sour taste coats my tongue as I force my stare back to Joey's and look at him in a whole new light. He's no longer the boy who gave me sweet kisses and was gentle as he took my virginity. No, instead he's a bigger fake than I am.

I broke his arm.

My gaze drops to his arm, disappointed to find it now back to its full health as he finally adds, "God, it must have been what? Almost three years?"

It takes everything in me to force a reply. "Yeah, it must have been," I say tightly, wishing I had just gone with Maddie to the bathroom.

The last thing I want to do right now is reminisce about the guy who I have recently discovered was a bigger prick than I ever knew. Hopefully this whole interaction is just a quick hello and I can get to Josh, head to the party at his house, and down an extra large drink and forget about Joey's entire existence with my dignity still intact.

"And look at you, you're hotter than ever, I forgot how gorgeous you are," he practically drools, once again leering at the body he was the first to touch, making his friends laugh knowingly.

The backhanded compliment does nothing but give me the ick, and panic flares in my gut as he steps forward and reaches out to touch my arm. I guess he also forgot how much people's touch can make me uncomfortable.

Yet as I brace myself, another hand curls around my stomach, pulling me away from him and back against a hard body. "I thought I told you to stay away from her." Josh's voice is like white hot fury in my ear, my entire body melting into the safety of him.

Joey's eyes flare in a mixture of surprise and fear, before he squares his shoulders and tosses back, "Relax, Peters, we were just talking."

Those fingers flex against my stomach. "Not to my wife, you're not, now fuck off back to where you came from before I break both your arms." His voice is casual, but I can still hear the threat there, and Joey looks at us in surprise.

"Your wife?" he questions, moving his stare back and forth between us, before the shock turns to anger.

It's only then that I remember something else about our brief relationship in high school. His jealousy over Josh. He couldn't stand the fact that I had a friendship with someone older and hotter than him, that I always had his back, and never let anyone talk badly about him. It was always a form of resentment for him, and now he sees the real secret I was harboring back then.

When his stare finally lands back on me he sneers, "Well, now it all makes sense, doesn't it? You certainly played the long game didn't you?"

My entire body burns with embarrassment and no words come to my defense, not one, because what would I even say?

Thankfully, Josh is here to have my back. "Don't fucking talk to her, Jockstrap, or this time it won't be only your arm I break," he warns, his words nothing but a depraved promise that makes my heart beat even faster for him.

I see his friends looking at us with a worried look in their eye, preparing for whatever is about to go down, but just as Joey looks as if he is going to grant himself a death wish, some other members of the team join the fray.

Archer strolls down the hallway with Alexander by his side, and Daemon on their heels, laughing and joking back and forth with his goalie until he reaches us, no doubt taking in the tension. He doesn't stop until he reaches Josh's side, Alexander and Daemon at his back, and when I look up at him, he takes in the look on my face and zones in on Joey.

"Do we have a problem here?" Archer asks, voice just as dark and lethal as my husband's, in a tone I have never heard from him before, and I have to put my hand over Josh's to stop it from shaking.

"I'm not sure, Gray," Josh casually replies, cocking an eye at him, before slowly moving back to Joey. "Do we have a problem here?"

Joey's friends have already stepped away, not having their friend's back in the slightest, as Josh's team came to have his, and when he notices, I see a deep anger there, before he finally relents. "Nope, no problem here," he replies casually, looking between all of us, before finally settling on only me. "I'll see you around, Hallie," he adds, turning on his heel and moving to leave.

"Next time you see her around, keep fucking walking, prick," Josh calls after him, his hand now harsh and brutal against my stomach as he holds me against him.

We all watch him leave and then before I can even speak, Josh has me spun around, my back hitting the wall, and him against me with his hands cupping my cheeks, forcing me to look up at him. "You okay, Tink?"

I'm already nodding, forcing myself to hold back my tears as I lie, "Yeah, of course I am."

Josh glares at me, his thumb brushing back and forth on my

cheek as he lowers his voice, "Don't fucking lie to me, Hals, remember rule number two on that list of yours," he muses, his anger barely restrained in his tone, yet still it brings me nothing but comfort.

"I'm okay now," I admit in a whisper, and he searches my eyes for the truth, one I can't give him. "I promise I'm okay, and you know I never lie to you, Peter," I add, the deceit slipping through my teeth and praying the mask he knows so well holds better than normal.

His stare stays on mine, not relenting for a second, and ignoring everyone else around us, as he holds my gaze and waits for me to break, but I don't. Not with him here giving me his strength, and I wish I could tell him that the only thing that could break me, is him.

"What's going on?" Maddie rushes out from down the hallway, storming towards us like a woman on a mission, and when I break her brother's stare to look towards her, I find Nova right at her back, both of them looking concerned.

"Nothing, I'm fine," I lie, at the same time Josh says, "She saw Joey."

Maddie looks between the two of us before she questions, "Jockstrap Jerkoff was here?" And all I can do is laugh, breaking the tension between everyone here as Josh laughs too, pulling me from the wall as he takes a step back.

"Yeah, but it's fine. Josh scared him away with threats to break his arm again, both this time." I playfully scold, only increasing my best friend's confusion.

"Again?" Maddie asks, flicking her stare between her brother and I, but Josh ignores her, nodding his head at Archer.

"Thanks for having my back, Gray," he forces out, and I know it must be killing him inside to get those words out, which is totally obvious to Archer as he grins.

"What are teammates for," Archer replies with a shrug. "You

might hate me, but I've still got your back," he adds, letting his eyes briefly move over to Daemon for a second.

"I don't hate you," Josh rushes to say, but Archer just raises his eyebrows at him, so Josh quickly corrects, "Okay so I admit I don't like you very much, but I don't hate you."

He's such a big fat liar.

Now it's Alexander who speaks as he collars Archer with an arm around his neck. "Don't worry, Peters, the weird fucker really grows on you, right Cap?" he asks, turning to Nova who stands protectively at Maddie's back.

"I don't know what you're talking about," Nova drawls with a smile. "I hate all of you, especially Peters." Which only brings a smile to my face, as the others laugh.

Yet Maddie acts offended on Josh's behalf. "Why do you hate my brother but not me?" she questions, and I already know Josh isn't going to like his answer when his smile turns wicked and full on intent.

"Because I doubt your brother would let me do all the despicable things to him that you let me do, Princess," he muses, and Josh's hand on my hip tightens as he curses.

"Darkmore, I swear to fucking god," he starts, making the rest of the guys laugh, and I know I need to end this little confrontation between them before it even starts.

"Come on, twenty-two," I purr, forcing his stare back to mine. "Let's get to the party so you can get me drunk and do despicable things to me too," I joke in an attempt to keep up our ruse and distract him at the same time, and to my surprise it works perfectly as his eyes turn from anger to pure heat.

"Oh gross," Maddie complains. "Come on, Charmer, get me to the party so I can drink away the memory of my best friend saying that to my brother," she snaps, dragging him down the hall.

"Anything for you, Grim," he tosses back, following after her like a lost puppy, as the other guys follow him too.

When I look back at Josh he is still watching me carefully, and just as I am about to open my mouth to ask him if he's ready to go too, he cuts me off. "Careful, Tink, because the next time you proposition me, I might just take you up on it," he warns before pushing away from me as if that threat didn't just fall from his lips, and all I can do is watch him leave. When I don't instantly follow him, he turns to walk backwards towards the door as he calls out with a smirk, "Well, are you coming?"

Fuck. I just might be.

And like a dog to his bone, my feet move towards him without my permission, making him smile even wider.

"This party is going to be fun," he adds, opening the door for me, and slipping his hand into mine as I pass by.

Even the December chill of the night sky can't cool me down as I walk with him side by side. "I really need a drink," I finally croak out, and all he does is laugh.

All in all it was a pretty standard Flyers game that I survived, now I just have to survive the afterparty too.

#18
JOSH
PUBLIC SHAMING

Two hours later and the party at my house is in full swing, yet the anger from the post-game confrontation is still clinging to my skin like a straitjacket. *Fucking Joey.* I'm not sure why his presence pissed me off so much, but when I walked out of the changing room and down the hall in search of Hallie, and I found her with him, I just saw red. Every fucking detail of the shit he said about her came rushing back, and not even the memory of the bones in his arm breaking beneath my fingers could tame me.

I was on her before I could even take my next breath, pulling her body into mine before that prick could ever lay another finger on her. The only thing that stopped me from hurting him again was her. Her body against me, her hand atop mine, both grounding me in a way I can't really explain or understand, I just knew I needed to protect her. Just seeing him made me act fucking stupid, and I haven't been able to look Hallie in the eye since we left the rink.

Careful, Tink, because the next time you proposition me, I might just take you up on it

What the fuck was I thinking saying that to her?

She's my little sister's best friend, my best friend, my fake wife, yet flirting with her is not only becoming easier, but also like a second nature, like I should have been doing it all along. Not that I can take all the blame, when she was the one putting such devious ideas in my head regardless of how made up they might be. This ruse is pushing against the boundaries of my restraints, especially given how long it's been since I've been with someone. I'm dripping with the need for release and itching for control, and it seems the band around my finger has sent me crazy, because it has me looking at her in a way I never have before.

Shaking those thoughts from my mind, I take another sip from my beer and pretend not to watch the way her hips sway as she dances with Maddie across the room. Long gone is the jersey with my name across her back, and now every prick is staring at the way that little white top of hers clings to her breasts like a second skin. They don't seem to care about the ring on her finger, and I seem to care way too much because I have to forcibly stop myself from going over there to show every prick here who owns her.

"You okay there, killer?" Gray asks, interrupting my thoughts, as he comes to a stop next to me and pours himself another drink.

I don't bother looking at him as I respond, keeping my eyes on my wife, while Maddie leans in and whispers something in her ear, before turning and leaving her alone. "I'm fine, Gray," I snap, not in the mood to make idle chit chat with him, but of course the fucker doesn't relent.

"For someone who just gained himself a smoking hot wife,

you look like someone pissed on your parade," he muses, just as Reign joins the fray.

"Don't fucking talk about my wife," I snap, making him smile even wider, my eyes still watching Hallie as a few girls approach her and start talking to her.

"He's right, Peters, you look miserable as fuck, do you want a cup of tea?" Reign asks, coming to lean on the counter beside me.

"Not everything can be solved with a cup of fucking tea, Alexander," Archer complains, as if this is an argument they have often.

"That's because you don't appreciate a good Earl Grey," he tosses back, and I do my best to drown them out.

Which isn't hard considering Hallie's gaze flicks from the group of girls to me, and then back again. And that's all it takes for me to know something is wrong, and I move my focus to the girls around her, noticing someone I didn't before.

Brianna.

"What the fuck?" I mutter aloud, making Gray and Reign stop their incessant argument, and follow my line of sight.

"Oh fuck me, Brianna's not starting her shit again is she?" Gray complains, tossing his drink back immediately before discarding it.

Again.

"What the fuck do you mean again?" I grit, turning towards Archer, and he holds his hand up in defense.

"Hey don't kill the messenger," he starts, and when I take a step towards him, he quickly adds, "She was giving Hallie shit in Econ a about you guys getting married."

His sentence is barely even finished before a fury like no other is flooding my veins. I toss my own drink into the sink and start heading towards them, ignoring the curses from both my teammates. I push through the crowds of people lingering around the downstairs of my house so I can get to her.

Coming behind them, as Brianna purrs, "What was it again, girls? Face down, ass up, and no speaking, that's how he likes it right? All of the control and none of the emotion." And it doesn't take a genius to figure out what they are talking about, not when I'm sure I have drunkenly sunk my dick into all of them at one point or another.

Something I had never cared about before, but when Hallie's eyes meet mine again, and I see sadness there, it makes me wish I could erase every single one of them just to see her smile.

Not bothering to even look at any of them, I keep my focus on her as I push past them and put my arms around Hallie pulling her in. "Everything okay, Mrs. Peters?" I ask, hating the stiffness I can feel in her body, but keeping her in my arms anyway.

"Oh Josh, there you are," Brianna coos. "We were just talking about you," she adds with a giggle that makes my skin crawl.

"Tink, everything okay?" I ask, ignoring Brianna completely, much to her dismay, yet still Hallie refuses to break her stare and look at me.

"Looks like the weirdo is broken again," Brianna jokes, making her little pack of friends laugh, and the wrath inside of me intensifies ten-fold. Especially when she adds, "Call me when you need a mistress," she winks, like it might make her offer more inviting. *It doesn't.*

"What the fuck did you just say?" I seethe, now giving her my full attention, causing more people to look our way, just as Maddie emerges from the bathroom and starts making her way back over to Hallie.

"Relax, Josh, it was a joke." Brianna rolls her eyes, her tone completely uncaring, as she examines her manicure.

"Yeah, at my wife's expense," I spit, my fingers now digging into Hallie's waist harder than I care to acknowledge.

"I'm sure she's heard worse, she's not exactly normal," she

snaps back with a cackle, only this time she is the only one laughing.

"Get the fuck out of my house." My voice is loud and clear as it booms across the room, being heard by everyone over the music, causing them all to look this way.

"What?" she stammers, her friends now looking wary as someone cuts off the music.

"You heard me," I say, voice cold and flat, and the shock in her eyes is clear as day. "What? You think just because you've laid on your back for half the guys on the team that it gives you some sort of status? Or maybe it's your daddy's money that makes you feel invincible. Well guess what, I don't give a fuck about either. You will not stand in *my* house and insult *my* *wife*."

From the corner of my eye I see Daemon descending the stairs, no doubt having heard the disruption, and he doesn't hesitate to start making his way towards us. Maddie also comes to a stop by my side, along with some other members of my team, all to have my back, to have Hallie's back.

Brianna is quick to try and claw back some face as she takes us all in. "Wow, looks like some of that control is starting to slip, Josh, you better be careful," she tosses back, thinking she still has any kind of sway here.

"And if you come near me or my wife again, or even think about disrespecting her in any way, then you better be careful, because I will ruin you so badly that even dear old dad won't be able to save you. Now I'll tell you again, get the fuck out of my house."

Her drink hits us before I can stop it, covering Hallie more than me as Brianna screeches, "Fuck you, Josh."

I pull Hallie back, furious at myself for keeping her in the firing line, but before I can even toss back a retort, Maddie is there, her hand cracking against Brianna's cheek so hard that her head spins to the side, but Brianna is quick to raise her own in response.

Before her hand can even move in my sister's direction, her wrist is snatched up by Nova. "Don't even fucking think about it, B," he warns in a lethal tone, and I see the flash of hurt in her eyes, as he comes to protect his girlfriend.

We all knew she favored him over the rest of us. He never gave her more than drunken trysts at parties, and now, here he is after claiming my sister to the world, and for once, I actually like the prick.

"Nova," Brianna quivers, her cheek red, yet her eyes turning even redder, but it doesn't work, not on him or me.

"You heard Peters, get the fuck out, and from now on you're no longer welcome at any of the hockey houses," he declares, dropping her wrist, and moving around her to get to Maddie, bringing them both to stand by our side.

"Nova, please," she begs one last time, and not a single person comes to her defense.

"You've crossed the line for the last time, so just go," Nova sighs, and I can tell he doesn't feel good about doing this, and I wish I could say I felt the same, but I don't.

Not when the girl in my arms is stiff and dripping in the bitch's drink, the words she also threw no doubt still swimming in her mind, and as Brianna huffs and turns on her heel to leave, I'm glad to see the back of her.

The entire party is watching this go down, and as Brianna leaves, their attention turns to us, and I can't stop myself from instantly guiding Hallie towards the stairs so we can get away from it all, thankful when I hear Daemon's lethal tone. "Turn the music back on. Now," he demands, and is obliged instantly.

The party comes back to life all around us, but my only focus is getting Hallie up to the safety of my room. She's silent as I guide her there, her body shaking slightly, but it's the tremble of my own that concerns me. An anger coursing through me that makes me feel like I am going to explode, and as we push into my room and I slam the door with a bang, she flinches.

I don't stop though, instead heading straight into the bathroom to grab her a towel, before storming back towards her. "Top, off," I demand, as she tries to dry it off with her hand, and her stare flicks to mine.

"Josh, really it's fine," she lies, moving around me to check her reflection in the mirror. I'm not sure what Brianna was drinking, but it has left a bright red stain down the front of her white top, and she now smells even sweeter than normal.

"Hallie, I've known you since you were nine years old, which means I know how much you physically despise the feeling of wet clothes against your body. In fact, I have been the audience to many lengthy debates on this topic from you more times than I can even count, so please respect your own damn rules, quit lying to me, and take off the damn top." I don't leave room for her to argue, moving towards my closet to grab her a shirt of mine to wear, and when I turn around I find her standing there in nothing but her bra and jeans, dabbing at her chest with the towel I got for her.

Fuck.

My wife looks good every day, she always has, but standing in the privacy of my room in jeans that showcase her thick thighs and gorgeous ass, while her tits are barely contained in the scrap of lace she is passing off as a bra, well it's safe to say I'm in trouble.

Ignoring my rapidly hardening cock, I move back across the room towards her, coming to a stop at her back as she stares in the mirror. I hold the shirt up in front of her, clearing my throat. "Here, put this on."

Her stare flicks to mine in the mirror, her skin tinted in a pink blush as she lets the towel drop and quickly grabs the shirt from my hand, muttering a quiet thank you. I don't turn around as she puts it on, not because I don't want to, but because I can't, like I physically can't make myself turn away from her. Not after what happened and why, I just need to make sure she is okay.

She slips her arms into my shirt, and of course it drowns her tiny frame, but she still rushes to button it up before she lets herself meet my stare in the mirror. I'm sure she can see the intensity there, hell, I can fucking feel it all around us, but she quickly focuses back on the shirt.

"Well this doesn't look ridiculous at all," she laughs, trying and failing to style it in any way, leaving her to just roll up the cuffs on the sleeves so her hands can pop out.

"I don't know, you look pretty perfect to me," I tell her honestly, and her stare snaps back to mine.

"Joshua," she laughs, my name falling from her lips like a prayer. "There's no one around, you don't have to pretend right now." Her words cut me a little, but it's the look in her eyes that tells me she really doesn't believe me, that hurts me more.

Before I can stop myself, my hands are on her hips and I am pulling her back against me until our bodies are tight against one another. "Does this feel like I'm pretending, Tink?" I ask, letting my very obvious erection for her dig into the bottom of her back.

All thoughts of her being my best friend have dissipated, and at this moment I can't understand how I have been looking at her for over ten years but not really seeing her.

Her eyes widen slightly, before she pulls away, and I start to panic that I have ruined everything, but then instead of moving from me, she turns in my hold, bringing her stare up to meet mine. "Why did you come over when you saw Brianna talking to me?"

Her question catches me off guard, mostly because the only thing I can think of right now is how good she looks in my shirt, the feel of her body against me, my hands on her hips, and her eyes on mine. "Because I knew she would be talking shit to you," I admit quietly, wishing I didn't know Brianna so well to know that.

I wish I could erase anyone that isn't Hallie right now, wanting nothing more than to feel her lips on mine, not caring that she's my best friend, or how long we have known each other. In fact, it only makes me want her more. Fake or not, the rings on our fingers mean she belongs to me and I belong to her.

"So? It's not your job to protect me, Joshua," she huffs, her hands moving up to my chest as if she's going to push me away, but I capture them in mine and keep her in place.

"First of all, it is my job to protect you," I tell her, knowing full well I have been doing it since the day I met her, and only just starting to ask myself why. "And second of all, I won't stand for anyone saying shit to you, especially because of me." Just because I have fucked around with half the girls on campus doesn't mean I want her tainted by it.

She deserves more than that, and she definitely deserves more than me, but I don't think I have the restraint to stay away from her, not when we were kids, and definitely not now.

"Why?" she whispers, her voice so quiet that I almost miss it, and the answer is simple.

"Because you're mine, Hals," I respond without thinking, her eyes instantly taking on a frown as I quickly add, "I mean, you're my wife, my best friend." Neither of them are far from the truth, yet somehow it still doesn't explain what I mean.

Her hand reaches up absentmindedly and her thumb skims the cut on my lip that I got from the fight in the game. "But none of this is real," she says in wonder, and my heart beats wildly in my chest.

I drop my forehead to hers, relishing in the feel of her touching me as I plead, "So? Let's break the rules anyway." Then

I am leaning down, bringing my lips towards the girl who I warned everyone else away from, but just as they are about to touch.

Knock. Knock.

"Hals?" Maddie shouts through the door. "Hals, it's me, let me in." And that's all it takes for Hallie to push away from me like she's on fire.

I blow out a breath, reaching down to rearrange myself before I move over to the door and open it to find my sister. Of course she doesn't take a second to read the room, or my mood, and just barges past me to get to her best friend.

"Hey, I just wanted to check if you were okay," Maddie starts, cutting across the room until she reaches Hallie, who is still standing by the mirror. "Do you need me to go get you some fresh clothes from home or anything?" she asks, her gaze dropping to the shirt of mine she is now wearing.

"I'm fine," Hallie lies with a bright smile, not even looking in my direction, as Maddie tries to come to her rescue.

And all I'm left with is the realization that I almost kissed my wife.

Fuck.

#19
HALLIE
CLOSET CONFESSIONS

I consider myself very lucky to have a best friend like Madeline Peters, but right now as she fusses over me after what happened downstairs, I am barely even listening to her. No, instead I am reeling from all the events of the last few hours. From the fight at the rink, to the run in with Joey, then the confrontation downstairs with Brianna. Yet all of those are overshadowed by the fact that he just almost kissed me. Josh Peters, my best friend since I was nine, and the boy I have loved ever since, almost kissed me.

He almost kissed me.

My gaze flicks from his sister to him, finding him still idling by his open bedroom door, not looking anywhere near as freaked out as I currently am. Why would he be freaked out? From the things those girls were saying, a barely not even happened kiss is probably nothing on his radar. My mind is swamped with the things Brianna and them were saying about what he likes, about his need for control and dominance to get off, and all I can do is compare it to how gently he just leaned down to kiss me.

"Are you sure you don't want me to run and get you another top to wear?" Maddie asks, cutting into my thoughts, and my stare snaps back to her, already shaking my head.

"Mads, seriously I'm fine, it was just a drink." I gesture to the shirt Josh gave me. "Besides I don't exactly feel like going back downstairs after that," I add, my skin still burning from the embarrassment and the feeling of the wet fabric clinging to me like a second skin.

In truth, it took everything in me not to react or show emotion, and if it wasn't for Josh being at my back, then I think I would have broken down and cried in front of everyone.

"I can't believe that bitch threw a drink on you," Maddie snaps, and I can't help but smile, as I flop down onto the end of Josh's bed, with her following suit.

"I can't believe you hit her," I laugh, still surprised by the fact that my best friend threw down like that.

"You're crazy if you think I was letting her get away with that," she tosses back, flicking her hair effortlessly, and I think I surprise us both when I reach out and throw my arms around her neck.

"Thank you, Maddie, you're a great friend," I mutter into her hair, and it's a few seconds before her arms finally return the hug.

When she pulls back she looks a little emotional, but she hides it with a smile. "Do you want to go home and eat ice cream while we watch some old *Grey's Anatomy*?"

My eyes instantly flick to Josh who looks conflicted, and I find myself about to say yes, but then he beats me to it. "She's sleeping here tonight," he says with finality, and Maddie shifts her stare between the two of us now, as if she is finally sensing some of the tension she interrupted when she came up here.

"Okay," she drags out with a weird smile, rising to her feet. "Then I guess Nova and I will have the house to ourselves tonight," she tells me with a wink, as I follow her towards the door.

"Yeah, like that stops you, I can hear you guys through my damn ear defenders," I toss back and she giggles, knowing full well I'm not joking.

"Okay, please get the fuck out," Josh groans, still holding the door open for her, and it only makes me laugh right along with her.

That is until she bids us both goodbye and is gone in an instant, Josh shutting and locking the door behind her, until we are alone again. That's when I realize the tension is still there, and not just that, but an awkwardness too, one we have never had between us before, and I already can't stand it.

"I'm going to get ready for bed," I rush out quickly, moving to snatch up my overnight bag and flooring it into his bathroom, closing and locking the door behind me.

Only then do I breathe fully for the first time since he almost kissed me, and still I almost choke on it. What the fuck am I going to do now? What is the protocol when your fake husband almost kisses you?

Not able to answer either of those questions, I just focus on getting ready for bed, stripping out of his shirt and my jeans, and then discarding my underwear, opting for a quick shower to erase the stench of Brianna's cocktail. I don't take my usual contemplate and cry shower, not wanting to freak Josh out with how long I am taking, and instead just wash my body as fast as I can, and then make quick work of getting dry.

By the time I have gotten dressed and brushed my teeth, I am so filled with anxiety and a nervous tension, that I almost wish I had taken Maddie up on her offer to go downstairs so I could have drank some more. Deciding that I am just being ridiculous, and that the almost kiss meant nothing, I fling open the door to find Josh lingering near his desk, and as soon as I step out of the way he mumbles something about a shower and slips into the bathroom, closing the door behind him before I can even say a word.

Well I guess that answers the question on how we are going to deal with this. Avoidance is key right?

I move towards the bed with the idea of just getting in it and going to sleep only to stop dead in my tracks, taking in some things that definitely weren't here when I went into the bathroom. There is now a fan sitting on the nightstand, an eye mask with matching ear defenders placed neatly on my pillow, and even a stuffed penguin similar to Percy that I have never seen before.

My eyes scan the rest of the room, and I notice the closet door slightly ajar, and when I investigate I find discarded boxes for all the items that indicate they are all brand new. No, there is no way he bought these just for me, yet when I lean down I find a receipt on the floor, and when I read it I can see that he ordered all these items the day after we got married. The morning after I stayed here for the first time and complained about how hard I find it to go to sleep, and my heart beats wildly in my chest. That feeling is only intensified when I flick my eyes around the rest of the closet and they land on a stack of books up high on his shelf.

Even from here I can see they are heavily tabbed, and with my curiosity getting the better of me, I lean up on my tiptoes to grab them. When I glance down at the titles there is no hope left for my beating heart.

What is Autism?
Girls and Autism

The Autistic Mind

Again I could try and convince myself he didn't get these for me, but as I flick open the first one, I find his name neatly scrawled across the first page.

Josh Peters, Age 11

The age he was when we met.

Tears burn in my eyes at the thought of him not only buying these, but also reading them enough to tab them, and when I continue to flick through the first one, the emotion thick at the back of my throat only increases.

Make sure to explain jokes if she doesn't understand them.
Explain exactly what you mean when you talk.
Loves loud music.
Hates getting her clothes wet.
Crunchy foods are best.
Likes to reread books and rewatch movies.
Collects penguins.
Subtitles on when she is watching TV

There is tab after tab marking countless paragraphs, all with his own little notes added next to them, and it leaves me totally and utterly speechless. It's then I hear the sound of the shower cutting off, and I rush to put the books back on the shelf in the same position as before, not wanting to be caught snooping. Then I pull the closet door back closed and rush back over to the bed.

I grab the eye mask and ear defenders and pull back the

sheets, eyeing the wide open space, and it's only then I remember the position we found ourselves in the morning after our wedding night. And it's with that thought in mind that I grab his extra pillows and build a wall between both sides of the bed, until I am satisfied I won't wake up rubbing all over his dick again.

Then I dive into bed with the new penguin, my mind still baffled about what I just saw in his closet. It's not just his attention to detail with the things he bought to make it easier for me to sleep here, but everything else too. He has books on autism, on girls with autism, and he doesn't just have them, he's read them. He's read them and tabbed them, and I can only presume it's for no other reason than to really know and understand *me*.

We have a great friendship, and I nearly threw it all away by letting him kiss me. That's the thought that is swimming in my mind when he opens the bathroom door and steps out, the steam surrounding his bare chest, as my eyes dip down to the V in his torso.

I don't know what's worse.

The fact he almost kissed me, or the fact I wish he would have.

He moves around the bed, not saying a thing about the additions he acquired, as he tosses his laundry in the basket, and then eyes the wall of pillows with a smirk. "Is that so you don't violate your husband with your ass again?" he asks, cocking a brow at me.

"No, it's so you don't come onto my side of the bed again," I snap, feeling grateful that we can just seamlessly fall back into our usual routine.

"I thought we established that both sides of the bed are mine," he purrs, shutting off the light so there is only a soft glow from his lamp, as he climbs in beside me.

Ignoring his manly scent fresh from the shower, I keep my

eyes firmly on the ceiling. "Carry on with your sass, and your wife will send you back to the floor with your sleeping bag."

Josh turns on his side and I can feel his stare on my face from beyond the pillows. "You want me down there on my knees again then all you have to do is ask, Hals, I've told you this."

A smirk threatens to burst across my face as I throw back, "Manwhore."

"Brat," he replies

"Asshole," I toss back.

"Drama queen," he adds, and I swear I can hear the lightness seeping back into his tone.

I shake my head in delight. "Goodnight, Mr. Peters."

He reaches over and turns off the lamp as I pull down my mask before he replies, "Goodnight Mrs. Peters."

And even the deep thump of the bass still blasting below us couldn't stop me from falling asleep happily tonight.

Silence lingers for I'm not sure how long, but it's long enough for either of us to fall asleep, until, "Hallie," he whispers into the dark, and I wish I could pretend I am asleep and ignore him, but I can't.

"Yeah, Joshua?" I whisper back in the blackness of his room, holding my breath for whatever he is about to say.

"I'm sorry I tried to kiss you," he tells me earnestly, his apology like a knife to the gut, and I am grateful he waited until now to say it, so the lack of the light can hide my tears.

I take a few slow, quiet breaths, before I finally force lightness into my tone and ask, "You mean tonight, or that day on the rock when we were kids?"

My answer only makes him laugh, one of my favorite sounds in the entire world, as I feel him shrug, "Both, I guess."

Tears stain my skin as I smile into my pillow, at the fact he is finally admitting trying to kiss me back then, and like an addict unable to quit their much needed fix, I snuggle into the new penguin he bought me and reply gently, "Then I guess I'm sorry for pushing you off that rock."

He doesn't respond, and I wait until I hear his breathing even out before I let myself drift off to sleep, and unsurprisingly it's to dreams of almost kisses, and a boy who has always owned my heart.

∼

When I wake up the next morning, I feel slightly less disoriented than last time, but as I slip off my eye mask, I still have to remind myself where I am. Thankful to have not woken up giving my husband a lap dance, I flick my stare to his side of the bed and find it empty. The time on the clock on his nightstand reads a little after nine, and I can only assume he must have gotten up to grab a coffee or something.

I climb out of bed and head to the bathroom, ear defenders still in place, as I curl my fingers around the door handle, and push inside. Which is where I come face to face with my husband. My very naked and wet husband who has his head thrown back, his eyes closed, and his hand on his very erect cock. And like the slut I am, all I can do is stand and stare as he strokes his fist up and down his length in what is nothing short of a porno.

Water clings to his skin as the shower cascades over him, and he's got one arm leaning on the wall, and the other wrapped around his dick as he thrusts into his fist again and again. I know I should leave, that this is a major invasion of privacy, and though my head is screaming at me to turn around and shut the door, it seems my feet aren't getting the message.

"Oh fuck," he groans, and it's deep and guttural, as he strokes himself hard and fast, his hips rolling towards his hand like he is imagining anything but.

Every part of me is on fire, and I must make some sort of noise, because all of a sudden his eyes fly open, landing on me instantly, as my name rips from his throat in a moan.

"Hallie."

Fuck. *Busted.*

#20
JOSH
BROKEN RULES

Cum explodes from my dick as I lock eyes with the temptress of my fantasies, my hand stroking my still rock hard cock. *Cum.* So much fucking cum. *What the fuck?* It goes everywhere, covering my hand, the glass, and the floor of the fucking shower. *Fuck, why is there so much?* And why is she still standing there just watching me fuck my fucking hand?

"Oh my god, I am so sorry," she finally splutters, pulling the door closed, thankfully with her on the other side of it, and all I can do is pant out my release.

Fuck.

All I wanted to do was escape her. Her scent on my sheets, her body in my bed, the image of her lips almost on mine, all of it driving me crazy all goddamn night long. So when I woke up hard as fuck, I thought it would be best to just sneak out of bed and take care of myself in the shower. With nothing but her candy scent clinging to me, and the image of her standing in my room in her jeans and bra, I was primed and ready to go.

Now here I am, covered in my own cum, and not a clue where to go from here.

I quickly rinse off, before grabbing a towel from the rail and storming back into the room, only to find her dressed and throwing her things in her bag, and I can't stop myself from yelling, "What the hell was that?"

Her entire body freezes, her eyes snapping to mine, only to widen when she realizes I'm only in a towel, and I see the moment she decides she is going to fight back. "What do you mean what the hell was that? What the hell were *you* thinking doing *that*, in *there*, with me right out here," she shouts right back, and if I wasn't so out of my mind because of her right now I might actually find this funny.

"Don't turn this back on me, you're the one who walked in on my private moment, Hals, not the other way around." A blush creeps up her neck as if she is recalling exactly what she saw. "Maybe try knocking next time," I add, in a huff, running my hands through my wet hair, as I try to rein in my temper.

"I didn't knock because I thought you were downstairs," she yells. "I was still wearing my ear defenders so I didn't hear the stupid shower, so maybe lock the door next time." Throwing all the blame at my feet, she continues tossing the rest of her stuff in her bag until she has everything and then closes it.

"I didn't lock the door because I thought I was safe, but I guess I forgot that my wife likes to violate me," I snark, and her entire body freezes, her stare snapping to mine, and I can see she is furious now.

"Oh my god, you're such a fucking asshole," she screams. "I can't believe I actually thought doing this with you would make us friends again. I hope the next time you jerk off that your fucking dick falls off." She moves to slip on her shoes and then picks up her bag.

"You're the only reason I was even jerking off in the first

place!" I shout at her back as she turns to leave, and she whips around to look at me with a humorless laugh.

"Look, I get that being fake married isn't ideal for your dick, but all I am saying is at least wait until I'm gone before you indulge," she grits, clearly misinterpreting the point I was trying to make.

She thinks I was in there jerking off because I can't go out and fuck someone else, because I am married to her. Is she insane? Why would I want anyone else when I could have her? Doesn't she feel this tension between us?

I watch her storm towards the door, ready to rip it open and leave me, and it's like every sane thought inside of my head evaporates, because one minute I am standing there watching her leave, and the next I am on her. My hand slams into the back of the door as she pulls it open, smashing it closed again, and then I am spinning her and pinning her up against it.

"For someone who claims to know me so well, I think you're being pretty fucking blind towards me right now," I tell her, pressing my body against hers and trapping her between me and the door. My cock is already hard again beneath the towel, and I press it against her stomach. "Does this feel like I want someone else? Do you think I was imagining anyone but *my wife* when I was stroking my cock in that shower?"

Pupils completely blown out, Hallie stares up at me in utter shock, and there is a voice deep inside my head that tells me to stop. To retreat back from the position I have her in right now, and not ruin our friendship, but the look on her face urges me on like never before. Her cheeks are pink and flushed, her lips wet from where she has slicked her tongue across them, and her chest pants heavily, her nipples straining against her top, and that's when I hear the other voice in my head.

Fuck it.

My lips are on hers before she can even take her next breath, stealing it right from her parted mouth as I kiss her in a way I have never kissed anyone before, and the second her lips are on mine, it's like everything in the world makes sense. My tongue strokes against hers and I push the bag from her shoulder, grip her hips, and pick her up, slamming her against the door with my mouth still on hers.

My tongue caresses her and I moan at the taste of her, our lips moving in tandem with one another, and I know this one kiss is going to change everything between us. There is no going back to being just friends after this. No, this one kiss is both ruining us and remaking us at the same time.

One of my hands cups her cheek and tips her head back so I can deepen the kiss, and the other stays gripped at her waist, holding her delicious weight against me, as her thighs clench around my torso.

Her hands aren't shy either, as she grips them around my neck and pulls me down into the kiss, like she thinks this will be our only chance to do this and she wants to make it count. And I kiss her like it is the only time, like she might disappear if I stop, pushing her harder into the door and letting her feel every inch of me against her. My cock is screaming for release again, but I can't stop kissing her, pressing it between her spread thighs and swallowing every gasp and moan that slips past her lips onto mine.

I'm not sure how long we stay lost in one another, but when I pull back to catch my breath, her lips are red and swollen, and all I want to do is feel them again. I lean back in, pressing a soft, gentle peck to them now, relishing in the panted breaths she is trying to catch as she stares at me.

"Hallie," I whisper as her legs slide down my body back to the floor, bringing my hands to either side of her head, and she shakes her head in a daze, as my towel drops to the floor.

"You broke rule number one," she whispers back, and I'm

about to laugh, but then she is pushing me away, and leaning down to pick up her bag. "I have to go," she mutters, pulling the door open before I can stop her.

When I rush to go after her, I realize I'm not even dressed yet, and I can't help but yell, "Fuck," as I hear the front door slam downstairs.

Another door opens down the hallway, and Daemon pops his head out, ignoring the fact I am freeballing with my dick out in the hallway, and just simply asks, "What did you do?"

And all I can do is sigh in response, "I kissed my wife."

"Well, fuck," he mutters, looking towards the empty space she just vacated.

Fuck indeed.

#21
HALLIE
RUNAWAY BRIDE

My mind is spinning as I storm from Josh's house and start making my way back home. The walk is only around ten minutes but it feels like it takes forever, and my heart thunders in my chest the entire time. He kissed me. Josh kissed me, and it wasn't just an almost kiss, or the lingering press of our lips like at the wedding. No, it was a full-on take your breath away kiss, and all I could do was run away. Not because it wasn't good, but because it was so good that I could barely even keep myself upright.

Crush is a fickle word, and doesn't even come close to describing how I feel about him, but as his lips pressed against mine, nothing else mattered. Not our title as best friends, or the rings on our fingers. No, the only thing that mattered was how perfectly he fit against me, how his lips felt against mine, and how it was both too much and not enough at the same time. Which is why I wrote the rules in the first place, not because I didn't want to kiss him, but because I knew if I did that I would fall even deeper into the pit that is Josh Peters, and well, now here I am.

I'm not sure what time it is, but as I reach the house and fling open the door, I'm grateful to find my best friend eating breakfast. "I'm in love with your brother," I gasp, letting out the only words that are on my mind, not caring about the repercussions, even as her eyes widen. Not to mention the look on her boyfriend's face as he sits beside her. "Hey, Nova," I add breathlessly, dumping my bag to the floor and closing the distance between us.

"Hey, Hals," Nova cuts in with a smirk, sipping his coffee as he flicks his stare between me and Maddie, waiting for her response. He is more than used to being present for our gossiping sessions lately, though I'm not usually the topic of them.

Ignoring him I focus solely on her, not caring that he can hear me as I add, "And I know I'm your best friend, and this is so breaking girl code, but I'm sorry I can't help it. I'm in love with Josh," I rush out, praying she can forgive me for this, but also knowing I won't be able to stop even if she doesn't.

"I know," she replies gently with a smile, popping another piece of bacon into her mouth, as Nova runs his hand up and down her bare legs.

"You know?" I question, not really sure if she is grasping the situation at hand. "What do you mean you know?"

Maddie puts down her fork and sits up in the chair, leaning towards me. "I mean I know you're in love with Josh," she says, as if it's the most casual thing in the world, and I can't help but feel both shocked and confused.

I have been friends with her just as long as I have been friends with Josh, and I never once thought I made my crush on her brother obvious. In fact, I treated them both the same, and then when he pushed me away, I treated him like I didn't care.

Our communication was solely name calling and snapping at one another. So how the hell did she figure it out?

"Since when?" I ask quietly, wondering when she discovered my biggest secret.

"Since we were nine." Four words and I feel like my whole world has been blown apart, and I can't say anything in return. "Come on, Hals, you didn't exactly hide it. Your eyes lit up every time he walked into a room, you're comfortable around him, and you've never given yourself a chance with anyone else over the years, despite having a lot of interest. It didn't exactly make me a genius to figure it out."

All I can do is stare at her in shock, and just as I open my mouth to respond, the front door swings open and I turn to find Josh stalking towards me. "Mads, Darkmore," he greets with a quick nod, before dipping down and tossing me over his shoulder effortlessly. "Excuse us, we're in the middle of a fight."

He doesn't even hang around to listen to their response, just turns and starts heading towards the stairs. "Put me down you fucking neanderthal," I scream, banging my fists into his back, but all he does is land a hard smack onto my ass, making me yelp.

"Not until you stop acting like a little brat," he tosses back, climbing the stairs with ease as if he isn't supporting any extra weight at all. In fact, he doesn't stop until he reaches my room, and only then does he put me back on my feet, slamming my door behind us. "Now where were we?" he asks, looking both frustrated and amused as he adds, "Ah yes, that's right, I kissed you and then you ran off like a chicken leaving me naked and alone."

I scoff at the mental image, ignoring what it does to my insides as I yell, "Yeah, well you broke the rules." I storm to my set of drawers, ripping open the top one and pulling out the pad that houses our agreement. "There it is in black and green, rule number one: no kissing," I tell him, not sure what I am really angry at. Am I mad because he kissed me? Or am I mad because the kiss was so freaking good?

"Oh my god you are the biggest drama queen I have ever met in my entire life," he snaps, moving to snatch the pad away from me and tossing it to the ground

"And you're the biggest asshole I've ever met in my entire life," I seethe, panting heavily, as his hands find my waist again and he pulls me up against him. "And why did you even kiss me, anyway?" I add, hating that my voice, though still shouting, is starting to lose its edge of anger.

"Because you're mine," he spits, his voice hoarse and almost breaking.

"I'm not yours!" I shriek back, hating how good those three words just sounded coming from his mouth. "This is fake, remember, none of this is real."

This time when he pulls me against him, I can feel the long, hard outline of his cock pressing into my stomach, as he brings his left hand up to curl around my neck. The other reaches down and entangles with my left hand, as his thumb finds the rings there. "These rings," he starts, flicking my wedding and engagement bands. "These rings mean you are mine, fake or not, in the eyes of the law you belong to me," he murmurs, dropping his forehead to mine, as his other hand gently squeezes my throat, until I can feel the bite of his own wedding band. "And feel this ring? *Fuck*, this ring means I belong to you, Hallie. It means you own me, so *that* is why I kissed you."

My heart is pounding out of my chest, every hair on my body standing on end as each of his words send me out into orbit with no way of ever returning. "But what about rule number one," I can't help but breathe, and all he does is smile.

"Fuck the rules, Tink." Then his mouth is on mine, robbing

me of any response, and I am both his wife, and a slut for the boy who is my crush, so who am I to not kiss him back?

Our mouths collide as my body ignites. He's kissing me, Josh Peters, my best friend, my husband, is kissing me, and just like that first kiss back in his bedroom, it's everything I need and more. His mouth is insistent, urgent, yet his lips are soft and smooth as they give me something I have been craving for years. He might be an asshole most of the time, and this might even be fake, but right now he's kissing me like he might cease to exist without the taste of my lips against his. Everything else around us melts away, and there is no fake marriage, no deal with his father, or no friendship to ruin. It's just me and him, and us.

Without tearing us apart, he pushes me until the back of my legs hit the bed and then I am falling, with him still on me, until my back hits the mattress and the kiss never falters. I can feel him everywhere, all at once, and it's too much, yet will never ever be enough.

"Fuck, Hallie," he growls, trailing his mouth down my jaw and onto my neck, as I squirm beneath him, searching for some much needed friction. "You taste so fucking good," he adds, coming back up and slamming his lips on mine.

I moan into his mouth, not caring if I run out of air, just not wanting this moment right here to end.

Knock. Knock.

"Everything okay in there guys," Maddie asks through the door, and Josh groans.

"Fuck off, I'm talking to my wife," he shouts back, and I can't help but laugh, as he comes back again, kissing and fucking my mouth with his tongue like I am the best thing he has ever tasted. Then his teeth sink into my lip, biting down hard until I yelp, like some sort of out of control animal.

Then he pulls back and looks at me in a way I have never seen, like he is seeing me differently, seeing us differently, and for the first time ever I feel hope that we could be something more.

"That was for running away from me, don't do it again, Hals, you're mine now," he tells me, pressing another gentle kiss to my mouth, making me swoon, before a coldness hits me as he pulls his body off of me and stands.

Sitting up on my elbows, my legs still spread wide to accommodate him, I pant, "Where the hell are you going?"

His eyes trail over every inch of my body as he bites his lip and shakes his head. "I've got practice and I'm already late."

I immediately sit up and glare at him. "You have practice? Then what the hell are you doing here?"

Josh bends down, cupping my cheeks and kissing me one last time. "I'm making sure my girl knows who she belongs to." And then with that, he is pulling back and tossing me a wink. "See you later, Mrs. Peters."

He saunters to the door, throwing it open, only to reveal Maddie on the other side, who looks between the two of us and states, "Nova already left."

Josh laughs, "As if I was going to go over there with that prick anyway." Then he is gone down the hall, and I wait until I hear the sound of the front door slamming, until I look my best friend in the eye.

"Ice cream and *Grey's*?" she asks, and I'm already nodding.

"Ice cream and *Grey's*," I agree, shoving off my bed and following her downstairs.

Which is how I find myself spending the morning holed up on the sofa with *McDreamy* and telling my best friend everything that has happened.

"Oh my god, I do not need to know that you saw my brother's penis," Maddie groans, fake gagging, as she discards the ice cream she was eating.

"You said you wanted the whole story," I point out with a shrug, and she shakes her head.

"Yeah, well now I don't want to hear another word, you guys are fucking gross."

"Oh please, like I don't hear Nova ringing your bell multiple times a night," I toss back, holding my hand up towards her. "High five by the way."

Her face is a picture of modesty, before she smirks and smacks her palm against mine. You should always high five your friend about great dick, it's good manners.

Then after a couple of hours of TV and gossiping, we decide to get our homework out of the way considering we will be busy tomorrow with another Sunday dinner spent at her parents, and by the time we have done that I am beyond starving. My stomach is growling for attention, reminding me I have only consumed ice cream so far today.

"Want me to make us some lunch?" Maddie offers, clearing away her books, but I am already shaking my head.

"No, I know exactly what I want, and nothing else will do," I tell her, tossing my own books into my bag and shoving it under the table as I stand and stretch.

"You know my brother's dick isn't on the menu right?" Maddie jokes far too easily, and I can feel the blush from the inside out.

"No you bitch, I meant a burger from this diner Josh takes me to," I recall, remembering the mouthwatering cheeseburger, fries, and milkshake I had the night he taught the kids at the community center.

We've been back a couple of times together and I have quickly become obsessed. Finding a new staple to add to my rotation of foods, and right now it's the only thing I want to eat.

"What diner?" Maddie asks, and when I tell her the name she still looks equally confused. "Oh, I've never been there before, but it sounds good, let me just go and throw some shoes on."

We both quickly get ready to leave, and then take the scenic route by the lake at the back of our house to get into town. It's a little chilly, but the fresh air is distracting me from checking my phone to see if Josh has messaged me. I'm not really sure where we stand after everything that happened this morning. I know he said I'm his, but I don't exactly know what that means. I mean, if we are being technical then my heart has always been his, and the ring on my finger only increases that, but it still doesn't mean I know where we truly stand.

By the time we make it to the diner, Maddie has complained at least a hundred times about how cold it is, but I barely even feel it. When we push inside, I'm glad to find it's not too busy, and I'm not surprised to spy two familiar faces as we head towards the counter to ask for a table.

"Hallie," Penelope shouts, spotting me instantly and turning her stool towards me in greeting, offering up her hand for a high five.

I have to hand it to her, we have only spent a few hours together over the last couple of weeks, and she caught on quickly to the fact that I don't exactly like being touched. Which, when you are helping teach a class of kids, is usually something that would be hard to convey. A lot of the little boys like to hug my waist when they score a goal, which I force myself to accept, yet the little girl noticed my discomfort and figured out why.

"Hey Penelope, how are you?" I ask, smacking my palm to hers, and she smiles holding up a book, as she rolls her eyes.

"My mom is making me read this," she claims, just as her mom comes from the kitchen.

"Reading makes you smart," she tells her, offering me a smile. "Hey, Hallie, good to see you."

"Hey Callia, good to see you too" I greet her, before focusing back on her daughter. "Your mom is right, reading is good for the soul, I love to read."

Penelope's eyes light up at my statement. "You do?"

"Of course, I read all the time, it's so much fun, you get to live so many lives in the pages of books," I tell her, and when I flick my eyes to her mom she mouths a thank you.

"Okay, well maybe this book isn't totally boring," she quickly switches up, before her gaze moves to Maddie. "Who's this?" she asks, cocking her eyebrows in the exact same way as my best friend, and I swear it's like looking at a miniature version of her.

"This is my best friend, Madeline, she's Josh's sister," I explain, and Penelope's eyes widen, yet Callia is staring at her in complete shock, though I'm not sure why. "Maddie, this is Penelope and her mom Callia, Josh teaches her at the center."

Like the perfectly trained daughter she is, Maddie holds out her hand for Penelope to shake. "It's nice to meet you Penelope, and you too Callia." She flicks her stare between the two, and Callia quickly snaps out her daze and nods at her with a smile, as Maddie adds, "And what's this about Josh teaching a class at the center?"

Crap.

It's only now that I remember that Josh didn't tell anyone about the class, yet before I can say anything, Penelope beats me to it. "Josh teaches me to play hockey, he's so much fun, he shows us tricks and explains the rules, it's awesome," Penny gushes, before moving her stare to me. "And Hallie has been teaching us how to beat Josh, that's even more awesome."

Pride curls in my gut at the high praise coming from the girl, and I quickly snap my eyes to Maddie and add, "I'll explain later." All she does is nod as, thankfully, Callia comes to the rescue.

"Do you want your usual, Hallie?" she asks, knowing I've

eaten the exact same thing every time I have come here, and I nod.

"What's your usual?" Maddie asks, and when I tell her she smiles. "Make that two of her usual please," she says to Callia with a smile.

"Great, why don't you find a seat and I'll bring it over," she tells us, a wary look in her eyes that I have never seen before, and I almost want to ask if she's okay.

"Or you can sit with me?" Pen says with a smile that says she would love nothing more, and before I can even look at Maddie to ask her, she is already pulling out a chair beside the little girl, making her smile even wider.

"Tell me about this book then?" Maddie asks, and from the gleam in Penelope's eyes, I know she is feeling the same thing I did when Madeline Peters first showed an interest in me, and all I can do is take the other stool and watch them in awe as a new friendship is born.

Callia doesn't take long to bring out our food, ensuring her daughter has some lunch too, but I find that she lingers a lot, watching us interact with Penelope like she thinks we might run off with her. Yet I suppose I would be the same if I had a daughter. You can never be too careful who you let into your life, so I can't really blame her.

We end up sitting there for over an hour, Maddie leaving Penelope starry-eyed as she talks about the fairy dollhouse she had growing up, as she switches her attention between the girl and her phone. "I still have it in my room at my parents' house, you can have it if you like, it's just there gathering dust."

Penelope's eyes widen, as her jaw drops. "Oh my god, are you serious? I've never had a fairy dollhouse before."

In the time we have spent together I have realized that Callia and Penelope don't have a lot of stuff, hell the book she has now discarded is clearly second hand, and though Penny is always dressed immaculately, Callia isn't. It doesn't take a genius to realize that anything her mom gets goes straight to her, and she is clearly killing it at being the best single mom she can be, but everyone still needs help sometimes.

"No, we can't accept that," Callia cuts in from the register, having overheard their conversation. "Thank you, but that's far too much."

Penelope's face drops and I can tell that she must know how hard her mom works for her, yet she's still a kid who just wants a dollhouse.

"Honestly, it's no big deal, I've been meaning to get rid of it for a while, and what better way than to give it to someone who can breathe some magic back into it," Maddie is quick to say. "I can even drop it off for you, it would be my pleasure," she insists with a smile, and just like with everyone, her charm does the trick.

"Please, Mom, pretty please," Penelope pleads, and I see the moment her mom caves.

"Okay," Callia sighs, and the little girl practically throws herself into Maddie's lap with tears in her eyes as she adds, "Thank you, Maddie."

"No thanks necessary," she tells her, arms round Penelope who is still half in her lap, squeezing the life out of her, which is how Nova finds us.

"Should I be concerned that I now have to share you with a child?" Nova asks with a smile, as he comes up behind us and drops a kiss to Maddie's head.

Penelope instantly sits up, eyes locking onto him as she blurts, "Wow, you're pretty."

Nova laughs, instantly declaring, "Hey kid, I like you already."

I turn to find not only him, but Alexander and Archer too, and hope surges inside of me as I flick my gaze past them but come up empty, and I can't help but ask, "What are you guys doing here?"

Nova eyes me with confusion given my tone, but still replies, "Maddie texted and said you guys were here, so we came for a late lunch."

Maddie turns and accepts another kiss from him, before turning to Penelope. "Pen, this is my boyfriend Nova Darkmore, and his friends Archer Gray and Alexander Reign." For some reason she blushes as she says Alexander's name, and he pointedly looks anywhere but at her, as she adds, "They play on the same hockey team as my brother." I'm sure her introductions are more for Callia than her daughter, who is eyeing all the boys with wonder.

"You guys know, Josh?" Penelope asks excitedly.

"Know him?" Archer jumps in like a jacked-up Golden Retriever. "Peters and I go way back," he lies boldly, making me smile. "I even went to his wedding."

Of course Penelope doesn't detect his bullshit as she gasps, "Wow, you must be best friends."

Archer grins, winking at me. "Oh, the bestest."

I lean over and smack the back of his head like I have seen his so-called bestie do before I ask, "And where is my husband?"

At my question his smile instantly drops, as he looks between his friends, and it's only then I notice there is a bruise on the corner of his left eye. All three boys look like they have a secret, but it's Nova that finally replies, "Josh is dealing with something, I'm sure he'll call you later."

With that, the three of them grab menus without another word, moving over to a booth so they can order some food, while Maddie bids a goodbye to Penelope so she can join her boyfriend. Meanwhile I am frozen to the spot, hands shaking as I pull out my phone in a panic.

> Hallie : Hey everything okay?

I might not be sure where we stand, but despite everything that happened between us this morning, he is still my friend first. His reply is almost instant.

> Peter Pan : No
>
> Peter Pan : Daemon isn't having a good day. I need to stay with him

Unease settles deep in my stomach, both with worry for his friend and for what this means for us. I have gotten to know Daemon a little better since Josh and I decided to do this, yet he's like an onion, you peel back one layer just to find another. I have barely yet been able to peel back one. Yet I know Josh has dug his way a lot deeper than I have with him over the last few years, so if anyone can help him with whatever he has going on, it's him.

> Peter Pan : You're still my girl, Tink

Butterflies attack my stomach as my heart pounds in my chest at the five simple words written on my phone screen.

> Hallie : Just take care of your friend, don't worry about me
>
> Peter Pan : You're mine to worry about remember
>
> Hallie : Psycho
>
> Peter Pan : Brat

> Hallie : Asshole

> Peter Pan : Mine

I don't respond, not really sure of what to say, yet I still keep my phone in my hand for almost the rest of the day. I joined Maddie and the guys while they enjoyed lunch, all of them conveniently not mentioning anything about practice. Then head home alone while Maddie goes off with Nova, with only one thought in my mind.

What the hell happened at that practice?

#22
JOSH
POWER MOVES

Spending the night trying to sleep on Daemon's floor to make sure he didn't do anything stupid wasn't exactly on my bucket list for last night, but he left me with no other choice. I was late for practice yesterday, and after Coach chewed me out I spent the whole time there thinking about getting back to Hallie and picking up where we left off. Yet the moment we left the ice and found an unwanted visitor waiting for my best friend, I just knew his breakdown was inevitable. If there's one thing I have learned about him in the last three years, it's that if he could, he would let the darkness win. Which is why there was no way I was leaving him alone.

Daemon didn't have the best childhood. In fact, from the few things I have managed to pry out of him, it sounds like he had it really rough. Mix that with the scars scattered across his body–that I have learnt to not ask about and pretend aren't there–well, let's just say, I get why he is the way that he is. So the moment I spied his older brother, Jasper, who I have seen only once before, lingering by the stands, I knew that I would have to fight against the darkness to keep my best friend.

After a slight altercation in the locker room, which I managed efficiently enough, I hauled him back to the house and locked us both away in his room, only coming out for food and nothing else. I knew if I left him to go back to Hallie, then Daemon would just go out and hunt for a vice that would only ruin him. So instead, I grabbed us a bottle of whiskey, tossed him his sketchbook, and then sat on his floor until his black became a little more gray.

By the time the sun came up this morning, I could tell he was back to his usual self, and though he didn't say it, he was grateful for my presence. We had a quiet breakfast together, and when I felt comfortable enough to leave him alone, it was almost time for the weekly dinner with my parents, which means I haven't seen Hallie since I kissed her. Which is how I find myself idling by the curb to pick her up before heading over to their house.

I'm not sure why I feel nervous. I mean, this is Hallie we are talking about, we've been friends forever. Except we aren't friends right now, not really, especially not after I kissed her. Fuck, why the hell did I kiss her?

Just as that thought resonates, she steps out of the house, looking as stunning as always, and every other thought in my mind disappears as I step out of the car to greet her. "Well, Mrs. Peters, don't you look beautiful today."

Her eyes scan me from head to toe in wonder before she smirks. "I wish I could say the same, Joshua, but you look like shit," she tells me, reaching the car and waiting for me to open the door for her.

"Always a pleasure to converse with you, Tink," I laugh, opening the door and then stepping aside to let her in as I add,

"Besides, I think I look pretty good considering I slept on the floor all night."

She brushes past me, her sweet candy scent lingering all around me as she muses, "You mean Daemon didn't invite you to share his bed? What a shame, I bet that could have been a lot of fun." The look in her eye is nothing short of flirtatious, as I slam the door and round the car, climbing inside.

"Contrary to popular belief, Hals, the only person who likes to violate me in bed is you," I tell her, pulling on my seatbelt.

"Oh you have no idea," she mutters under her breath, before she turns to me and asks, "How is Daemon? Is there anything I can do to help?"

If she wasn't already one of my favorite people on the planet then this would do it, because of the selfless way she cares about other people. Hell, we are only in this situation right now because of how much she cares about Maddie and I, and that includes putting up with the bullshit dinner we are on our way to right now.

"Hallie, I appreciate you for saying that, but unfortunately there isn't anyone who can truly help Daemon at the moment, not yet anyway." I don't voice out loud that I'm not sure that anyone will ever be able to help him, because that thought is just too sad.

By the time we make it to my parents' house, I have forgotten the woes of my friend's childhood, and am faced with the ones of my own. I park my car in its usual spot, gripping the wheel in frustration at having to even be here, as Hallie rubs her hand on my shoulder.

"Come on, twenty-two, we will be in and out before you even know it." She pats my arm, and then climbs from the car before I can even respond, forcing me to do the same.

Meeting me on the other side, she holds out her hand for me to take, and I do, pulling her into my side and tugging on my tie, as I prepare for the usual onslaught of comments from my father. Yet when I look at my wife, all the stress and anger building up inside of me dissipates. My heart stops thundering in my chest, and instead, all I see is her.

"In and out before I know it," I agree, taking a deep breath to settle myself, before I turn to her and add, "Just one more thing first." Then I am on her, pushing her up against the side of my car, and capturing her mouth with mine, her gasp allowing me to slip my tongue past her lips instantly.

Our mouths move in tandem with one another, our kiss like a volcano finally getting to erupt, as I pour myself into her. I kiss her like I'm starving, and she kisses me back the same, rolling her body against mine, and I can feel my dick hardening in my pants, as she moans onto my lips. My hands roam up and down her curves, wishing that I could just take her here and now, as I let my fingers slip between us and trail up her inner thigh.

"Josh," she gasps, making my dick go from half-mast to fully stiff in a second, just as my fingers graze against her panties, finding them already damp.

Fuck.

I rub tiny circles against the fabric, leaving her panting and moaning into my mouth, as I swallow every delicious sound that slips past her lips until her body is shaking. Only then do I let my fingers slip into the fabric and graze against her bare pussy, relishing in how soaked she is for me.

"Fuck, Tink, who knew you'd be such a good girl for your husband," I muse, slowing down my movements until she is trying to chase more friction with her hips. "Ah, ah, we are going to be late for dinner if I let you come." I pull my hand away from her, and the groan she lets out is ungodly.

"And you are going to be punched in the dick if you don't," she whines, looking up at me with her pupils completely blown out in a daze, and all I can do is smile.

She has never looked better, and I can't wait to get her home and lay her out like my own personal feast, and it's with that thought in mind that I bring my wet fingers up to my mouth and lick them clean. "Mmm, tastes like mine."

"You're such an asshole," she snaps, pushing me away and fixing her skirt, before moving to storm around the car and up to the house.

I quickly catch up with her, pulling her hand back into mine. "And yet for some reason you married me, sounds like you're the problem," I toss back similar words to which she once said to me, and her eyes snap to mine, a mixture of lust and anger swirling in them.

"God I hate you, Joshua Peters."

"No you don't, Hallie Rose Peters."

We make our way into the house, and are guided to the table where we find my mother, father, grandmother, and sister, all sitting in an unbearable silence. I used to try and keep the flow of conversation going, but I have found that in recent weeks I have no desire to be part of their bullshit show anymore.

"Josh, darling, there you are," my mother coos, always trying to keep the charade of our family life together. "I hope you're hungry."

My eyes stray only to my wife as I respond, "Oh I am starving." Making my new wife blush, and all I can think about is seeing the rest of her body stained that color.

"Good, then let's eat," my father booms, and I swear that not even he can ruin my mood today.

The dinner is nice enough, and now that they are catering to Hallie's food preferences, I have no need to make another scene. It's like Hallie said, we just need to get in, get it over with, and then get out.

Simple.

Or it would be if my father wasn't Mayor Hugo Peters. He is in the middle of prattling on about some 'lesser' man in his office, when he remarks, "Any man that gets on his knees for a woman is pathetic in my eyes." His statement isn't all that unusual, but it's the tone of his voice that grabs my attention, and when I move my stare to his, I find him watching me with a smirk. A smirk that tells me he knows something, and it's only when his stare flickers over to Hallie, who is totally oblivious, that the hairs on the back of my neck rise up, as he adds, "I saw an interesting piece of television the other day."

My mind flicks back to the day we were in his office, and I instantly know what he thinks he saw, and even though it wasn't real, anger courses through my veins all the same. "I'd be careful about what comes out of your mouth next," I warn, only making his grin wider, and I can feel every defense against him snapping into place.

Hallie freezes beside me, only now starting to sense some tension in the room, and I can feel my sister's stare burning into the side of my face, but I don't look at either of them, keeping my focus solely on the man who raised me. There is a mixture of disgust, and what he thinks is pride, as he glares at me, but I don't back down, not when it comes to this, not when it comes to her.

"You forget how good I am at keeping secrets, Joshua, especially when it comes to family." He raises his glass towards us at his words, and from the corner of my eye I see my mother flinch, yet another person damaged by his misdeeds.

"I'm not sure banging every woman with a pulse in your office counts as a skill, father, but hey, what do I know about politics," I toss back, ignoring my mother's gasp, and focusing solely on him.

I even ignore Hallie as she slides her hand onto my thigh in an attempt to ground me, but it's no use, not with him. He's an expert at finding my weak spot and exploiting it, and clearly having her by my side doesn't make a difference.

"Based on your recent choices, I'd say you know more about politics than I thought," my father adds, sipping his drink slowly and eying me over the top of the glass. "In fact, I'd be happy to bring you down to the office and show you where we both know you are going to end up."

I'm on my feet so fast that the back of my chair hits the floor, and the table between us shakes, but before I can explode at him, Hallie is right there beating me to it. "Oh my god, I can't believe the time, I'm so sorry but we promised my dad that we would attend a small business function at my parents' house, so we must be going."

My chest is heaving up and down as years of wrath and resentment threaten to burst out of me, but there she is standing at my side and sliding her hand into mine. She stares at my father with a polite but firm smile, and it will only take one word. One wrong word aimed towards her and I will not be responsible for my actions.

Thankfully, whatever my father sees on her face, or mine, is enough to have him responding, "Best listen to your wife and run along, boy."

I continue to stare him down until Hallie pulls on my arm, and like a magnet my body moves towards hers, as she bids everyone at the table a goodbye and pulls me from the room. She doesn't stop until we get outside, and it's then I can hear her saying my name, snapping it really, her face getting up in mine to try and bring me back down, but it's no use. I'm too far gone right now, too wrapped up in my fury to even see straight. All I can do is get her in the car and start driving, and I don't say a word, not until we are back at her house, and in her room.

My breathing is still ragged as I storm back and forth in front of her bedroom door as she leans her back against it. She looks as if she isn't sure whether I will stay or go, whether she will stay or go, and all I can do is snap, "I fucking hate him, Hallie, I hate him so fucking much." She doesn't flinch, she has heard this particular rant many times over the years, so I'm sure she is used to it.

"He's an asshole, but we know this, so why are you letting him get to you?" she asks gently, and just the sound of her voice helps me breathe again.

"Because no matter what I say or what I do, he always has the power, he's always one step ahead, and I know Lincoln has said that he has found some stuff, but will it be enough? Will it ever be enough?"

Lincoln called me on Friday and said he wants to see me next week, when I'm free to go through what he has found, and at first I was excited. Finally, *finally* I would have something to begin my father's downfall, but does it even matter? My father has survived every single thing that has ever been thrown at him, including a scandalous affair, so why will this be any different?

"For once I just want to feel like I have the power. I hate feeling like everything is just out of control." I know my tone is harsh, that she doesn't deserve my outburst, but it seems like she is the only person willing to see the real me and stick around for it.

That point is only proven when she moves off the back of the door and closes the distance between us, forcing me to a stop, and pulling my face down towards her. "Then tell me what I can do to help you feel in control," she pleads, her eyes searching mine, and almost instantly she has me held captive in her stare. "Tell me what to do and I'll do it, Joshua. I'll do anything for you."

Her words aren't meant to be provocative, but the second they leave her mouth it's like my entire body comes alive. My attraction for her is heightened, as the lust and anger battle inside of me. "Don't say shit like that to me," I warn, knowing I'm not in the right frame of mind to be with her right now. No, right now I would only take what I need for myself, and she doesn't deserve that.

Yet of course she pushes me, just like always. "Why? Because it's true? You know whatever you ask of me, I'll do. Hell, I'm here right now as your wife and all you had to do was ask." She throws up the hand that houses my ring, and it's like a bull seeing red as something inside of me snaps.

"On your knees," I command her coolly, taking a step back and shrugging out of my suit jacket before tossing it aside. She doesn't move, not right away, yet I hear her sharp intake of breath as I add, "Remember when you said you would get on your knees if I asked," I remind her, removing the cufflinks from my shirt, and rolling up my sleeves. "Well, now I'm asking you, Hallie. Get. On. Your. Knees."

I move towards her chair in the corner, undoing my shirt as I go, until my chest is completely on display. Only then do I turn towards her and lower myself into the seat. She still hasn't moved, but once I am sitting, I see her prepare herself to walk towards me, and when she goes to move, I lift up my hand, halting her in her tracks and then point to the floor. "Ah ah, on your knees, Tink, crawl to me like a good little wife."

#23
JOSH
CRAWL COMMANDS

My command hangs in the air around us, coated in anticipation, yet our eyes never break away from one another. I watch her as she absorbs my demands, and turns the words over in that pretty little head of hers, never once letting her mask slip. *What is she thinking?* No doubt she is contemplating the pros and cons of submitting to me, making a list in her head of all the reasons why she shouldn't do this, and the one reason she should.

Because she's mine.

"What's the matter, Tink, are you scared?" I taunt, knowing that just as easily as she pushes me, I can also push her in return.

"I'm not scared," she is quick to gasp out, barely saying anything at all, yet telling me everything all the same. She *is* scared. Not because she doesn't want this, but because she does.

All the signs are there, I see the rapid rise and fall of her chest, spy the glazed look in her eyes that I now know means she is turned on, all the way down to the fidgeting of her hands. She wants to give me the power, she wants me to have the control, and who am I to deny my wife anything?

Tell me what to do and I'll do it, Joshua, I'll do anything for you.

"Then lose the dress, and get on your knees, Hallie, I won't ask again."

As if on instinct, her hands reach down to the hem of her dress and slowly start to pull it up, inch by delicious inch, revealing her smooth and silky skin. I spy a familiar peak of black lace as the dress comes up over her hips, only to be followed by a matching bra as she pulls the fabric off over her head. My eyes scan every inch of her, as my hands grip the arms of the chair so tight that my knuckles turn white. For a moment I think I have never seen anything better, but then she lowers herself down, her knees hitting the floor first, and then her hands coming out in front of her until she is on all fours.

Fuck, she is a goddess.

I thought she might refuse me, or at least hesitate long enough to tell me to go fuck myself, but watching her drop into position has to be the best thing I have ever seen in my life. My cock is rock hard, straining against my pants, as she starts to crawl towards me, her hips swaying with every move. Her bedroom is silent except for the pounding in my ears, as our eyes watch one another in complete and utter fascination.

"Is this what you want?" she asks boldly, licking her lips as she moves towards me, and I have to blink a couple of times to process the powerful image before me.

Hallie Rose Sanders is on her knees for me.

No, Hallie Rose *Peters* is on her knees for me.

Fuck, I'm a lucky guy.

"No," I hiss, gripping the chair even tighter. "This isn't what I want, it's what I need" I tell her, watching as she gets closer and closer. My entire body is pining for her touch, just so desperate for her to have her hands on me that I almost can't get out my next words. Especially when she finally reaches me and kneels at my feet, her eyes looking up at mine, patiently awaiting her next command. "Undo my pants and take out my cock." My voice is low and lethal, yet she obeys me instantly.

Her hands shake slightly, as she reaches out and slowly begins to unbuckle my belt while I watch her every move. Her fingers are meticulous in the way they work, removing my belt first, and then slowly unzipping my pants, until she can reach inside and feel the length of me. Her eyes widen when she realizes how hard I am for her, my chest already heaving in breaths as I await the feel of her skin on mine, but she doesn't hesitate. She wraps her hand around the base of my cock, as I lift slightly, helping her with pulling down my pants and boxers.

When my cock is finally free, she stares at it for a moment and then looks at me expectantly, and it's only then that I realize she is into this. This game I've created, she wants it, maybe even needs it in the same way I do, and I am more than happy to play with her.

"Now spit on it," I instruct, relishing the way her eyes snap from my cock to me.

"What?" she splutters, only making me harder, knowing that no one has ever pushed her this way before.

"You heard me, *wife*, spit on my cock and get it nice and wet." I'm surprised by how quick she is to follow my demands, as she leans forward, opens her mouth, and spits on the head of my cock, using her hand to stroke the salvia up and down my length until I hiss. Fuck, just her hand feels good, I can't imagine what her mouth or pussy is going to feel like. "Now suck me into that pretty mouth, Hallie."

Her smirk is devilish, as this game of demands comes to a head, and I almost come on the spot when she purrs back, "Yes, Mr. Peters."

Oh fuck.

I watch as her mouth closes around my crown, my fingers almost breaking the arms of the chair as I force myself not to rush her. I'm sure she can feel my cock thickening against her tongue, as her warm, wet mouth sucks me inside. Never have I wanted to plunge my dick deeper into someone's throat before, but the tentative way she sucks on me is so unbelievably inviting that I can't stop her.

She pulls back, letting her tongue flick across my head in barely there licks that do nothing but make me feel more out of control, and it's only then I finally snap, forcing one of my hands to grip her chin. "Don't tease me, baby, not when I am already so desperate for you."

My words seem to delight her as the hand at the base of my cock flexes as she asks, "You're desperate for me?" She pairs her words with a slow stroke of my cock that leaves me ready to beg for more.

All I can do as she looks up at me with a surprised yet aroused smile on her face is nod. "Do you have any idea what you do to me, Hallie? What it feels like to see my ring on your finger as it's wrapped around my cock. I'm so beyond desperate for you that I can't even put it into words."

Then before she can respond I roll my hips into her hand, mesmerized by the way the diamond I put there sparkles as it moves on me. As if she can read my mind, she pushes her fingers further around my cock, ensuring I can see both rings, as she strokes me up and down, only then does she lower her mouth around me. Her teeth scrape against my underside as her tongue swirls around me like I am her own personal ring pop, and I throw my head back and groan.

Her mouth feels unreal, and the thought that it belongs to me just does something that I can't explain. She's mine. *My wife.*

My head snaps back down and I watch as she eagerly bobs up and down my cock, making my balls draw up in response.

Slowly I roll my hips again, teasing us both as she works me with both her hand and mouth. My eyes follow that damn ring as she works me over, and I can't help but thrust harder into her mouth, as her eyes look at me in wonder.

"You can take more of me," I tell her, sitting up in the chair and pushing my hands into her hair to guide her. "Come on, baby, relax that throat and let me all the way in." She doesn't look convinced yet still follows my instructions, as she hollows out her cheeks and begins taking more of me into her mouth. I watch as she slowly swallows every inch of my cock, both of us moaning in unison as I hit the back of her throat. "That's it, baby you feel so fucking good, this hot little mouth was fucking made to take my dick."

Slowly I roll my hips again, then again, thrusting into her mouth over and over, getting faster with every snap of my hips. I hit the back of her throat once more and she moans again, her tongue caressing my shaft as I begin to fuck her mouth roughly. Spit coats my dick as she chokes around my length, the vibrations of her moans going straight to my balls as I feel them drawing up.

"Yes, Hallie, fuck yes," I praise, pushing her back and standing to my full height so I can plunge myself deeper. She doesn't falter, taking my movements with ease, and keeping her eyes on mine. "Look at you, look how fucking perfect you look, Mrs. Peters, sucking your husband's cock so fucking good."

I can see her entire body flush under the praise, and I can't wait to taste every inch of her. My thrusts are punishing now as I pound into her mouth, my movements becoming sloppy, as I can feel my release starting to dance up my spine.

"I'm going to fill this pretty little mouth with my cum," I tell her, and she nods her head between my hands, as I continue to fuck her, taking every slam of my hips like no one ever has before. "Yes, Tink, just like that," I groan, watching as her head bobs back and forth on my cock, and when I hit the back of her throat once more and my eyes lock on that damn ring, I am fucking gone.

I explode in her mouth, spurting hot, long ropes of cum down her throat until I can barely fucking stand, and like the good little wife she is, she swallows me down without being asked.

When she pulls back, I can see her mask slamming back into place, like she wants to pretend she didn't just fucking ruin me for anyone else sucking my dick ever again, and I won't allow it. I drop to my knees, with cum still leaking from my cock, and slam my lips to her, tasting the remnants of myself on her tongue, as I plunge my own into her mouth, kissing her with force. She kisses me back, hands coming around my neck and fisting in the bottom of my hair, until I am groaning and panting against her.

"Do you have any idea how fucking sexy it is to kiss you and taste my fucking cum on your sinful little tongue?" I ask, kissing her again and sucking her tongue into my mouth until there isn't a trace of me left. She moans between my lips and I swallow the sound, wanting more, needing more, as I pull back and slip my hand down into the lace of her panties.

Her pussy is soaked and I groan against her as my finger finds her clit. "Did you get wet sucking my cock, baby?" I ask, teasing her pussy with the pad of my finger, my throat aching for another taste of her. One lick of my finger before dinner was nowhere near enough to satiate my need for her.

"Joshua," she gasps, moving her hands to my shoulders and clinging to me as her body begins to shake.

"That's it, say my name, Tink," I tease, as I bring my free hand up to curl around her neck, holding her in place against me, as my fingers massage her clit.

"You're such an asshole," she moans, bringing her lips back to mine and I smile against them.

"If I'm such an asshole, why are you about to come all over my fingers?" I ask, pushing my hand down so I can slide a finger inside of her, making her breathless in my arms, as my thumb moves to her clit. "Look at you, turning into such a pretty little mess for me." I drag my mouth down her jaw, kissing and sucking the skin of her neck until I can reach her ear. "I can't wait to clean you up," I add in a whisper, fucking her with my finger, and pretending not to notice how delicious and tight she feels.

"Fuck, Josh, I'm going to..." her words trail off into a scream as her pussy constricts around my fingers, squeezing me in way that has my freshly sucked cock twitching.

"You're so fucking pretty when you come for me," I tell her, coaxing her through her release, as her body trembles, and her pussy soaks my hand in her cum. Only when she is done screaming do I pull my hand back and plunge it into her mouth, pressing down on her tongue. "Taste yourself, baby, I want you to remember exactly what it tastes like when I make you come for me."

Then I reach down, grip her hips in my hands, and pull us both to our feet, picking her body up against mine until she wraps her legs around me. Walking us towards the bed, I toss her into the center of the mattress, crawling up between her legs, and ripping the panties from her body.

"Lose the bra," I tell her, and she scrambles to do so, as I dive in and take one long lick of her sweet little cunt. "Now play with those perfect tits while I make you come on my tongue," I command, lifting her legs so they are over my shoulder, until her pussy is pressed against my face.

"Josh, please," she begs, and when I cock a brow at her she groans.

"Please what, Mrs. Peters?" I ask, teasing her lower lips with a flick of my tongue, reveling in the way she presses her hips down in search of friction.

"Please taste my pussy, Mr. Peters," she breathes, tweaking her hard nipples, her body writhing against the bed already, and once again my hand locks in on that goddamn ring.

Oh, I am so well and truly, fucked.

#24
HALLIE

SWEET SLEEPOVERS

Josh's thumb trails up and down both sides of my pussy, spreading the wetness already there, and my body reacts as if he didn't just make me come less than a minute ago. Then his head dips down, and the swipe of his tongue is completely ruthless as it licks up and down my slit, before swirling around my clit. My pussy throbs against his mouth as I feel myself getting wetter and wetter for him.

"Such a beautiful, needy little cunt, baby, and who does it belong to?"

The word baby falling from his lips should be a sin, my body writhing against his tongue and my sheets as I gasp, "You, it belongs to you."

His eyes flick up from between my legs to meet mine, his smile wicked, as he shakes his head and purrs, "Such a good fucking wife for me." His fingers part my lips, his tongue sucking my clit into his mouth gently, not giving me a chance for his dirty words to digest before he is feasting on me like a man starved. "You taste so fucking sweet, Tink," he groans against my pussy, his breath hot and his tongue deliciously wet.

"Fuck, Joshua, yes," I moan, unable to keep my cool as he licks, bites and sucks my pussy, until I am aching for him. When I pant his name again in nothing short of a desperate plea, he sucks my clit again, and I watch in awe as he brings his left hand up and sinks his ring finger inside of me.

A guttural moan tears from my throat now as he swirls his tongue around me, his finger rubbing that sweet spot inside of me. "So fucking tight for me, baby, I can't wait to feel this sweet little cunt clenching around my cock." He fucks his finger in and out of my cunt, while his tongue continues its pattern of gliding up and down the length of my slit, and then lapping against my clit even more.

The feel of his ring inside of me is another level of hot, and all I can do is spread my legs wider for him, praying he sinks in even deeper. Then he is going at me even harder, his tongue working my clit until I am crying out for him. I roll my hips against him, trying desperately to meet every swipe of his tongue, and he groans, pulling me against him even harder.

His tongue and finger fuck me in a tandem until I am completely at his mercy and desperate to come again. "Give it to me, Hals, I know you want to," he growls against my cunt, and his words mixed with the flick of his tongue, and the depth of his finger, have me exploding against him.

I come hard, the orgasm pulsing out of me everywhere as I scream his name and roll my hips against his mouth. "Yes, yes, right there, yes," I pant out, gushing against his face, and he laps at me greedily.

"That's it, good girl," he praises, his pace never relenting until I am completely spent beneath him. Only then does he rise from between my thighs, crawling up my body and bringing his mouth back to mine. "You're so fucking sweet." The kiss is slower this time, like he is savoring the taste of us, until I am melting against him, ready to go again, but much to my dismay, he pulls back and bites his lips with a smile. "What the hell am I going to do with you?" he asks, rubbing his nose against mine, and I can feel his cock pressing into me, and I can't help but squirm.

"A repeat of what we just did would be preferred," I snap, feeling both satisfied and needy, and he barks a laugh.

"See this is why you're one of my favorite people," he tosses back casually, pushing off of my body and moving to sit on the end of bed, cracking his neck, like his tongue and words didn't just obliterate me.

Feeling a sense of dread in the pit of my stomach at the thought that what we just did means everything to me, and nothing to him, I move to push off the other side of the bed, and quickly grab my robe.

"I'm just going to freshen up," I tell him quickly, darting out of my bedroom towards the bathroom before he can respond, and not stopping until I am on the other side of the locked bathroom door.

When I look in the mirror, I find my cheeks completely stained pink, my neck and chest not faring much better either, and I can feel myself starting to panic. *Oh my god.* What the hell was that? How did we go from talking about his father to me on my knees for him, to his head between my thighs? This is bad, really bad, we will never recover from this. How am I ever going to look him in the eye again after I just crawled to him? How can I look myself in the eye when I not only did it, but absolutely loved it?

I spend my days trying my best to remain in control of everything, from picking clothes that won't irritate me, selecting foods I am comfortable with, to avoiding physical touch from the majority of people as I guide myself through my day. Hell, my whole sleeping schedule is centered around an entire routine, my whole life is. So relinquishing that to Josh, letting him take over, not thinking about anything but pleasing him, fuck it was refreshing. I felt free, yet I know it has ruined everything.

This was just about helping him feel some sense of power in his life, now we go back to being just friends, spouses, nothing more. Which is why I stay in the bathroom for a good twenty minutes, showering, brushing my teeth, and washing my hands three times, before I finally bravely go back to my room. That should be enough time for him to slip out and then text me an excuse for why he had to leave.

Yet when I stroll back into my room, I find our clothes tidied away, the lights turned down, and Josh sitting up in my bed, still shirtless with Percy snuggled under his arm. My TV is on and he has the next episode of *Criminal Minds* lined up ready to go. His eyes flick to mine, and the smile he offers me is almost coma-inducing. There is no trace of panic or regret, just the face of the same boy I have loved since I was nine.

"You don't mind if I stay, right? I thought I could watch you fawn over *Dr. Reid*," he muses, patting the spot beside him on my bed, as if he didn't just have me spread out on it. My heart races at the memory, but my feet are moving towards him before my mouth can even form a response.

It's only when I reach the bed that I spy a pair of pajamas laid out for me, along with some fresh underwear, and when I flick my eyes back to him, he is watching me carefully. I know that if I told him to leave, he would in an instant, yet for once I don't want to be alone. I like having him in my space, I always have, and I'm glad he didn't slip out without saying goodbye, no matter what just happened between us.

My throat still aches from taking him, and I have to swallow thickly as I untie my robe and slip it off, so I can put on the stuff he left out for me. His eyes flare wide as it hits the floor, his stare trailing over every inch of my skin like it's the most beautiful thing he has ever seen in his life, and for some reason I don't feel shy. I don't rush to cover up, I let him see me, all of me, taking my time to pick up the panties and step into them. Shimmying my hips as I slide them up my legs and into place, and only then do I reach for the Fairfield U tank he picked out for me, slipping it over my head.

My nipples are hard and begging for attention, and if he stares at me like this any longer I am going to be back on my knees, only this time I will be begging. That thought is only intensified when he reaches down to adjust his now hard again cock and curses, "Fuck, who knew putting clothes *on* could be so erotic."

I laugh, sliding into the sheets beside him, surprised to realize he is only in his boxers, and I can't help but think how easy it would be to slip them down and climb on top of him. The thought has me rubbing my thighs together, those two orgasms I've already had clearly are not enough when it comes to him.

With his stare still on me, the only thing I can think to say is, "You stole Percy."

Josh scoffs, "I don't think it counts as stealing if I am the one who got you the damn penguin, but let's just say I'm enjoying joint custody for the night." Then he lifts up the arm holding him and pulls me into his body like it's the most normal thing in the world for us. "Now be quiet and watch your little boyfriend," he adds, picking up the remote and pressing play, and I laugh.

"You sound jealous," I muse, keeping my eyes on the screen, even when I feel his gaze burning into the side of my face.

"What do I have to be jealous of, Tink?" he asks, reaching across my body, picking up my left hand, and tapping my wedding ring. "You belong to me now, remember, which means the only boyfriends you are allowed are fictional." He places my hand down and taps it like that's all he needs to say, focusing back on the screen.

Butterflies swarm my insides, as I try to do the same, yet casually reply, "Oh well that's good, because there are a lot of those."

His head snaps back to me. "How many?"

I shrug, pretending I am following what is happening on the TV screen. "At least a hundred that I can think of off the top of my head."

I don't see his reaction, but he stares at me for a few seconds, before blowing out a breath. "Damn, that's some tough competition."

Smirking, I snuggle more into his side as I mutter, "Oh you have no idea."

For the next couple of hours we cuddle up together watching TV, and it's probably the most relaxed I have ever seen him. That point is only proven when I turn to ask if he is ready for another episode, and I find him sleeping softly beside me, Percy tucked under his chin. I can't help but smile as I look at them, reaching for my phone and snapping a picture, before I quietly slip out of bed. I make quick work of going to the toilet, turning off the TV, and getting back into bed ready for sleep, and as soon as I turn on my side, he reaches out in his sleep and pulls my body into his.

Dreams don't come easy after that, because for once my reality is better.

∼

MY SLEEP IS RESTLESS, and when the sound of an alarm that isn't my own starts blaring, I curse into my pillow, as Josh unwraps himself from around me. I flick my eyes open to watch him reach over and turn it off, and then, like a psycho, he just instantly climbs out of bed. There is no hitting snooze, no waiting for him to fully wake up, nope, he is just up and out of bed.

I keep my head on my pillow and my eyes closed, ignoring him as he darts around the room, slipping back into his clothes with ease, before leaning down and whispering, "Hals, I've got to get home and get changed for class."

My eyes flick open to meet his, and I nod, feeling a lot more nervous to be around him than I did yesterday. Maybe my post-orgasm haze has worn off. He pauses a moment, looking a little unsure, before he nods back and then turns to leave, and when the door closes behind him, I can't stop the sense of dread that creeps over me.

Before that feeling can fully take over, my bedroom door flies back open and he storms towards me, his lips slamming to mine before I can take another breath. He kisses me with more intensity than yesterday, if that's even possible, before he pulls back and smiles at me softly.

"Meet me after practice today? We can go to the center together." His question lingers in the air between us, and all I can do is nod, making his smile even wider. His lips meet mine again and I curl my hands around his neck, feeling desperate for more of him, for more of us, and when he groans into my mouth, I almost drag him back into the bed. "Fuck, Tink, you really know how to kick-start a man's day," he grits, standing up and adjusting his hard cock behind his pants.

"You haven't seen anything yet," I boast back without thinking, and his eyes darken.

"Trust me, Hals, what I have seen will be imprinted into my mind for eternity," he says with a wink, and I blush as he backs away from the bed and adds, "Until later, wife."

Then he's gone, taking my heart, and my orgasms, with him.

#25
JOSH
RINK RENDEZVOUS

Walking out of Hallie's bedroom, with her half-dressed body still between the sheets begging to be touched, is one of the hardest things I have ever had to do. Every cell inside of my body was begging me to climb back in next to her and spend the day with my cock buried deep inside her, but here we are. Today is the last day of classes before Christmas break and I have multiple assignments to hand in, which is the only reason I walked out of her room this morning.

Yesterday was a whirlwind, but the shit show of a dinner at my parents' house was soon erased from my mind with the image of Hallie on her knees crawling towards me. *Fuck.* Never have I wielded that power over someone, and never have I enjoyed it more. She was so fucking perfect, her mouth like a heaven I have never felt, and from the way her pussy felt stretched around my finger, I know sinking into her sweet cunt will be a dream.

I feel myself hardening in my jeans at the thought, and I am grateful for the desk I am sitting behind so I don't fucking embarrass myself in front of the whole class. I am barely listening to my business professor, too distracted by my wicked thoughts of my wife, when my phone starts to vibrate in my bag. Knowing that my actual phone is sitting in the pocket of my pants, it means that it's my other phone going off, the burner one that Lincoln Blackwell gave to me.

We have spoken a couple of times but he said he wouldn't contact me again until he has everything he needs. Well, I guess this means he has everything.

I discreetly reach down into my bag and locate the phone, pulling it out beneath the desk to make sure no one pays too much attention to it, and then click on the new message lighting it up.

> Unknown : I've got what you need. Come to the office tomorrow.

> Josh : I'll be there

There is no response after that, not that I'm surprised. Lincoln doesn't strike me as a man of many words, yet his message leaves my body buzzing. He's found it, whatever it is, it's enough for my father's downfall, and that thought excites me more than it should. After years of his tyranny, and political bullshit about family matters while he sticks his dick in anything other than my mother, I can't wait to witness his downfall.

The rest of the class passes in a blur, and as I make my way over to the gym for practice, my mind is dizzy with the possibilities of what he might have found. Even the cold tension of the locker room can't seem to snap me out of it, although I do note that Archer actively avoids looking at Daemon after what happened. Coach spoke to them both separately about the incident, and whatever Daemon said to him seemed to cool him down.

By the time we all hit the ice we are one big happy family again, or more like estranged cousins at least, but hey, it works for us. After a killer workout, I am working on some drills when Levi finds me.

"Hey man, missed you at the house last night," he says, coming to a stop beside me, watching me work.

I keep my focus on what I'm doing as I reply, "I spent the night at Hallie's." My voice is loud enough that Gray and Reign hear it and holla at me like a pair of idiots, causing Coach to snap at them both.

Levi watches me quietly, before he moves in a little closer and lowers his voice to only be heard by me. "You're taking this a little far aren't you?" he asks, and my stare flicks over to him in question. "Playing house with Sanders," he explains with a shrug. "Look I get all the shit with your dad, and she is fucking hot, but come on, this is a little much don't you think?"

Fire and resentment burn up inside of me as I give one of my best friends of almost eight years my full attention. "We've been friends a long time, Levi, and trust me when I say that's the only reason you are still standing right now," I spit, causing most of the other players on the ice to turn our way. "But I will only tell you this once, stay the fuck out of my business, and keep your eyes off my fucking wife."

I turn away before he can respond, or I can do something stupid that we will both regret, ignoring every prick that stares at me as I storm off the ice. Coach yells my name but practice is almost over anyway, and I will not be held responsible for my actions if I stay on that ice. So instead I hit the showers early, trying and failing to let the scalding water erase the anger inside of me. Yes, Levi might have some fucking insight on my situation with Hallie, but he hasn't got a fucking clue about what goes on between us, our friendship or otherwise, so he needs to mind his own fucking business.

By the time I turn off the shower, the locker room is occupied by the rest of my team, most of them giving me wondering looks, but I ignore them all and start getting changed. I pray that Levi doesn't say another word to me, otherwise Coach will be dealing with another Flyer on Flyer fight in here for the second time in less than a week.

Once I'm dressed, I storm out of the gym, irritation clinging to me like a second skin, but as soon as I get outside, my eyes land on Hallie, and everything else immediately melts away. She is leaning against the wall, dressed in her usual class attire of an oversized sweater and leggings, and when her gaze collides with mine and she smiles, I have never seen anything more perfect.

As if sensing my mood, her face turns into a frown as she takes in mine, and she is instantly moving towards me. "Is everything okay?"

With any other person, I doubt she would even notice the shift in their mood, but since the day I met her she has always been attuned to my emotions, just like she is with Maddie. I swear sometimes she is the only person in the world who truly knows me.

Just as she voices her question, the door behind me bursts open and I find Levi with Daemon not far behind, as if he was coming after me and Dameon tried to stop him. We lock eyes, and whatever is in my stare has them both pausing as I turn back to Hallie and respond, "Yeah everything is fine, let's go."

Gripping her hand in mine, I entwine our fingers and pull her away from the gym towards my car. I can feel her stare on the side of my face, and I know for a second she doesn't believe me, the thought only proven when she softly squeezes my hand in hers three times. *Are you okay?*

Not giving her an answer, I wait until we reach my car and then turn to find her stare still filled with concern and, without restraint, I lean in to capture her mouth with mine, letting her kiss erase any other bullshit. She tastes just as sweet as she always does, and a part of me wonders what I would do if she were no longer my wife, no longer *mine*. Our dynamic has changed completely and we haven't exactly discussed what it means, but all I know is that right now she is the only thing that can ground me.

When I pull back, I look down at her and just breathe her in. "I am now," I finally respond, and a small smile pulls at the corner of her perfect mouth.

The drive over to the center is filled with her usual chatter as she tells me all about her day and the apparent 'best nachos ever' she had for lunch, and it's only once we arrive that I realize she has fully turned my mood around.

"I've got a meeting with Lincoln tomorrow," I say casually as I pull into the parking lot, and her head snaps towards me.

"Want me to go with you?"

Her question throws me as I turn off the engine and look towards her. "Why would you want to come with me?"

"I don't know, to support you I guess," she shrugs, tossing her bag into the back of my car as she takes off her seatbelt. "Besides, if you don't take me I'll punch you in the dick again," she adds cheerfully, before climbing out of the car.

I'm on her heels in an instant, pulling her into my side. "Such a brat, do I need to fuck that pretty little mouth of yours again to get it to behave," I purr, and her eyes flick around the lot where parents are still arriving.

"Joshua," she scolds my name in the same way she always does, pushing me off her and walking away.

"You better stop saying my name like that," I toss back, and she scoffs as we reach the door, but as she moves to open it, I pull her against me and add in a whisper, "Because every time you do it gets me hard as fuck."

Her soft gasp is like music to my ears, as I recall all the delicious sounds she made while she was writhing beneath me yesterday, and all I want to do is pull more from her, but right now I have a class to teach. I open the door, rejoicing in the scowl on her face as I hold it open for her, then we move inside to get started.

We find the usual hustle and bustle of students Hallie has become accustomed to in the last couple of weeks, and they are all crazy excited to see her again. Once their parents note my arrival they start heading out, and I instruct the kids to lace up and head onto the ice.

I see Hallie's stare flicking across them all, and I know instantly who she is searching for. "Penelope isn't coming tonight, Callia texted me this morning, she is just getting over a sickness bug from the weekend."

They have formed quite a bond already given Pen is usually the only girl in my class, and I know it's been nice for her to have Hallie to look up to. It has really managed to bring her out of her shell, which is just another reason for me to be grateful to Hallie.

"Oh no, I hope she's okay," she mutters, dropping onto the bench so she can change into her skates.

"I'm sure she's fine and will be back with us after Christmas," I say as I watch as she laces them.

She doesn't even notice she has my full attention as she pulls her hair into a clip, and then flashes me that sunshine smile, as she purrs "See you on the ice, Coach."

The next two hours can only be described as pure torture, as Hallie skates around the ice with all the young boys following after her. She looks like some sort of ice princess leading her court, and it's basically like I don't exist as she teaches them yet another trick that I taught her. They only give me their attention when she insists on playing a game of teams, and of course all of them want to be on hers. *Little traitors.* Reluctantly, some of them come over to my side after some gentle pleading from her, but all I want to do is wipe the smug look off of my wife's face.

"You're going down, Mr. Peters," she coos, skating to the center to meet me, her team of boys fanned out at her back.

"I think we have already established how much I enjoy going down, Mrs. Peters," I purr, and I know if her cheeks weren't already pink from the cold, that my comment would make her blush. "Bring it on."

Our sticks smack against one another as we fight for the puck, and I manage to steal it first, much to her dismay, and before she can steal it back, I am gone. Skating towards my team and shouting out plays as I pass it on to one of the young boys. Pride floods my insides as he accepts the pass with ease and his face fills with determination. I've taught them a lot in the last year, but they have taught me a lot more in return.

The boys start running tricks and flying around the ice with ease, and when my gaze collides with Hallie's I can see the same look on her face that I'm sure she can see on mine. This is a bunch of kids that love to play a game that can easily turn into a passion, and I'm sure Hallie remembers as well as I do what that's like. I was just a kid when I discovered ice hockey, but it changed my life forever. I was also just a kid when Hallie discovered me playing, and lately she has changed my life even more.

By the time the parents arrive to pick up their kids at the end of the lesson, all of us are all skated out, and Hallie and her team beat us nineteen to twelve. Although she definitely used some sly tactics to bag herself that win, ones that were downright easy to spot, yet they worked on me like a charm.

Once we wave off the last kid, I turn and find Hallie stepping back onto the ice and pushing off to skate around the sides. When I join her she whizzes past me with a smile as she yells out, "I hope you're not going to be a sore loser, Mr. Peters, it was a fair game."

A scoff leaves me as I push off to skate after her. "A fair game? Is that what we are calling you cheating?"

She spins on her heels to watch me follow her like a damn dog. "I do not cheat, I simply just used distraction methods, it's not my fault you allowed them to work on you."

I skate faster, making her do the same, but where she might have the skill, she doesn't have the speed, not to out skate me anyway, and I catch her with ease making her yelp. "Hallie, if you brush this body against me, of course I am going to be distracted," I growl, spinning her, and pulling her ass against me, as my hands grip her hips, all the while still gliding us around the ice.

"You're just jealous I scored more goals than you," she gasps, and with every move my cock gets even harder.

"Oh is that right?" I ask, skating us to the middle where the kids left a few pucks and sticks dumped at the end of the lesson. "Okay well let's see how good you are at scoring when you're distracted," I tell her, pulling her into position in front of me, so she can line up to take a shot.

She peeks over her shoulder to assess me, but I ensure my face remains clear of the devious plans in my mind. Just like I knew she would, she moves us into position to take a shot, but as soon as she does, I move my hands from her hips, sliding them beneath the top she is wearing until my fingers graze her bare skin across the band of her leggings. Her entire body reacts as she jumps at the contact, only bringing her ass harder against my cock, and even with the multiple layers in the way I groan.

"Joshua," she gasps, flicking her eyes back to mine once more, and I grin.

"What did I tell you about saying my name like that, Tink?" I ask, teasing my fingers along the waistband of her leggings, before dipping them inside and reaching my hand down to cup her. "Now, I thought you were going to demonstrate your goal scoring skills again, huh?" I massage her pussy gently, stroking my fingers over her ever so slowly, savoring the way she melts against me like putty in my hands. "Come on, Mrs. Peters, show off for me."

My words have their desired effect, because she looks entirely motivated as she focuses back on the puck and the net, squaring her shoulders. My entire body is molded to hers which means every time she moves, I move with her. I feel everything, everywhere, and being the one who taught her how to play, I know when she twists her body that she is preparing to strike. *So I do the same.* I push my middle finger past the lips of her pussy and press down on her clit, making her entire body jolt.

The puck flies out in front of us as her stick strikes it, but it goes wide, missing the net completely as she moans in my arms. "Now who's not playing fair," she breathes, leaning her head back against my chest, as I tease her clit with the pad of my finger.

I lean down to inhale her scent, circling my finger as I kiss a path up her neck to her ear, as I whisper, "I don't play fair, Hals, I play to win." I bite down on her earlobe, pulling it between my teeth, delighting in the moan that falls from her lips. "Now line up your next shot and see if you can score with my fingers inside you," I instruct, sinking my hand down until I can slide my finger into her cunt, groaning at how tight she feels as she grips me.

My palm grinds against her clit, rubbing it again, faster this time, enjoying how her body reacts to my touch, even as she scrambles to try and line up another shot. She strikes again, but so do I, sinking a second finger into her, reveling in every gasp that passes her lips.

"Oh you missed again, Mrs. Peters. What ever am I going to do with you?" My fingers don't stop their assault, fucking her hole and rubbing her clit in tandem, hurling her towards the edge.

"Please, Josh?" she begs, throwing her head back against me and closing her eyes, as she begins to wind her hips against my hand.

"Please what, baby?" I whisper, trailing my tongue up her ear, as my fingers fuck her harder.

"Please make me come," she moans, the sound echoing around the rink, and I don't even care that I haven't locked the door. Let someone come in here and see exactly what I do to her.

"You're so fucking pretty when you beg me, Hallie." Her body begins to shake now, and I know she's close, and my eyes can't look away for even a second, not as she begins to fall apart beneath my touch. *She's fucking magnificent. And she's mine.*

"God you're an asshole," she huffs, rolling her hips against my fingers, fucking them even harder, and I sink my teeth into her neck, sucking hard on the skin, as she starts to spasm around my fingers.

"And you're a fucking goddess," I praise, coaxing her orgasm from her. "Now come for your husband."

My demand sends her over the edge, a scream tearing from her throat as she rides my fingers into oblivion. I feel the gush of her release against my hand, her clit throbbing against my palm, and fuck I want more. Without pause, her pussy still convulsing in my hand, I skate us towards the goal post, my hand never letting up as she rides out her orgasm against me.

"You know after yesterday, all I wanted to do was lay you out on the bed and take my time fucking you. I wanted to have you spread out beneath me when I sunk into your sweet little pussy for the first time, fucking you deep into the mattress until you screamed out my name, but I don't think I can wait another second," I explain, pulling my fingers from her pussy and bringing them up to her face, rubbing her cum between my fingers. "Look at the mess you made of my hand, wife." I press it against her lips and to my surprise, she opens them up and sucks my fingers into her mouth, swirling her tongue around them like she did my cock.

"It's been a long time since I fucked anyone," I add slowly, pressing my cock into her ass and letting her feel what she does to me. "And the idea of fucking my wife gives me more pleasure than you can imagine, Tink."

My lips trail along her neck leaving little kisses across her skin as she gasps, "It's been a while for me too." And I throw my head back in a groan, thinking about anyone else having her before me.

"Fuck, don't tell me things like that, baby." My heart is pounding in my chest, my cock aching to be let out of my jeans, and with my wife pressed against it, all I want to do is fuck her. I want to possess her, control her, erase anyone else that isn't me, until she is mine and only mine.

"Why not? We said no lying, remember?" she whispers, turning her gaze over her shoulder at me and I get lost in her stare. "And besides, you said it first,"

"Yes, well, I'm a jealous psycho, I thought we covered that," I muse, stroking my hands down her arm, and moving them until they can grip the top of the goal post on either side of her. "And because it makes me think things I shouldn't, like fucking you here and now without a condom."

Her gaze fills with heat as it continues to hold mine, and I feel her fingers tighten around the pole beneath my own. "Oh, well a good boy would ask before doing such a thing."

My smirk is wicked as I let my teeth sink into the juncture of her throat again as I ask, "And what makes you think I'm a good boy?" My tongue laps against the mark I know I have just left, as her ass continues to writhe against me. "Trust me, Hals, there is nothing good about me."

"That's not true," she instantly disagrees, and all I can think about is shutting her up with my cock, and I can't help but smile as I think about her spread out in front of me, half bent over the goal post.

"Okay you're right, my wife is pretty cool," I tease, letting my hands trail back up her arms until I reach her hair, moving until I can take out her clip and let it fall down across her shoulders

"I hear she's pretty funny too," Hallie tosses back without pause, flicking her hair over one shoulder to once again stare at me.

"That's true, she always knows how to make me smile, she always has," I tell her truthfully, knowing that in just a few short weeks I am already in way too deep with her, for either of us to escape this unscathed.

"Joshua?" she whispers, voice like honey as she uses my name like a question.

"Yes, Mrs. Peters?" I respond, knowing that whatever she is about to ask I will give her, I will give her fucking everything if she asked for it.

"Please fuck me."

Three words, three simple words, and I am completely done for. I'll never be able to step onto the ice again without thinking of her spread out and begging to be fucked.

I think being married might be the best thing that has ever happened to me.

#26
HALLIE

HOLES AND GOALS

My question lingers in the air between us, the tension scolding hot in comparison to the ice beneath us, but I wait with bated breath for his answer. I knew I was playing with fire during the lesson, especially with the kids around, but from the moment he left my bed this morning, all I could think about was how much I needed him. Yesterday was just scratching the surface. I know that, I've been with guys before, none of them possessing the ability to make me come. Yet Josh not only did it, he ruined me, not just with the out of this world orgasms he gave me, but with the power and possession he used to control me.

Now here we are again, way beyond the lines of friendship and deep within this forgery of a marriage, but I can't stop, and I hope he feels the same. That hope is hanging by a thread as I wait for his answer though, my hands fisted around the top of the hockey net as my breath comes in quick, short pants.

Just when I am about to think he will never answer, his hands reach down and start to spread my legs out on the skates.

"I wanted space the first time I fucked you, but it seems you are more of a brat than I thought," he grits, almost sounding angry, but I know him well enough now to realize that he is just as turned on as I am. His gaze flicks to mine as he undoes his belt and frees his cock from his jeans and demands, "Hold on tight, wife."

Then he moves his hands to my hips, gripping them roughly, before he slowly skates backwards, taking my hips with him until I have no choice but to bend over to keep my grip on the bar. Only then does he release me, leaving me almost at a ninety degree angle, my arms stretched out above my head holding the pole, and my legs spread wide.

Anticipation burns through me as he rips down my leggings and panties in one swoop, lining his cock up with my pussy. "Hallie, the next time I fuck you, I promise to take my time and give you exactly what you need," he vows, brushing the tip of his dick up and down my slit until my juices coat his shaft. "But first, I am going to ruin you for anyone else." Then he slams into me with one quick, hard thrust, stealing the air from my throat, as my hands almost slip from the pole.

"Fuck," he growls out, his fingers crushing around my hips to the point where I know there will be proof of this moment left on my skin, and all I want is more. "You're so fucking tight."

I have barely even caught my breath when he does it again, and then again, spearing me with his cock, and stretching me in a way I have never experienced. He pulls all the way back to the tip, and then slams into me over and over, never relenting on his punishing pace, and from this angle I can feel every inch of him as he slides inside me. His fingers were nothing compared to how long and thick his dick feels as it fucks me, and the sounds spilling from my throat do nothing but spur him on.

"Joshua," I moan, unable to form any more words than that, and a deep groan rips from his throat in response.

"You are so fucking tight, baby," he spits, his fingers digging into my hips even more, as he pulls me against him, fucking me harshly, and the word baby sends butterflies flooding through me. "And look how well you fucking take me," he praises, snapping his hips against my own, and all I can do is hold on like he wanted.

My chin rests on top of one of my arms so I can watch him as he fucks me, his focus only on where our bodies meet, as his cock plunges into my pussy. My eyes take in the rise and fall of his chest with every powerful thrust, the strong hunch of his shoulders as he grips my hips, his dark stormy eyes as he watches himself fuck me. It's mesmerizing. The way he looks at me with such lust and affection and care, yet the way he fucks me like a savage without a care in the world. It's addicting, and I know it's wrong, that we should stop, but I can't, because I have been addicted to him since the moment we met, and the high has only gotten sweeter.

"Fuck I could get used to this, Hals," he moans, eyes flicking to mine, and the only thought it in my mind as he continues to pound into me is, *so could I.*

This wasn't just fucking, it was something else entirely, something I had never experienced before, and without him, I probably never will again.

"Joshua, you feel so good," I moan, unable to stop watching him, and the moment his name leaves my lips it's like a switch is flipped inside of him, and somehow be begins fucking me even harder.

So hard that I can barely breathe, let alone talk anymore, as he takes me hard and rough, toeing the line between pleasure and pain, and if I could I would ask for more. I love this, love being at his mercy, not caring if the whole town walked in here and found us fucking like this. I will never be able to watch him play hockey again without thinking about the way he is moving inside of me right now.

Sparks light up my insides as I feel my body hurtling towards another release, the deep fucking of his cock hitting that sweet spot inside of me that I've only even been able to find with one particular vibrator. I'm going to come again, I'm going to come while he fucks me. Joshua Peters, my husband, is going to feel my pussy convulse around his cock as he takes me, and the thought brings me a thrill like no other.

I start to roll my hips, meeting him thrust for thrust, and the feel of him inside me paired with his hands holding me like he will never let me go has me racing towards the finish line. "Josh, I'm gonna come," I gasp, delighting in the way my words affect him.

"I know, baby, I can feel your pussy sucking me in," he snaps, his eyes locked on mine as he leans forward, pushing his hand into my hair and fisting it tight. "You look so fucking pretty with my cock inside of you, Mrs. Peters." He pulls my head up, as his chest hits my back, and his fucking turns absolutely savage.

"Josh, don't stop, please," I beg, not caring how desperate I sound, not to him, no, he already owns me in every way possible anyway.

"I'm not stopping until you give it to me, Tink, so give it to me, come on your husband's cock and show me exactly who you belong to," he grits the words into my ear, his voice like gravel scraping against my bones, and that's all it takes.

He asks and I give.

My entire body spasms, my insides coiling tight as a wave of pleasure rips my body to shreds, making him curse. I scrunch my eyes tight, pushing my head into his touch and my pussy against his groin, as a scream tears from my throat, bouncing off the plexi around us.

"Baby, keep looking at me please," he begs, with my orgasm

never stopping, and my eyes snap back open, colliding with his own, and the look in them almost ends me. I have never seen him look more open and vulnerable, and at this moment none of it feels like pretending. "Fuck, fuck, fuck," he groans, ripping his cock from me, his hand taking over as he jerks himself roughly, until he is coming all over my ass with a groan.

My legs almost buckle with the aftermath of his assault, but before I can even drag my skates across the ice to bring my legs together, his knees hit the floor. Then his fingers are massaging my ass cheeks, spreading his cum into my skin like he is branding me.

"Fuck, Hallie, if I had known how good you look covered in my cum, I would have stolen you as my wife a long time ago," he purrs, before leaning forward and lapping his tongue against my skin, cleaning himself off of me.

"If I knew how good your cock was, I would have let you," I laugh as he pushes me back towards the goal so I can stand back to my full height. Then he pulls my leggings back into place and gets back to his feet as I turn towards him and add, "It would have given my sex toys a break if I had."

If I thought his stare looked satisfied, it's nothing compared to how his eyes gleam now as he asks, "Toys? As in plural?" He molds his body against mine, pushing my back into the very pole I just held on to as he used my body like his own personal toy. "I will have to look at this collection of toys, see if they are good enough for my wife," he muses, bringing his mouth to mine, and slipping his tongue between my lips until I can taste his salty release against my own.

"I thought you'd be jealous given they are your competition," I mumble into his mouth, enjoying how he just takes from me without asking now.

He pulls back and laughs. "If you think there is any competition for the way I just made you strangle my cock as you came all over it, then you're not as smart as I thought you were." He kisses me again, before pulling back and fixing both of our clothes until we look like we didn't just fuck like animals on the ice.

"You think I'm smart?" I ask, not hiding my smirk as he drags me towards the edge of the rink.

"Well you agreed to marry me, so not that smart," he snaps back, pulling me off the ice and down onto a bench. Then he drops to his knees once again and starts untying my skates for me.

I watch with rapt attention, enjoying the view more than I care to admit as I casually reply, "From the orgasm I just had, I'd say it's the smartest thing I've ever done." His eyes shoot up to mine, and there is a wicked sparkle in them that tells me he knows just how much I enjoy having him on his knees for me.

He finishes up with my skates, passing me my shoes, before pulling off his own, and then standing to leave. "Come on wife, I want to feed this wicked mouth of yours," he grins, and I try my best to hide the elation I feel every time he calls me his wife.

It doesn't sound fake or forced, it just sounds true.

"With cock?" I tease, trailing after him, and savoring the way his fingers feel entwined with mine, and he barks a laugh.

"No, with two cheeseburgers, fries, and a milkshake, because despite how much I would love to silence you with my cock in your mouth again, you get cranky when you aren't fed, so hurry up," he commands, pulling me in front of him, and then landing a hard slap to my ass as I pass.

"Keep that cock away from me and that will make me cranky too," I toss over my shoulder, ensuring to sway my hips as he follows me to the car door.

His eyes are lighter than I have ever seen them when I turn and wait for him to open it, especially in comparison to when he walked out of practice earlier, and the smile he offers me is nothing short of glorious. "Noted," he nods, pulling open the door and offering his hand for me to step inside. Then he leans down and pulls me in for another kiss before he adds, "I would apologize for breaking rule number one, but I'm not sorry that I know what these lips taste like, Hallie Bear."

Then he pulls back and closes the door like he didn't just ruin my pussy *and* my heart.

∽

THE NEXT DAY we make the drive into Black Hallows together, and I swear I can still feel him everywhere. I was right, there are bruises on my hips from the way he held me against him, marks on my neck from where his teeth sunk into me, both a delicious reminder of our tryst on the ice, but neither of them compare to how my pussy aches for another taste of him.

Last night we went for dinner and then back to his house, where we found it practically heaving with guests celebrating the last day of classes before Christmas next week. By the time we made it to bed I was dead on my feet and Josh ordered me straight to sleep. Then this morning we rushed to get ready so we could make the meeting with Lincoln on time.

I'm not sure what to expect when we arrive. Josh hasn't given much away when it comes to the mysterious man helping him, so I can't help but feel nervous. Especially when we pull up to an office that looks nothing short of high class. When we enter we are welcomed by a young woman who Josh greets as 'Eliza', and then we are ushered straight to an office down the hall to meet the man in question.

What I don't expect is to come face to face with two blond gods who look to be in the middle of some sort of heated interaction. One of them is brooding and broad, wearing glasses that make him look like some sort of Clark Kent, and the other is tall and lean with a stare that looks like he would murder you for just one wrong word. Both are dressed impeccably and dripping in wealth, and as we enter, the one with the vicious stare snaps away from the other one.

"Sorry, Mr. Blackwell, I didn't realize you were occupied," Eliza stutters, seeming nervous, as she flicks her stare between the two of them.

"It's okay, Eliza, Mr. Donovan was just leaving," the Clark Kent one responds without looking at us, confirming to me that he is who we are here to see.

The other one, Mr. Donovan, looks ready to kill him still, but turns toward us and nods, "Mr. and Mrs. Peters."

I'm not sure how he knows us but to my surprise, Josh replies, "Asher, good to see you again."

The tall, lethal blond doesn't respond, just brushes past us and exits the office without another word, and I watch as Eliza pulls the door closed behind them with a soft smile. I guess this must be their usual behavior, and I can't help but smile back as I turn towards Lincoln Blackwell.

"Sorry about that," he offers, gesturing to the chairs in front of his desk. "You must be Hallie?" he adds, offering his hand out for me to shake, and when I take it, I'm surprised it feels rough in mine.

"It's nice to meet you," I reply with a smile, and he looks at me in a way I can't quite decipher, almost as if he is assessing what I just said. It doesn't make me feel uncomfortable, in fact his presence is cold yet inviting.

"You really mean that," he tells me, and I look towards Josh in confusion, but he just shrugs as we take our seats.

"Yes, of course I really mean that," I laugh as I turn back towards him, and then he looks between Josh and I as if seeing us with fresh eyes, as if he is sensing something he didn't before, but he quickly shuts it down.

"Well, thank you both for coming, I know it was short

notice," he replies stiffly, moving towards a large box in the corner and bringing it back over to the desk. "Like I said I was away for a close friend's wedding, congratulations on your own by the way," he muses, dropping the box on the desk in front of us. "We are quite busy at the moment, but I did manage to find a lot of useful information for you." He taps the box before taking a seat behind his desk and watching us closely.

The box is bigger than expected considering I didn't expect a box at all, a few pieces of paper maybe, or a file, but not a whole box. What the hell has Hugo Peters been up to? Not that I should be surprised. I mean, I'm only here because the plan to marry his daughter off was botched, and he forced Josh's hand into mine. So whatever skeletons are in his closet, I shouldn't be surprised really.

"All that box is stuff you found on my father?" Josh asks, not moving from his chair to inspect it any closer, and I can tell even from his nonchalance that he is nervous about what's inside.

"Yes, there were the easy finds, like the affairs and underpaid taxes of course," Lincoln replies without emotion, keeping his focus on my husband as he adds, "And then there was the deeper stuff like embezzlement, bribery, corruption, you know the usual." His tone is as casual as you could get and I have to silently remind myself that this is what he does, picks people's secrets apart for a living.

"Is it enough?" Josh questions, and I know what his question means, he wants to know if what Lincoln found is enough to really do it. He doesn't want to dig through his father's wrongdoings and play his games, he just wants to win.

"If given to the right people then your father is looking at spending a long time behind bars. It would take a couple of weeks to leak it without a trace, but yes, it's enough." Again his words are said with no emotion, as if he doesn't have a care in the world, and I mildly find myself wondering if he cares about anything or anyone.

Josh is silent beside me and I know he must be asking himself if this is what he truly wants. He hates his father, I know that, hell, even I hate him, but is hate enough of a reason to send him to prison for the rest of his life?

"How much?" Josh finally asks, and for the first time I see Lincoln frown a little in confusion.

"I'm sorry?" he replies in question, looking between the two of us, but I keep my focus on Josh.

"How much more is all this information going to cost me?" he snaps, leaning forward in his chair and still making no move to look into the box. He is offering money without even finding out if the information is worth it.

"Have you always been this cynical?" Lincoln finally responds, and without thinking I reply, "Yes," at the same time Josh replies, "No."

Josh snaps his head towards me as Lincoln smiles. "The downfall of being raised by the elite I've come to learn," he laughs, as if it's his own private joke before focusing back on us. "There is no extra fee, I quite enjoy helping take down a Mayor," he replies coolly, and it's only now that despite his youth I see him for what he really is, *ruthless*.

"Well okay then, pull the trigger," Josh finally says, standing to his feet and moving to leave without even looking at anything Lincoln found.

I also stand but Lincoln halts us in our tracks as he adds, "There is one other thing." He reaches into his desk and pulls out a file that clearly wasn't packed away with whatever is in the box. Josh halts behind his chair as Lincoln looks between us before finally saying, "There is another marriage deal on the table."

"That's impossible," Josh spits back instantly. "My father

agreed that if I married Hallie then he would leave Madeline alone."

Lincoln looks slightly nervous now, and I know whatever he is about to say is going to change everything. "The marriage deal isn't for you or Madeline, it's for someone else. A child."

Josh is already shaking his head. "No, you must have it wrong, it's just Maddie and me," he starts, but it's as if he remembers who he is dealing with here because then he spits, "What the fuck do you mean a child?"

Lincoln flicks open the file and pulls out the top piece of paper, sliding it onto the desk towards us. "I matched your father's DNA to another child, a little girl, she lives in Fairfield, I think you might know her."

Her. Realization slams into me almost instantly, and without even looking I know exactly who Lincoln is referring to, and I know it's about to break my husband's heart.

Josh reaches out and snatches the paper off the desk, about to read whatever is on it as Lincoln finally adds, "The marriage deal is for Penelope Barratt, your little sister."

#27
JOSH
DNA DISCOVERIES

My mind is reeling as I stare down at her name on the piece of paper in my hands, yet still it doesn't sink it. I have another sister, a little sister, a younger sister, one that I know, one that I spend time with regularly, and one I am only just finding out about. *Penelope is my sister.* I stare down at a picture of her birth certificate with her name right alongside Callia's, the father's name left conveniently blank, and when I flick my stare back to Lincoln, he passes me another piece of paper. This one is a DNA test that proves in black and white that she is my sister, well my half-sister.

I automatically start doing the math, and start shaking my head in disbelief even more. "Penelope is almost eight, Callia is in her early twenties," I say out loud, trying to work out how much of a scumbag my father really is.

Lincoln clears his throat. "Callia Barratt did a summer internship for your father when she was sixteen. She worked under him for three months, and Penelope Barratt was born eight months later."

Bile rises in my stomach. "She was a fucking child," I spit in fury, as I start to pace back and forth behind the chair I vacated. "She was still in high school for fuck's sake, and you're telling me my father fucked her and got her pregnant?" I flick my stare back to the paper again and still I can't believe it. "Does she know?" I ask, coming to a stop and focusing back on Lincoln. "Is Callia certain that my father is one hundred percent Penelope's father?"

Lincoln nods. "She went to your father when she found out she was pregnant and he paid her off to have an abortion, but she took the money and left for a while. Since she's been back I'm not sure if they have seen each other, but clearly your father knows she never had the abortion, because a deal is already in place for Penelope to marry when she comes of age."

A deal, a fucking deal, that's what it always comes down to with my father, doesn't it? Not his children's wellbeing, but what he can exchange them for in fucking business. I think back to the conversation I heard about him having to wait on a return for his investment and it's only now that it makes sense. I thought by stepping in and marrying Hallie that I would end all of this, but clearly he is always one step ahead. *Well, not this time.* No, this time I won't let him win, this time he doesn't get to come out on top, and there will be no more fucking deals.

"Take him down," I demand. "I don't care what you do or how you do it, but I want my father gone and I want every single person in the state to know exactly what kind of man he is."

Blood means nothing to me, not anymore, not when it comes to him, but for Maddie, and now for Penelope, I will do whatever I can to protect them, and to do that, he has to go.

Lincoln smirks, not a big one, but enough of one to tell me that to blow the horn on my father will be a pleasure. "Consider it done."

I nod, gesturing to Hallie for us to leave because I don't care about all the information found, as long as it's enough to stop my father, but then I find myself halting in my tracks. "What about the marriage deal?" I ask, and Lincoln looks at me in question. "You said the deal was already done, so what about the man who has signed the deal for Penelope?"

I mean what kind of man signs a fucking marriage deal for a seven year old child?

Lincoln's smirk turns completely dark and twisted as he replies, "Oh don't worry, I'll deal with him too, and it will be my pleasure."

From the look in his eye I don't think I want to know what that means, so instead I just nod and move to leave. "Call me when it's going down," I toss over my shoulder, knowing now with confidence that Lincoln can do this.

Hallie slips her hand into mine but I can't even look at her right now, my mind is still reeling from all the information I just received, and there is only one place I know I need to go right now.

"Do you want to talk about it?" she asks, rushing to keep up with me, while also waving goodbye to Eliza as we leave.

"What's there to talk about, Hallie? It's not like I wasn't aware my father was a fucking piece of shit human, all that Lincoln confirmed in there is that more people were lying to me than I thought."

I don't mean to be angry towards her, but right now the only thing I can focus on is the fact that Callia has been bringing her daughter to my class for almost a year, and not once has she bothered to tell me who she really is. I've been teaching Penelope, driving her to the diner, having dinner with her, all ample opportunities for her mom to tell me she was my fucking sister, but she didn't.

Opening the car door for Hallie, she climbs inside without a word, and then I jump in the other side. Silence stretches between us as we begin the drive back to Fairfield, and I can feel her staring at me, but my focus remains on the road.

"It's okay to be mad, Josh," she whispers, and all I can do is nod, because I am mad, and the last thing I want to do is take it out on her.

By the time we pull up at the diner, I know Callia will have already started her shift, and though Hallie has told me a hundred times that this is a bad idea, and that I need to calm down first, I can't. Turning off the engine, I climb from the car and storm inside, Hallie hot on my heels, and as soon as we are through the door, Callia is smiling our way.

It only takes a second, one second for her to see the look on my face, and her entire relaxed persona changes, her eyes flicking around the diner as we approach her.

"You know," she whispers, looking nervous, and even though I know she was a victim in all of this, I can't help but still be mad at her.

"You mean I know that I have a sister that you never told me about? Yes, I know," I spit, not caring how rude I am being right now.

"Josh I'm so sorry," she breathes, looking both stressed and relieved as she leans over the counter slightly and lowers her voice. "I wanted to tell you a hundred times, but I was scared of what your father would do. I even almost told Maddie when she dropped off the fairy house for her the other day, but I just couldn't get the words out."

Hallie steps in closer beside me, and I know she is trying to show her support, but I don't think even she can calm me down right now.

"It's been almost a year, Callia. A year, since I have been coming here, since Pen has been coming to the center, and you couldn't get the words out? What the hell am I supposed to do with that?" I snap back. "She's my *sister* and I didn't know, for the last year I've been teaching her. *I didn't know, for the last seven years."* I add, shaking my head as I try to keep control of my temper.

I have been looking out for Maddie before I was old enough to even know what being a big brother meant, I just knew I had to protect her, it was in my blood. The weight of my wedding ring feels heavier than usual as I remember just how far I am willing to go to protect her, and all the while there was another little girl left defenseless.

Before she can respond, a man appears like a ghost beside me, placing a firm hand on my shoulder, "She said sorry, so why don't you take a step back."

His voice is firm and full of authority and Callia looks nervously towards him and mutters, "Angel, it's fine, really."

The man, Angel, whatever kind of name that is, doesn't even look at her as he responds, "No, it's not fine."

I look him up and down, noting he is around the same age as me, yet his eyes look far more haunted, as I reply "And you are?"

Now his stare flicks to Callia and then back to me before he replies, "Just a concerned stranger." Which is complete bullshit because I just heard her refer to him by name, but whatever.

I open my mouth to tell him this is a family matter and to mind his own business, but before I can get the words out, another voice hits my ear. "Josh, Hallie!" Penelope squeals, coming from the direction of the bathroom, and my entire world shifts.

When I lock eyes with the little girl I instantly see it. I mean, it's so obvious I can't believe I didn't see it earlier. Hallie even said after she first met her that she reminded her of Maddie as a kid, and she's right. The blond hair, the blue eyes, the perfect amount of sass and shyness, they are so alike that I can't believe I missed it. I've always liked her, but when I look at her now I don't just see my favorite kid in my class, I see my sister. She's a part of me, and always will be, and right then the anger just seems to slip away.

"Hey, Pen," I manage to choke out before clearing my throat, and I can practically feel Callia's panic from across the counter. "How are you doing? Your mom said you've been sick."

Penelope doesn't stop until she climbs onto the stool I am standing next to, and it's only then I notice the discarded book and milkshake. "I'm feeling better, but I'm sad I had to miss class yesterday," she tells me with a smile, and all I can do is stare at her in disbelief.

She's my little sister.

It's only then that Hallie squeezes my hand three times. *Are you okay?*

And I don't know if I am, but instead of answering her, I keep my focus on Penelope. "Well I have the keys to the center, so maybe one day this week we could have an extra lesson since you missed out," I tell her, and her eyes widen in excitement, and when I flick my gaze to her mom, she is watching us with a soft smile.

"Oh my god are you serious?" she gasps, looking to her mom for approval. "Can I Mom, please?" she pleads, and Callia nods.

"Of course you can, sweetheart," she sighs, and I know she must be struggling to keep her emotions in check the same way I am.

"Yay, you're the best," Pen tells her, and as if Hallie can feel the tension between us, she quickly steps in.

"What are you reading this week?" she asks, as I nod my head towards the other end of the counter, gesturing to Callia for us to speak alone.

We both move in unison until we can't be heard by the little girl, and when we come to a stop she is the first to speak. "Josh, I'm sorry that you had to find out this way, but Penelope and I have basically always been on our own, and I planned to keep it like that. When a friend told me about the class your name wasn't even mentioned, it was only when we arrived that first night that I realized, and by that point she was already too excited and I didn't want to ruin it for her." I can hear the desperate plea in her voice for me to believe her, and I can't help but feel bad for how I came blazing in here. "I'm sure you've seen by now what a shy kid she is and you guys just clicked, and well, I wanted her to have her family, even if she didn't realize it."

It's only then I take a step back and truly think about what happened. She got pregnant when she was sixteen, and all my father did was try and erase his mistake. She has raised Penelope alone ever since, and I have seen how amazing she is at that and she's barely older than I am. The last thing she needs is me making her life more complicated, especially after what my father has already done to her.

"No, I'm sorry, I shouldn't have come in here the way I did, the whole thing just took me by surprise and I lost my cool, like father like son I guess," I huff, taking a seat at the counter in front of her, and just taking a second to let myself absorb all of this.

I'm surprised when her hand comes out to rest on top of mine as she replies softly, "Josh, you are nothing like your father, trust me." Her tone is firm, and I see the truth and pain behind her eyes and it kills me.

What happened between them? Did he rape her? Take advantage of her? There are a hundred awful scenarios floating around in my head, and I can't leave here without knowing the truth.

"How bad was it?" I let myself ask. Her knowing smile is sad as she pulls back her hand, flicking her eyes to the side towards the man who interfered in our conversation, who is still watching us silently.

"Not as bad as you're thinking," she tells me firmly, offering me little relief. "I had a shitty childhood and your dad took a chance on me. He made me feel special, and I was young, stupid, and smitten. It took me giving birth to realize what a dumb kid I had been and well, by that point I wasn't on my own anymore, so I didn't have time to feel sorry for myself."

This time when I look at her I feel no sorrow, because the only thing staring back at me is a strong woman who did what she could to survive the hand she was dealt. Do I wish I would have known about Penelope earlier, so I could have helped her more than I already have? Of course, and going forward I will do whatever I can to make their life better, and that starts with erasing the stain of my father.

"Well, for what it's worth, I'm sorry you had to deal with all that alone." I slide off the stool, ready to head back to the girls, but once again Callia places her hand on top of mine, halting me in my tracks.

"For what it's worth, I'm glad she has you as her brother, even if she doesn't know it yet." Emotion clogs my throat at her words, and all I can do is nod in response.

Yet.

When I move back to Hallie and Penelope they are deep in conversation about the book, and Callia laughs at how animated they are both being, telling us she will bring us our usual. Which is how I find myself having yet another dinner with my favorite student, only this time it's with my sister too. We make plans to have an extra lesson during the week, and I tell her I will invite Maddie along too, she is going to hit the roof when she finds out about this, but Penelope is ecstatic at the news. Callia is more relaxed than I have ever seen her as we say goodbye, and it's already harder than normal to say goodbye to Pen too.

It's why I can't help but pull out the burner phone from Lincoln and shoot off a text to him.

> Josh: Take him down whatever means necessary but the girl remains untouched and off limits.

His reply is instant.

> Unknown : I wouldn't do it any other way

By the time we make it back to the house I can tell Hallie is worried, and though my shock has dissipated, my anger is still palpable. Not towards Callia or her situation, but at the whole way my father dealt with it and kept it hidden. He knew, he knew Penelope existed, and instead of letting us get to know her as a sister, his only interest was marrying her off to the highest bidder.

"How are you feeling?" Hallie asks softly, as we push into my room and I close the door, and honestly, I'm not even sure how to answer her.

"I don't know," I tell her truthfully, knowing she will value my honesty over anything else, and she smiles softly, as I take a seat on the end of my bed and drop my head into my hands.

She comes to stand in front of me and brushes her fingers through my hair freely. "Do you want to talk about it?" I'm already shaking my head beneath her before she has even finished her sentence.

I don't want to talk about it, I don't want to talk about any of it, not until I have fully wrapped my head around the whole situation, and it's only from years of friendship that Hallie seems to understand exactly what I am saying, without me having to convey the words.

"Then how about a little distraction instead." Her words pique my interest enough to lift my head up back towards her, and I find her smiling coyly at me.

Thanks to the meeting we had earlier, she is dressed in a black dress that hits just above her knee, tied neatly around her waist, paired with tights and black heels. I've seen her dressed like this a hundred times thanks to the summers she spends working for her father, but right now in the confines of my room, with my ring on her finger, it feels very, *very* different.

Everything with her these last couple of weeks feels very different if I am being honest with myself, and I don't look too closely at the reasons why. Instead, I watch with rapt attention as she reaches for the bow at her waist and tugs on it gently, undoing it, pulling her dress open and revealing what's underneath. My mouth goes dry as I take in the black and emerald lace bra that encases her full, round tits, letting my stare drag down her stomach towards the matching panties. *Fuck.* The tights aren't tights at all, but stockings held up by flimsy little straps, and my cock hardens to an almost painful amount, as I take in the sight of her. *She is fucking breathtaking.*

"What kind of distraction?" I manage to croak out, fisting my hands into the bedsheets beside me as she smirks, my mood rapidly changing.

"Whatever kind you need, Joshua" she purrs, pushing the dress off her shoulders and climbing into my lap, and fuck me I am so gone for her.

I'm not sure when it happened or even how, but when I look at her it's like I can truly breathe. My heart beats evenly in my chest, just like it always does, but now even my mind is clear. She calms me, grounds me, and when she stares at me with that sunshine smile, she fucking floors me.

"All I need is you," I tell her, the confession falling from my lips easier than I intended, and I don't miss the way her eyes widen at my statement. She really has no idea the effect she has on me lately.

I bring my hands to her hips, holding her firmly against me

as she continues to brush her fingers through my hair. "Tell me what to do to make it better," she whispers, and it's only now that I realize she is offering me the power I constantly crave. "Command me, Joshua, tell me exactly what you need from me and it's yours."

Fuck. I don't think she realizes how perfect she is for me, how seamlessly her body fits against mine, to the point I almost think about sending my father a thank you note for forcing my hand in marrying her.

"Take off my shirt," I demand, my mouth aching to be pressed against her own, as her hands drag slowly from my hair, down my neck, to the collar of my shirt.

Her fingers are meticulous in the way they slowly flick open every button until she can push the fabric off my shoulders, her skin brushing against mine in a way that drives me crazy. I don't think I have ever wanted anyone more than I want her right now, and I can't help but push my hand up her own chest and curl it around her neck.

"Now kiss me," I demand, pulling her towards me by her throat, and my lips are on hers before she can even open her mouth to respond.

My tongue caresses hers and she gasps into my mouth, as I squeeze her neck gently, holding her in place as I tongue fuck her mouth with my own. Fuck, she even tastes like sunshine, all hot and sweet, and just begging to be owned, and the metal of my ring thrums against the pounding pulse point in her neck. Her hips roll against my own, and I know she can feel the hard length of me pressed between the apex of her thighs when she moans into my mouth.

I swallow every sound she makes and push for more, slipping my free hand down to her ass and squeezing it tight. The image of it painted in my cum as she was bent over in front of me on the ice yesterday, is seared into my mind forever. Yet knowing that I am about to fuck my wife, in my bed, does something to the caveman pounding inside of me. Yesterday was quick, ruthless, rough, but tonight won't be like that. No, tonight I am going to spread her out and fuck her until she is a whimpering mess beneath me, until she is mine.

When I slip my hand into the back of her panties and push it down, I find evidence of just how much she is enjoying my mouth on hers. "Is this for me, Tink?" I ask, pushing my fingers right between her ass cheeks and groaning at the sloppy mess of her cunt. "Does my tongue in your pretty little mouth get you wet for me?" I add, kissing her until I am panting and breathless.

"Everything about you gets me wet," she gasps, writhing in my lap to the point where I know my dick is leaking pre-cum in my pants.

My hand continues to hold her in place by her throat against me while the other massages between her ass cheeks, spreading her wetness all over her pussy without ever touching where she needs me most. I let the tip of my finger slip into her hole, teasing her with quick short thrusts, until she is dry humping me so good that I am about to come without her even fucking touching me.

When I start to pull my hand out, the pads of my fingers graze against her back hole and she flinches slightly. "Has anyone ever taken you here, wife?" I ask, bringing one of my fingers back to tease her tight rim and she huffs, shaking her head. "Good, because now you belong to me, and I don't like people touching what's mine."

My words seem to delight her as she kisses me again, robbing me of my breath and sanity, until she pulls back and scrapes her nails down my chest, reaching my pants. She unbuckles them without a word, her lust-filled stare burning into mine until she can reach inside and pull out my hard and aching cock.

I push her off my lap before she can wrap her hand fully around me, and she frowns in confusion until I push the shirt from my shoulders, and then let my pants fall down to my ankles, kicking them off at my feet. She moves to wrap her arms around me again, but I stop her once more, dropping to my knees at the foot of my bed until she is towering over me in her heels.

My mouth presses feather light kisses down her thighs until I reach the first fixture of her stockings and snap it open. I repeat the motion until they are all unfastened, and she watches me with keen interest as I slide her panties down her legs, my eyes never leaving hers.

"Do you like seeing your husband on his knees for you, Mrs Peters?" I tease, brushing my fingers over her now bare pussy and savoring the way her body starts to tremble beneath my touch. I sink my fingers into her wetness and she groans as I bring them back to my mouth and suck. "You're the sweetest fucking thing I have ever tasted, baby," I breathe, lapping at my fingers like they are my last meal.

Only then do I rise to my feet and reach to unclasp her bra, letting her fucking magnificent tits fall out until she is in nothing but the stockings and matching belt. I reach down, picking her up by her thighs with ease, and then fall back onto the end of my bed, bringing her with me. I smile as she moves to grind her bare pussy against my dick, and fuck if it's not tempting to just sink inside her instantly, but no, first I want another taste of her.

"Bring that delicious pussy here, Hals, I want to fucking drown in it," I breathe against her mouth, pulling on her hips until she has no choice but to move with me.

I don't let go until her thighs are straddled on either side of my head and I have the most perfect fucking view in the world as I spread her open for me.

"Josh," she gasps, looking nervous, and fuck me if it's not absolutely adorable.

"Don't go shy on me now, wife." I wink, pairing my words with a slow leisurely lick of her cunt, making her entire body flinch.

At the taste of her, my cock throbs so hard that it physically aches to be inside of her, but I keep my focus only on the sweet, glistening Nirvana in front of me. When I flick my tongue against her again she pants, her hands flying to my hair and gripping it tight in a way that pushes her tits together gloriously. It's that sight that undoes me, making me dive in like a man starved, as I fuck her cunt and swollen clit without pause. Licking and sucking on her sweetness until she is writhing against me without a care.

She is dripping all over me, begging and pleading until I bury my tongue inside of her and become addicted to the sounds of her pleasured cries. I fuck her with my tongue, lapping at her cunt until her entire body starts to tremble, only then do I return to her clit, sucking it roughly between my lips and letting it graze against my teeth.

"Joshua," she cries, pulling my hair until I think she might rip it out, but still I don't let up. "Don't fucking stop," she begs, and I almost laugh against her pussy. Stop? As if I could ever fucking stop.

Isn't that what being an addict is? Not being able to stop, and I am pretty sure I am now addicted to her.

Her pleas turn into screams as I force two fingers inside of her, keeping up my attack on her clit, as I slowly fuck her with my hand. In and out, harder and harder until she is slamming her hips to my face and mouth in search of her release, and fuck I want to give it to her. I have never wanted to give anyone anything more in my life.

Eyes closed, head thrown back, hands fisted in my hair, and

tits begging to be fucked, it's all I can do not to explode, as I feast on her sweet cunt until she's almost crying out in relief as her orgasm hits her. I don't stop fucking and sucking on her until she can barely keep her body upright, only then pulling back, pressing soft, gentle kisses to every inch of her cunt, before letting her collapse on the bed beside me.

"Fuck," she pants, struggling to catch her breath, and the look in her eyes as she watches me lick the taste of her from my mouth is sinful. "Now what?" she asks, like a needy little brat, and I have to smirk, as I lean off the bed and look down at her.

"Now, I'm going to take my time showing you who you belong to, does that sound good, Mrs. Peters?" I ask, not really searching for an answer, but still she bites her lip and nods.

"That sounds like exactly what I need, Mr. Peters," she purrs, making me fall deeper into my new found obsession.

I am so fucked.

#28
JOSH
DEAD MAN WALKING

I've lost count of how many girls I have fucked, and that's not me trying to be a dick, I just never cared for any of them. They were a means to an end, something to pass the time while I dealt with my father's bullshit, and right now I can't even remember a single one of them. Hallie is spread out beneath me on my bed with my ring on her finger, and fuck she has never looked so good.

Usually the news of my father's misdeeds would have sent me into a spiral, but she has managed to push it out of my mind with ease, and not for the first time. Hallie has had the ability to consume me since I was eleven years old, and in just a few short weeks of not pushing her away, everything has changed. We still have the same friendship and shared jokes from before, but gone is the distance, and in its place is something I never thought I'd have, least of all with her.

Her hair is splayed out across my pillow, and I know it will only increase the stain of her sweet scent on my bed sheets that I have become accustomed to. Her eyes are glazed, her pupils blown out in lust, as she stares up at me with a hunger that I'm sure mirrors my own. There is no mask on her face tonight, just the smile that first drew me in, and a need that rivals how desperate I am for her.

I move until I am settled between her parted thighs, my thumbs skimming the bare skin across the top of her stockings, mesmerized by the way she breaks out in goosebumps beneath my touch. Fuck. How the fuck did we get to a place of such magic between us.

"Are you just going to stare at me, or are you going to fuck me?" she asks, delighting me in a way she always does, and my heart starts beating wildly in my chest.

There is something happening inside of me, something that I have never felt before, something I don't even know how to name. It's like there's an electricity thrumming within me, a fluttering deep in the pit of my stomach, that only intensifies as I lean down on one arm and fuse my lips to hers. She doesn't just taste like sunshine, she tastes like mine, like she always has been, and it's unnerving. Her lips are soft and wet, and I feel like I could kiss her forever and never get bored, but as my body presses into hers she moans into my mouth, making me groan.

I pull back and she is panting heavily, her chest heaving in an attempt to catch her breath, and the sight of it is addicting. I always want this, I want her here beneath me, her mouth on mine, her hands in my hair. I could feel the scrape of her rings against my skull, and it made me feel like I was going insane for her, yet I never want it to stop.

"I told you, Tink, I'm not fucking you, I'm owning you," I finally respond, sliding my dick up and down her slit until I am drenched from her release. Fuck she's wet, all warm and slick, and my throat burns to taste her again. I want to taste her forever.

"I don't feel much owning going on," she purrs, pulling me in for another kiss and grinding her hips on my cock like she is as desperate as I am. She's blind if she thinks there is no owning going on here, she owns me completely.

"Such a brat," I breathe against her mouth, lining my cock up with her opening but then pausing at the tip.

"Such an asshole," she gasps back, pushing her hips down in an attempt to get me inside her further, and I can't help but laugh.

Then I push inside her slowly, inch by glorious inch, as her wet heat wraps around me like a fucking vice, making her cry out in appreciation. I tense at the tightness of her, she is fucking dripping for me, and I can feel her clit swelling against my cock as I roll my hips against her, before I begin a slow assault. My pace is tortuous, but I want her to feel all of me, I want her to remember exactly how I feel moving inside of her until she remembers me and only me.

I'm already desperate to come, the feel of her just too damn fucking perfect, but I want to stay inside her for as long as possible, forever if she'd let me. A thought that stuns me, yet I know instantly this is more than either of us are willing to admit to one another, to ourselves, I knew it yesterday on the ice. Hell, I knew it on the ice when I was fucking eleven years old.

"Joshua," she cries, reaching her hands up to cling to the back of my neck as she meets my every thrust, and fuck, the way she says my name is something I will never be able to erase.

I know she wants more, needs me faster, harder, but I want her moans, I want to drown in her pleas of pleasure until I can't fucking breathe. "Beg me, baby, beg me or I will stop," I demand, slipping my tongue back into her mouth and swallowing her moans.

"Harder, Joshua, please," she begs freely, and fuck I want to come. I want to mark every inch of her skin until there is no mistake on who owns her. I pick up the pace, drawing my cock completely out of her, and then slamming back inside in one slick thrust, pounding into her again and again, and she takes every last bit of me without complaint. "Look at you," I breathe, leaning up to watch as my cock sinks into her, her pussy swallowing me whole. "Look at how fucking well you take your husband's cock."

I have never been territorial before, never wanted to be, but with her it isn't just a want, it's a need. I can't think about whoever had her before me, and thinking about anyone coming after me makes me want to squeeze the life out of something. *She's mine.*

"My husband fucks me so good," she purrs, throwing her head back and closing her eyes, letting the pleasure take over, and her words send me blind with lust.

My hand snaps out before I can stop it, gripping her chin firmly between my fingers until her eyes snap open. "Say that again," I demand, my pace never relenting as my cock continues to fuck her deep and slow.

"You fuck me so good," she gasps, eyes aflame beneath my power, and it does nothing to decrease my need for her.

"Don't be a brat," I grit back at her, my anger and lust fighting to come out on top. "You know what I want to hear, now be a good little wife and say it again."

Her left hand slides up my arm, her ring glistening in the light and making me feral as she whispers, "My husband fucks me so good."

Any control I thought I had left snaps, as I release her chin and snatch her left hand up with my own, our rings clashing together as hard as we are. Then I am fucking her, owning her, pounding into her sweet little cunt as hard and fast as I can possibly manage, until she is crying out beneath me.

Her mewls, moans, and screams are like a fucking symphony, and I don't even care if the rest of the house hears.

Let them. Let them listen to exactly how good I fuck my wife, how much she loves taking her husband's cock, how much I love giving it to her. Yesterday on the ice was nothing compared to this, that was a quick fuck. This is life-altering sex I will never recover from, and if I am going down then so is she. So with my hand tightened in hers, I lean down and kiss her once more, her moans captured between my lips as her pussy tightens around me in the most incredible way.

"That's it baby, squeeze my dick," I growl against her lips, snapping my hips until I can feel my own release dancing up my spine. "I want your cum dripping down my cock, Hallie, I want to feel this sweet little pussy strangle my dick until I can barely fucking breathe."

My words have a scream tearing from her throat as her body starts to shake beneath my own, and it takes everything I have to not come on the spot as she falls apart around me. Her orgasm is mind blowing, her pussy practically chokes my cock until I get exactly what I asked for. I struggle to catch my breath as I lean up and fuck her hard and fast, watching as her tits bounce up and down. I can't help but lean down and lap my tongue against one of her nipples, sucking and pulling it between my teeth until her body shakes even harder.

One orgasm bleeds right into two, and fuck she looks stunning filled with my cock, her hand gripped in mine, as I pound her into the mattress. My tongue flicks her nipple rapidly before I sink my teeth around it and bite down until I leave a mark, only making her scream more. Fuck I want to leave my marks all over her, and when instead of pulling away, she pushes her chest up for more, I feel myself ready to blow.

"Fuck, Hallie, fuck," I move to pull out, but her thighs clamp around my waist and she leans up and kisses me deeply.

"I'm on the pill," she whispers, holding me against her, my cock never once stopping. "Fill your wife up with your cum."

Fuck. Me.

Seven words and I am completely done, my cock exploding as I slam into her one last time, my cum flooding her pussy at her request.

My body collapses on top of hers and I know I need to move, that this is probably more than she can handle, but fuck, it's more than I can handle too. I can barely catch my breath as I desperately try to suck in air between my teeth, and when I feel her move beneath me, I go to move, yet she surprises me by bringing her fingers back to my hair and combing them through it gently.

I'm not sure how long we lie there, but I rest my head on her chest, my cock still inside her, as I listen to the deep thrum of her heartbeat. Her hands keep up their gentle playing of my hair, and I honestly don't think I have ever felt so at peace.

"I don't think something fake is supposed to feel like this," Hallie eventually mumbles, and I lift my head to find her eyes already on me. Her face is the most open I have ever seen, a million feelings written right there for the world to see, and yet for once I can't work out a single one of them.

"Feel like what?" I ask, not really sure what I'm asking, or if I truly want the answer, and she smiles softly.

"Like I can only breathe when you are near me," she admits softly, and that wild thumping of my heart is back again, her words sending a thrill through me.

Is this still fake? Are we still playing a game? Because if we are, the rules have disappeared out the window and I'm not sure if I am winning, or if I am going to lose bigger than ever before.

"I don't think it's supposed to feel like this either, but you've fucking ruined me, Hals." My admission hangs in the air between us, and I can barely remember what it was like to only see her as my friend. Have I ever seen her like that, or was it always more?

Hallie opens her mouth to respond, but a loud banging on my door startles us both. I know that knock, it's from the only person who even knocks on my door, and only ever when it's important. I climb off of Hallie, throwing the blanket over her until she is completely covered, before grabbing a pair of shorts off the floor and quickly pulling them on.

When I pull the door open I find Daemon staring at me blankly, his eyes not even flinching at my lack of clothing. "Your father is here." His words are barely out before my father appears at the end of the hallway, stalking towards me like a predator would his prey.

Daemon moves back slightly, but not in fear, no, I know from experience that he is preparing to step in if necessary, and I can't say it won't be. My father never comes here, and I don't just mean he doesn't stop by regularly, I mean he has literally never come here before, not even once.

"Good evening, Joshua," he snarks in that airy mayoral tone of his, and I have to remind myself of the audience we have. It's the only reason he is being so cordial.

"Father," I grit through my teeth, trying to get a hold on my temper. "To what do I owe this unexpected surprise?" I can't ignore the panic in my gut as I wonder if he has found out about my meeting with Lincoln, or worse, my time spent with Callia and Penelope, but I keep my cold mask firmly in place.

"Oh I was working late again so I just thought I'd pop in on my way home and say hello," he muses, and I hear Daemon's grunt of disapproval at his bullshit, but thankfully my father doesn't.

My eyes catch on the pink stain of lipstick on his neck and I roll my eyes, working late my fucking ass. Yet before I can respond, he moves until he is standing in the doorway, Daemon tensing beside me, no doubt having already seen what I was trying to hide, as my father's eyes travel over my shoulder landing on Hallie barely covered in my bed.

My father's smile is wicked as he purrs, "Hallie my dear, didn't expect to see you here." His tone tells me he definitely wasn't expecting to see her here, and it's almost as if he is here to check up on us.

I take a step directly in front of him, blocking his line of sight completely as I snap, "She's my wife, why wouldn't she be here, the question is why are you here?"

My father laughs without a trace of humor as if he has found something delightful and unexpected. "I heard an interesting rumor this week," he purrs, like he is talking to one of his lackeys, and my fingers clench for a taste of his blood.

"That makes two of us," I toss back casually, not giving anything away to him, not like I used to, not when he is standing in my house and I can feel the support of my best friend and my wife.

I can also feel the lingering presence of Levi and Landon down the hall, and from the guilty look on his face, I know Levi is the one who let him in here in the first place. I'll deal with him later.

"Apparently you made quite the threat to a Miss Michaels, and she thought I should know what kind of son I am raising, she was quite informative."

Brianna. Of fucking course, I should have known. I wonder if she ran to her daddy first or mine.

"Is that who left that lipstick on your neck? Because if so I hope you enjoy sloppy seconds, she's been through half the team at least ten times over," I toss back, not giving him an inch of anything to work with, and I can see his patience floundering.

"Jett Michaels is one of my biggest investors, and you almost cost me that fucking relationship because you couldn't play nice with his daughter. I taught you better than that, Joshua," his tone is dripping in so much disappointment that it almost drowns me.

"I'm sure the satisfaction of riding the mayor's dick cheered her back up," I drawl, hitting him where I know it will anger, his pride, and his hands fly out just like I knew they would.

He throws me back against the door, forcing it to bang against the wall, and his only saving grace is the fact Hallie has somehow slipped out of bed, and tossed on one of my jerseys with her leggings to cover herself. It's the only thing that keeps me from attacking him. I want his anger, I want his rage, I want to look him in the eye one last time and let him feel like he owns my whole fucking world, just before I rip it all out from under him.

"Watch your fucking mouth, boy," he snaps, revealing the man I know all too well, and for once Daemon surprises me, he doesn't attack, no instead he silently holds up his phone and starts recording him.

"Go on, hit me, I dare you, let's see what your precious little voters think about that," I taunt with a smile, and only then does he notice the phone, releasing me instantly. I push off the door and allow my height to tower over him. "I'm not as easy to keep in line anymore, Mayor, so if I were you I'd watch your back."

I see the moment his fists clench and I prepare myself for the hit, it won't exactly be the first, but before my father can decide one way or another, Daemon's hand lands on his shoulder with a thud. "You need to leave, now," he warns, his tone like icy death, and whatever my father sees in his eyes makes him visibly swallow.

It only takes a second for him to regain his composure though, straightening his suit, as Hallie comes to stand beside me, slipping her trembling hand into mine.

"How's your father these days, Mr. Forbes?" he asks, focusing on my best friend like he is a new bug he wants to squish beneath his expensive loafers. "Been to visit him in prison lately?" The question is meant only to taunt Daemon, throwing his past in his face like that, and I panic at the thought it might push him into his usual darkness.

Yet my best friend only smirks as he replies coldly, "Not since the day I put him there." His response makes me smile, because soon we will have more in common than we already do.

When my father grunts and steps back he sees that he is now surrounded. Hallie is at my side, holding her head up high, a mask of disapproval that I know isn't fake covering her face. Daemon is staring my father down like he will gut him on the spot if he makes one wrong move, and Levi and Landon are watching from down the hall as if they have never truly seen the truth of their mayor before, and they haven't.

I know the moment my father realizes he made a mistake by coming here, because for the first time in my life when he brings his stare back to mine he looks wary of me. Not once in his arrogant life has he ever taken a step back and looked at the family I have built for myself in my team, at how they would have my back. No, instead he's floundered at parties and fundraisers, telling anyone who will listen that I am following in his footsteps. Taking him down is going to be more enjoyable than I thought.

"You can see yourself out," I tell him dryly, not giving him any more ammunition, and also not wanting him here for another second longer.

My father's face is that of thunder as he turns and stalks down the hall and towards the stairs, and none of us move until we hear the slam of the front door. Only then do I share a look with Daemon, who nods before slipping back off to the comfort of his room.

Landon looks at me in horror as if wondering if my father has always been that way, and Levi moves to step towards me, an apology no doubt on the tip of his tongue, but I halt him in his tracks. "Not now," I spit, pushing back inside my room with Hallie and closing the door behind us.

Before I can even open my mouth her lips are on me, her body pressing against me, and every ounce of tension within me disappears instantly. Her hands slip between my own and she squeezes it three times. *Are you okay?*

My own hand squeezes her three times in return. *Yes, I'm okay.*

Only then do I pull back and bring my gaze to hers. "Now where were we?" I ask with a devilish smile, dipping down and picking her up until her legs wrap around my waist. "Ah that's it, I was about to lick my cum clean from your pussy and then fuck your pretty little throat in the shower." I pair my words with the hard slap of her ass, and just like that, my father's visit is forgotten about, and I lose myself in my wife yet again.

I definitely need to remember to send him that thank you note.

#29
HALLIE

DREAM TEAM

Without classes to keep us apart, Josh and I spend the next few days wrapped up in one another, and I have never been more sated in my life. Whatever green light that flashed between us to kick-start the physical side of this whole fake marriage, has been beaming ever since. Josh hasn't kept his hands off me, and reminds me multiple times a day exactly who I belong to. We fuck in the shower, in the car, in the kitchen, on the stairs, and that's after Maddie banned us from our house until we get ourselves under control. Her words, not mine.

If I had my way, I would never have control again. I would give it all to Josh and live happily ever after, but every time I have that thought, another darker one hits me. After the visit from his father the other night, Josh has been in constant contact with Lincoln, conspiring with him about his plan to take his father down, and all it does is remind me that this whole thing has a deadline.

I'm not sure what Josh's plans are after dealing with his

father, but I'm sure our imminent divorce will be discussed at some point, and I don't even think years of masking could prepare me for it. I love him, I love him so fucking deeply that it makes my heart physically ache, and somehow not having him at all was easier than what we are now. Before I could lie to myself, I could tell myself it was all one-sided and there was never any hope between us, but then he came into my room and dropped to one knee, and gave me so much hope that it made me sick.

We haven't discussed what we are, yet the word wife falls so freely from his lips that I have almost convinced myself this is all real. We sleep together, we wake up together, we eat together, and we fuck so much that I can still feel him even when he isn't inside me.

I am so deeply, and madly in love with him, and it's honestly both the best *and* worst thing that has ever happened to me.

"You ready, Tink?" Josh asks, striding into the bathroom where I am applying my last coat of mascara, sending my stomach into somersaults.

He looks just as stunning as always with his blond hair perfectly tousled, and his blue eyes sparkling with mischief as he comes to a stop behind me. His hands freely landing on my hips, like I am his to touch however he pleases, and I am I guess, but how freely he lets himself have me is still taking some getting used to.

"Almost," I smile, praying he doesn't see the sadness still lingering in my eyes at the thought of losing this, but thankfully he is too distracted.

Today is the day we are going to the center and putting on an extra lesson for Penelope. Ever since Josh found out about her, he has been in constant contact with Callia to coordinate seeing his sister, and apparently the little girl hasn't stopped talking about today since we last saw her at the diner, earlier this week.

The morning after we discovered the truth, we both went over to my house and sat Maddie down and told her everything, and sadly she didn't even seem surprised. I guess, like Josh, she is used to her father's shitty behavior by now. She agreed to come with us today so she can also use the opportunity to get to know Penelope better. Yet much to Josh's dismay, where Maddie goes, Nova follows, and with Nova comes both Alexander and Archer. The two of them heard the words ice rink and were instantly sold, complaining it was their last chance to have fun and skate before going home for the holidays. That only left Jake Harper, whose girlfriend has already left for the holidays, so of course he was in too.

Their presence meant Josh also invited Daemon, and once Landon and Levi got wind of it, well, they were down too. None of them aside from Nova know the girl's true relationship to the Peters, and they were all surprised to learn that Josh teaches a class in town. To my own surprise they all showed genuine interest in it, and told him if he ever needed help all he had to do was ask. I'm not sure how Josh feels about them all coming today, considering he claims to hate half of them, but I think since Maddie and Nova started dating he has come around a little. Plus, Archer is so hell-bent on them all being best friends that I don't think my husband has much of a choice.

"Come on, baby, if you take any longer I am going to bend you over and fuck you raw until I ruin all this pretty makeup," he purrs, sinking his teeth into the side of my neck, as his hands squeeze my hips even tighter.

"You already fucked me last night and this morning, wasn't that enough?" I tease back, not missing his erection now digging into the back of my ass, and it almost distracts me from his words.

"It will never be enough," he mumbles into my hair, and

when his eyes find mine in the mirror, they are more serious than I have ever seen them.

I open my mouth to respond, to ask him what this all means, but Landon beats me to it, as he yells out from the hall, "You guys better not be fucking in there again, we are going to be late."

My smile is quick in response, as I close my makeup bag and push off the counter so I can slip away from him. "We better go, I don't want to keep Penelope waiting."

We head over to the rink with Daemon, Levi, and Landon all piled into the back of Josh's car, so any chance to finish our conversation is lost, and by the time we arrive, I spot Callia and Penelope already waiting outside. I can already tell the little girl is bursting with nerves and excitement, which only intensifies as we step from the car and she spots us.

All the guys are dressed in their Flyer jerseys, and I can't help but drool a little at the sight of my husband, as he pulls my hand into his. I try not to blush beneath his touch, I really do, especially given all the ways he's touched me this last week, but it doesn't work. I still remember the way he made me feel when we first became friends, he lit up my entire world, and when he pushed me away, it was like a hole was punched through me.

I know I should prepare for that distance again, that we won't always be entwined like we are now, but all I can do is enjoy the weight of his hand around mine. Right now there is zero distance between us, and I plan to enjoy every second, right up until the moment he breaks my heart.

"Josh!" Penelope calls out, waving frantically at him, just as Maddie and the rest of the guys arrive too.

"Hey, Pen, I hope you don't mind but I brought some friends to make our practice extra special," Josh replies, gesturing to everyone around us, and to my surprise, he looks like he actually means it when he says the word friends.

The little girl downright blushes when she spots all the guys walking towards her, not that I can blame her, especially when her eyes zero in on Nova. Yeah, you and every other girl out there kid. Maddie flicks her eyes to me with a smirk, and I mouth the word sisters to make her laugh. They are really going to be two peas in a pod.

"Can you beat them all?" Penelope finally asks, flicking her eyes back to Josh, making Alexander and Archer howl in laughter.

"Only in his dreams kid," Archer grins, holding his hand up to the little girl for a high five, as Alexander lets his gaze trail over Callia with a keen interest.

"And who might you be?" he purrs, tossing her a wink, and Josh cuts him a scathing look.

"Eyes back in your head, Reign, don't even think about it," he snaps, only making Archer laugh even more as Alexander shrugs.

"Alright, Peters, don't get your knickers in a twist, I was only being friendly," he tosses back, his gaze still firmly on Callia, making her blush beneath his attention.

Alexander Reign is a player through and through, and I mildly wonder if there is any girl that would refuse him. It would certainly be fun to see.

Penelope is of course completely oblivious to him hitting on her mom, yet still looks up at him with a frown. "You talk funny."

Now all the guys burst out laughing, as Alexander feigns annoyance in a way that only someone British could as he replies, "I grew up in England."

This switches Penelope's mood up instantly, as she starts bombarding him with questions, and Josh rolls his eyes as he pushes past him to get to the door. It seems he doesn't like sharing his little sister's attention, and I can't help but smirk as I trail after him. We wait while he unlocks the door and heads inside to turn on the lights, before we move inside to follow him.

I still can't believe the owner allows Josh to have his own set of keys. I met him during one of the lessons as he usually opens up for Josh, since he's always coming from practice and he doesn't want the kids waiting outside, and he looks at Josh with a twinkle of pride in his eyes. Josh says it's because of his last name, because of who his father is, but I know that's not true. I know the owner sees him exactly as I do, a man with a passion for the game who just wants to share it. Which is why we are here now, letting ourselves in, because he trusts the boy with the love for the game.

Once inside, the guys all change into their skates as Callia helps Penelope with hers, and then Josh introduces each of them one by one. I can see reservations behind her eyes, and I can't say I don't relate to her shyness or being the center of attention, but the guys soon sweep her off her feet. Like utter children themselves they all quickly start fighting for her attention, bragging about their skills, and I see Callia's eyes shine with tears at the amount of attention her daughter is getting. It must have been really lonely for her, and I smile as Maddie slides up beside her and links their arms together in comfort. That little girl's life is about to change for the better and she doesn't even realize it yet, but her mom does.

I flick my eyes back to the boys, where they are all still fighting over who is better, and I shake my head with a laugh. I don't know why they are even bothering, after a year of teaching she already adores Josh, and she is making eyes at Nova like he hung the damn moon, but still they try, and Pen loves every second of it. The only person not vying for her attention is Daemon, who is watching Penelope closely, like he's afraid she might break or something. His stare reminds me of the same protective one whenever Maddie is in trouble, and I wonder if he has any siblings of his own.

It's clear that all the guys are going to fall in love with her the same way Josh did, the same way I did, and as they get ready to move onto the ice I remind her to show off all her tricks, as I lace up my own skates.

Maddie takes a seat in the stands with Callia, and then I head onto the ice where the guys are already warming up. It's quite a sight being in the middle of eight hot hockey players as they stretch out their bodies on the ice, and I can't blame Penelope for staring at them in awe. *You and me both, girl.*

Once we are all warmed up, Josh tells Pen that we are going to be playing teams against each other like we usually do in class, before mildly threatening all the guys that if they knock her over he will break their hands. Then he makes both Pen and me captains, and I gracefully allow her to pick first. She nabs Nova instantly, making Josh fume. Which I only add to when I name my first pick as Daemon.

Josh glares at me with an incredulous look. "Really, Tink, it's like that is it?" he asks, his wicked expression making Daemon smirk softly, as he comes to stand beside me.

Penelope then takes pity on him by choosing him next, and I then pick Archer, before she picks the one with the 'funny voice', leaving me to steal Levi. Josh then pushes her to nab Landon, making Jake mine.

We all move to take up our positions, but Josh glides towards me and taunts, "You're going down for that, wife."

I can't help but gleam as I brush against him and purr, "But I thought it was you who enjoyed being the one going down." My voice is laced in innuendo, as his eyes darken with so much lust, that I swear I can still feel the phantom of his touch from our early morning tryst in the shower.

His fingers find that same spot on my waist that they always do, as he leans down and presses a kiss to the side of my throat. "You know the rules, Tink, you want me on my knees then you better ask nicely."

My skin burns even on the cold chill of the ice, as I whisper, "I thought you preferred me on my knees?" My words have him groaning into my neck, and I'm sure he is thinking about the last time we were on this ice together.

"Don't push me, wife," he grits, and I know if we were alone here right now that I would be having another fantasy come to life on this very ice, especially when his teeth nip at my throat.

I tip my head to the side to give him better access, but he pulls away too quickly, leaving me feeling horny and needy. "Come on, Joshua, you know the saying, happy wife happy life," I tell him with a shrug, as he circles around me on the ice.

"What about having a happy husband?" he questions, letting his fingers trail around my waist, as one of the guys yells at him to hurry up.

"Hmm, how about you let me win this game and I'll make you a *really* happy husband and let you score a goal again." I gesture towards the net he bent me over a few nights ago, and his eyes widen in surprise.

"Are you flirting with me Mrs. Peters?" he questions, his tone laced with both shock and lust, that I can't help but laugh at as I skate away.

"For years now, Joshua, it's about time you noticed," I toss over my shoulder, before joining my team with only one thought in my mind.

My husband is going down.

Archer offers me a high five as soon as I reach him, and Daemon watches him with that dark, detached gaze of his, but Archer just ignores him completely. I'm still not sure of the dynamic between them, because every time I think I have worked it out, they change it up, but there is definitely some history there. I don't know Jake that well, he lives in one of the other hockey houses, but I've seen him around campus with his girlfriend, and Levi has been around since Josh was in high school, so it shouldn't be too hard to wrangle them into a good game.

"I hope you're ready to win, boys," I gleam, flicking my gaze across all of them, surprised to find them all giving me their full attention.

"Come on, Hals, you really gonna make us try to win against them?" Levi asks, flicking his stare over to the other team.

"What's stumping you, Jones, is it the seven year old they've got?" Archer asks, causing Daemon to drop his head to hide a smirk. "Or are you still scared of Cap?"

Levi scoffs, and I cut in before they can start some bullshit argument. "I don't care how we do it, just that we do. If Josh beats me he will never let me live it down." My eyes flick over to the man in question, finding him leaning against the goal post he took me against, watching me with a smirk.

I can see Penelope gesturing wildly, keeping her team in check, and I can only imagine the trouble she is going to be in with boys when she gets a little older. Josh is definitely going to have his hands full, but his eyes are still on me, and I watch as he frowns when Archer slings an arm around me.

"Why don't you kiss me again, Sanders, that will distract him," Archer teases, his eyes on my husband, as he offers him a little wave of fingers, and I blush furiously.

Before I can respond, or Josh can react, Daemon's hand lands on Archer's shoulder causing his head to snap towards him. "Don't even think about it." His tone is completely lethal, yet for some reason Archer's eyes seem to widen in delight, like he won something.

"Why? Does your friend not like sharing his toys like you do?" he tosses back, and my own eyes widen in surprise. Yet before I can even take my next breath, Daemon has him gripped by his jersey and smashed against the plexi glass, panting heavily as he stares at him in a rage, but Archer only smirks. "Careful, Forbes, don't poke the bear."

I have no clue what is happening between them, but the anger is pouring off of Daemon in waves, and the rest of my team curses. From what Josh has told me, this is a regular occurrence between them, they have a relationship similar to the one Josh has with Nova, but this isn't the time or the place. I skate up beside him and place my hand on his shoulder gently. I know he doesn't like to be touched, we have that in common, and though I don't know his reasons why, I can't help but feel right now he needs it.

When his stare snaps to mine, his eyes are almost black as they take me in, like he is no longer here with us, yet still I softly whisper, "Come on, Daemon, Penelope is watching."

As soon as the words leave my mouth he releases Archer like he has burned him, his stare filling with regret as he snaps his gaze over to the other team. Thankfully Penelope is too preoccupied with Nova, who has swooped in to teach her a trick, but it's the disappointment in my husband's eyes that I know will cut through Daemon the most.

I know the moment he sees it, because his stare drops to the floor and he moves as if he is going to skate away, but I immediately step in his path. "Leaving will only make it worse," I tell him softly, and his eyes snap up to mine, and what I find in them can only be described as pure heartbreak. It's at this moment that I wish more than anything that I knew what happened to him to make him the way he is. "We all make mistakes," I add in a whisper. "It's how we fix them that counts."

For a moment I almost think he is going to ignore me entirely, and I can feel Archer's stare burning into us in question, but then Daemon nods. It's small, and only once, but it's there, so I take it as a win. When I skate us back over to the team, I give Archer my best death glare, but his delight seems to have dissipated as he watches Daemon like a hawk. Ignoring them both, I make a game plan, and each of them cuts in with their ideas of how to be careful in terms of skating around Penelope.

Then it's game on, and the tension in the air is quickly forgotten as we all go head to head. Josh is just as much of a force on the ice as he always is, and with Nova on his team, it's like they are unstoppable, especially with the help of Landon. Their only downfall is Penelope, who is too busy falling in love with her older sister's boyfriend to actually care about scoring any goals. She is well and truly under the Nova Darkmore effect. Even Alexander isn't much help with his focus on Callia instead of the game, much to Josh's displeasure.

My team is faring a little better at least. After his outburst, Daemon's focus is stone cold, to the point you'd think this was an NHL final and not a friendly match between friends. I can't help but feel he needs this to burn off his emotions, and wherever he moves, Archer isn't too far behind. The more I see them together, the more confused I get. It's like they hate each other, but are also drawn to one another, and no one else seems to notice but me.

By the time the game is over we scrape a win with five points to four, and the victory is sweet when I spy the look on my husband's face. It's soon wiped off with a grin when Penelope tells him that this has been the best day ever. The look in her eyes as she stares up at him is priceless, and I know that whenever Callia decides to tell her who he really is, that she is going to be delighted.

The rest of the guys filter off the ice led by Nova, who immediately zeros straight in on Maddie, like he can't stay away from her too long, but I find myself lingering on the ice, chasing the feeling I had when I was last here.

Which is how my husband finds me.

"Should I be impressed or concerned that you easily managed a team of four hockey players to victory?" he drawls, pulling me in by the loop of my jeans until his body is flush against mine.

"Well I had an excellent teacher." I smirk, leaning my head back on his shoulder so I can meet his gaze. "Or maybe the ice was making me feel inspired," I add, skating us around the goal post with a spin.

"Oh, is that right?" he smiles, bringing his hands to my hips, squeezing them tightly, and I mildly wonder if his touch will be ever enough. "Tell me in detail exactly what inspired you, wife?" he demands, his teeth once again dancing up the skin of my neck, even as he forces us to glide around to ice.

"We have an audience," I whisper, my eyes dancing across the guys through the plexi glass, as they watch us move, not that I care, I want them to see how much he owns me.

"You're just lucky my sisters are here, otherwise I'd already be showing my teammates exactly who you belong to," he warns, his words lighting me up from the inside out.

"I wonder if my next husband will be as possessive as you," I muse out loud, and I feel his entire body flinch, but he quickly shuts it down, spinning me out from his body until I am turned towards him and skating backwards.

"Please, we've already covered that I'm a jealous psycho, remember? I'd get rid of any future prospects so fast that they'd never get the chance to be the future Mr. Hallie Rose Sanders." His words drop from his lips effortlessly, like he barely even thought them through, and my heart beats faster in my chest. "You're lucky I didn't rip Gray's arm off his fucking body earlier," he adds, and the threat towards my friend shouldn't thrill me, but it does.

"Archer is my friend, you know that, besides I'm your wife, so anything else is irrelevant," I tell him truthfully, amused that he is still so blind to how far gone I am for him.

There has never been anyone else, only him.

"No it's not, it's infuriating," he snaps, staring Archer down like a jealous asshole, as he adds, "Like I said, he's lucky I don't lay you out in front of him and show him how you like to be fucked."

Panties ruined.

His words send a rush of attraction through me, and I find it hard to breathe as I ask, "And who do I belong to?"

My words are just the taunt I wanted them to be, making his eyes turn dangerously dark. "Don't fucking push me, Tink." That temper of his is burning just as bright as always, yet still I smile as he brings us to a stop in the middle of the ice.

"I think I like pushing you," I tell him honestly, and the only thing in my mind is rule number three on our list. Absolutely no falling love. What a stupid, pointless rule, because I have loved him since the moment I met him, and with his eyes on mine, and my hips in his hands, there is no escaping that feeling.

"Yeah I think you like it too," he grunts, finally pushing us towards the edge of the rink so we can finally get off the ice, and his fingers flex around my waist as he grits, "But don't worry, I'll punish you for it later."

His words send a thrill down my spine as he pulls us down onto a bench to discard our skates, and when I meet Maddie's eye she is watching us closely.

In fact, when I look at all of them, I find all of their eyes on us, and I can't help but feel self-conscious, something to which Josh notices instantly as he snaps, "What the hell are you all looking at?"

Nova rolls his eyes at Josh's typical temper, tucking Maddie into his side, and the rest of them pretend they are looking elsewhere, but to my surprise it's Archer who responds to him. "You two skate together like your bodies are magnets to one another or something," he replies in nothing short of awe, and I can't help but blush at his statement.

I'm not sure what I expected him to say, but it definitely wasn't that, and I don't know if it's his words, or the fact that it's him saying it, but Josh is quick to pull me to my feet beside him and snap, "And? We have been skating together for almost a decade, and she knows how to do it better than any of you assholes, so leave her alone."

I don't bother pointing out that they weren't insulting me or him in any way, not that it would matter, and instead focus on Maddie's smile as Josh starts to lead us all outside. It's a smile I have never seen before, one that tells me she knows something I don't, and I remind myself to ask her about it later.

For some reason I leave the center feeling lighter than I have in weeks, and we all head over to the diner to have what Alexander is calling afternoon tea. It's the first time some of them have been there, and I recommend my usual order which most of them take me up on, and with Callia not working for once, she gets to enjoy it with us too.

By the time we are done, Penelope has every single one of them wrapped around her finger. I almost feel sorry for Callia, because she now has eight brooding and protective hockey players looking out for both her and her daughter, but hey, that's the dream right?

#30
HALLIE
TRUTH OR DARE

The next morning is Christmas Eve, and I wake up early to find Josh still sleeping soundly beside me, his arms wrapped around me like a vice. We spent last night once again losing ourselves in one another, until I felt utterly boneless, and only then did he let sleep claim him. I run my hands through his hair, memorizing the way he pushes deeper into my touch, even while he sleeps. It's moments like this that I will miss the most, the quiet in the midst of this tornado we have let ourselves get swept away in. The storm is almost over, and I can see the sunshine rising over the horizon. Question is, *how will I survive it?*

I slip out of bed silently, pulling on the jersey he discarded last night when we got home, and letting his scent surround me as I tiptoe from the room. It's early, so early in fact that I know that apart from Daemon, the rest of the house will still be sleeping, which is why I don't mind slinking down to the kitchen. I've gotten comfortable being at the house in the last few weeks, and the guys are more than used to seeing me around now, so they barely even bat an eye.

Daemon doesn't even flinch anymore as I enter the kitchen, even with his headphones on, and to my surprise he slides a fresh cup of coffee across the counter towards me, as if he was expecting me. I smile in thanks, more than used to his silence in the mornings now, and instead of lingering and making him feel like he has to talk to me, I head into the living room to enjoy my coffee.

The armchair in there has recently become my own, and I get comfy, wrapping one of Josh's blankets around my legs, and enjoying the early morning winter sun pouring in through the windows. It isn't long before Daemon takes a seat on the sofa facing the same window, and we both listen to the soft trickle of an instrumental playing from his phone.

I'm not sure how long we sit there, but it's long enough for my stomach to rumble, and at the sound, Daemon instantly rises to his feet and heads back towards the kitchen.

"You don't have to cook for me," I call out instantly, knowing that is exactly where he is going, and he freezes between the threshold of both rooms.

When he looks back at me, I can see an internal war going on inside his head, before he softly responds, "I like to cook for the people I care about."

His words render me near speechless, because out of all the things I thought he was going to say, it wasn't that, and it's only now that I truly take him in for the first time today. The dark marks beneath his eyes are more prominent than ever, like he hasn't slept properly in weeks, and my heart aches for him. I haven't forgotten about the comments Hugo Peters made to him the other night about his father, and I wonder what other secrets he is hiding in that mind of his.

I know he opens up to Josh, but I also know it isn't much,

and I find myself wishing he had something more with someone. That someone could come along and see all of his broken pieces, and somehow work out how they fit together. I know I can't say that to him, that the honesty would probably make him uncomfortable, so instead I keep it simple.

"You care about me?" I wonder aloud, knowing my question could send him into another spiral of silence, and I can see his body rocking back and forth on the spot, like he isn't sure whether he should answer the question or run.

"You're my best friend's wife," he replies simply, like that's enough explanation in itself, and when I continue to stare at him in wonder, he adds, "Josh is the closest thing I have to family these days, the closest thing that counts anyway." I can see how hard it is for him to admit that out loud, and I force myself to hold back the tears at whatever happened to him to make him this way.

"But you know the truth about us," I dare to reply in a whisper, despite all the times he has seen something more than fake between Josh and I, he has known from the beginning that it was nothing more than a ruse.

We stare one another down, and I see his eyes trail over Josh's jersey and blanket, at how comfy I am in his house, with his friends, his rings still wrapped around my finger, and he smirks. "I see everything," is all he responds with a nod, before turning and heading into the kitchen without another word.

By the time the smell of bacon and pancakes has surrounded me, the rest of the house slowly comes to life. Levi is first, Daemon's cooking making him like a bloodhound I have come to learn, before Landon slinks down beside him at the island, still half asleep. Neither of them grumble more than a good morning in my direction, as they sulk over their coffees and talk about heading home to see their families. Daemon is the only one staying home for Christmas, and though I invited him to spend the day with Josh and me at my parents' house, he politely declined, and Josh told me not to push him on it.

When Josh finally strolls down the stairs, his eyes instantly land on me, his smile predatory, as he stalks towards me without a word. I open my mouth to say good morning, but his lips on mine rob me of anything other than being able to gasp into his mouth, as his tongue starts to stroke against mine. He kisses me like he wants to keep me, with nothing but possession and power, and I never want to be kissed by anyone but him ever again.

When we pull apart I find all three guys watching us, Landon with a smirk, Levi with worry, and Daemon with an intensity I can't even begin to describe. Thankfully Josh ignores all of them, and heads into the kitchen to fetch us breakfast without me even moving from the chair.

I'm handed a plate of pancakes topped with sprinkles, and when I flick my stare towards Daemon in question, he shrugs with a blush. "It's Christmas," is all he responds, tucking into his own breakfast, as we all enjoy our food together.

Once we are done, all the guys disperse from the kitchen. Levi and Landon moving to get ready to head home, and Daemon because, well because he is Daemon.

I stay cocooned in my blanket in the chair, quietly reading on my phone, as Josh reaches me and gestures for me to let him in the chair with me. I don't bother following his command because just as I expect, without even waiting for me to answer, he reaches down and picks me up, steals my spot, and then places me onto his lap effortlessly. He tucks the blanket back around us, and positions me on his lap sideways so he can nuzzle into my neck. I try to stay focused on my reading, I really do, but it seems that my fictional boyfriends are for once not as intriguing as my husband.

Especially when his hands start to run up and down my bare

legs in slow, sensual strokes. When I look at him he is watching me closely, and I do my best not to squirm in his lap under his stare. I can feel his erection slowly growing against my ass, and I know the moment that he knows I feel it, because he smirks at me wickedly. My eyes flick back to my book with a focus I don't currently possess, trying and failing to ignore him, but that only intrigues him more.

"What's got you staring at that screen so hard, Hals?" he asks, kissing the side of my neck gently, as his hands start to brush up my inner thigh. When his eyes drop to my phone and he spies what I am looking at, they widen in surprise and delight. "Are you reading porn while sitting in my lap, Mrs. Peters?"

I blush furiously, yet still manage to keep my voice strong as I reply, "Technically I was reading it before I sat in your lap, you're the one who disturbed me." I've been reading for the last thirty-minutes as I enjoyed my pancakes and he and the guys chatted away in the kitchen none the wiser.

"Are you telling me you have been sitting here with my teammates all morning reading smut about..." his voice trails off as he takes in more of the words on my phone. "Wait, how many guys are there?" he asks, voice incredulous, as he reads a particularly spicy scene in the why choose romance I am currently in the middle of.

"Three guys," I whisper, not because I feel self conscious, but because his hands are dangerously close to finding out just how much fun I have been having while sitting here. "She doesn't pick, she is in a relationship with all of them."

His eyes flick to mine as his hand tightens around my thigh. "At the same time?" I nod, making his eyes darken with lust. "Is that what you want, wife, three men worshiping you?" he asks, resuming his stroking on my leg, only this time he gets even higher, his fingers brushing against the damp lace of my panties. "Should I call my teammates down here and let them watch as I make you come?" he adds, slipping his fingers inside and groaning at how dripping wet I already am. "Fuck, I think you would like that," he grits, massaging my pussy gently, and my eyes flick to the stairs in a panic.

"Joshua, they could come down at any minute," I gasp, as he brushes his fingers against my clit.

"Isn't that what you want?" he purrs, licking a strip of skin up my neck, and I tip my head back to give him more access.

"What happened to my jealous, psycho husband," I pant, not wanting to be caught, yet not caring if we are. He is barely even touching me yet his fingers are like magic.

"Oh, no one is allowed to touch you, Tink, you belong only to me" he grumbles against my neck, licking and nipping at the skin there, as if he is imagining it's my pussy. "But I'd let them listen to you scream my name while I make you fall apart." He pairs his words with a gentle circling of my clit and I can't keep in the moan that spills past my lips.

"Joshua, please" I pant, desperate for him to move his finger even faster, yet he continues to tease me until I feel like I am losing my mind.

"That's it, baby, let them hear you beg," he teases, rubbing my clit with his middle finger until I am writhing in his lap, my phone now being crushed between my fingers until I fear it might break.

I open my mouth to beg for more when footsteps start to thunder down the stairs, and then Landon appears, with Levi hot on his heels. They are both heading out to see their families, Landon to see his sister, and Levi to see his dad, both who don't live too far from one another, so they are driving together. They barely even pay us any notice as they dump their bags at the door and head into the kitchen to grab some supplies for the road.

If it wasn't for the blanket across our legs they would see my parted thighs, my pussy dripping as Josh glides his fingers through it. I try to clamp my legs together, to push him off, but all it does is send my husband wilder. His fingers pick up their pace, mixing between toying with my clit and sliding down to sink inside of me, all the while his friends talk back and forth in the kitchen, completely unaware.

"Look at them, Tink, they have no idea that I am playing with your pretty little cunt," he whispers against my ear, making my entire body shudder. "Should I make you scream for me now? Should I let them hear how perfect you sound when you come?" My entire body burns beneath his touch, and I don't think he will have much choice in making me come, I'm already halfway there.

With their focus in the pantry pulling out snacks, Josh moves me slightly so his hand can fully sink down with ease, as he slips his finger into my cunt all the way to the hilt, and then starts to slowly grind his palm against my clit. I hold back another moan, biting my lip so hard that I taste copper on my tongue, yet still I grind my hips against his hand.

"I can feel your pussy squeezing my finger, baby, do you like the idea of being watched, of being caught with your pussy all filled up?"

Fuck. Who the fuck taught him to speak like this?

His words have my brain short-circuiting as my body begins to tremble, but I think I'd rather die than have him stop touching me right now.

My cheeks start to heat and I feel his chuckle as he slips another finger deep into my pussy, praising me as I clench around him. "Such a good little wife."

When the guys turn towards us, it takes everything in me to swallow my moans, and I focus on my phone like it's the most interesting thing in the world, as Josh pretends to laze around beneath me.

"You guys heading out?" he asks, his tone appearing completely casual and unaffected, as his fingers continue to sink in and out of my cunt.

"Yeah we want to get on the road before the traffic gets too crazy," Landon replies, but it's Levi's gaze I can feel burning into us.

"Okay, well drive safe," Josh tosses back, giving them that typical guy nod, and turning his attention to my phone, as if whatever is on it is also interesting to him.

"Merry Christmas guys," Landon calls over his shoulder as he heads out, and after lingering for just a second longer, Levi follows after him too.

Josh doesn't even wait for the front door to fully shut, before he is slamming his fingers in and out of me, and rubbing his palm against my clit like his only mission in life is to make me come. His other hand snatches around my throat and turns my head so he can capture my mouth with his own. Then he is fucking me with his hand, capturing every gasp and moan, while his friends are still right outside.

I come so hard I swear I black out for a second, but he doesn't relent, just continues to fuck me through my orgasm until I am grinding and panting against him like a horny little slut. Then before I can even catch my breath, he rips the blanket off us, pulls my panties to the side, and then frees his cock, pumping it twice, before lining it up with my pussy and slamming me down onto it.

The moan tears from my throat freely now, as Josh sweeps my hair to the side over my shoulder, and leans back in the chair and starts fucking me from below. "Fuck, this god damn jersey" he groans deeply, his hands spreading my ass cheeks, as he no doubt watches himself sink inside of me. "Do you have any idea how fucking good it feels to fuck my wife while *our* last name is spread across your back?" he grunts, fisting his jersey, and pulling it tight against my skin, as I grind my hips into his. "You look so fucking good in it, Hals," he adds with an almost pained moan, like he has been holding in that truth for far too long.

My eyes flick towards the window where I can clearly still see Landon and Levi loading up the car, as I moan, "Joshua, they could still catch us," I gasp, his cock hitting that place inside of me, as he releases the jersey and leans up to bring his chest to my back.

I continue to grind into his lap, my chest heaving as he cups my tits through the fabric, toying with my nipples until they are hard and aching. "Someone already has," he grunts into my ear, his pace never relenting, as his left hand closes around my throat, his thumb pushing my head to the right where I meet the dark and stormy eyes of his roommate.

Daemon is standing frozen on the threshold of the room, his eyes taking in every inch of the scene before him, and I can't stop the clenching of my pussy in his presence. *Fuck. What the hell is wrong with me?*

Granted he can't exactly see anything, I am drowned in Josh's jersey so both my tits and pussy are still covered, but it doesn't take a genius to figure out why I am grinding in his best friend's lap. I expect Josh to stop, or tell Daemon to fuck off, but I watch as Daemon's eyes collide with my husband's, and they have some sort of silent communication.

I can't read the expression on Daemon's face, his mask blanker than my own, just like always, yet Josh's hand flexes around my throat possessively. "Stay," Josh commands, and I should be embarrassed, maybe even ashamed, but when his eyes flick back over us both and turn heated, I can't help but bask in the forbiddenness of it all. Especially when Josh's mouth is still hot on my neck as he breathes, "Daemon likes to watch."

His words force me back to the night of Halloween, because of course I already know that Daemon likes to watch. I remember vividly what it felt like when he watched Archer kiss me and feeling more free than I did then, I can't help but smile, as I reply, "I know, I remember." Josh squeezes my throat in response, the heat of his ring blinding, as he silently pleads for more information. "He was there during truth or dare," I add, still slowly riding him under the watchful eyes of his friend. "He watched as Alexander dared Archer to kiss me."

The hand around my throat flexes again at the mention of kissing his teammate, and he grunts, grinding his cock into me a little harder until I moan. "Does my wife want to play again?" Josh asks, letting his other hand slip beneath the hem of his jersey so he can play with my clit. I'm nodding before I even realize, marveling at how Daemon's body turns to stone at our conversation. "Truth or dare, Hallie?"

Not yet confident enough to pick what I know he wants me to, I can't help but gasp out, "Truth." I feel his smirk against my ear, his harsh, moaned breaths only sending me even more wild for him.

"Do you like my best friend watching you? Do you like knowing you belong to me and that I can own you like this? Do you like feeling his eyes trail over you while you ride my cock like a fucking goddess knowing I won't let him or anyone else touch you?"

Fuck.

"Yes," I moan, clenching around him, his filthy words making me even wetter. "Yes, yes, I like it."

Josh's hand is dripping between my thighs, playing with the mess I am making for him, as he purrs, "Good girl." I know the moment his eyes flick back to Daemon, watching him, warning him, yet his friend doesn't move an inch. "Now let's play again, truth or dare, Hallie, and you already used your truth."

His hand slows his pace against my clit making me groan, as I grind my hips down into him silently begging for more. I know

I won't get it, not until I give him what he wants, no, what he needs, and fuck I have never felt more powerful. He might have all the control, but he is giving me a freedom I have never even thought was possible.

My eyes collide with Daemon's again, and I swear I can see amusement there, like he is trying to convey some sort of message, not that I am in any position to decipher it right now. Josh's hand is slick as it sides up and down my pussy, giving Daemon everything, yet showing him nothing. It's exhilarating, and all I can do is smirk as I breathe, "Dare."

Josh's voice is stained in nothing but pleasure as he demands, "I dare you to come on my cock while my best friend watches."

Fuck.

The sentence has barely fallen from his lips before he starts pounding into me from below, and when I try to move my own hips again he tightens his hold. Then he is pumping into me from below, driving his dick so hard into my pussy that the only sounds in the room are our pleasured breaths, and the wet smack our bodies. The sound is obscene, and I just take it. I take every inch of his cock, as his best friend watches, and I have never been more turned on in my life.

Daemon surveys us with keen interest, but his eyes bounce between the two of us, like he can't quite choose where to look, and when my pussy starts clenching at the thought of him enjoying seeing both of us, Josh uses the hand around my throat to pull my stare back to him.

"I think that's enough looking at my best friend, wife, I want your eyes on mine when you come for me," he grunts, shoving my hips back down on his, and all I can do is stare at him and let him see what he does to me.

"Joshua," I whisper, wanting this little moment only for us, and his eyes sparkle, as he feels me getting ready to fall apart around him.

"Come for me, baby, I love feeling you squeezing my dick," he murmurs against my mouth, grinding our hips together, until I am shaking against him, as my orgasm takes over completely.

"Fuck," I scream, flexing my own hands on his knees and bouncing up and down on his cock, as I ride out my wave of pleasure, only spurred on by two manly grunts as they watch me.

I know the moment that Josh is ready to explode, because he releases my throat and grips my hips in both hands, slamming me back down onto his cock roughly. I toss my head back against his shoulder, closing my eyes, too sensitive to see or do anything but take him, and with one last snap of his hips, he is coming with a loud groan.

I am panting and breathless against him, my whole body trembling from the aftermath of his onslaught, and when he trails his mouth up my neck, all I can do is purr like a damn kitten.

"Fuck, Tink, what the hell am I going to do with you," he grits against my skin, his words burning like fire, and when I open my eyes to look at him, I find him staring at me intensely. "You okay?" he asks softly, and my eyes flick over to where Daemon was standing, but I find him already gone.

"Have you ever done anything like that before?" I whisper, and I don't know why but he barks a laugh, like what i just said was the funniest thing he has ever heard.

"Hallie, I have never done anything like what I do with you," he murmurs, pulling me in for another kiss as if he can't stand not having the taste of me in his mouth. Yet I'm not sure what he sees on my face, because he sighs gently, pulling us back into the chair, his cock still inside of me, as he adds, "Fucking for me was always just an outlet, I was in, out, then gone. You're the only person I have ever had more with, or wanted more with."

His words light me up inside, only now that my lust haze has passed, I can't help but wonder why he let Daemon watch us, no matter how hot and enjoyable it was.

"How do you know Daemon likes to watch?" I ask, searching his stare, as his hands start to rub all over my body again.

"It's his thing," he shrugs. "Never with me before, but I've heard rumors about him, hard not to sometimes." I mean he's not wrong, there is more gossip at FU than there was in high school, there is always something, yet I remember the night on Halloween.

Daemon was watching Archer not me, and just now, his eyes didn't stay on me, they trailed over my husband too. So was he watching me, or them?

Those questions aren't mine to answer, nor are the answers my concern, so instead I focus back on Josh as I ask, "And what's your thing?"

"You," he replies instantly and without thought, and I blush harder than when he just fucked me in front of his friend.

"Then why did you just let your best friend watch me come?" I question with a smile, not sure if I will ever be able to look Dameon in the eye again after what just happened. Thank god Landon and Levi didn't realize what we were doing as they left.

"Because I know you're mine," his answer is just as quick as the last, and hope soars inside of my chest. "The whole town could watch me fuck you and it wouldn't make you any less mine, you've got my ring on your finger and my last name, you belong to me and no one else," he adds, and his words shouldn't delight me, they shouldn't have me feeling needy to let him fuck me again, but apparently I don't have a limit when it comes to my husband. "Now stand up so I can watch my cum drip down your legs, wife," he purrs, pushing me off his dick and to my feet, his growl scraping against my very soul, as I feel his release sliding down my skin. "Turn around," he commands, and I do instantly, looking down at him, but his eyes remain firmly between my thighs.

Then he is dragging his fingers through his cum, collecting it up, before rising to his feet with it dripping from his ring finger. I know his next demand before he can even voice it out loud, and I open my mouth and wrap my lips around his finger, licking it clean completely, making him groan.

When I pull back, his lips are on mine before I can take my next breath, and for the first time since this started, I forget about the rules, I forget about the deal, and I let myself feel that this is all real. That feeling only intensifies when he dips down and picks me up, wrapping my legs around him, and moving towards the stairs.

"Come on, wife, you can swallow my dick in the shower like you just did my finger, before I lay you out and show you the only person who will ever own you again is your husband."

I've never agreed to something so fast in my life.

#31
JOSH
PENGUIN PJS

If someone would have told me three months ago, that I'd be waking up on Christmas morning with my wife wrapped around me naked, I would have laughed. If they'd have told me that my wife would be Hallie, I would have thought they were downright insane, yet here we are. Yesterday was easily one of the best days I have ever had, from the public claiming of her on the sofa, to watching her head bob back and forth on my dick, while I fisted her wet hair in the shower, and don't even get me started on the ten orgasms I gave her with my tongue. Yes, ten, one for every year I have known her. I'm a gentleman like that. Yet none of that compares to how it felt when I sunk my dick inside her and took her nice and slow, her body trembling, and face stained in tears of pleasure.

Fuck. That image isn't one I will forget anytime soon.

We also enjoyed a quiet dinner with Daemon, which to my surprise wasn't awkward in the slightest. I've known Daemon for a long time, and despite our strong friendship he still keeps me at arm's length, but that doesn't mean I don't notice things about him, whether he wants me to or not. I've seen him around girls, I mean they practically throw themselves at him, yet I have never seen him indulge with any of them. Most people presume that whatever dark secrets are lurking in his past are the reason, but I think it's something else entirely. Which is why when I saw him come down the stairs yesterday I didn't stop, because I knew he'd enjoy the show without showing any true interest in my wife.

No, I've figured out he's interested in chasing something different entirely.

Hallie is still sleeping softly in my arms, and all I can do is watch her like some sort of stalker. The eye mask is still firmly across her head, and Percy is tucked dutifully under her arm, but the only thing I can truly focus on is where her legs are tangled with mine. The weight of her body against mine is like a drug, and despite the fact my father will soon be in prison, and our deal will no longer be required, I can't see myself letting her go.

The thought plagues me for almost an hour until she begins stirring in my arms, her ass rubbing on my very interested dick, just like it always does. When she tries to move, I nuzzle her neck one last time, before I loosen my arms and let her stretch out. When she pushes the mask off her eyes, she blinks a few times before she focuses on me and groans.

"Why are you watching me sleep you pervert?" she grumbles, turning over and tucking her head into my chest.

I still marvel at how comfortable she is with me, how easily she lets me touch her, how much she seeks it out, and it's all I can do not to beg her to stay in this bed with me forever. My hands reach down to her hips and pull her against me, wrapping one of her thighs over my waist, and tucking her against me even tighter, yet still it's not enough. *Will it ever be enough?*

"Maybe your snoring woke me up," I tease, and her fingers

reach up and pinch my nipple sharp and tight until I yelp. "Ow, what the hell was that for?"

She shrugs in my arms. "It's too early, I don't have the energy to dick punch you yet."

My cock leaps at just the mention of the word dick, and I lean down and press soft kisses to her ear as I ask, "Is it too early to do other stuff to my dick?" I roll my hips against her, letting her feel my erection that is no longer just morning wood, and completely for her.

"You're insatiable," she murmurs, pushing her hands around my neck, and lining my jaw with kisses.

"Nope, just addicted to the feeling of my wife's pussy wrapped around me," I tell her truthfully, rolling her onto her back, and spreading her thighs so I can rest comfortably between them.

"Then fuck me nice and slow, husband, I want to make sure you can feel me squeeze every inch of you."

Fuck, her mouth is wicked, which is how I find myself sliding my cock up and down her slit, before slowing sinking inside to the hilt. Her pussy spasms around me instantly, and I do exactly what she asked. I fuck her slow, with long, steady snaps of my hips, until she is begging for more, yet I don't stop. I can't stop, not until she has come twice around my dick, and only then do I grind my hips against her in small but quick circles, until my own release fills her up completely.

I drop my forehead to hers, letting our panted breaths mix together, until I can finally breathe again. Then I kiss her slowly and sweetly. "Merry Christmas, Hals," I whisper against her mouth, and she smiles, and for once I don't dread this damn holiday.

Once we both climb out of bed and shower, Hallie insists on us wearing the matching pajamas she bought us covered in penguins, and we head down to the kitchen to search for coffee and breakfast.

"I hope you got me more than your dick for Christmas," Hallie scolds as we reach the kitchen, and to my surprise there is already bacon and eggs keeping warm in the pan.

Daemon is sitting at the counter nursing what I am going to presume is around his fourth cup of coffee, while reading an old and battered copy of *The Great Gatsby*. He offers us both the slight tip of his head as a good morning, but when his eyes scan across us, I see a ghost of a smirk tug at the corner of his mouth. "Nice PJs," he grunts, turning the page and focusing back on his book.

I snort a laugh at my wife, ignoring Daemon, because these pajamas are awesome and comfy as fuck, and pour both me and Hallie a cup of coffee.

"Hals, don't act like my dick isn't the best present you've ever had, but I knew you'd chop it off if I didn't get you actual gifts, so yes I got you more than my dick for Christmas," I muse, turning round to lean on the counter and find her blushing furiously. Fuck she looks good in the morning, even covered in penguins.

"Such a good husband," she coos, picking up an envelope on the table with both our names on it, and slipping out a piece of paper from inside.

"What is it?" I ask, sipping my coffee, and she doesn't even look up, her eyes tracking every part of the paper in awe.

I shove off the counter and move to peer over her shoulder, only to find a sketch of us from our wedding day. It's so detailed that it may as well be a black and white photograph, and I don't know what I am more surprised about, the fact it's such a good drawing, or the fact he even let us see it in the first place.

"This is amazing," Hallie finally breathes, devouring every part of it, before her eyes dance up to meet mine and then flick over to my best friend. "Daemon, is this from you?" she asks, and his eyes flick to hers nervously, before he nods gently.

Daemon never shows anyone his art, in fact I think outside of me and his art professor, Hallie is the first person to see it in years.

"He's an amazing artist, not that he ever usually shows anyone his work," I reply, giving him a stern look, and he grunts, but I just can't get over how unbelievably talented he is and the fact that he chooses to hide it.

"Daemon this is breathtaking," she smiles, shaking her head in disbelief, and looking at the piece of art as if it is the most precious thing she has ever been given, before she adds, "Although you kind of stole my idea." She rolls her eyes, taking the picture with her, as she moves to the small Christmas tree we have set up in the corner, and grabs one of the boxes.

We always buy each other a present on Christmas and birthdays, we always have, but I'm not sure if my gift this year is overstepping the mark a little. I just hope it can allow us to broach the topic of being more than just a business deal.

I let Hallie go first, and when she slides the present over the island towards me, her smile is smug. "This might be the best present I ever got you," she preens, and my interest is thoroughly peaked.

I put my coffee down and rip into the paper, revealing a long, flat, slim box, and when I take off the lid I find a picture from our wedding.

"It's a wedding picture," she offers pointlessly, coming around the island to stand by my side to admire it with me.

"I can see that, Hals, but this is just a picture of you, I'm not even in it," I laugh, flicking my stare between her and the picture, and she rolls her eyes.

"Joshua, if you're so desperate to see yourself, look in the mirror, this picture is perfect," she grumbles, moving to slide into one of the seats, and taking a drink of her coffee.

I flick it around to show Daemon and he smirks again, the biggest one I have ever probably seen from him on a day that he hates so much, before I focus back on the photograph. She's right, the picture is perfect, it's one of the only ones the photographer took of her alone, and she looks absolutely stunning, but she looks just as stunning right now perched on the chair in her penguin pajamas, sipping her drink.

"Why do I need the picture when I have the real thing?" I ask, moving to drop a kiss to her shoulder, before I head to the tree to grab the gift I got for her.

"It's to put with the other two in your room, so all your future conquests know that you belonged to me first," she teases, and now it's my turn to roll my eyes. She really has no idea how deep in this thing I am with her.

I slide the small, wrapped box onto the counter in front of her, and then move to plate us both some breakfast as I toss over my shoulder, "I thought we already covered that the only Mr. Hallie Rose Sanders will be me, so stop trying to get rid of me." I place the plates in front of us and take a seat at her side, watching as she gently unwraps the gift with shaking hands. When she sees the black velvet jewelry box, her eyes instantly flick to mine and I laugh, "Don't worry, it's not another ring."

Daemon snorts, but there is no humor on Hallie's face as she focuses back on the box. Flicking it open she reveals a small, dainty chain, silver in color because she never wears gold, with a little letter J dangling from it. The letter has a small green diamond at the bottom to match her ring, and I panic slightly at her silence. Maybe she hates it? Maybe it's too much?

Her eyes flick to mine and I see the question in them before she even voices it, so I quickly rush out, "It's from that Taylor song you like, you know the one about wearing his initials on a chain round your neck."

"Not because he owns me but cause he really knows me," she whispers, and I nod at the sound of the lyrics, as her focus turns back to the necklace.

"Josh, I don't even know what to say," she starts, and panic curls in my throat. "You don't have to say anything," I'm quick to say, and I swear I can feel Daemon's smirk from here in my panic.

"It's beautiful," she cuts me off, pulling it from the box, and instantly passing it over to me, before giving me her back, and swiping her hair up to allow me to put it on. My hands are steadier than I feel as I pull it around her neck and fasten it, before she lets her hair drop, and looks down on it. "It's perfect, I love it, thank you," she tells me, turning round and pulling my head down to hers.

The kiss she gives me feels permanent, like she is trying to tell me something without words, except I don't know what it is. In fact, the only thing I do seem to know lately is that I seem to have developed very real feelings for my very fake wife.

After breakfast, I hand over the gifts I bought for Daemon, a new sketch pad and some pencils, and to my surprise, Hallie hands him a vinyl from one of his favorite operas. He blushed furiously, much to my amusement, before slinking away back to his room to hide away for the rest of the day. Once we are dressed, Hallie questions whether we should check on him before we leave, but I shake my head. I don't know what his issue with Christmas is, but I do know that he always spends it alone, no matter how hard I try to coax him into it. I know he will be grateful for the gifts from us, but I can't help but feel bad as we leave the house and he stays behind all alone.

The drive over to Hallie's parents is familiar enough to me, which is a good thing, because the amount of times my eyes stray from the road over to my wife is a crime. Of course she is fidgeting nervously in her seat, insisting we play the same song on repeat, as she babbles to me about how she knew what to get Daemon for Christmas. She's nervous, that much is clear, but for the life of me I can't work out why. Beth and Jeremy are amazing people, and even better parents, it's why I went straight to them after Thanksgiving, because I knew they'd understand. So, I'm not sure what Hallie is so concerned about.

By the time we arrive, Hallie is talking so fast that I can barely keep up, and when she jumps from the car before letting me open the door, I know something is really up. She rushes towards the front door, but before she can ring the bell, I grab her waist, spin her, and pull her body against me.

"Okay, spit it out, Tink," I demand, and she tries and fails to put a blank mask on her face, as if I don't know her by now.

"Spit what out?" she huffs, looking anywhere but at me.

"Whatever the hell is bothering you," I snap, feeling irritated that we even need to be having this conversation. She's normally the one person who can tell me anything.

"Nothing is bothering me," she quickly lies, and I almost laugh at how bad she is at it.

"Now, now, remember the rules, don't lie to me, baby." Her eyes soften at the term of endearment, but still she pulls her lip into her mouth and nibbles on it nervously.

"We have to act normal while we're here," she breathes, finally staring up at me. "My parents know this is fake remember, so we can't be you know, touching and kissing in front of them and stuff, they will ask too many questions."

Her request shouldn't gut me, no matter how unexpected it is, yet still it does. Of course she's right, I came to this very house and asked for their permission to commit this ruse and promised them I would protect their daughter, and that nothing would happen to her. Except I happened to her. She sleeps in my bed almost every night because I insisted on taking her, not caring for the repercussions, and it's a bitter pill to swallow.

I release her instantly, already nodding my head. "Sorry, yeah, of course, I wasn't thinking what it would look like." I turn away from her, not wanting her to see the look in my eyes, as I reach out and ring the doorbell.

She watches me carefully, but before she can say anything else, her mom is ripping open the door with a wide smile.

"Ah, there you guys are, come in, come in, I've been so excited for you to get here," Beth gushes, ushering us both inside, before pulling her daughter in for a hug. "Merry Christmas, Sweetheart," she greets Hallie, before pushing back and holding her at arm's length, checking her over just like she always does.

When her eyes flick to mine they lighten even more. "Josh, dear, look at you, you get more handsome every time I see you," she coos, pulling me in for a warm hug of my own, which I can't help but reciprocate.

"And you get more beautiful," I tell her truthfully, almost the mirror image of her daughter, and she smiles and rolls her eyes in just the same way as Hallie.

"Hey, you've got your own wife now, Peters, stop hitting on mine," Jeremy calls out, as he walks down the hall from the kitchen. "Looking good, son," he adds, and I hold my hand out for him to shake, but he bats it aside and pulls me in for a hug just like his wife.

I've always liked Hallie's parents, and for some bizarre reason, they have always liked me too, and I can't help but feel happy knowing that she had it better than I ever did growing up. "It's good to see you," I reply, smacking his shoulder, before we pull apart, and he turns his focus to his daughter.

"There's my Hallie Bear," he smiles, cuddling her tight, before pulling back and ushering us all back to the kitchen with him. "Thank god you're finally here, your mother has been driving me crazy all morning," he complains, heading over to the sink to wash his hands. "Why don't you girls go relax in the den and us men can finish off the cooking."

Hallie looks at me a little alarmed, but I'm already slipping out of my jacket and rolling up my sleeves.

"Dad, Josh didn't come here to help you cook," she complains, looking more nervous than I have ever seen her, and Jeremy looks at her with a smile.

"Hals, this might be the only son-in-law I ever get, I need to get my money's worth out of him."

Hallie rolls her eyes. "Don't be ridiculous, he won't be the only son-in-law you ever get," she sighs dramatically, discarding her own coat.

Oh yes I fucking will be.

"I thought we already covered that I'm going to be the only Mr. Hallie Rose Sanders, Tink, don't make me let my jealous streak out," I tell her sternly, and her mother laughs, taking a seat at the counter to watch as I start working beside her husband.

Hallie reluctantly takes the seat next to her, both of them ignoring her father's request to head to the den. I quietly start chopping up vegetables as Hallie snaps, "No, the only thing we covered is that you're a psycho."

I keep my focus on my knife skills as I reply, "I think I've been a very calm husband so far."

Her scoff is adorable. "Oh, is that what we call breaking people's bones?"

My smile comes easy as I remember how good it felt to feel Joey's arm break beneath my fingers, I only wish I'd have done it again when we saw him at the rink. "Technically I wasn't your husband when I did that," I shrug, as her mom flicks her stare between us in shock, as she gasps in question, "You broke someone's bones?"

Hallie looks delighted at her mom's interest, turning her stare towards her as if she expects her mom to be on her side. "Remember Joey," she asks sweetly.

"You mean Jockstrap Jerkoff," her mom nods, and I snort a laugh as Hallie huffs, but I don't know why, the only person who could have told Beth that nickname was her.

"Yes, well, Josh broke his arm back when I graduated high school, it's why I never heard from him again," she tells them, like a total little narc.

"He's lucky that's all I did," I tell her carefully, before flicking my stare to Jeremy's as I explain, "He was talking shit about her to his dumb friends."

Jer barely even pauses as he holds his hand out for me to fist bump. "That's my boy."

When I look back at Hallie she huffs again, as she mutters, "You're such an asshole."

I ensure my smile is sweet as I respond, "And you're such a brat."

I feel her parents watching us, flicking their stare between us and each other, and I kick myself internally after what Hallie said outside. Although I'm not sure I can hide how much I enjoy being married to their daughter, I remind myself to try and not act like this thing is real.

Even if I think it is.

By the time we've had dinner, Hallie has argued with me no less than thirty times, much to her parents' amusement, and when they keep agreeing with me, she only gets angrier. I excuse myself to help her mom with the dishes, leaving Hals and Jer to talk business with one another, yet still I can't help my eyes from flicking over to her every few seconds.

"Being married suits you," her mother comments from my

side, and my gaze snaps from her daughter to her, to find her already watching me. "For the first time since I have known you, that darkness that surrounds you seems a little less black."

I ensure my voice remains calm and steady as I reply, "Your daughter just has that effect on people I guess, she's like a ball of sunshine."

Beth watches me and I try my best to keep my face blank, but still she offers me a knowing smile as she passes me another dish to dry. "That ball of sunshine is happier than I have ever seen her," she whispers, flicking her stare over to her daughter, and I can't help but do the same.

Hallie is reading over a file with her dad, pointing stuff out and talking animatedly about what she would do if she were to invest in them, and I swear I have never seen her look more comfortable or at ease. Gone are the anxiety and nerves she had on the way over here, and Beth is right, for once, she looks completely and truly happy.

Could this thing between us actually work?

Is there a world where I can take down my father and still keep her?

Could we forget the deal we made, rip up that list of rules, and just continue on as we have been, but no longer faking it?

I guess there is only one way to find out. First I have to take my father down, and then ask my wife if I can keep her.

#32
HALLIE
BAD OMENS

The week between Christmas and New Year passes in a blur, and the more phone calls Josh excuses himself to take with Lincoln, the more on edge I become. Apparently the downfall of his father will start as soon as we ring in the new year, and I have never felt more afraid in my life. Josh hasn't given me any indication of wanting this thing between us to end, yet still I live in limbo wondering when the walls of this fake marriage will come crashing down.

Tonight is New Year's Eve, and Hugo is throwing a huge party to celebrate not only the new year, but our wedding too. Which means not only has he invited half the town, but also all of Josh's teammates. When Josh got wind of it, he went crazy, frantically calling Lincoln to work out if this is some kind of ploy on his father's end, but I wasn't surprised. Mayor Hugo Peters only ever does things to make himself look good, and he couldn't exactly throw a party for his son and not invite his team.

I'm standing in front of the mirror in Josh's room, staring at myself in the short white dress I picked out for the evening. The material is silky and sheen, hugging tight around my torso, with pearls encrusted across the chest, and flared out with a pop at my waist. My hair is twisted up into an elaborate bun, with a couple of my curls framing my face, and I went heavy on my makeup as always, giving myself a silver smokey eye and a soft pink lip. For any wedding party I look perfect, for my own wedding party I look like a fraud.

A sound at the door draws my attention, and I flick my eyes up to meet Josh's in the mirror. He is leaning on the doorframe looking even more handsome than usual in his dark tuxedo, and it's all I can do not to drool. Especially when he pushes off the door and stalks towards me until his chest is pressed against my back, his lips dropping to the bare skin of my shoulder.

"How the hell did I land a wife so beautiful?" he asks, kissing up my neck and pulling me in by my hips.

I try not to let the butterflies in my stomach affect me as I tip my neck to the side and softly reply, "You got on your knees and begged me to marry you."

His smile is instant, as if remembering the moment as well as I do, before moving to stand in front of me, and tucking one of my face-framing curls behind my ear. "And I'd do it again in an instant," he tells me firmly, not a speck of dishonesty in his tone. "You look beautiful, Mrs. Peters," he adds, dropping a gentle kiss to the side of my mouth.

"You don't look so bad yourself," I manage to choke out, making him smirk.

"Come on, we need to leave, because if you keep looking at me like that, I'm going to ruin your dress, makeup, hair, and pussy, and I know you spent a long time getting ready." His words make me blush, his hands never leaving my skin as he guides me towards the door, and I half wonder how much damage he could really do if I let him bend me over the bed before we leave.

Unfortunately we really do have to go, and by the time we make it downstairs hand in hand, the rest of the house is already waiting. All dressed in some form of suit or tuxedo of their own, Daemon, Levi, and Landon, are all idling by the door for us, ready to go.

When they hear our footsteps their eyes all flick towards us, but Levi is the first to break the silence as he blurts, "Wow, Hals, you look beautiful."

My blush only deepens as I feel Josh's hand flex in mine. "Eyes off my wife, Jones, I don't want to have to get your blood on her pretty dress."

For a second Levi looks as if he is going to say something, but his eyes flick between the two of us then quickly meet the floor, and the tension in the air is thick so I quickly rush out, "Are we ready to go?" The guys all nod, and we head out to make our way to the Mayor's mansion.

When we arrive, the whole place looks like a winter wonderland with decorations and lights placed everywhere. There are multiple valets parking cars, and guards checking the list of names as people enter. Of course we are ushered in without pause as the noted guests of honor, and I can already feel my throat itching for a drink to get me through this night.

"Is this really where you grew up," Landon groans in awe, but from the look in his eyes, I know he remembers the visit from Josh's father just as well as I do.

There was a steep price to pay to grow up here.

As soon as we enter the main dining hall where the Mayor always hosts his parties, I spy Maddie, Nova, and the rest of the team already taking up space on one of the long tables across the back of the room, and I head straight there.

"Hals, finally," Maddie groans, lost in a sea of testosterone. She looks more than pleased to see me, as she makes space for me to sit down next to her. "You look beautiful."

"So do you," I reply, admiring the soft satin length of her black gown, that looks perfect against Nova's black suit. The two of them look as if they have stepped right off a runway, and I'm sure her father is somewhere glaring daggers at the two of them, at least that's what I can guess from the snarl on Nova's face.

"Mr. and Mrs. Peters," Archer drunkenly drawls. "Great party, thanks for inviting me."

Josh lets his stare flick over him only once before he replies dryly, "I didn't"

The rest of the guys take their seats, and for some reason there is a tension in the air I can't understand. I mean, sure I get why Nova is pissed after what Hugo did to his mom, and of course Josh would rather be anywhere but here, yet the rest of the team seem on edge too. Archer is already completely off his face, and Daemon looks at him in disgust. Alexander looks bored, Landon looks intrigued, and Levi looks downright pissed off.

When the waiter passes with a tray of champagne, I quickly snatch one up, downing it in one gulp before the taste of it can actually register. Then I survey the rest of the room slowly, taking in the number of notable businessmen and politicians, and I can't help but wonder what they will all soon say about their precious Mayor.

An elaborate dinner, which I barely touch, is followed by more drinks, and by the time Hugo has made some bullshit speech about love, marriage, and unity, Josh looks ready to explode. So Daemon hauls him off for a walk around the grounds to calm down, but I doubt the December chill could thaw the ice already surrounding him this evening.

I turn my focus to Nova, where he leads Maddie around the dance floor, as Hugo watches them with nothing but contempt, and I find myself looking forward to watching him fall. When his eyes flick my way, I even hold my drink up in cheers, before taking a sip and never letting myself drop his stare. By the time he looks away from me he looks nothing short of pissed, and I roll my eyes at what a pathetic piece of shit he is when it comes to his children.

I'm lounging by the bar, sipping on some cocktail named after Josh and I when Levi finds me. "Hals, there you are, enjoying your party?" he asks, signaling to the waiter for another drink.

"I've had root canals more fun than this," I reply dryly, and he laughs like it's the funniest joke he ever heard. I can't help but drag my stare over him now, noting how on edge he seems as his eyes flick around the room wildly. "Is everything okay?" I ask, causing him to snap his stare to me, and what I see in it makes my stomach jolt, and my eyes quickly drop down to my drink.

If I'm not mistaken, I would say I could see attraction burning there, towards me of all people. No, I'm being silly, I'm bad at this sort of thing, I've probably just had too many cocktails. At least that's what I tell myself, but then I feel him flick his eyes over me again as he replies, "You really do look beautiful tonight."

I open my mouth to respond, to say what, I'm not sure, but thankfully I am saved when Josh and Daemon slink up beside us. "Tink, there you are, I was starting to worry I wouldn't find you before midnight," he grins, leaning down to kiss my cheek, but my eyes stay on Levi, who has gone from smiling to scowling.

Josh doesn't seem to notice, but Daemon is watching Levi like he can dissect every thought with just his mind, and when he moves his attention to me, I know he feels the tension. I subtly shake my head before smiling up at Josh. "My lost boy always finds his way back to me."

His smile mirrors my own, but his eyes are glossy, as he reaches out and literally boops my nose. "And I always will,

Hallie Bear," he drawls, and it's only now I take in his disheveled suit, and the whiskey on his breath.

I flick my stare to Daemon. "Is he drunk?" I ask, and he nods just once.

"I'm not drunk," Josh snaps, and Daemon rolls his eyes.

Shaking my head, I focus back on my husband who is still smiling at me like I am his everything, and I swallow thickly as I intertwine our fingers. "Come on, husband, I think it's time you took me for a spin round the dance floor." He obliges instantly, which is how I know just how drunk he really is, because he pulls me to the center of the floor and wraps his arms around my waist.

"Two minutes to midnight," someone calls around the room, and Josh smiles as he starts swaying us from side to side.

"If I took any longer I think Levi would have been kissing you at midnight," he grunts, and when our eyes meet I realize he doesn't miss a thing.

"You saw him?" I ask nervously, wondering why he didn't say anything, but then his hands flex around my waist, and I understood why. He doesn't have to say anything because he knows that I belong to him. I have told him myself that anyone else is irrelevant, but does that mean our deal is irrelevant?

"When it comes to you, Hallie, I've realized that I see everything," he tells me earnestly, and I swear his eyes have never looked so serious before. Yet I'm not sure if it's the whiskey talking, or him.

"Well it doesn't matter anyway, I don't kiss boys at midnight on New Years, it's a bad omen," I reply casually, even though my heart is thundering inside my chest, and when I flick my stare over his shoulder, I find his father watching our every move.

"Oh and why is that?" he asks, pulling me in even closer until I can feel every hard ridge of his body.

We are so close now that I can feel his breath on my face as I stare up at him, and despite the music, my voice is low when I reply, "Because I don't want to start the year with someone I won't be ending it with. Hence no kissing boys, boyfriends or anyone else for that matter."

His grin is downright feral and wicked as he asks, "And what about kissing your husband, is that a bad omen?"

Sometimes, I instantly say in my mind, but when his left hand reaches up and lands on my cheek, and I feel the weight of his ring, everything else just fades away.

The countdown begins, everyone chanting around us, but the only thing I see is him. "Hallie, I..." he starts, as the cheers ring out, but I slam my lips to his, stealing whatever he was about to say with a kiss, because even if I can't keep him forever, I can still keep this moment.

Our mouths move in sync, kissing one another has become as natural as breathing, and it's all I can do not to break down and cry. I feel him everywhere, as I curl my hands into his hair, and he holds me against him like he never wants to let go. My tongue caresses his own, and I swallow his deep groan, enjoying his rough touch, as he tries and fails to get me even closer to him.

When we pull apart, the words are right there on the tip of my tongue. Just three little words that if I say there is no taking them back, and I want to. I want to say them, I want him to hear them, but what about rule number three? What about what he said in return?

Don't worry, Hals, you already know I'm not wired to find and appreciate something as simple as love.

His words from Thanksgiving come rushing back, and bile rises in my stomach as I open my mouth, but the only three words that come out are, "Ready to go?"

He blinks back from me as if he was expecting me to say something else, but then puts a lazy smile across his mouth. "Sure, baby, I'm ready. I'll go find Daemon and meet you at the door, okay?" He drops a kiss to my head, before he disappears into the crowd, and watching him leave hurts more than it should.

No, I can't do this anymore. The second we get home I am going to tell him, even if it kills me.

I make my way through the crowd, not bothering to say goodbye to anyone, considering I watched Maddie and Nova slip out just as Josh and I made our way to the dance floor. As for the rest of the team, I'm sure they are around somewhere, but I don't have the energy to find them, so instead, I do what Josh asked and go and wait by the door for him and Daemon.

"Leaving so soon," a smug voice curls around me, and I turn to find Josh's father strolling down the hall from his office, looking me up and down, his eyes zeroing in on the letter J that dangles from my neck.

"Mayor Peters," I greet with a smile as fake as his. "The party was amazing as always, but yes we are heading out."

He doesn't stop until he is right in front of me, his proximity sickening, as he purrs, "Hallie, we are family now, I think it's time you called me Hugo."

My cheeks ache from keeping my smile in place but still I nod and correct myself. "Hugo."

His own smile is approving now, as he assesses me closely before adding, "I'm so glad you married my son." His tone is filled with charm and I almost snort.

"Yeah I'm sure you are," I reply as sweetly as I can manage, flicking my stare back towards the party and praying Josh comes and saves me.

"No really I am, and not just because of the validity your last name holds," he explains, as if saying bullshit like that is the most natural thing in the world, and I guess in his world, it is. "But because out of every girl I put on that list of names, yours was the most well-suited to him."

My heart starts pounding in my ears as his words wash over me. "List of names?" I repeat, my hands beginning to shake, and his smile turns wicked.

"Yes, you know the list of names I gave my son, of approved women he could choose a wife from. I mean, you were in excellent company of course, Dear, but out of everyone I am so glad he chose you."

I suddenly find it hard to breathe as I am vaulted back to the night Josh proposed, my mind dissecting through every single word he said to me.

My father will leave Maddie alone as long as I marry someone of his choosing.

That's what he said, those were his exact words, I didn't mix them up or mishear them. That is exactly what he said to me.

And he chose me?

I asked him outright, so sure I got him wrong, and he nodded. There wasn't a mention of a list, or any other names, he said he needed to marry me and I agreed. I agreed because I thought he had no other option, and despite my feelings for him, and how much worse it was going to make things for me, I wanted to help.

How fucking stupid was I?

Hugo is still staring at me in delight, as if he orchestrated this entire thing, and it takes everything I have not to cry. Instead I put a smile on my face and respond, "Oh yes, of course, that list."

The lie slips off my lips with ease, as Josh and Daemon appear from the ballroom and head towards us, Josh's eyes already lined with anger as he takes in his father's proximity to me.

"Everything okay?" he asks, his focus solely on Hugo, and for once I'm thankful for his lack of attention.

"Yes, everything is fine." Four little words, one big lie, yet

Josh doesn't let his gaze stray towards me to see if it's true or false.

Daemon stares at me like the lie is written right across my face, and all I can do is drop my eyes to the floor.

"Then let's go," Josh snaps, slipping his hand into mine, and without another word, the three of us are leaving his father behind and climbing back into the car that brought us here.

I'm not sure where Levi or Landon are, but at this moment I don't care, because the only thing I can focus on is the list of names. The whole ride home that's my only thought. From the car, to the sidewalk, all the way up the stairs, my only focus is that stupid list of names.

Once we reach Josh's room, Daemon is still watching me quietly, but then he bids us goodnight and heads down to his room.

My heart is still racing, and as Josh leads us into his room, and drops down on the end of the bed, all I can do is flick my stare around. From my eye mask on the pillowcase, to my penguin in the sheets, from the fan on the nightstand, to my pajamas thrown over the chair. My presence, this fake marriage, it's everywhere, staining this room like a fucking disease with no cure, and it was all a bigger lie than I could have ever imagined.

Yet I don't break, *I snap.*

#33
HALLIE
LIAR LIAR

I storm to his desk and start ripping open the drawers, rifling through every piece of paper inside like a woman gone mad. Except I'm not mad, I'm just in love, which I guess is worse. Josh jumps to his feet as I discard the first drawer and move onto the second, not caring for the mess I am making, not when my heart is breaking inside of my chest.

"Hals, what the hell are you doing?" Josh asks, stumbling to my side, but when he touches me I flinch away from him, making him step back as I rip through the second drawer.

"Where is it?" I snap, my voice hoarse from holding back tears, and my hands shake as they fumble through pages of notebooks in search of what I am looking for.

"Where is what?" he pleads, completely bewildered by my behavior, and it makes me want to scream.

"The list," I demand. "Where is the list?" I toss the second drawer aside, and yank open the third, which completely falls to the floor before I can even look in it.

"What list?" He looks genuinely confused, and I don't know

if that makes this whole thing better or worse, I simply square my shoulders as I turn to face him.

"The list of fucking names you chose me from," I scream, my voice breaking with emotion, and I watch as his face transforms from confusion to regret.

"Hallie, I can explain," he pleads, taking a step towards me, but I instantly step back, swiping my hand up to catch the first tear from my cheek as it falls.

"Explain what? How you could have picked any girl to run off into the fake sunset with, but you chose me? Don't bother, Daddy dearest already filled me in." I back away towards the bookcase, continuing my search there, and he rushes to my side and moves to place his hand on my shoulder.

"Don't, I can't even fucking look at you right now." I snap away from him before he can reach me, pulling books off the shelf and flicking through each of them like I have completely lost the plot.

At this point I think I have.

"Baby, please," Josh begs, and when I snap towards him and he sees the tears pouring down my face, he looks broken.

I'm sure he can see it now, the truth, the reason I agreed to all this in the first place, but I don't care anymore.

"Was this all just some big joke to you?" I ask with a scoff, shaking my head, as I try to stop myself from crying. "Did you just look at this list and see my name and think *wow I can easily make Hallie marry me without effort so why not pick her*?"

He's already shaking his head, stepping towards me again, but I step back. "It wasn't like that, I swear."

"Then what was it like, Josh?" I yell back, rage and heartbreak at war inside of me. "Tell me why you did this to me? Tell me why you picked me and ruined our friendship?" My questions are basically pleas, and no answer will change the outcome. It's not like he did it out of love, it's not like his heart beats the same way as mine.

"I did it because you were the only person on that stupid list I even liked, let alone cared for. I thought doing this with you was the best choice, the only choice, and I was right."

His face looks more serious than I have ever seen it, yet right now it means nothing. "You thought lying to me was the best choice?" I ask, my voice trembling, my hands shaking, but for once I don't back down. "You thought making me believe I was the only person who could help you was the best choice? Do you honestly think I would have gone through with this if I didn't think there was another way to help you? I thought I was saving Maddie."

"And you did save her," he reassures me, once again trying to get closer to me, but I can no longer bear it.

"And *you* lied to me," I whisper, letting my heartbreak show all over my face, even when I can see how much it hurts him

"Is the lie even relevant now?" he asks, emotion staining his own voice, as he pushes towards me again. "Does the list even matter, look at us, Hallie, this isn't exactly fake anymore."

A choked laugh leaves me. "Isn't it? Because I had very few rules when you asked me to marry you, and one of them was not lying to one another."

I don't move when he reaches me this time, no longer having the energy to fight against him. "What do you want, baby? Tell me and I will give it to you," he pleads, searching my face for a solution to all of this, but I think it's too late for anything to save us now.

What I want he can't give me, but it's taken me this long to realize it. "I want the boy from the ice that day," I admit softly, as his thumb captures one of my tears. "I want the one who proposed to me with a ring pop, the one who bought books on autism and hid them in his damn closet." His eyes widen with every one of my truths, but I can't stop. "I want the boy who would have never ever lied to me."

I push him away from me and move towards his desk, searching through the papers again, with my hands a little calmer, it doesn't take me long to find it, and when I do it hurts even more than I imagine. There are almost thirty names on the list. So many girls I know Josh has history with, including Brianna, and he could have picked any one of them.

When I turn back to him he looks as crushed as I feel, but the weight of the list in my hands is too heavy to care. "You used to be my favorite person in the entire world, did you know that? Just one look from you and my entire world would tip on its axis, and you never even noticed, did you?" My eyes hold his, as I let my truth pour out, no longer caring for the repercussions. The worst has already happened, and instead I focus on packing my things into my bag so I can leave.

"You think I didn't notice you?" he asks, shaking his head in disbelief, as he desperately follows me around the room. "Hallie, you have been one of the most important people in my life since the day I met you. I think about you every time I step out onto the ice, every time there is a Taylor Swift song on the radio, and every time I see something green. How could I not notice you? You're in me, you're a part of me, and I wouldn't change that for anything."

When I turn back to him I wish I could still see the boy from the ice, but right now he is too similar to the man who raised him. "Except you did change that," I exhale softly, zipping up my bag and lifting it onto my shoulder. "You changed it the moment you picked my name off some list like it meant nothing to you, and now there is no going back."

I move towards the door, but he snatches my hand up in his. "Baby, please don't do this," he begs, but I snatch my hand away as if it's on fire.

"Don't touch me," I snap, far too loudly, not caring if anyone hears, they no doubt have already heard more than enough to know what is happening in here. "Just, let me go," I add, slipping off my rings, leaving them on the table by the door. Then without waiting for a response, I leave a room that feels more like mine than my own ever did, and don't look back at the boy who still owns my heart.

When I reach the front door, Daemon is waiting silently, my coat clutched in his hands, clearly having heard everything, but when I meet his stare, his eyes tell me an even more bitter truth.

"You knew, didn't you?" I ask, and he smiles so sadly that it almost breaks me completely. He holds out my coat for me to put on, and then opens the door and steps out to walk me home, just as Josh comes barreling down the stairs.

The look in his eyes kills me, but I turn and leave without another word, because I realize that even though he will always be my first love, all I ever was to him, was just his first wife.

#34
JOSH
BULLSHIT BETS

There is an ache in my chest so painful that it feels as though someone has taken an ax to it, and I'm not entirely convinced they haven't. Even the whiskey and champagne burning its way through my system does nothing to dull the pain, not when I just lost her, not when I just watched her walk away without looking back. The weight of her rings crushed inside my palm makes bile rise up the back of my throat, and I feel my legs go out from under me. I slump down on the stairs and don't move until Daemon comes back alone, and when he meets my stare, I know it's even worse than I thought.

"Is she okay?" I force out, bringing my hand up to clutch my chest, as if just my touch alone could take the pain away. It can't, because it's not hers.

"No," Daemon replies, not stopping to say anything else, as he brushes past me and heads back upstairs without another word.

I guess Hallie isn't the only person I've disappointed.

I'm not sure how long I sit here, but it's long enough for the sun to rise the next morning, and the alcohol to dissipate out of my system completely. I should probably feel something, anything that isn't this giant, gaping hole in my chest where the sun once shined, but I don't. The pain only intensifies with every passing second, until I can barely breathe. I need to see her, I need to find her, and make her understand why I did this.

Do I even really know why I did this?

I think back to the moment my father gave me the list of names, trying to remember what I felt, but I can't, because the second my eyes landed on her name I knew this was only going to end one way. There was never going to be anyone else that I wanted to make my wife, and not because it wasn't practical, but because she was the only choice my heart could make. I mean, she's my best friend. *Was my best friend.*

My palm opens up and I look down at the rings I picked out for her, the ones she gave back to me, not caring about the cuts now staining my skin, and just wishing they were back on her finger. No, she isn't just my best friend anymore, and I don't think she ever has been. She's my wife and I need to get her back.

I don't even bother getting changed, I just grab my keys and drive straight over to her house, not caring that it's barely even 7am. I can't wait any longer, and as soon as I arrive I head straight up to the door to knock. I do it lightly at first, just a normal knock, but after a minute with no answer, I knock again, and then again, until I am pounding on the door so hard that the neighbor comes out.

Ignoring their disgruntled complaints, I pull out my phone and call my sister, but her phone is off, so I call the next best thing. It rings only twice before it connects, just like I knew it would. "Hector," I greet Madeline's bodyguard. "Where is my sister?"

"Good Morning to you too," he drawls, more than used to my snappy attitude, but right now I can't handle his jokes.

"Where is she?" I ask again, and he huffs.

"Where do you think? I'm parked on your street. Didn't you just see me when you left the house?" he asks with a laugh, and I tip my head up to the sky and silently curse.

Of course, Maddie is with Nova, which means Hallie is there, she wouldn't have wanted anyone other than her best friend last night.

"Thanks," I snap down the phone, not bothering to stay on the line and explain myself.

No, instead I jump right back into my car and drive back across campus until I reach Hockey Row. As soon as I pull up I spot Hector's car that I so clearly missed when I left, and I ignore his smirking face, as I storm past him up to the house. This time when I knock on the door I'm not gentle or quiet, and too impatient to give a fuck.

"Alright, keep your fucking dick in your pants," an irritated voice shouts towards the door as they stomp towards it, and when they open it, I meet the pissed off eyes of my captain.

"Where is she?" I snap, in no fucking mood to speak to him, but all the prick does is smirk.

"If you're looking for your sister, she's in my bed, if you're looking for your wife, she's in my best friend's bed," he purrs, like a cocky asshole, and I fight the urge to punch him.

"Nova, if you don't move out of the way, I will make you." I don't want to threaten him, despite how much I hate the bastard, not when I know it would upset Maddie, but right now the only thing I care about is my wife.

"You can try," he taunts, leaning on the doorframe like I am in no way a threat. "I'll even let you get in a free shot."

"Why?" I question, and his honesty surprises me.

"Because I fell in love with your sister," he admits freely, and it almost makes me like him, but then he adds, "And now she lets me do unspeakable things to her."

"Nova, I swear to god," I start, and whatever he sees on my face has his own softening.

"Look man, I'm sorry but she doesn't want to see you. You know what you did and she needs time, so you're not coming in here right now."

He doesn't even wait for my response, just slams the door in my face, and then locks it for good measure, like he thought I wouldn't listen to him. I wasn't going to, but fuck him for knowing that. So all I can do now is plonk myself down on the porch and wait.

I watch as Hector switches shifts with Maddie's other guard, Julian, both of them eyeing me warily, and I remind myself to speak to Lincoln about hopefully keeping them on, or finding them similar work elsewhere when everything with my father goes down. Then I watch as people stumble home from parties, or head out for a run, and all the while, the only thing on my mind is Hallie.

Two hours pass with me just sitting there, before the door opens behind me and I snap my head around in hope, yet the only thing I find is my sister's sorrow-filled eyes. "Hey, I brought you some coffee, you look like you could use some," she smiles softly, taking a seat beside me, and I take it in silent thanks.

"Is she okay?" I ask desperately, and the pity in my sister's eyes is sickening.

"No of course she isn't," she says sternly, before she throws the question back at me. "Are you okay?"

A humorless laugh slips out of me as I toss back, "No, of course I'm not." I take a deep slug of the coffee, yet it does nothing to erase the pain in my head or my heart. "What do I do, Mads, how do I fix this?"

She eyes me with concern before she asks, "Your friendship?

Or your marriage?" I don't respond, because honestly, I'm not sure how, yet it doesn't stop her from pushing me for more. "How could you do this, Josh, to Hallie of all people? She loves you so much that she would do anything for you, you know that. I mean, she's so in love with you that she agreed to your stupid plan to marry you."

My gaze snaps to hers as she finishes speaking, but I am already shaking my head. "Hallie isn't in love with me," I'm quick to reply, the words tasting sour on my tongue, and Madeline scoffs.

"Hallie has been in love with you since she was nine years old, and you've been in love with her too," she tells me slowly, like she is talking to a child.

"I'm not in love with her," I deny far too quickly, not admitting that I'm incapable of loving anyone, and she shakes her head with a laugh.

"Josh, from the moment you met her it's like the two of you were magnets. I was her best friend, but you were her whole world. Are you going to tell me it wasn't the same for you?" she pushes, only making the pain in my chest worse. "Think about it, you never let anyone say one bad word about her, you protected her, fought for her, defended her, you even made a campus-wide no dating rule for her—"

I cut her off, "Yeah, because I care about her, because she's my—"

"She's your what?" she asks, cutting me off in return, and all I can do is stare at her blankly.

When I don't respond, my sister takes the now empty mug from my hand, and smiles at me sadly. "Maybe you should figure out what you want before you lose her forever."

She doesn't wait around for me to say anything else, just taps my arm in comfort before rising to her feet and heading back inside. The lock sliding into place like a fucking deadbolt across my heart.

I think about everything she just said, about Hallie being in love with me, about me being in love with her, and the question she just asked me, only coming up with one answer.

She's my everything.

The realization hits me like a freight train. I love her. I'm in love with her. That's what this pain in my chest is, it's not from hurting my friend, it's from my heart cracking open in my chest at the thought of losing my wife. *Fuck.* I am so madly in love with her that I never even saw it coming.

How the fuck am I going to fix this?

The question plagues me for hours as I sit there on the porch, my heart inside of the house behind me, and when I spy Daemon coming out of our house with Levi and Landon hot on his heels, I prepare myself for their onslaught.

"Hey man, I brought you some lunch," Daemon says quietly, offering me a lunchbox and a drink, and I thank him with a smile.

"You look like shit," Landon smirks, and I can't help but laugh, as I take the cap off the water and take a drink.

"I feel like it too, brother," I tell him truthfully, and all three of them look at me in wonder.

"What are you even doing here?" Levi snaps coldly, and my eyes flick to his in confusion, and Dameon watches him warily as he adds, "Give up on the fucking ruse, man, it's getting old."

"What the fuck is that supposed to mean?" I snap, at the same time Landon asks, "What ruse?"

The door opens behind me and I snap around to find Gray and Reign, coming out to see what all the arguing is. When I realize Hallie isn't with them, I ignore Landon's question in favor of my old friend, who looks at me with nothing but pure contempt. "Come on, Josh, you can't exactly be surprised, she wasn't going to settle for your fake bullshit forever."

It's only now I see it, too blinded by his friendship to ever notice it before. He likes her. "I'd be very careful about what comes out of your fucking mouth next, Jones," I warn, because one wrong word about Hallie and I won't give a fuck about how long we have been friends.

Levi scoffs, "Please, we both knew it was only a matter of time before you fucked everything up, like father like son."

Landon's eyes widen in shock, but it's Daemon who steps up to Levi and warns him with a voice like death, "You need to walk away. Now."

From experience, I know that it will only take one more word for Daemon to absolutely lose his shit, and for once I won't stand in his way. Not with the bullshit pouring from Levi's mouth, not with the way he is looking at me as if he despises me. I stare him down, daring him to say one more word directed at me, but his gaze flicks to Daemon as if he is completely beneath him.

"Don't even get me started on your father, Forbes, Josh's may be a piece of shit, but yours is a fucking murderer."

The punch lands before he can stop it, the fist moving so fast none of us even spot it until it's too late, only Daemon hasn't moved an inch. When I turn my head to the side I find Archer staring down at Levi, his whole body shaking with rage, as he spits, "Get the fuck away from my house, or the only murderer around here will be me."

All of us are frozen on the spot as we stare at Archer in utter shock, before Levi does the first smart thing today and scrambles back away from him. When I bring my focus back to Daemon, he is staring at Archer with a look I have never seen before, and it's only now I understand what Hallie meant when she said their dynamic was interesting.

I think it's more interesting than any of us have ever realized.

"What the fuck is going on out here?" Nova stalks onto the porch, flicking his stare across all of us, and when his eyes land on his best friend, he looks nothing short of confused.

"Josh, you're still here?" Maddie asks, coming from the front door to join him, and I know from the multiple sets of eyes on me that they don't have a clue what is going on.

I open my mouth to speak when my ringtone cuts through all the tension, and when I pull the phone from my pocket, I find my mom's name flashing across the screen. I send it straight to voicemail, and only now notice the multiple texts and calls from her and my grandmother, leading to only one conclusion. The Mayor has finally fallen.

I flick my stare to Madeline and announce, "Dad has been arrested." Shock flows through my teammates, but Maddie just stares at me with nothing but relief. It's finally done. With that in mind, before any of my teammates can say anything I add, "My father is a lying, corrupt, piece of shit, who tried to force Maddie into a business marriage. I ruined it, but my father forced me to take her place. I was told I had to pick a wife, and Hallie's name was on the list of approved choices. I picked her because she was my friend, and I knew I wanted an ally as I took him down." Reign, Gray, and Landon all look at me like I have gone insane, but Maddie, Nova, and Daemon already know all this, so I force myself to add, "I have since realized that I am madly in love with my fake wife, and I need to fucking fix it, so I am not leaving here until I see her."

I expect some backlash, maybe some pissed off rant about what I did was wrong, but what I don't expect is Gray to groan, the anger leaving him completely as Reign bursts out laughing. "I fucking knew it," Reign brags, jumping onto his friends back and rubbing his knuckles on his head. "Pay up, you little prick."

My stare flicks between them in confusion, before Gray

sighs, "Reign bet me your marriage was bullshit, I bet him it was real."

If my chest wasn't still burning with pain I would probably laugh, but instead I reply, "Then I guess we all lost, because my marriage may have been bullshit, but it was somehow the realest thing I have ever felt."

All of them look at me in stunned silence, before Nova nudges Maddie. "You heard your brother. Go and fetch his wife, the man is in love."

And to my surprise, she turns on her heels and heads back inside.

Hmm, I guess Nova Darkmore isn't so bad afterall.

"Fuck, I love watching her walk away from me," he grits, his voice laced in lust as he rearranges himself in his shorts.

Nevermind. He is a prick.

#35
HALLIE
WEAK BABY

The smell of the bed sheets beneath me are fresh but unfamiliar. Archer changed them when I arrived, before making himself a bed on the floor and lending me one of his jerseys to sleep in. When Daemon led me here last night instead of home I was confused at first, but when we reached the door, he explained that Maddie was inside. My best friend knew as soon as she saw my face that something was wrong, and when I broke down in her arms she let me stay there and cry for over an hour.

All the guys in the house avoided us thankfully, until it was almost 2am and Nova and Archer came down and insisted we get some sleep. Maddie left me reluctantly, but Archer promised he would look after me, and he did. Yes he still made a joke about me being the only girl to ever sleep in his room without fucking him, but even his attempt at humor couldn't save me. I was already at the bottom of the abyss of Josh Peters, and just like I knew at nine years old, there was no way out.

Archer's room is almost identical to Josh's, yet looking

around it I feel nothing. I always thought the worst pain you could feel was physical, like getting hit by a car, or losing a leg, but nothing can compare to your heart being ripped out of your chest.

I'm curled up in the center of his bed, and haven't moved since I laid down here in the early hours of this morning. Not even whatever commotion is going on outside could get me to move, nothing could. So when the bedroom door opens and in comes my best friend, I don't even flinch.

Maddie lays down on the bed beside me and brings her face up to mine. "What's happening outside?" I ask to distract my mind from the constant pain, before she can ask me any questions.

"My dad has been arrested, I guess whatever Josh orchestrated has finally happened, my mom is calling us non-stop."

Lincoln must really be good at his job for how fast it has happened, and I can't say I feel sorry for Hugo, he deserves every single thing coming to him. I just wish her words brought me some comfort, after all, the only reason I even went through with this marriage was to get to this outcome. That was the plan all along, marry Josh, save Maddie, and take his father down. So why do I feel like I haven't accomplished anything?

"I'm sorry," I whisper, because I'm not really sure any other words would suffice. Hugo Peters may be an asshole, but he is still her father.

"Don't be sorry, Hals, you saved me, you and Josh. If it weren't for you guys I'd be engaged to Bradley Thorne right now, or maybe even someone worse," she scoffs in disgust, and knowing what she has with Nova, I can't say I blame her.

"Is there anyone worse than Sad Brad?" I question, and she smirks.

"Jockstrap Jerkoff?" she tosses back, but the reminder of Joey only causes the pain in my heart to hurt even more.

"Is that all that happened? I thought I heard arguing?" I ask, changing the subject again, and she cringes a little.

"Oh, well, Archer punched Levi in the face," she replies casually.

"What the hell, why?" I snap, and she smirks, knowing she has got me hook, line and sinker.

"Levi started talking shit to Josh, and then when Daemon tried to cut in to defend him, he turned his wrath on him, so naturally Archer punched him." So many words, yet one of them feels as if she physically punched me in the gut.

"Josh is here?" I ask in a whisper, and she nods, smiling at me like I am an idiot.

"Hals, he's been sitting on the porch for hours, says he isn't leaving until he talks to his *wife*." She exaggerates the word wife with a smile, and if my heart wasn't hurting so much then maybe I would smile back. "The guys have been guarding the door and not letting him in, but I don't think he's going anywhere."

Fuck. I'm going to have to go and face him.

I lift myself up off the bed as Maddie follows, and I cringe slightly when I pass the mirror on Archer's wall and see how shitty I look, but I might as well get this over with. Walking down the stairs feels like walking to my death, and when I reach the door, I hear the guys arguing just outside on the porch.

"Sorry man, it's not my fault your wife wanted to sleep in my bed," Archer purrs, like the cocky asshole I know and love him to be.

"Gray, I swear to god, if you don't stop saying shit about her, I am going to fucking kill you, and trust me I won't be sorry," Josh replies darkly, and his voice scrapes along my bones like a phantom touch.

"Damn, after I just defended your honor and everything," Archer tosses back, as I step onto the porch. Josh has his back to me, so he doesn't see me right away. Nova and Alexander are just to the left of the door, and Archer is on the stairs closer to Daemon, but looking up at Josh.

"Really, you wanna go there, or should we talk about why you really punched him?" Josh snaps back, and I see Archer's entire face freeze in a panic. There is a secret there, one he is probably not done chasing the truth for yet, so I decide to put him out of his misery.

"Hi," I all but whisper, but a bomb may as well have detonated for how fast Josh reacts to my voice.

His head snaps around and his entire face softens as he takes me in. "Hals," he breathes in pure relief, like just seeing me is the cure to everything, and when I look him over I note he looks just as bad as I do.

"Can you guys give us a minute?" I ask no one in particular, my voice a little louder this time, and the remaining guys scramble like their asses are on fire to give us some privacy. "You shouldn't be here," I tell him as soon as they are gone, making his face fall. "Maddie told me what happened with your dad."

My words already have him shaking his head. "Hallie, do you really think I give a fuck about my father, he can rot in hell for all I care."

I can't help but smile softly at his outburst, because some things never change. "I meant you should go be there for your mom and grandma, they're your family." I move to stand beside him on the porch, and he looks at me like I have lost my damn mind.

"The only member of my family I care about right now is standing right here with me," he snaps, looking so desperate and sad that it kills me to see it.

"Josh," I start, but he cuts me off. "No, Hallie, just let me say this, please," he pleads with a sigh, and I close my mouth and nod. "You're right I shouldn't have lied, and I'm sorry I did, but honestly if I didn't, I never would have realized how much you truly mean to me. You're my best friend, but you're also so much more than that." My heart starts to beat wildly in my chest at his every word, and I have to swallow thickly to keep myself from crying. "I was so fucking blind, Hals I mean, I banned anyone from dating you, I broke that prick's arm, I lied to make sure you married me, that isn't something a friend does." His hand reaches up and presses hard into his chest like he is in pain as he gasps, "You're so much more than a friend to me, Hals, you make me feel..." he trails off like he can't quite find the right word.

"What? What do I make you feel?" I plead, both desperate to know the answer, and not sure I can survive it.

When his eyes collide with mine again, they are so intense that I feel like his stare strips me bare. "Weak, baby, you make me feel weak." He takes a step towards me, closing the distance between us, and when he touches me, I don't shy away from it. "I look at you and I know I don't have to be strong all the time, like the power I have learnt to demand and crave just to get by under my father's bullshit is irrelevant, because with you by my side, I feel invincible."

The tears are falling freely down my cheeks now, and he cups my face with his hand and swipes them away. "You know I still remember the first time I saw you, you stormed into the middle of my game with a big smile and a whole lot of attitude. Your hair was in pigtails, and you had on that ridiculous, yellow fluffy coat that you insisted on wearing every day that winter, and you looked just like sunshine," he smiles, and now my heart aches for a whole different reason.

"You remember that?" I ask in disbelief, and he nods, pressing his forehead down to meet mine.

"When it comes to you, I remember everything, and it took you walking away from me last night to realize why." I can feel his breath on my lips, the warmth of him so alluring after just hours apart.

"Why?" I breathe, the one word almost a struggle to get out, as my heart feels ready to explode.

"Because you're my everything, baby. You always have been, and I want to be yours."

Fuck. His words are ripping me apart from the inside out, and I can't help but shake my head in his hands. "But you told me you weren't capable of falling in love," I whisper, and the smile on his face is my utter downfall.

"Then I guess I need to apologize for breaking all of your rules, Tink, because I am so unbelievably in love with you," he laughs, as if his admission didn't just set my entire body alight. "Are you in love with me?" he asks with a smile, as if he already knows the answer, and I can't help but smile back.

"Since I was nine years old," I admit to him freely for the first time, and it's like a weight has been lifted off my chest.

"Then kiss me, baby, because I can't take another second of your lips not being on mine." His mouth slams to mine before I can even respond, the kiss robbing me of my answer, and my breath.

He tastes of whiskey and coffee, but for the first time ever he also tastes like mine, and all I can do is kiss him back.

When he pulls back he looks at me with nothing but passion as he says, "I love you, Hallie Bear." Five words and my heart ceases to exist completely.

"I love you too, Joshua," I smile back, the words still feeling weird to say out loud.

Then he surprises me by dropping to one knee and pulling out my rings. "Again, I don't have a ring pop on hand, but I'm hoping these will do." He reaches for my left hand and holds it up in his. "Hallie Rose Peters, will you please stay married to me, no rules, no deals, no fucking lists. Just you, me, and Percy."

I'm openly crying now, too emotional to hold back my tears as I nod. "Yes, I'll stay married to you." My hands shake as he slides the rings back into place on my left finger, not caring how crazy this whole thing is, and I hear hollers and cheers coming from inside the house, and when I turn towards the window I find Nova, Maddie, Archer, and Alexander all pressed up against the glass with huge smiles on their faces.

Josh laughs, giving them the finger as he rises back to his feet and kisses me again, only when he pulls back this time and flicks his eyes over me, they turn dark. "Now can you please do me a favor?" he asks, fisting his hands at my waist.

"Anything, you know that," I tell him truthfully.

"Take off Archer Gray's fucking jersey so I can light it the fuck on fire," he grits, pulling on the fabric around me.

I bark a laugh at his request, forgetting entirely that the jersey I'm wearing has the number thirty-one on it, and not twenty-two. Especially when I know my next words are gonna send him even crazier. "I can't take it off, I'm not wearing a bra underneath."

His eyes darken even more with both anger and lust, and he doesn't even pause before dipping down and tossing me over his shoulder. "You're gonna pay for that, wife," he snaps, slapping my ass and making me yelp, as he marches us across the road to his house. When he kicks open the door, Daemon and Landon snap their heads towards us, but Levi is nowhere to be seen, not that Josh seems to care. "I suggest headphones, or going on a long walk," he snaps, as he moves towards the stairs. "Because I'm about to remind my wife exactly who she belongs to."

When we reach his room, he doesn't stop until we are in the bathroom, only then does he drop me back to the floor. He discards his jacket, before leaning into the shower and turning it on full. I move to take off the jersey, not wanting it on for a second longer, but Josh bats my hands away, then reaches into a drawer beneath his sink and pulls out a pair of scissors.

"Joshua!" I say in surprise, but it doesn't deter him. In fact, his name falling from my lips only seems to spur him on, as he brings the scissors to the collar of the fabric by my neck and forces them through until it splits.

Then he sets the scissors down, takes his hands and rips it completely down the middle until my tits are bare to him, pushing it off my shoulder like it offends him. "This is your one and only warning, Tink, if I ever see you in another jersey that isn't fucking mine, you will be sorry."

His threat thrills me, and I can't help but feel the need to taunt him in return. "I thought I looked pretty good in it, maybe I should take a page out of one of my books and build myself a hockey harem," I purr, slipping out of the leggings that Maddie let me borrow until I am completely naked before him.

"It's like you want me to march over there and break another arm in your honor," he grits, his eyes trailing over every inch of skin I have on display. "We've already covered that you're mine, but it looks like one night in another man's bed has left you confused, but don't worry, I know just the solution."

I watch in awe as he takes off his shirt and unbuckles his pants, undressing until he is also completely naked and my mouth is watering. Only then does he dip down and pick me back up, this time wrapping my legs around his waist, before walking us into the shower. The heat of the spray is nothing compared to the warmth of him, and as the water washes down around us, I never want to be away from him again.

"You really love me?" I ask, still in shock from his confession, and his smirk is both sinful and filled with love.

"Hallie, I think I've loved you since I was eleven years old," he admits softly, pressing me into the wall of the shower. "But now I'm going to fuck you so hard that Archer fucking Gray will hear it from across the road."

And true to his word, we don't get out of the shower until I feel like I can barely walk, and he has made me come around his dick three times.

Then he deposits me in bed, while he helps Daemon cook us some food and returns phone calls to his mom and grandma. Hugo was arrested on multiple charges, and none of the law officials in his pocket have come to his aid. Josh's mom is distraught, but I think she will come around after some time away from her husband, and his grandma has already asked to speak with both Maddie and Josh about their trusts.

Which means the only thing left to do is curl up with my very real husband, and Percy, while we watch some *Criminal Minds*.

Fuck, it feels good to be Mrs. Joshua Peters. For real.

#EPILOGIE
JOSH
TRICK PLAY

The crowd is going wild as the score is tied at four all with only a few minutes to go. Nova is screaming orders across the ice like a man on a mission, and Gray and I fight to get him the puck. When I flick my gaze to the stands, I find my wife sitting on the edge of her seat, with my sisters on either side of her.

After the news of my father's arrest made the press, the town went crazy. So many people came forward with stories about him, and the hole I pushed him down got even deeper. Lincoln pulled strings to ensure he wouldn't be granted bail, and he is set to stand trial in a couple of months. My mother was upset at first, and insistent on standing by his side, but the more people that came forward, the more affairs were revealed. It seems the only thing my father could ever actually do well was adultery. When I told my mother about Penelope it was the last straw, she filed for divorce the very next day.

My grandmother was a whole different story. From the moment her son's crimes were common knowledge she abandoned him instantly, not wanting him to bring down the good name of the family in any way. Maddie and I met with her the day after New Year's, and were finally given full access to our trust funds without any bullshit stipulations, and the money that was set aside to leave to my father was divided evenly between us. She even set up a trust for Penelope and gave Callia full access to it, even though she tried to refuse it of course.

When Pen found out who Maddie and I really were she was over the moon, and has since become a regular staple at our houses in the last few weeks. We eat dinner together multiple times a week, and nearly half the team joins me on Monday nights to help teach her and the others down at the center. It seems everything has worked out great.

When Gray finally steals the puck from the other team I hear my wife screaming at him to get it down to the net. I quickly switch direction and skate towards where she is sitting behind the plexi.

"Did you forget my name, Tink?" I yell, making her stare flick between me and the game, as the crowd around her begins chanting my name.

"I think there are enough people cheering for you, Joshua," she scoffs, gesturing to all the people in her section, and I smirk, ignoring Coach as he yells at me from across the ice.

"Trust me, Hals, the only person I ever want screaming my name is my wife," I tell her with a wink, before pushing away from her and moving to steal the puck from Gray.

"What the fuck, Peters?" he grunts, skating faster to keep up with me. "I thought we were friends now you asshole," he adds, trying to take the puck back from me, but I use one of the first decoy tricks I ever taught Hallie to keep it away from him.

"You kissed my wife, Gray, we will never be friends," I toss over my shoulder, as the clock starts running down, and I put my eyes on the prize.

We skate towards the goal as he fends off the opposing team, until my shot is clear to take with ten-seconds left on the clock. My heart is pounding wildly in my chest, we need this goal, we need this win, if we get it, we are heading straight to the Frozen Four. I let my eyes flick over to Hallie for just a second, and that's all it takes. One look, one-second, and my heart starts to beat steady again as she grounds me completely.

She screams my name, and I take the shot.

The Flyers win the game.

By the time we get to the afterparty at Nova's the energy is electric, the entire team buzzing from the win, yet all I want to do is sneak off with my wife. Maddie is in the kitchen with Cap curled around her, and whatever he is whispering in her ear has her blushing. I grit my teeth as I shift my focus to the other guys. Gray, Reign, Harper, Daemon, and Landon are all standing around the island with Hallie, taking shots.

Levi is nowhere to be seen of course. After what happened, the house took a vote, and we asked him to move out. Now we only see him during practice and games, and not once does he ever look up. I guess Archer's right hook was very effective.

When Gray spots me walking towards them, he raises his glass and drunkenly asks with a smirk, "How about a game of truth or dare?"

Hallie instantly smacks him in the back of the head. "Don't make me punch you in the dick, Arch," she snaps, downing her shot, and then sinking into me as I curl my arms around her waist from behind.

"Did you hear that, Peters, now she wants to see my dick too," Gray winks, and if he were anyone else, he wouldn't still be walking, but I am more than used to their friendship by now.

Besides, Archer Gray isn't a threat, not to me anyway.

"Want me to break his arm for you as well, Tink?" I drawl

The Puck Decoy

against her ear, relishing in the full body shudder that she lets out.

"I think I would quite enjoy that," she purrs back with a smile, and Archer acts offended.

"Fuck off, you two assholes still owe me a jersey," he complains, and I hide my smirk in her hair, because I definitely set that fucker on fire, and Daemon helped.

I flick my stare to my best friend and find him already watching me with a knowing smile, but Hallie distracts me as she turns in my hold and leans up to press a kiss to my lips. She's drunk, I can taste the sweet taste of liquor on her lips, and I know if I don't get her out of here now, that I will be dealing with her grumpy and hungover tomorrow.

"Come on, husband, take me home and do that thing with your tongue I like," Hallie purrs, stirring my cock to life against her, and my sister groans.

"Oh my god, please kill me so I can erase the memory of my best friend saying that to my brother," she mock gags, but then Nova leans in again.

"How about I do that thing with *my* tongue that *you* like," he whispers, far too fucking loudly, and my dick now feels like it wants to shrivel up and die.

"Okay, on that fucking note, we are leaving," I snap, dragging Hallie away from the island, and ignoring all of their protests at our departure.

I keep my hands on her hips and guide us through the party, accepting congratulations on winning the game as we go. When we reach the door, she pauses and flicks her eyes up to look at me.

"Want to go fuck on Archer's bed to get back at him for being a prick?" she asks, and fuck me if I didn't already love this girl, those words would do it.

"Hals, as much as I would love to defile you up there and let this whole party hear you scream, tonight I want you all to myself." I turn her back towards the door and push us out into the cold air to head back to our house.

Yet when we reach the front door, she turns to look at me and smiles drunkenly. "I still can't believe I got my lost boy to fall in love with me," she laughs, the sound making my heart soar. "I'm so in love with you, Peter," she adds, throwing her hands around my neck, and bringing her body against mine.

"I'm so in love with you too, Tink," I purr, leaning down and capturing her lips with mine.

I don't get her to myself after all. I fuck her right there against the door, while the party rages on across the road behind us, but they don't even notice.

All the tricks I've learnt, and my wife is still the best decoy I've ever played.

THE END.

#BONUS
ARCHER
CUM BUDDIES

The first week of classes has barely even ended and I've already got a hot, wet mouth wrapped around my cock. *Fuck I love college.* The girl whose name I have now forgotten sucks me down like a champ, and I tip the bottle of whiskey in my hand back and relish in the burn it leaves in my throat, as I get ready to blow my load down hers.

Her hair is gripped lazily in my hand as I guide her bobbing head up and down my cock. I can still hear the deep bass of the music thrumming from the party just outside in the halls, but who was I to turn down an eager mouth. Not that I didn't see plenty of action in high school and through the summer, but there is just something extra sweet knowing that my parents aren't going to accidentally walk in and see me with my cock out. Not that they ever cared.

Just as I have that thought the door opens and I curse, my fingers flexing in the girls hair. "Fuck off this room's occupied," I groan, not even bothering to lift my stare from the eager mouth wrapped round my cock, and to my surprise the girl doesn't even flinch at the sound of the newcomer.

It's a dark and husky detached tone that hits me in return. "This room is mine, so why don't you fuck off."

My eyes snap up instantly, finding an unamused green stare that is just as dark as his tone. He's easily at least 6 '2, and with jet black inky hair that's ruffled in all directions on his head, and tattoos flowing down his arm. He looks like some sort of fallen dark angel. He surveys the scene before him with zero emotion, like finding us like this in his room doesn't affect him in the slightest, and all it does is piss me off.

"It's Forbes right?" I ask, trailing my eyes over him once more, as the familiarity hits me through my whiskey haze. "Freshman Flyer like me?" I add in a groan, as my cock hits the back of the girl's throat. "I'm Archer."

His stare remains uninterested, even when it flicks down to the girl on her knees, as he quietly replies, "I don't care what your name is or who you are, just get out."

There's no way in hell I'm moving before this girl has swallowed my cum, so I pour the last drops of whiskey down my throat, before discarding the bottle. Then I lean back on what I can only now presume is his bed. "I don't mind if you watch, and you don't care either, do you babe?" I ask the girl, tugging on her hair gently, and using the term of endearment only because I can't remember her name.

The guy, *Forbes*, or whatever the fuck his name is, might appear unaffected, but I can see the firm line of his cock beneath his shorts like a fucking beacon of light.

"Or you could join us if you like?" I drawl, gesturing to his dick, and it earns me a pissed off grunt, his eyes never leaving mine.

His stare unnerves me, but the girl lets my cock fall from her mouth, turning her own stare over her shoulder to appraise him.

She looks delighted at the sight of him, not that I can blame her, I'm as straight as they come, and even I can appreciate how handsome he is.

"I've got three holes for a reason," she purrs, tone laced in pure seduction, and my eyes meet him again in a challenge.

I see him toying with the idea in his head, before he places down the black book in his hand and moves towards us. The girl watches him with keen attention, and when her hand reaches out to caress his chest, he snatches it up in his own, his movements faster than lightning.

"Don't touch me," he commands, throwing her hand back towards her, yet sliding his own hand into her hair beside mine and forcing her mouth back to my cock.

My eyes remain on him, even as she sucks me back into her mouth, and it feels even better than before, yet I watch in fascination as he pulls the shirt off over his hand and reveals a chiseled, tattooed and scarred torso. My stare dances across every mark in wonder, but his focus is now solely on the girl separating us.

He reaches down and undoes his belt, freeing his cock, before sliding a condom from his pocket down his length. Only then does he touch the girl, and only enough to pull her underwear to the side and sink his cock inside of her. I know the moment he does because she moans around my cock, and the vibrations send me into a fucking spiral.

Then he is fucking her roughly and wildly. There is no slow build up, no calm and collected pace trying to savor the moment. No, there is just pure, ruthless fucking, and all I can do is accept every snap of his hips as it pushes her mouth deeper onto my cock.

Fuck.

His focus is on where his dick is sinking into her pussy, chasing nothing but his release, yet I can't take my eyes off of him. Even in the midsts of fucking he still looks cold and detached, yet when my cock hits the back of her throat again and I moan, his eyes snap to mine.

Then our stares are transfixed on one another as we fill two of the girl's holes, and every rough snap of his hips only makes me harder. I've never had a threesome before, the opportunity having never presented itself, but fuck if this is what it feels like, sign me the fuck up for more.

His force makes her mouth choke around my cock, and my hand tightens in her hair, as I begin fucking her mouth just as hard as he is fucking her pussy. The girl gags and moans like this is the best night of her fucking life, yet I barely even remember she is even here. I'm too intrigued by the mysterious nature of my new teammate.

His hand slips back into her hair, so close yet not touching mine, then he is guiding her mouth up and down my cock until I am gasping and moaning beneath them.

"Fuck that feels unreal," I curse, making the girl moan even louder, as she grips my cock at the base and jerks me at the same time as she sucks me, but I'm not fully convinced that my words are for her.

Yes it's her mouth wrapped around me, but I've had plenty of fucking mouths choking on my cock before, and none of them have felt like this. This isn't her, it's him, and his eyes seem to delight at my statement, yet there still isn't a trace of happiness anywhere on him.

Just a stare like cold death as he fucks us both without mercy. I know the moment he reaches that spot inside the girl, because her movements become sloppy as she starts gasping around my cock. I see the second she starts to come from the tight set of his jaw, and he only fucks her harder through her orgasm.

Then a deep guttural groan rips from his chest, making my cock spasm, as he pulls his dick out of her, rips off the condom, and then cums all over her bare back with the jerk of his hand. I am mesmerized as long spurts of cum paint her skin, and I have never been more jealous of anything in my life. I want that, and it's with that thought in mind that I rip my cock from her mouth, stand to my feet, and jerk myself over her until she is covered in both of us.

The girl remains boneless beneath us, no doubt still reeling from her own orgasm, but he stares at me with a look I can't decipher, as I pant to catch my breath after the best orgasm I have ever fucking had. Then with his eyes still on mine, he leans down and licks up both our cum.

My eyes widen in disbelief, but he looks so unaffected by the whole thing that I can't think of a single word to say to him.

"Oh my god, that was amazing," the girl purrs, standing up from all fours, and looking between us with glazed eyes. "Seriously, anytime you wanna do that again, all my holes are open."

Fuck I love college.

Before I can open my mouth to respond, my teammate simply replies, "No, thank you." Then he reaches down and passes her her shirt and gestures towards the door.

I'm sure she looks just as bewildered as I am, yet she grabs her top and slinks it back on without another word, before moving to the door with a shrug. "Oh well, hockey teams have a big enough roster, onto the next I guess." Then she is gone, and he is staring at me like I came in here and fucking killed some puppies.

"Are we cum buddies now?" I laugh, aiming to lighten the mood, yet his gaze remains sharp and unaffected.

"You're done, you can leave now." He pairs his words with holding his door open wide until I have no choice but to move towards it.

I barely pause past the threshold, turning to say, "Okay see you around." But the door is already being closed in my face, and somehow I hear the sound of the lock being slid into place over the music.

What the fuck just happened?

I pull my phone out completely bewildered as I stagger my way through the party, and pull up my new teammate's number who told me to text him if I needed anything. Kind of like if there was an emergency, and well, this feels like an emergency.

> Archer - Is it gay to cum on another guy's cum and then watch as he licks it up?

The message is read almost instantly and I'm thankful to see the typing bubbles appear just as quick. I know I had a good feeling about him, and that I could count on him in my time of need.

> Nova - What the fuck?
>
> Nova - Were you dropped as a child?
>
> Nova - We just met
>
> Nova - What the fuck is wrong with you?

And that's how I become best friends with Nova Darkmore, and mortal enemies with Daemon Forbes.

AFTERWORD

Thank you for reading The Puck Decoy

Are you ready for more yet?

Archer and Daemon's story is up next!

The Puck Chase

ACKNOWLEDGMENTS

Rebels,

Can you believe we have come to the end of another book? Like how did we get here?

Did we enjoy our time back in Fairfield?

First, I want to thank you my readers because without you I would not be able to live this little life that I love so much. Creating these stories is a passion and being able to do it with such amazing support is something I will never take for granted. Thank you for always being so kind, so patient, and so unbelievably amazing to me. I love you all more than I could ever put into words.

To my husband who is always by my side, and my daughter who is half the reason I wrote Hallie in the first place. Thank you for always showing me the most love in the world, especially as I am writing this note while you two are enjoying the first day of our vacation without me. I will forever feel blessed to have you both in my life and I love you both so much.

To Duchess, my number one cunt. You know these characters just as well as I do, and you are always there for my crazy vibe sessions, whether that be supporting my chaos, or telling me my ideas are absolute bullshit and helping me come up with better ones. I appreciate you more than you could ever know, and I know bitches are gonna try come for your man a little more after this book. So again this is another official announcement that Daemon Forbes belongs to you.

To Sam, I'd say sorry for how many times I complained about the absolute insane pressure this book was on me, but you've told me to stop apologizing so much at least a thousand times so maybe I should listen ey? I am so grateful to have you as best friend and I cannot thank you enough for always being my sounding board when I am going insane. So for all the times you have listened to me vibe and rant, and for every Edward Cullen Tik Tok you have sent me, from the bottom of my heart, thank you.

To Dean, my alpha, my signing assistant, my best friend (and most definitely not my husband LOL) thank you for always taking an interest in my work and listening to me ramble, and thank you for always telling me I should take a break (even though I never listen). You're the best Joben... Oh and I definitely set another deadline don't kill me!

To my amazing proofreaders, Zoe and Trinity, thank you for accepting my insane tight deadlines and still delivering the best work possible. I could not stay sane without you guys and your messages gave me both humor and relief. I love you guys.

And finally to my Street Team and all of the ARC sign ups, thank you so much for hyping me up and supporting me. I will forever be in your debt and I adore you. Thank you so much.

ALSO BY G.N. WRIGHT

FAIRFIELD U SERIES

1. The Puck Secret

2. The Puck Decoy

3. The Puck Chase - Coming Soon!

THE BLACK HALLOWS SERIES

1. Revival of a King

2. Revenge of a Queen

3. Rebellion of a Kingdom

4. Reckless Rebel

5. Ruthless Rebel - Coming Soon!

THE HALLOWED CROWS MC SERIES

1. Distrust

2. Dishonor

3. Disloyal

4. Disarray

THE KINGHOOD SERIES

0. - Tainted Crown - A Kinghood Novella

DEADLY GAMES AT BSU (co write)x

1. All Bets Are Off

ABOUT THE AUTHOR

G.N. Wright is a self published author of dark and contemporary romance. She lives in England with her husband and daughter. When she isn't writing she can be found reading, listening to music, and spending time with her family.

She enjoys a good social stalking so be sure to check out all of her links below!